The Woman in The Tree: The True Story of Camelot

By Natasha D Lane

Prologue

"Do you think this is really necessary?" Robin watched Arthur place her chamber items in a large pouch. She played with the charm bracelet he had given to her several months ago as a ninetieth birthday gift.

Arthur didn't turn to look at her when he replied. "Completely, Gwynevere," he said.

She took in a sharp breath. "You know I hate when you call me by my first name."

"Oh, I know," he replied, a smile in his voice.

She rolled her eyes. "Maybe he won't come. Maybe it was all a mistake."

"No. We are sure of his intentions and his plan. You must leave."

"Can you stop?" She sat up from the corner.

He was silent.

"Arthur, stop, please."

He continued to march around the room, packing away her belongings.

"Will you at least feign interest in my words?"

He tossed a wool scarf into the pouch and turned towards her closet.

"Stop it, now!" Robin shouted, stomping her foot and glaring at him from across the room.

All the shuffling ceased and the only sound was the crackling fire. Finally, he had stilled.

Robin sighed. She released her stance and walked to him. He turned to face her and brought her into his arms. She sunk into him, pressing her forehead into his neck and her face into his chest. She took in a deep breath.

He must have walked in the gardens today.

"I do not enjoy ignoring you, Robin. It's only because I must finish preparations for your journey."

He lifted his face to the top of her head. She smiled, and he kissed her forehead.

"And since you refuse to pack, I must do it for you. The midnight bell will ring soon. You must be on your way. Liz is already waiting."

He pulled away and begin stuffing the pouch once more.

Robin ran her hands through raven black hair and closed her eyes. She could feel a spell coming on but didn't wish Arthur to take notice. Her "weak constitution," as the doctor called it, already had Arthur and her uncle Terryn watching her every move. Now that she may be gone from them for some time, having a fit before her departure would only worsen their concern.

She cleared the fog from her head before snatching the pouch from Arthur's hands.

"I think that's enough," she said. "During our speedy exit, I do not want to be weighed down by all the items you consider necessary for a 'young lady.'"

Arthur sighed. "Well, you would know better than I, wouldn't you?" He winked and smiled at her.

She pursed her lips and narrowed her eyes. "Such sexist humor does not fit you, Arthur."

He shrugged. "If it ruffles your feathers a bit, it fits me just fine."

Robin tossed the pouch at him. "You will carry my things, then. Since I'm such a frail and delicate lady."

He gave her a grin. "Are we ready then?"

She held up a finger and moved to the fireplace. There was a loose stone in the mantle which she pressed inward. As she pressed, a stone on the right side of the fire place jutted out. The stone was long and hollow and inside were two glistening daggers.

Robin grabbed them, placed them under her cloak, and pushed the top stone in again.

Arthur stared wide-eyed.

"And how long have you had those?"

"Since I came here all those years ago. They belonged to my parents. Figured I'd never have a chance to use them but they do fit the oh-so-dangerous feeling of tonight. Do you agree?"

"You never told me about them."

"Well, we all have our secrets, don't we?" She raised a brow and gestured towards his sword. "Like where you got Excalibur from. You've never told me the full story."

He cleared his throat. "As you said, we all have our secrets. Let's go."

Arthur tossed the pouch over his shoulder and stepped into the hallway with Robin at his heels.

"Let it be known that when you and my uncle are proven wrong, I was the one who thought this whole concept ridiculous."

"And when you realize your uncle and I have saved you, let it be known you were wrong."

Robin rolled her eyes. "Cadfen hardly speaks to me. We were only close as children. And even if he were planning to claim me as his, as you say, why me? My cousin Morganna is the direct heir. It would make more sense to wed her."

"Morganna is being taken a different route. Only as a safety precaution though. Yours was the name he listed in his journals."

"And I've told you those journals could have been planted. Many men are jealous of Cadfen's station. He's been loyal to my uncle for years. Why would he cause a riot now?"

Arthur was quiet for a moment. He took slow steps and occasionally looked behind them.

Robin itched to pull at his hair for a response.

"I don't pretend to, nor would I ever want to, understand the ways of traitors."

She took in a hard breath. Calling an esteemed soldier a traitor was a high insult, especially coming from a knight. Still, of high station or not, such a crime was punishable by lynching, skinning, or worse.

"We're here," he said.

The pair stood in an abandoned room whose only décor was a dining set and a bed. The first-floor chamber had once been Terryn's playroom as a child. Now it housed a hidden tunnel.

Terryn and Robin's father Allen constructed the passage when they were older and had used it to sneak away from the castle. Their parents never discovered their mischief.

Robin could hear Arthur grunting from under the bed.

"Need help?" she asked, peeking below the bed frame.

He shook his head. "Only a few more stones. Then follow me down."

Several minutes passed before Arthur emerged again. He was dusty, sweaty, and smiling.

"What's so funny?" she said.

"Nothing really. I'm just very relieved the hole is big enough for you."

Robin pounced at him. He rolled out of her range and crawled under the bed before sticking a hand out and waving her under.

"Come along."

Thanking Trithian she wore a slimmer dress, Robin followed Arthur down the tunnel. She had to admire the engineering of it all. Earth had been pushed back and rocks now protruded forward in specific areas. Each rock was the perfect distance from its companions, making the climb down relatively easy despite the narrow passage. Her father and uncle had done well.

At the bottom, Arthur jumped down and waited for her to fall. She dropped into his arms and he placed her on the ground before taking her hand in his.

They moved on the rocky path beside the river until they reached a gate. Robin could see Liz's blonde curls bouncing around as she paced in front of the gate.

"Liz?" Arthur whispered in the darkness.

The pacing stopped. Robin's green-eyed chambermaid turned to stare into the tunnel.

"If that's Arthur and Robin, I have to say, you two are slower than snails. The bell's about to ring."

Arthur grabbed the key from his belt loop and unlocked the gate. Immediately, Liz pulled Robin into a hug and tucked a dark strand of hair behind her ear.

Arthur nodded towards Robin. "This one never makes anything easy."

She snatched the pouch from him.

Liz smirked. "We make it a point not to."

The young women giggled while Arthur shook his head.

"All right," he said amongst the chatter. "Listen, you two. Hike to the highest hilltop and wait for the signal. If you see a flame in the highest bell tower— "

"*When* we see the flame," Robin corrected him.

"*If* you see the flame," he said, pointing his gaze directly at her, "wait for me and my men at the hilltop. We will come and escort you back to the castle. Try and stay hidden until then, yes?"

They nodded.

Arthur spoke again though he was slow to let the words fall from his lips. "And if the flame is not lit by three-quarters past the hour, then..."

His gaze fell on Robin. She reached for him, but Liz intercepted her arm and looked into her eyes.

"We will be fine, my lady," she said.

She turned to Arthur. "More than fine, my lord. If we do not see the flames by three-quarters past, I will make sure Robin and I head north, going around the woods, not through as specified, to King Herald's castle. I have packed provisions."

Arthur cleared his throat and turned his head downward. "Yes. Thank you, Liz. Your hands are the most trustworthy to leave Robin in. Both of you, please, stay safe."

A loud echoing ring sounded from the castle. Robin looked up to the bell tower into the starry night sky.

Not one cloud. That must be a good sign.

"It's time." The words had come from Arthur.

Robin turned back to him and smiled. "Short, blonde hair just above the brows. Blue eyes like the seas of the east."

He shook his head and clasped her face in his hands. "Hair as black as a raven's feather, eyes as icy as the northern castle, small pink lips and a nose as flat as a cat's."

She pinched him. He still pulled her to him and their lips melted into one another.

Arthur was so warm, so soft and the smell of the gardens fumed from him like fire from a dragon-- all encompassing. Robin could feel her heart racing and her flesh begin to tingle when--

"Excuse me." Liz tapped on Robin's shoulder. "Love is great, however we do have a plan we should see to, hmm?"

Arthur's face was red as a beet. Robin had to cover her mouth to stop from laughing.

He straightened himself. "Uh...yes. Sorry again, Liz. You're very right. Wait for the signal and I will ride up to escort you both." He chanced one last look at Robin, then disappeared into the tunnel.

"We shall be off then." Liz tightened her cloak and started for the hilltop.

Robin followed behind her. She pulled her hood up and widened her strides to stand beside her friend.

"Are you all right, Robin?"

She bobbed her head. "Yes. I'm fine. I only want this whole ordeal to be over, so we both can return to our beds and Arthur can stop worrying. He's good at that, you know?"

Liz nodded. "Most men are. Only thing is they don't like to admit it." She nudged Robin in the side and the friends grinned.

Robin rested by the hilltop just beyond the road. Liz, like Arthur, thought the cover of trees was a necessary measure in case the king's plan failed.

Robin had scoffed at the thought. *The plan cannot fail if there is no conspiracy.*

She turned her head to Liz who was behind her braiding her hair.

"Liz, don't you think this whole thing is ridiculous?"

"What do you mean?" she asked, picking a flower from the earth and twisting it in with her friend's dark waves.

"This claim against Cadfen. He would never betray my uncle," she said. "I told Arthur the same, but he disagrees. What do you think?"

There was a slow exhale behind her.

"It does seem unlikely. But I understand why your uncle would be concerned about you and Morganna's safety. You are the last descendants of the throne."

Robin gave a dry chuckle. "More like she is. I've never wanted to be queen. Those desires belong to Morganna alone."

The echoing sound of the bell tower moved through the forest. Robin smiled. She turned to Liz.

"Now Arthur will see I am right." She leaned forward, then crawled to the edge of the road where the castle was in view.

"Stay still, Robin. I'm not done with your hair."

"I'm sorry, Liz. I want to see the flames, so we can be done with this night."

She watched the highest bell tower. Within minutes, a flame burst to life and delight spread across Robin's face.

"You see?" she said, turning back to look at her friend. "My uncle and Arthur were wrong. Cadfen is a good man." She directed her eyes back to the bell tower, a smug smile on her face as the flame grew brighter and brighter until the whole tower was ablaze.

Robin's eyes filled with twirling oranges and reds that spread from the tower onto the castle roof, turning her home into a maze of the colors.

Her eyes burned yet Robin could not look away.

"Something's wrong," she whispered.

She reached behind her. "Liz," she said, spinning around, "something's— "

Her breath caught in her throat as the scream sought to erupt from her.

It was an odd feeling--the warmth of her blood and the cold of the dagger plunged in her thigh. But where had the dagger come from?

She turned to Liz. Her beautiful lady-in-waiting was smiling.

"Liz," Robin breathed, "something...something..."

"Yes, something is wrong, my lady. The fact King Cadfen isn't willing to kill you disturbs me, as well." She gripped the dagger in Robin's thigh and twisted. Back and forth she moved the dagger, digging deeper into Robin's flesh, turning the pale white a disturbing red.

Robin stared as Liz deepened the cut and blood trickled down her leg. She held shaky hands above the wound as if she was attempting to keep the pain from spreading. But it refused and when Liz twisted at just the right angle, moans of pain hitched in Robin's throat, until she swore she could feel the knife scraping against bone. And then she cried out into the night, her entire body quivering as blood and agony rolled from her gash.

Finally, Liz pulled the dagger out. Robin took in a sharp breath. She glanced from Liz to the dagger. This was her chance. She couldn't wait.

Robin gritted her teeth, trying to force the pain into a normal sensation, before jumping to her feet and moving to the road. With only two steps taken she was again on the ground.

Liz leaned over her and showed Robin's hair wrapped in her fist.

"You're not going anywhere, my lady. King Cadfen's men should be here shortly."

"Traitor!" Robin spat, steeling the trembles in her voice.

Liz shook her head. "You would be doing the same if our positions were reversed."

She tugged Robin by her hair and pulled her so she leaned against a tree with one shoulder popped up in the air and the other slammed at an angle into the ground.

Liz sighed. "Won't be long now."

"You don't have to do this," Robin said through clenched teeth. Her eyes burned and she wasn't sure if it was from the pain of Liz's betrayal or the physical assault.

She attempted to turn completely to look Liz in the eyes. As soon as she moved, Liz pulled her the other direction.

"You can let me go," Robin breathed, watching with horror as blood continued to pour from her thigh. "Just let me go."

The blood was coming so quickly it had even started to stain her thick, purple cloak. She moved her hand to feel the spot, unable to believe all of it was really spilling from her. But when Robin placed her hand down she felt the cool of metal instead.

Deep breath.

"Say I escaped or something," she begged.

"I can't," Liz stated, her voice devoid of tone. "This is the only way. Struggle all you want."

"No, thank you."

"What?" Liz moved her gaze down to her prisoner.

In one smooth motion, Robin slashed through her own hair and leapt for the road. The pain in her thigh took her down. The lady-in-waiting leapt onto Robin and begin to drag her back into the woods. Robin moved to lay on her back, so, they were facing one another. For a moment, gazing into Liz's eyes, she hesitated. That meadow green made the whole moment surreal.

But then the green darkened to the color of pig dung and all Robin felt was rage.

She moved the dagger upward in an arc and felt pleasure erupt in her chest as it sliced Liz's cheek. Red spilled from the wound, splattering Robin in the process, and despite the maid's efforts to cover her cheek, the blood continued to ooze down her arm.

Liz wailed into the night, her body shaking with each breath. The only thing louder than her scream was the sound of approaching horsemen.

Both women stilled.

Liz turned to her lady and grinned. "As I said, they'd be here shortly."

Robin could hear and feel the horses get closer with each step. The earth trembled and the vibrations ran through her like small thunderstorms--frightening her.

"Here!" Liz screamed. "I have her here."

As she raised up to wave the men down, Robin rose with her. She dug her dagger into Liz's gut, pulled it out and pushed her shocked body to the side.

Standing on a wobbling leg, Robin peered down at her old friend, now bleeding from two wounds. "Always disarm your enemy, you doxy."

And then Robin ran off, away from her pursuers and north towards the woods. But she could hear them close behind. The sound of hooves grew louder and louder, the once peaceful night plundered by the foreboding sound of the traitors.

"Come on, boys! We've almost got her."

No. Robin moved faster, ignoring the blasting pain in her leg until she didn't feel it at all. Her burning chest had gone cold. Her arms that once ached from the struggle were numb. All she could feel, nearly all she could hear, was the rapid thumping of her heart.

And then, she was at the woods. She moved to go around the forest when she caught sight of what was after her. Five men on horseback, approaching at quick speed, a bloody dagger raised in the air held by a still wailing Liz. All coming for her.

No time. Robin spun to peer into the woods. Every story she had ever been told as a child warned her not to go inside. Even her uncle's men marched around the forest when they left the castle. Still, Arthur had gone in once and came back. She could too.

Plus, as her uncle always said, "We are becoming a country of science not witchcraft."

There was no more time. She pushed into the trees and shivered as laughter greeted her ears. She wasn't sure if it was Liz from the other side of the tree line or maybe something else...

The forest was thicker than she imagined, and Robin found herself bumping into a tree no matter which direction she chose. Her eyes tried to adjust to the darkness but unlike the road there was no moonlight here. The slivers of light that managed to touch the forest floor disappeared as soon as she spotted them. It was as if the forest was swallowing the light. Like it didn't want her to see what was coming next.

Robin continued to force her way through the forest, stopping every now and again to listen for horses or shouting. Neither was ever far away.

She pressed on until that odd sensation spread through her back--that odd feeling of hot and cold, caused by her warm blood and a chilly metal. She slumped against a tree and reached behind her. The feathery end of an arrow tickled her palm.

"She's there, boys. Right there!"

Lord, please, no.

Robin shoved away from the tree. She attempted to pick up her speed once more but her body did not agree. Her pace slowed yet the world wouldn't stop moving, no matter how often she rested. And they were always there. The men, Liz, always calling after her.

"Come on, boys. I see her now."

"Please, help me," she whispered into the black forest. She could feel herself slumping to the ground. "Please."

She pushed forward and wrapped her arms around the tree to stop from falling all together. As her arms encircled the trunk, she noticed there was something missing. The tree was not full. There was a hollow portion in front.

Robin stumbled to the tree's other side and moved her hands around. It was there. A hole big enough for her to climb into and hide.

She didn't hesitate.

Robin crouched down and then moved up inside the gaping hole, pushing herself as far to the side as she could get. With the darkness, the thickness of the woods, and the odd angle Robin stood, her pursuers were not likely to see her. She sunk into this thought, allowed it to bring her some peace. Soon her heart rate slowed. Her eyelids became heavy and Robin fell asleep.

Robin's entire body felt rough and bruised. She opened her eyes despite better thinking and was greeted by a ray of gray sunlight that still managed to blur her sight. She hissed and looked away into the darkness, leaning her head back and taking in the scent of the forest.

The Cursed Forest, she thought. *The place no one is ever supposed to go...except Arthur...Arthur.*

Her eyes filled with scalding tears as everything came back to her. Liz's betrayal, the burning castle, Cadfen's men, the arrows in her...

Robin turned to her right, reaching for her back only to have her motion stunted. She then tried to turn from her left and found she could barely move.

She felt around her middle. Where her waist had once been there was the rough exterior of tree bark. Robin moved her hands across the wooden surface. She shook her head and stepped forward, ready to duck out of the hollowed tree and make her way north.

There was a quick snapping sound. Robin paused.

Is that from me?

She moved, and again, she heard the snapping of wood. But what frightened her even more was the slow creaking noise and the palm of pressure that spread across her upper-body. She traced the direction of the bark and found it had sprouted upward and out over her chest.

Robin took in a deep breath. The wood creaked once more.

The young woman lunged forward towards the exit but even as the bark snapped apart it was replaced by the creaking. She thrashed in the alcove, banging her head and hands in the process of trying to escape. Repeatedly she thrust herself towards the opening, letting out screams that seemed to be swallowed by the tree, the monstrosity that only tightened its hold.

"No," she shouted. "No!" Robin tore at the bark until she could feel the soft wool of her clothing. And as soon as she felt that material, as soon as her heart beat slowed, there was the creaking sound teasing her ears. Another layer of the tree was formed.

A gurgling cry erupted from the pit of her fear. The young woman ran her hands over her face and pulled at her hair as her pain, apprehension, and misery erupted into the forest. She felt warm streaks across her cheeks but she was unsure whether the warmth was from her tears or her bleeding fingernails.

Robin dug into her scalp and screamed again, begging, pleading for release. It couldn't all end like this. There were those that had to be reprimanded, the public had to be saved from Cadfen's unfit rule, her cousin who would need consoling. It couldn't end with her uncle dead, perhaps Arthur too, and her, imprisoned in a tree for eternity.

No, no, no.

Her thoughts became words and she began to speak them.

"No, no, no."

She repeated the mantra again.

"No, no, no."

She spoke loud enough to drown out the steady creaking of the wood. First, it covered her chest. Then, up to her shoulders. The bark traveled down her waist, as well. Large, steaming tears slid down her face, but she could do nothing to stop it.

No one will ever know what happened to me. Arthur...he has Excalibur. He must be alive. He'll look for me.

The thought set on fresh heat behind her eyelids. Robin leaned her head forward and pressed her palms over her eyes. A small patch of cool touched her cheek. She reached for her wrist and fingered the several pieces of metal that hung from her charm bracelet. She held the middle piece between her thumb and forefinger.

"Dragon," she said.

The tree creaked but she focused on the feeling of the charm.

Arthur's gift for my nineteenth. His last gift to me.

She held her wrist tight in her hand and took a long breath.

There was the slightest sound of moving wood.

"Someone has to be alive," she croaked into the darkness. "Someone has to be and if it's Arthur, he'll look in these woods and see the bracelet. He'll know I'm here."

He must.

Robin closed her eyes. She counted the charms on her wrists all the while the bark continued to encompass her. There wasn't much time now.

With what little movement she had left, she stretched her right arm out of the alcove and into the gray sunlight. The bark around her shoulders tightened but she pushed through until it snapped and her arm was almost fully extended.

The charms still twinkled a bit in the sun and the shimmers made her smile.

The tree seemed to have increased its speed because the same arm she had just stretched out was turning into a branch in front of her. Her fingers became immobile.

"Find me," she whispered as the bark gripped her throat. Soon, she could make no sound. Soon there was only the thinning vision of the gray sun patches. Then, there was nothing.

Chapter One

Alistair bit his lip. He gripped the reins as he raced south to the middle kingdom's capital, Camelot. His eyes watered as the wind whipped past him, but he had not time to stop. He had wasted his morning finishing up an odd job for an innkeeper who he now perceived to be more of a crook than anything else.

"Ten shillings for seven hours," he barked out. "Nearly missed my actual job helping him and all he agrees to give me is ten shillings. Merchants, they're all a bunch of damn criminals!"

Fred, his horse, neighed and Alistair nodded, satisfied with his companion's response.

"And what makes it worse, Fred, is I have three more packages to drop off today. I'll be late to them all because of him. If I lose…"

The young man let his words trail off but they had already implanted in his mind.

If I lose this job, we won't make it through the winter.

He let out an angry grunt and lightly kicked Fred in the side. The horse picked up speed and Alistair lowered himself so his lips were by the horse's ears. He gritted his teeth and tried to keep his hold on the reins light so he didn't hurt Fred.

"We're going to make it. Forget about what I said. No matter what comes our way, we've got one another."

Fred huffed. As streams of air spiraled from his nostrils, Alistair could feel his companion press further on, faster than before.

Alistair stroked Fred's side. He forced a smile onto his face. "Come hell or high water," he said. "Come hell or high water."

The pair continued to move south and soon the path to Cadfen's capital came into view. The path directed travelers around The Cursed Woods. Even those unfamiliar with the land would naturally move towards the smooth walkway instead of the ominous trees.

Alistair wasn't aware of anyone who didn't know about the forest, any child who didn't hear bedtime stories of horror detailing what lay in wait behind those trees. But they had become just that. Bed time stories. Alistair's own mother had terrified him with tales of witches and goblins who ate little children that wandered in the forest.

But the time of witches was gone. There hadn't been an attack in over a decade.

He reached up and ran his fingers through the patch of silver in his hair, always an odd contrast to the rest of his hair that was pitch black. His aunt had called it a witch's curse, the only thing the blasted creature left him the night she tried to take his soul.

Alistair shivered at the thought.

The demons are extinct now. There is no longer anything to fear.

The pair grew closer to the forest. He could see the outline of trees very well now.

Despite the stories now serving the sole purpose of keeping children in line, a chill ran through him and the patch began to itch.

It hates this place as much as I do it seems.

The path to Cadfen's capital, Camelot, was to their left but at the speed they were going, Fred and Alistair were going to pass it soon.

Taking the path will extend my journey. Cutting through the trees will shorten it.

The forest wasn't too far now. The twisted trunks and branches were visible. On the other hand, the road to Cadfen's castle was slowly disappearing.

"They are only bed time stories," the young man said, his eyes splitting looks between the road and the trees. "And as King Cadfen says, we are a country of science not witchcraft...what do you think?"

Fred was quiet.

"Should I take your silence as a yes?" Alistair pushed on.

The horse continued his gallop.

Alistair glanced to the left again. Then back at the trees.

"Do you trust me, Fred?"

His companion huffed.

The young man nodded. "Then we're going straight through."

Alistair watched as the road disappeared from his sight before turning forward as they broke through the first line of trees.

Something wasn't right. Alistair felt it as soon as they entered the woods. It was like something had settled on his skin. Yet, just as soon as it settled, it had been washed off, a cold bucket of water rinsing the grime away. Still, he knew it was out there, whatever it was, maybe only a feeling, waiting to latch onto him again.

He shook himself. Paranoia did men no favors.

Alistair swallowed the ball in his throat and forced his back straight as they made their way.

At least I'm making good time. I'll be ahead of schedule even.

He took a breath and nodded. Yes, he was fine.

Fred couldn't gallop like he did in the open fields. The woods were thick with nature, but the horse kept a steady pace and maneuvered as needed.

Alistair reached forward and stroked Fred's face. "This rest will do you some good, huh, Fred?"

The forest was noiseless aside from Fred and Alistair, but even they had started to melt into the disturbing peace of the trees. Their breathing had lowered until it was inaudible. Alistair had stopped any chitchat. He placed his hand forward on Fred's chest and allowed himself to get lost in the rhythmic beats. The pulse was familiar. He had done the same thing with Fred's mother when he was a child before his parents sent him to the northern kingdom.

It was August, meaning his uncle and cousins would be celebrating the northern New Year. Ice shingles would be hung around the town and the fishermen would be working double shifts in preparation for the feast. He hadn't heard from his cousins for some time. He gazed upward to spots of sky.

"I wonder what they're up to," he said.

When he looked ahead once more, there were several small flashes of light and then nothing.

Alistair pulled on the reins and Fred came to a stop. He leaned back, then, moved his head up and down again. The small flashes appeared. They were coming from his left. He performed the movements a third time before nudging his horse over and going forward. The lights were no longer flashing. Now, they were glimmering in one spot above a tree branch.

Alistair and Fred moved towards the tree where the branch protruded. He dismounted Fred and walked to the tree. The sunlight was to his back revealing the source of the light flashes.

He reached for the branch where a leather charm bracelet hung. The material seemed to be old with signs of fading from the red leather. But the charms were perfectly intact.

The largest charm, the middle one, was in the shape of a dragon.

Alistair fingered the figures, before turning to the sun spots to see the light play off them again. They had to be made of good metal to have lasted so well in the elements. The carvings were detailed, too, particularly the dragon. The beast looked real enough to step off the charm and into the world.

The young man held the bracelet over his head and stared at it. His patch of silver was itching horribly but he ignored it. "I'm not sure what young woman left you. It doesn't seem she's here now. Probably a good thing, considering all the stories about this forest. Wouldn't be surprised if she fainted with fright."

Alistair felt Fred nibbling at his hair. He waved him away and stepped to the side. With one last look, he slipped the bracelet onto his wrist.

It's not my most masculine attire but maybe it'll bring me some luck.

The horse pulled at his hair again and this time Alistair hissed in pain as Fred tugged hard at the roots.

"Fred! What are you--" He had turned, hoping to twist out of his companion's grasp but Fred wasn't the one holding his hair. Actually, the horse hadn't moved from where he had dismounted him.

Alistair's blood went cold. He widened his eyes at his horse and the animal neighed, eyes roaming upward.

Alistair inhaled. It did nothing to calm his nerves. Slowly, with his eyes closed part of the way, he moved his head and looked up at what was holding him. For a moment, relief slipped in and Alistair could feel his blood running warm again. It was the twigs of a branch that had gotten stuck in his hair. Nothing more.

But then he felt another tug and saw that the tips had turned into fingers--human fingers. A weightless pit of a feeling settled in Alistair, leaving him in momentary shock, before bursting into tendrils of fear that ran through him.

He jumped forward only to find himself sideways on the ground. He tried crawling away yet whatever thing held him dragged him back, towards the black hole the branch protruded from. He screamed and grabbed at the earth, clutching onto anything that would slow his departure. The creature was relentless though. The harder he pulled, the stronger its grip. Alistair continued to scream.

Fred rushed over. He grabbed his owner's leg in his mouth and attempted to pull him away from the tree's grasp. The scene went on for several minutes. Alistair hanging like a wish bone, being pulled on either end by Fred or whatever creature was trying to pull him into the alcove.

And then, almost as suddenly as it had begun, the tree released him. He dropped to the ground with his patch burning, both from the pulling and the itching.

He scrambled away to his horse, reached into his satchel, and pulled out a small knife. It was old, rusted, and wouldn't do much, but it was the last thing that belonged to his parents and the only thing he happened to have on him. Blades were expensive.

The branch was a full arm now, poking out from the opening. The arm flexed, reached out into the air, and, finally, sunk back into the darkness.

Alistair waited. He wasn't sure if he'd be quick enough to mount Fred before the monster decided to come for him again. He *was* sure that it would be able to out run them in the forest. The land belonged to it, not to them.

Alistair took a shuddering breath. Was this going to be his last stand?

He peered at Fred who stood loyally by his side. Bile rose in his stomach when he realized he had signed both their wills. He gripped the knife with all his strength and just as a high-pitched gasp echoed from the tree, Alistair dove forward, rusty knife at the ready.

The monster crawled out from the tree's hole. He curved the knife downward. The creature stared up at him with dark hair and blue eyes that reminded him of northern shingles, and smooth pink lips. He twisted his wrist and the knife landed in the tree instead of the young woman's neck.

She watched him. Her chest rose and fell rapidly as she glanced from him to the knife he held in his hand.

"Was that for me?" she asked in voice that was scratchy and seemed out of practice.

Alistair's own chest was rising, as well and he could only nod in response.

She inclined her head. "I scared you?"

"Honestly, miss," he said, holding in a gulp of air and then releasing it one big puff. "You're scaring the life out of me right now and I'm trying to decide if this is a nightmare or if I've eaten some spoiled meat."

There was a small upward movement by the corner of her lips. She started chuckling but quickly stopped and placed a hand on her chest. Her breath began to come out in wheezes.

Alistair looked her over. Her thin fingers were grasping at her chest as she tried to gain air. There were no claws, no red eyes or fangs.

"Are you all right?" he asked.

She shook her head. "No but I'm better than I've been in some time. It just hurts to laugh...and speak."

Alistair nodded again yet remained silent. Women emerging from trees wasn't his area of expertise.

Fred walked over to the stranger and nuzzled her hair. She grinned and smoothed her face against his nose.

Alistair tensed and tightened his grip on the knife. He waited for the woman to strike, to puncture Fred with her branches. Nothing happened. Instead, she stroked his nose.

"I love horses," she croaked.

Alistair reached up to scratch his silver. "Well, he's always been one for the ladies."

He expected another chuckle or at least a giggle but her face had lost all emotion. Her eyes were fixated on his right wrist where the bracelet hung.

He peered at the charms. *So, this is the young lady you belong to?*

"Here," he said. "I assume this is yours." He removed the bracelet from his wrist and dropped it in her shaky, open palm.

She clasped it to her chest and closed her eyes as her face distorted. Then, with an unsteady breath and now glossy eyes she turned to him. "What is your name, please, sir?"

"Clark," he said.

"Clark?"

"Yes."

"That's an odd name around here. Are you from another kingdom?"

"No."

She narrowed her eyes. "What's your real name, *Clark*?"

He stared at her for some time. Then, he sighed and dipped his head to her. "You catch on quickly. Well, my real name I will not give you. There is power in names and I'm still not certain what you are."

"You mean a witch?"

He hesitated. He wasn't supposed to believe in witches. No one was anymore.

"What if I give you my name?" she said, continuing the conversation.

She tried to slide the bracelet on her wrist. Her fingers were staggering the effort. She toyed with the charms instead.

He shrugged. "I'll still be Clark. I still would like to know who nearly scared the soul out of me."

"All right," she said. "My name is Robin."

"Hm."

"What? Do you not approve?" There was that small turn of her lips again.

"No, it's not that," he said with a wave of his hand. "Actually, I think it's a lovely name, only it's not common for this day and age."

Her fingers froze. The charms became stagnant. There was a tense silence before she said, "And what day and age is this exactly?"

Alistair's eyes darted between Robin and the tree. The tree was thick and large with twisted branches that stretched out into the branches of its kin. Robin, in contrast, was small with some height to her. But the way she gripped the charms, the way her eyes had begun to flatten when she looked at Alistair...she was reaching out just like the tree, only not with branches this time.

"The year is four ninety, miss."

She stared at him. Then, Robin's back arched forward and she released a choking gasp that brought streams of tears down her cheeks. She pressed the charms to her and heaved out hoarse sobs as her shoulders shook.

Alistair moved towards her but stopped and stepped back. He glanced at Fred and raised a brow. The horse stepped beside Robin and nuzzled her hair again as she wept.

If she wanted us dead, I guess we'd be dead by now. Unless she's a patient witch.

He shook himself. His uncle Garron would have his head if he saw him now. A young lady was crying and he was standing frozen like a frightened child. Tree lady or not, she had done him no harm.

Alistair kneeled beside her and slowly pulled her into his arms. She seemed to barely notice. She didn't flinch or tense. She only fell and continued to sob.

"It's all right, miss. Whatever it is that's ailing you, you're not in the tree any longer and that's good news, isn't it?" He had pushed her to his chest and was rubbing her arms. She cried for several more minutes and then her weeping turned into silence. He tried to look down at her, praying she hadn't fallen asleep from exhaustion but her face was turned into his neck.

"You are a kind man, Clark," she said without looking up. "You've freed me from my prison, answered all my questions, and even comforted me. Still, I'm afraid I must call on your kindness again."

He nodded. "First, I didn't free you. I'm not sure how you got out. However, I'm more than willing to assist you. What can I do?"

"I need you to take me to King Terryn's capital, Camelot."

Alistair paused, his motions of comfort coming to a halt.

How does she know about the old king?

He gave a few airy coughs. "I'm sorry but I've never heard of any King Terryn. The land we're on belongs to King Cadfen. There is King Herald in the North, the two kings Essen and Issin in the Eastern realms and King Orof of the South. No Terryn."

"Is that what he's told everyone?" she said. Her breathing was coming out in rapid wheezes again.

"He?" Alistair asked.

"No one." She moved her head to stare up at him. "No one. Please, just take me to Camelot."

"I can do that. I have several packages to deliver there."

She gave him a small smile and nodded. "Let's be off, then. Shall we?"

Chapter Two

Neither Robin nor Clark had spoken since they left the forest. On Robin's part, she was eager to return to the land she had once called home even if such was the case no longer. Her blood heated her chest like coals in a hot fire as she thought of what happened that night. She hadn't been there but if Cadfer was king, Robin was certain her uncle and his men were dead. Maybe all of them.

She clutched her charm and shook away the thoughts of Arthur covered in blood.

He had Excalibur with him. The sword has saved him more than once. Why would this time be any different?

"You should try and move your legs, Robin, if you plan on getting them to work properly again."

Clark glanced back in her direction before turning to the road ahead.

Despite her best efforts, Robin felt a blush creep up her face. When she had tried to stand to mount the horse, her legs collapsed under her. She had tried to push herself off the ground and her arms shook horribly. Clark had to help her on and he even put the bracelet around her wrist.

Even now, she couldn't grasp the reins correctly and it was taking much of her strength and focus to hold onto Clark.

The tree had sustained her over her ten years of imprisonment. However, what it gave it also took back. Her body was out of practice. She had lost agility, speed, strength, and, temporarily at least, her mobility.

What labored her mind the most was she wasn't sure how long it would take for those things to return or if they ever would. So, she began to kick her legs, though the movement that occurred would hardly qualify.

"We can still make it, Fred. Race horse or not, you're the best. Come on!" Clark lightly slapped the horse's side.

Robin could feel the beast pick up speed. She smiled. Clark seemed kind and he treated his horse well, better than some royal trainers she had seen. Still, she was uncertain how much longer she could rely on his kindness. True, Clark was a messenger, meaning he was paid well enough, but by the looks of his clothes and the rusty knife he had tried to stab her with, he was not a wealthy man.

I won't put him out for too long, she thought. *Once I'm strong enough, I'll go in search of anyone who survived Cadfen's betrayal and together we'll re-take the kingdom. I'd love to see dear Elizabeth again, as well.*

She grinded her teeth at the thought and put more effort into her leg movements.

Clark turned back to her. "Follow my lead."

"What?"

"Everything I'm about to say isn't true but I need you to pull your hood up and play along."

She looked past him. A few yards away were four guards lined in front of a moat surrounding Camelot. Something of Cadfen's doing obviously.

Clark's words suddenly made sense to her. Without a second thought, Robin pulled her hood up and leaned against him.

As they approached the moat, one of the guards stepped out and held up a hand. They came to a halt.

"Business?" the man asked in a familiar voice. Robin fought the urge to turn and see if she knew him.

"Messenger. Packages for the baker Henry, the seamstress Odila, and the cobbler," Clark said, breathless from the ride.

"City of origin?"

"Satbury. The farthest north you can get before King Herald's land."

"Right," the guard responded. "Please, let me see your seal. Who's this you got here?"

"A new arrival for Lord Kensington."

There was a roar of laughter. Robin could even feel Clark force out a few chuckles.

"That old man," said one of the guards. "I don't know how he keeps up with all his *packages.*"

"He needs to start sharing with the rest of us. He's got more than enough to go around," said another.

A man grunted. "That's the truest statement I've ever heard. When he's doing books for the shop, I could keep his ladies occupied."

There was another bout of deep laughter.

Robin's stomach twisted. These men were pigs and Cadfen had let them loose. Uncle Terryn outlawed brothels unless the people there were present of choice and mind. But this, what these men were discussing was something entirely different. This was sex slavery.

"All right, here's ya seal, boy. Go on in."

Following his permission, the slow sound of the drawbridge greeted Robin's ears.

"Thank you, sir." Clark nudged the reins and Fred moved through the gates to the capital. As the gates closed behind them, Robin pulled her hood back a bit and sat up. Immediately, she looked south and there the castle rested as before. Four towers on each corner of the castle wall and the keep rested back, dead center with varying chambers on either side. The Camelot flag flew from each peak. It was if nothing had changed.

"Did you hear me, Robin?"

She forced her eyes away from the castle.

"What?"

"Go on, Fred,' said Clark and the horse started through the city.

Robin gazed around her. A few businesses and shops had been replaced, as well as some new structures added. People milled around the streets, bartering for goods, talking shop, others having lively discussions about the day. Nothing out of the ordinary.

"I said I'm sorry about what I told the guards," he stated. "I couldn't think of another way to get you in without suspicion."

"It's fine," Robin replied, peering around the city. "I know your words were for show. Who is this Lord Kensington?"

"He's the most sought-after treasurer in Camelot," said Clark. "Only works with the finest businesses. He also owns all seven, uh, male intended establishments. Many of the girls brought here are for his own entertainment though. If the guards ask him about you, he'll just figure he missed one."

Robin scoffed. "Male intended establishments? You mean brothels. Or better yet, let's call it what it is. Sex houses where the participants are kept there against their will. Am I correct?"

Clark loosened his grip on the reins and placed his hands on Fred's back. "He knows his way from here. And yes, you are correct, Robin. Many of the women and children--"

"Children!" She jumped in her seat, her body temporarily forgetting it was imprisoned for ten years. Her hands became fists and she felt a boiling disgust rise in her.

He has children...working in the brothels? How could he ever-

"Robin?"

The disgust in her stomach had forced her mouth shut.

"Yes," she answered through gritted teeth.

"Would you agree it is not in our best interest to draw too much attention to ourselves? You know, with me being from

Satbury and you rolling from a tree only a few moments ago."

"Uh-huh." She flexed her fingers, wishing more than ever she could get them around Cadfen's neck.

He had taken her home, taken the city's dignity. He had taken everything.

"So..." Clark gave her a glance.

What was he saying to me?

"How do you think screaming as we enter the city qualifies?" He raised a brow.

She closed her eyes and tightened her fists before taking a deep breath which did nothing to calm her.

"Yes, I'm sorry. You're right," she said, jaw still tight. "I was lost in my mind for a moment."

"Another thing, Robin."

"Yes, Clark." She tried not to bite the words out at him.

"Breaking the rider's chest bone of the horse you are also riding is highly ill advised."

With a gasp, she pulled her arms back from his chest and lightly placed her hands on his shoulders. Clark had not been the one to wrong her. Cadfen had. She would save her rage for him, yet her body was not in complete agreement.

Children.

The sickening feeling rose in her stomach again. This time it was not hot and angry. Instead, the churning felt heavy and dense. The mobility her body had gained when rushed with energy faded and sunk, drawing her with it. Robin could sense the airy feeling smooth over her head. She grew slack and though she tried to tighten her grip on the horse, she could feel herself falling.

Fred jerked to the left. A hand wrapped around her wrist and then she was resting lopsidedly against Clark. There was a slick sweat on her brow.

He encircled himself using her arms and pulled her up a bit.

"Children," she wheezed into his ear. "My uncle, Arthur, everyone...he's taken them all."

A tremor ran down Clark's spine.

"Robin, you misunderstood what I said. The children aren't being sold. They serve food and clean."

She raised her own brow. "Then, they're not..."

He shook his head.

A sigh escaped her. That was one less thing to press on her mind.

"Look, I'm almost to my first stop. You should tell me where you want to go."

I have nowhere to go.

"You're obviously feeling worse than we thought. You need help, a physician perhaps."

"It's a simple spell. The doctors have already told me I have a weak constitution. It will pass."

He nodded. "Fine. Well, I don't want you fainting in the city. You're likely to be stomped by another horse before I can dismount."

Clark closed his hand around her wrists. "My cousin from the north used to have fainting spells, too. Focus on me, the hold you have on me. Everything else will be a blur. I'll be your center."

She nodded and tightened her grip. Through his clothes, she realized how slim Clark was. His small frame was enshrined with muscle, probably not acquired through any formal training but it was still present. His abdomen rose and fell with his breathing. His shoulders flexed every now and again.

Robin turned and stared up at him. His hair was the same shade as hers, aside from the streak of silver. His eyes were a strange shade, as well. Not a dark brown but a deep purple that shone when caught in good light.

She inhaled. Clark smelled like warm hay in the sun. Memories of her childhood rushed to her but she pushed them into a dark corner. She was here in Camelot with Clark and Fred. If she could focus on that, her mind would as well.

I will not faint.

Again, she turned to look out at the city. There was no immediate sign of mistreatment. Actually, the townspeople seemed happy going about their day. There was no cloud of gloom hanging over their heads. They were content...with Cadfen.

Tears threatened to spring from Robin's eyes. She pulled closer to Clark and they receded.

Robin scolded herself. She needed to be smarter and not let her emotions get the best of her. What had she expected really? Blood smeared across the road and walls? People hanging from posts?

No. Cadfen was a traitor, not stupid and before *that* night's events, Robin hadn't ever seen him be cruel. His political mindset and skill on the battlefield were what got him ranked so highly among the foot soldiers, only a class below the knights like Arthur. Uncle Terryn had respected him, trusted him, maybe even confided in him more than he should have.

Where Robin had expected the scent of death and decay, there were the smells of sweet bread, roasted meat, and fire.

Fred came to a halt.

"Be right back," Clark said. He dismounted slowly, so she would have time to adjust her hold on the horse. He ran into a shop with open shutters. Inside, Robin saw several spinning wheels and lines of fabric. In a matter of minutes, he was back with a small envelope and a wide smile.

"Gotta a few extra coins." He climbed back onto Fred and they were off again.

Immediately, Robin wrapped her arms around him and pulled forward.

As they reached the next stop and Clark dismounted, Robin noticed a man standing outside a building across from the baker.

He had large eyes, a toothy smile, salt-and-pepper hair, and a beard to match. Most distinctly, there was a golden chain around his neck. A chain that Robin knew came from his wife.

"Mathius," she meant to say the name to herself but it came out much louder.

He glanced at her, squinted his eyes, and shook his head before walking the opposite direction.

She watched him until he was out of view, hoping he would spin around and race to her side, suddenly realizing who she was. But he didn't. He disappeared and Robin was left looking like someone had shot an arrow in her chest.

She shook the thought away. *In the back was bad enough.*

From the same building, several other men stumbled out. None of them wore armor but from the build of their bodies and the way they carried themselves, even with ale in one hand, Robin guessed they had to be knights. In fact, she knew they were because she recognized them. It may have been ten years, yet still she knew their faces. These were four of the first sons from some of the highest respected families in Camelot, groomed since birth to be knights. Gavin, Aaron, Petsin, and Lyle.

They were boys when she had been imprisoned in the tree. Now they stood as grown men.

Robin examined the building. There was no sign or title on it. But considering the state of its inhabitants, it was not completely abandoned. Probably some bootlegger who couldn't afford the tax and was hiding out until he either saved enough or was caught. Not exactly a respectable place for knights to be, on duty or not.

As the four made their way to the street, they pushed each other up and puffed out their chests. Robin applauded their attempt, still noting they looked like fools trying too hard to *not* be drunk. Something else tugged at her, as well.

If these boys and Mathius were working under Cadfen, could that mean their families had been involved in the plot to overtake the kingdom?

The light airy feeling returned to her head. She fell forward on Fred and tried to control her breathing. Clark was still speaking with the baker.

"Well, hello, there, miss."

Robin turned to her right. Gavin stood in the street in all his drunken glory, his fists on his hips and his chest pushed forward like a rooster. He grinned.

Robin raised a brow.

"Are you in need of some assistance? A lady should not be out too long in this sun. Where's your rider?"

"Uh- "

"No, no, don't speak," he slurred and blundered his way closer to her. "Conserve your energy."

He held up a hand and placed the other over his chest.

"These are my men." He gestured to the three behind him. "The strongest men you've met, I'm sure. And me?"

He flashed that grin again and leaned elbows first on Fred as he gazed at her.

"Well, I am sure I'm the most handsome man you've ever met and I'd love to have a beautiful lady like you by my side."

Perhaps on another woman it would have worked. Those green eyes, that smooth orange hair that peaked perfectly at his brows and complimented skin that was as pale as if he was from the north... well, they were a dangerous combination.

Maybe someone younger, who hadn't known Gavin since he was small and hadn't changed his diapers would have succumbed to his "charms." Robin did not.

Instead, her cheeks grew hot and with all the ferocious authority of an older sister she said, "Gavin Webb, I do not know what harlots you are accustomed to *swooning*. But I can assure you I am not one of them. Your mother would have your nose if she saw you now. If I were not in a current dilemma, I'd have the mind to go tell her right away."

His eyes bulged. "Uh, wait, who-"

She shook a finger at him. "I'm not done. Any woman who falls for the little act you put on is not for you, Gavin. You need a lady who can see through your foolery and flattery in order for her to make you a better man. Whatever female company you are keeping, *change it*."

All four men stood rigid. She was certain her speech had

sobered them up a bit faster than normal. They shot glances at one another and, then at her.

After a few pregnant moments, Lyle turned to Petsin. "I haven't received a whacking like that since my sister left for the covenant."

Robin opened her mouth to ask about Susan, his sister, but she quickly bit her tongue. She had already drawn too much attention to herself, the very opposite of what Clark had advised. If they recognized Robin, they were doing a good job of hiding it.

But if Mathius is alive and the boys have become knights...could Arthur--

Suddenly, there was a chesty laugh. Gavin proudly stood with his head thrown back as deep chortles erupted from him.

Robin sighed. Gavin had always been a bit of a gaudy fool. It was both comforting and disappointing that much hadn't changed.

Miss," he said placing his eyes back on Robin. They roamed over her. Her skin crawled.

He crossed back a leg and bowed. As he stood straight again he grabbed her hand and kissed it.

Robin pulled her hand free and glared down at him. He only grinned, the drunken gloss of ale still swirling in his eyes.

"Is everything well here?"

Robin and the men snapped their necks back to see Clark standing outside of the baker's shop. He crossed his arms. Slowly, he moved his eyes to Robin.

"Robin?"

She looked from him to the four men. A woman and four drunks was not the most respectable scene.

Robin went to answer, yet before she could, Gavin had pushed off from Fred and was raising his hands.

"Apologies. Didn't know the lady was accounted for. You're a lucky man, my friend."

Clark loosened his stance. "No harm done. You all have a good afternoon."

He calmly mounted Fred, knocked his sides and they were off again.

Robin pulled her hood closer before turning back to Gavin and the others. They were still milling in the street. She turned to Clark and wrapped her arms around him.

"You sure you're all right? You still look a little sick," he said.

She nodded. "Yes, I'm fine. Those men...I know them."

"How?"

"From before."

"Before what, Robin? From when you lived here? Are they childhood friends?"

She chewed on her response. How much could she really tell him? What if he thought her mad or, worse, what if he turned her in? Arthur had said Cadfen wanted her as a wife. As soon as he discovered she was a live, he'd claim her, Robin had no doubt. He had done worse, hadn't he?

So who am I to trust?

"Was my question too personal?" he asked.

Robin looked him over.

God be with me.

She cleared her throat. "No, not at all. Clark?"

"Hmm?"

She took a deep breath. "I need to tell you something."

Chapter Three

Alistair couldn't believe the day he was having. On one hand, he still managed to make good time on his deliveries, so his job was secure for the winter. Some of the usual clients were even feeling generous and tossed extra coin his way, all of which he planned to put in his savings.

On the other hand, he was nearly scared to death when Robin pulled herself from the tree, an act he was still trying to wrap his mind around.

People don't just pop out of trees. Well, she didn't really pop out of it. There was a branch first and, then, her arm like she had been part of the tree. How the hell did that happen?

His gaze found Robin who was eating broth in the corner across from him.

She hadn't posed any direct danger but in the process of trying to help, he had lied to the Camelot guards twice--they were confused when he departed with her still on his horse and stopped him for questioning--an act that could have gotten him executed if she had stirred up trouble. Not to mention, she had inadvertently become his responsibility after she admitted she had been lying to him and was homeless.

What did I really expect though?

The woman had emerged from a tree, and from the way she reacted when he told her the year, she must have been there for some time. He wondered when she had been trapped. She didn't look much older than himself. More importantly, how had she been trapped there? Turned into a tree?

He snatched a glance of her again and shook his head. The days of witches were over. Perhaps she had been cursed before the witches disappeared. Any family or friends she may have had were likely either dead or moved on somewhere new.

Alistair didn't want to admit it. Since their meeting in the woods, he knew she was going to drag him into something. His silver patch hadn't stopped itching since they met and his aunt had warned him the itching was a sign. He had thought it was only because of the forest, a sort of leftover from before when magic reigned.

Robin was not a witch. He was pretty sure on that. Instead, it seemed like whatever had gotten her into that tree had left a kind of magical residue over her, hence the perpetual itch.

And now, he reminded himself again as she sipped broth from a chipped bowl, she was his to care for. It was the only proper thing a man could do, after all.

He sat across from her and listened to horses snoring below as she finished her meal.

When she was done, she put the bowl to the side, wiped her mouth with the tip of her cuff, and smiled at him.

"Thank you, Clark. It was very good."

He nodded. "Not exactly filling though."

"No, no, it was fine," she assured him. "Actually, it feels wonderful to eat something for myself instead of drawing from that tree."

"Is that how you survived all this time?" He had wondered exactly how a tree-woman ate.

She nodded. "The first week I was terrified I'd die of starvation. Instead my hunger abated. Soon I was rarely hungry at all. I don't think my appetite will ever be what it was."

"I'm still sorry I don't have more to offer you. When I returned to the middle kingdom most of my money went into my parent's burial and my new lodgings." He gestured to the small room they both occupied.

"Is that how you ended up here?" She moved her eyes around the tiny space he called home. He bit back the feeling of shame rising in his chest. Alistair didn't have many friends in the middle kingdom meaning he didn't often entertain guests. Living in a questionable room above a horse stable was fine for him. For a young lady? He wasn't so certain.

"You're lucky."

Robin pulled him from his thoughts. She was now sitting cross-legged and leaning out the window. Her hair had been pushed to the side.

In the torch's glow he could see the light blue lines of her veins run across her neck like glowing webs knitted across northern snow.

Her lips curled up again as she stared out the window. Still, her arms trembled a bit when she leaned forward. The rush of energy she experienced in Camelot had helped her body regain some mobility, but nothing would replace actual practice.

"I suppose it's time for me to tell you." Her sight moved to him.

"I don't want to push you to do anything, Robin. Though knowing exactly what I've gotten myself into would be helpful."

"Of course. I only need you to promise me one thing."

"I think I can do that," he said and sat a little taller.

"What I'm about to tell you sounds like a child's tale but it's the truth. That being said, you must swear not to have me put away." She moved forward and extended her hand. Her blue eyes were pushing into him with a deadly seriousness he hadn't felt since his aunt Una had caught him eating her southern chocolates.

The memory made him shiver and for a moment he hesitated. He glanced from her hand to her eyes, before offering up his hand, as well.

They shook.

"Good." She straightened and pulled her shoulders back. "My full name is Gwynevere Robin Leingard. I prefer my middle name. King Terryn, the rightful king, the man who should be ruling now is-*was* my uncle."

She paused and kept a steady gaze on him. If she was expecting a reaction, he was not going to give her one. His uncle had informed him to never let anyone in the middle kingdom know he had memories from the time before. And considering he really didn't know Robin well, despite his duty and growing fondness for her, he repeated what any citizen of the middle kingdom would say.

"King Cadfen has always been king."

The hollowness that appeared in her eyes was disturbing. She swallowed and then ran her hands through her hair, before taking a deep breath.

"Every king has a predecessor. Terryn was Cadfen's predecessor."

"I've never heard of him," Alistair lied.

"So, what do you think, then? Cadfen was born king and will rule forever?"

The lie was turning into a tight ball in his throat. "Of course," he mumbled.

Robin's eyes widened. She closed them and took in a shuddering inhalation. When her eyes were fixed on Alistair again, he could see the brewing storm behind her icy blue.

She clenched and unclenched her fists. "All men are mortal, Clark."

He nodded. "Yes, but Cadfen is not a man. He is a king."

Robin shot up from where she had been sitting. Her fists were balled and her chest was heaving quick, short bursts of air. Her whole body shook, angry tremors running all over her when she finally said, "Cadfen is no king!"

The horses neighed and snorted below them.

"Cadfen," her voice was reaching a deafening pitch, "is a mur-
"

Alistair moved without thinking. He didn't want to hurt her but the words she had said, as well as the ones she was about to speak, could have them both tortured and boiled alive for treason. He pushed her into the wall and moved his hand over her mouth.

Her eyes had grown round. However, this time, their size was not from a riveting speech.

Robin was scared.

She looked like a rabbit caught by a dagger--absolutely frightened. She began to buck under him and Alistair didn't have the heart to hold her.

She squirmed away and pushed herself into the corner beside the door.

Alistair showed his palms and took a step towards her.

Robin reached for her cloak. From under one of the folds she pulled out a jeweled dagger and held it out.

She set her jaw. "I may not be a soldier but I'm sure I can slice you up quite well if you ever lay your hands on me again."

Fight had replaced flight apparently.

Alistair stopped his march. "Robin, I'm sorry."

"You will be if you move any closer." She pulled the dagger back and relaxed her stance. A slow exhale eased from her. She moved the dagger in front of her and angled it upwards while her other arm was held out from her side. She flexed her fingers.

She's not all talk, I see.

"I didn't mean to hurt you," he said. "But what you were about to say, what you said, if anyone heard any of it, the guards will be here shortly and we'll be killed."

"I can speak my mind," she retorted.

"Not in Cadfen's kingdom."

A pained look flashed across her face. "That man is a monster."

Alistair made no movement. "Most just call him king."

Robin said nothing, only took in a bit of air and kept the dagger at a good distance. Alistair was silent, as well. He remained standing with his hands up, palms ahead, waiting for Robin to make the first move. After all, she was the one with the dagger. He didn't want to spook her and end up with his throat slashed...or worse.

While they continued to assess one another, Alistair also examined her weapon. No fraud in the world could make something so fine. The dagger was obviously royal-forged with a handle designed to create a good hold for the wielder. He looked between the dagger and Robin.

Of course, Alistair had never met anyone of the royal family. He was a commoner. Not to mention, he was already up north with his uncle when Cadfen took over. But even before then, King Terryn, Princess Morganna, and Lady Robin had seemed like mythical faeries more than real people. He could only remember hearing a bit of news about her, well, more like a rumor. Arthur Pendragon, one of Terryn's top knights, was courting her.

Could this really be her?

The way she spoke, the dagger, even her dress and cloak, though filthy from years in a tree, alluded to her being high-born, a golden child as some jokingly said about royals.

"Do I have to slice you with it or is the dagger proof enough?"

He sighed and lowered his arms. "You can't blame me for being skeptical, Robin."

"But you haven't called me a liar. And you haven't run out of here to report me to the guards, so you must believe some of what I'm saying." She released her stance and hid the dagger under her cloak.

He nodded. "That's a fair assumption. You also had a dagger pointed at me. There's that to consider, as well."

"I'm going to believe the dagger had the least influence," she said and took a seat in the corner. "Now that you believe me, how do we get others to believe me too?"

His shoulders sagged at the use of "we."

"Someone from before has to be alive. He couldn't have killed them all, could he?" She had her hands folded tightly in her lap, her pinched eyes looked at him. There was water building in them.

He moved to sit beside her but she pushed away and turned to face him.

"I just need you to try. Try to remember what happened before he was king."

The lie had built in his chest now. It pounded at his rib cage. "My only memory of a king is Cadfen."

She muffled a sigh with her hand and wiped at her eyes. "Nothing, then?"

He shook his head.

She took in a long breath. "Fine. Then, I am here to tell you what you think fact is false. I don't know how he's doing it, but my uncle Terryn was king before Cadfen. Cadfen was one of his loyal soldiers. For a reason which I will never understand, he betrayed my uncle."

She wiggled in her small corner. Her feet tapped the floor.

"I'm not sure where it all went wrong," she said, staring into the torch's light. "There was a rumor Cadfen was a traitor. I didn't think it was true, but Arthur and my uncle slipped Morganna and me out the night he was supposed to attack. I left with my chambermaid, believing everything was going to be fine. And then, it wasn't."

Alistair remembered when the news of King Cadfen had reached his uncle. No one in the north, King Herald included if rumors were true, could believe a foot soldier had ascended the throne. Not without some foul play. But as his uncle pointed out, none of that really mattered. What mattered was the citizens of the middle kingdom did not protest.

No one raised arms or argued. It was like Terryn had been wiped off the face of the earth, right out of the scrolls.

"My chambermaid, Elizabeth," Robin continued, "she had been working for Cadfen the entire time. She attacked me and tried to hold me prisoner. Apparently, Cadfen intended to make me his bride. As if I'd ever agree." The last words left her mouth like a painful joke.

"Anyway, I escaped from her and my pursuing guards. The forest, I-I had always thought they were mostly fairy tales to scare children. And...well, I was scared, so I ran straight in, hoping to lose them and make it to the northern territory."

Alistair let her take her time. But he had to admit, he was feeling a little anxious himself at her tale. If what she was saying was true, Terryn was definitely dead and any still loyal to him likely had been killed, their bodies probably burned. Robin was alone.

Her eyes were fixed on the torch like she was in a trance. "I kept running. I moved my feet as quickly into the earth as I could but they were so close. Then, they shot me in the back three times. I was bleeding and they were closing in on me. I thought the tree would keep me safe until they left and I could make my way north. Instead, when I woke, well, I think you know the rest."

He nodded but did not make eye contact with her. Her story played out perfectly along with King Terryn's sudden disappearance. Men don't just up and vanish, well, a few have been said to have when they stepped into The Cursed Forest but he was sure Terryn did no such thing.

"So, do you believe my story?"

Robin had scooted a bit closer. She was almost leaning directly above the torch and a misshapen shadow crossed her face, leaving only one eye exposed. In that one eye, there was a disturbing desperation, a vengeful need.

Alistair let a chill run through him and then stood. "I see no reason not to," he said with a breathy exasperation.

Suddenly, she had a hold on him. Her arms coiled around his neck and pulled with such strength he questioned where she got it from.

"Thank you, Clark," she whispered into his shoulder. "Thank you for believing me."

He placed a hand on her head and pressed his cheek into her hair. She smelled like fresh soil and water, the scents from his childhood. Except, what Robin had been through was far from innocent. She had suffered, been nearly killed and even though he didn't want to divulge all his secrets just yet, one fact was unmoving--he had to help her.

He patted her head one more time and then gently moved her back.

"I guess I'll have to start calling you *my lady* since you don't like Gwynevere."

She shook her head. "Only my parents can call me Gwynevere. Everyone else called me Robin and I hope you will do the same. The use of *lady* would be a little odd considering our situation, as well."

"Fine. Robin it will be."

"Yes." The biggest smile spread across her face. "And now we need to make plans on how to take my home back. There has to be some--"

"Robin?"

"Yes, Clark?"

"I think sleeping is your best option currently."

"But we--"

"Are you even sure Arthur would still be in the middle kingdom? Maybe he fled north."

She sighed. "No. He never submits. Arthur, if he's hiding, it'll be somewhere close by. Somewhere no one would think to look. This is why we should start--"

"Robin?"

"Yes, Clark?" The word came out as a slow breath.

"Have you ever heard the story of the sleeping bear and the sly fox?"

She narrowed her eyes. "No, but what does a fairy tale have to do with anything we've discussed?"

He cleared his throat. "Nothing, really except my mother used to tell it to me to help me sleep. I think it may do the same for you."

She chuckled. "It's sweet but I'm not exactly a child anymore."

"And I'm not exactly a mother yet I'm willing to give it a go."

More importantly, you can hardly run much less take back Camelot.

She paused and turned back to the window.

"Robin," he said, "there is nothing that can be done now that can't be done tomorrow. Here." He gestured to a tattered mat that lay on the opposite side of the room. There was a blanket and a few badly kept pillows.

"I'll sleep on the floor and tell the story until you drift off."

Robin examined the ratty mat. "Are you sure?"

"As sure as the sun rising tomorrow morning."

She looked at the mat again. Her shoulders seemed to slack some and her eyes glazed over a little. It had been a long day.

"I guess you're right," she said with a sigh.

She curled up on the makeshift bed and pulled the covers over her. Immediately, she began yawning and Alistair had to hold back a laugh.

"What's this story?" she asked. "The sly fox must be the hero in the end." Another yawn.

He positioned himself so he was sitting with his back to the wall and his side by Robin's head.

"I'm not one for spoiling tales. You'll just have to listen."

"Mhm," she grumbled.

"Once upon a time, in a forest covered in white, there lived a bear."

Chapter Four

obin awoke in a sweat. She tossed the covers off and searched her body for arrows. She had been bleeding. She knew she had. It had pooled out of her like she was hung up in a butcher's shop. Where were the wounds?

She rubbed her abdomen, searching for a soft red spot leaking her life into a puddle all around her. There was nothing.

She checked her back. The same result. But she knew she had been hit! She knew she was dying and that Cadfen's men were after her. Why couldn't she find the damn spot?

"Alistair, do you ever have fun?" A woman's voice.

Robin looked up from her body and took note of the strange room she was in.

There was more chatter from outside. She crawled to a window and peeked over the edge, before craning her neck out.

"I think only the rich have time for fun, Maddy." A man's voice, followed by a chuckle.

Robin couldn't see the young woman properly. She had a hood pulled up. What she did see was long hair an odd shade of black draped across her shoulder.

Robin stared at the man. He seemed more familiar than the woman, but his back was facing her. She couldn't be sure. He had black hair with a streak of silver towards the front, reminiscent of the moon.

And he smells like warm hay bathed in the sun...how do I know that?

Robin's head swam as too many memories fought for dominance in her mind.

I was in the forest and-no. I left. I escaped from the tree. But how?

"Alistair?" the young woman asked.

She's calling him the wrong name. He's Clark, not Alistair.

"Hmm?"

"Do you have a friend over?"

The man turned and stared up into the window, right into Robin's eyes. Immediately, she pushed back from the opening and curled on to the mat. Her head had turned into an ocean and she was drowning. She felt as if the ground was uneven beneath her, shifting somehow.

Purple? Why are his eyes purple? Why do I know that?

All she could see were those purple eyes. Then, they turned blue and the man's hair turned yellow.

And it's shorter too. Just above his brows. And he'll smell like a garden. This other man smells like a garden, he...his name, he's Arthur. Arthur.

She could see him standing right in front of her.

Why does this feel familiar?

"Robin, are you well?"

The image faded. Instead of Arthur, Clark, or Alistair, as the young woman had called him, was standing in his place, his hair dark like hers and mid-neck length.

"Robin?"

She shook herself and took a deep breath. "Uh, yes, I'm fine. I'm sorry, Clark. I didn't mean to scare you."

"No harm done. I was doing some work for my landlord below." His eyes scanned the room and landed on the covers tossed to the side. He turned back to Robin.

"Did something frighten you?" he asked.

Yes, forgetting where I was.

But she didn't want to think about that. Instead, she said, "In the tree, I didn't dream. I've forgotten how...terrifying they can be."

He nodded. "Sounds more like a nightmare than a dream."

She laughed though it sounded hoarse because her throat was so dry. "I'd agree with you yet I don't know what's worst. The nightmare or waking and realizing it's a reality."

"Maybe both are just bad enough," he said. "Are you hungry?"

She shook her head. "No. As I said, my appetite is another thing that damn tree has taken from me."

"Water?" He raised a brow.

Her throat pulsed at the very mention. "That sounds wonderful."

"Be right back." He grinned and stepped out the door, leaving it open behind him.

Robin got up and closed it. She returned to the mat and heaved a heavy sigh.

Why did I forget where I was? Why couldn't I recognize Clark? No, not Clark. Alistair. The girl called him Alistair.

She closed her eyes and pinched the bridge of her nose, sorting through her thoughts, and then she remembered.

As the door opened, Robin narrowed her eyes at the young man.

"Your name is Alistair, not Clark."

Alistair paused mid-stride and watched her. Robin jutted out her chin, crossed her arms, and smiled up at him. She had known she was going to get his real name eventually.

Alistair ruffled his hair and shrugged. "At this point, I guess it doesn't matter. Fred and I are sure you're not a witch."

"Well, I'm glad that issue has been cleared up at least."

He squatted next to her and placed a bucket at her side. "Your voice sounds worse than an ax on stone. Here."

He placed a small tin cup in her hands and tapped it with his fingers. Another grin pulled at his lips. "I even got you the royal mug."

She pulled the cup away and batted at him. "You're such a jester, are you?"

He sat across from her, ankles under his thighs. "Well, Fred can't talk with me and I need to find a way to make myself laugh. I believe I do a fine job, actually."

"Oh, look at that. Funny and full o' himself. Very charming, Alistair, very charming."

He bobbed his head, the big grin still bold on his face. Robin sighed at him before dumping the cup in the bucket and scooping out water. She raised the cup to her lips and at the first drop she knew she was extremely dehydrated. Water had never tasted so good and suddenly she couldn't have enough. With every mouthful she took down, it felt like her throat became drier, begging for more.

She continued to pour water in her mouth, not caring but actually enjoying the dribbles that rolled down her dress and cooled her. And then, the bucket was empty. Robin licked her lips, her throat feeling somewhat satisfied. She stretched, pulling her neck back and finally sat against the wall, her knees laid to the side.

"Should I fetch another bucket or bring you the whole well?" Alistair stared at her with a curved brow and a gaping mouth.

Robin blushed but pinched herself to stop all the red from rushing to her cheeks. "I guess I need more water than food now," she said, glancing at the empty bucket before returning her eyes to the young man. "Can I ask you something, Alistair?"

"Of course."

She waited a moment, letting the words take their best form before she spoke. "Your eyes. I've never seen purple eyes."

"You noticed, then?"

"The color is quite definitive in the sunlight."

He laughed. "It's not exactly common."

"Exactly, so why are your eyes that color?"

"To be honest," he said with some exasperation, "I'm not too sure. My parents told me I was born earlier than expected. They attribute it to that."

Robin tapped a finger on her thigh. She had seen premature children before but never with purple eyes.

Alistair stretched his back and placed both hands on his knees. "Now, are you remembering yet?"

She stopped tapping. "Remembering what?"

Though he didn't sigh, the muscles in his face tensed for a moment. He ran a hand through his hair and blustered out a breath.

"I suppose it'll take more time," he said.

"What will take more time? What are you going on about?"

Alistair's gaze fell to the floor before his shoulders slacked and he stared back at Robin.

"I mean that we've had this conversation. You wake from a nightmare. I come to check on you, you ask about my eyes. . . Do you not remember any of it?"

A tight feeling wrapped around Robin's chest.

"I-I...no."

"Do you at least know where we are? How we met?"

"Yes! Of course. You pulled me from that tree. We're in Satbury at your home."

He nodded. "Good. And how long have we been here?"

"We only arrived last night."

His face muscles tightened again. He shook his head.

"No, Robin. It's been a week."

A chill rushed over Robin. She had to close her eyes. She reached for her bracelet and began fingering the dragon charm. She tried to look at Alistair once more yet she couldn't bring herself to do it.

I'm losing my mind. And I'm not even trapped in that damn tree anymore.

Alistair cleared his throat. She watched him from her peripherals.

"It'll come back with time, Robin. Here, I brought you these." He slid a bundle of clothes across the floor. "They're clean and fresh. They're a bit big for you but I thought you may want to get out of that dress."

The clothes he'd given her consisted of a stained white tunic and washed out brown pants along with a pair of leather boots Robin knew she couldn't fit. They were, with all respect, peasant clothes, similar to what Alistair was wearing himself.

She smoothed her hands over the rough material, noting every time a stray thread got caught in her nail. Then, she felt her own dress, before pulling the clothes close to her chest.

"Thank you, Alistair," she said. "Out of all the gifts I've ever received, I am most thankful for this. Your patience, as well. I know this must be hard."

He shrugged. "Life's pretty hard. I'm used to it. Plus, what was I supposed to do? Leave you in the forest alone?"

"You could have," she said, finally turning her head and meeting his gaze. "I'm a stranger to you. You owe me nothing."

"You're definitely not a stranger, Robin."

"What do you mean?"

Alistair stood and moved across the room to sit beside her. He pointed at her eyes.

"Your favorite color is blue like your eyes. It was your mothers too. Your favorite food is chocolate berries from the south, just like my aunt. Once, you got sick eating too many as a child."

"How do you know all of that?" she countered, gawking at him.

"Like I said, it's been a week in Satbury and you like to talk. Especially in your sleep."

She blinked, turned away from him and looked down into her lap, chuckling a bit. "It seems you do really know me."

He propped his head up on a fist and gave her a wide grin. "We've had more than enough time. Now, are you ready?"

"For?"

"Think, Robin. Try to bring back the memories. What have we been doing every time you wake up?"

She closed her eyes. Everything before that morning was an empty space.

"Anything?"

She sighed and set her sights on him once more. "No. The only thing I'm feeling is the pain in my legs. Lord, why--"

Her hand paused above her calf. She stared up at Alistair.

"We walked yesterday. For me to practice. I fell when we were walking."

His lips curved up and he nodded vigorously. "Yes! I told you you'd remember."

Robin clutched her hand over her chest. She clenched her teeth together because she was sure if she smiled too much she'd never be able to stop.

She turned back to the clothes in her arms. "I'll put them on right now. Then, we can go on our walk?"

"Of course. Come down when you're done." Alistair left the small room and closed the door behind him.

Well, you did something right, Robin. Focus on that. One day at a time.

Robin undid the straps on the back of her dress and began to slip it off. Quickly, she changed into her new clothes and stepped into the shoes. She climbed down the ladder that led from the room to the stables. Alistair was at the bottom waiting for her, and as she stepped down, he offered his hand.

She squeezed his hand and peered up at him.

"What's on the agenda for the day? Don't forget you promised to help me find Arthur."

"I know. I know," he said walking out of the stables. "Seems there are certain things you didn't forget."

"A promise is a promise, Alistair."

Alistair tapped the horseshoe on the stable doors. "The best place to get any information is from the innkeeper and the women at the ale houses," he said. "But we'll need to be discreet. Saying the wrong name can get you killed and Arthur isn't common. I also have some deliveries I need to make."

Robin followed behind him, darting her eyes around the stable doors. "Where did your friend go?"

"Who?"

"The young woman you were here speaking with."

"Oh, Maddy. I asked her to excuse me when I saw you had woken. She stops by occasionally."

"Hmm. Where's Fred?" she asked, walking beside him.

"He's in the back stables with a few other horses. All the deliveries are local for me today. No need to disturb him."

"Why do you keep him in the back?"

"The landlord requested he be kept there, so no one who wants to rent a horse gets him confused with one of his own. He also likes his horses to have a certain look, fancy and all that. It was part of the deal when I started renting from him."

"I see. I bet Fred is better than any of those other horses."

Alistair chuckled. "You and I are in agreement there. Watch where you step by the way. Everyone doesn't clean up after their horses."

"I can smell that," she replied.

"I'll pick the packages up from here. Wait a minute."

He ran into a stone building filled with enough people, Robin thought it might burst.

The local Chancery.

The townspeople stared at Robin while she waited. She held her chin high and ignored their gawking. Apparently, a woman in trousers was still not a common sight.

She set her eyes ahead and watched Alistair through the window. He seemed accustomed to the crowd as he maneuvered through it quickly. Within a few minutes, he was at her side once more, his satchel stuffed with packages.

"More pickups than deliveries. Let's be off," he said and headed down the road.

Robin looked around her. Satbury, even when Terryn was ruler, was the second largest town in the kingdom and it didn't seem to have stopped growing. Not only were the roads full of people, but the structures were becoming larger, as well. Some of the town's center had even been replaced with wooden buildings versus stone.

Of course, she didn't expect this to be the case with the serfs who lived on the outskirts of town.

Alistair huffed beside her.

Robin gave him a once-over and noticed how the bag dragged down with the newly added weight.

"Let me help you carry a few." She reached for the parcels but he stepped back.

"It's fine, Robin. I like the weight."

"Wouldn't you rather give your shoulders a rest?"

"My uncle's a fisherman from the north. When I lived with him, he'd take me out to work, too. He'd always say a heavy catch means a good day's work."

"Hmm. Do you know your shoulders seem to broaden when you talk about your uncle?"

"You're very observant."

"A lady has to be, especially in my situation."

"Well, I am not one to argue with a lady." He smiled and knocked on the door of a tiny stone home. Said door was a plank of wood. They had only just left the town center.

Robin rested her hands on her hips and tapped her fingers. She swung her shoes out and in across the earth, before starting to tap it, as well. Poverty was something she was unfamiliar with. Alistair, quite the opposite.

"What's wrong?" he asked.

She briefly glanced at him. Then Robin sighed and crossed her arms.

"There was something you told me...about your parents. I

know they used to live here in Satbury. Still, there was something else you told me."

"I told you they died," he said and handed a package to the elderly man who opened the house door. The man thanked him, and closed the door.

Her mouth was dry. How could she have forgotten his parents died?

You're quite the guest, Robin. Well done.

"I lived with my uncle for most of my life. When my parents passed, I returned here. Is it coming back a bit now?"

"Some, yes." Robin stumbled to the side, nearly stepping into a pile of smelly brown. She could see the corners of Alistair's lips turn up even as she scrunched her face in disgust.

She trusted Alistair. There was no doubt about that. She also had little choice if she were being honest. But the more they knew about one another, the better they'd be able to work together. It was the same theory Arthur had offered to her uncle Terryn. He had been trying to persuade the king to form a group of Camelot's most skilled and trusted knights; men who would work for the kingdom outside of the traditional hierarchy. He had wanted them to be called the Knights of the Round Table. Robin had thought the name lacked luster.

She pulled her mind back. "When did you leave to the north, then?"

He dug out another package and placed it beside a home where no one had answered.

"I was six."

"And when did you return?"

A vein pulsed in his neck. "Just this year."

Robin stopped walking. She stared at his back as he moved past her. "Sixteen years? Have you told me this, as well? I'm forgetting everything."

Alistair's strides came to a halt.

"No, this is a new addition to our conversation. Though, I'd rather not discuss it."

Perhaps too much, Robin? She pinched herself for not minding her own business.

Robin walked up behind him and placed a hand on his shoulder. "I'm sorry," she said. "Sometimes I let my curiosity get the best of me. I shouldn't have pushed you like that. You wouldn't have done it to me."

"It's fine," he replied. "Look, I'd rather not tell you exactly why my parents sent me away. I lived with my uncle until I returned this year to bury them. That's all there is."

And with that said, he gently moved her hand from his shoulder and placed it at her side.

Chapter Five

Robin was certain the tavern maid had heard Alistair the first time. Still, the woman insisted on leaning close to him with her breasts all but falling into his face. Honestly, Robin wouldn't have blamed Alistair for liking the woman.

She was pretty, a beauty under the lantern's light and built with much to offer the male gaze. But Alistair, being the gentleman he was, kept his eyes fixed on her face--his own was a little red-- and repeated the name.

"Arthur," he said. "He's a friend of mine that said he'd be passing through here some months ago. I haven't heard from him. Does the name sound familiar?"

She puckered her lips. "The name's a bit outdated for anyone that's come around here recently. What's he look like?"

"Very blue eyes," Robin chimed in. "Like the ocean. And short hair last time we saw him. Blonde."

The tavern maid didn't even glance in her direction. She did, however, start to nibble on her bottom lip in thought.

"Blonde, blue eyes, named Arthur?"

They nodded.

"Doesn't ring any bells. Then again, I do prefer brunettes."

She smirked at Alistair and lightly touched his hair. "I'll let you know if I hear anything though." Her finger trailed down his cheek.

Now Robin could feel her own face flush. When did women become so bold?

With another smirk and a wink, the tavern maid left their table, knocking her hips from side to side as she did so.

Alistair's face was a bright red and his mouth had flattened into a hard line. Robin covered her own mouth to stop from laughing. A few giggles still found their escape though.

Alistair cleared his throat. "Well, uh, seems like we're having no luck here. Should we move on to the inn?"

"But we haven't talked to all the ladies yet, Alistair." A smile played on her lips and her eyes crinkled at the corners.

He refused to make eye contact. Instead, he pulled at his clothes, before standing to leave, keeping his eyes on the table.

"Four are...uh, four are more than enough, I think. Perhaps, he's going by another name. If he were in the area, he'd have to step into town at some point." Alistair's eyes were still fixed to the table.

Robin laughed a bit but nodded. "That is a possibility. Or maybe he's been taken in by another king."

"That's true though the lower eastern king, Issin, is no more since Essen drove him out."

Robin could feel her eyes bulge. "What do you mean--"

"Those damn refugees!" A large man slammed his mug so hard on the tavern counter, Robin jumped. Both she and Alistair turned their attention to the bar where he sat with several other large men of a similar build.

"Because Issin couldn't keep his kingdom intact, we have to suffer all the consequences." He swayed in his chair.

"Alistair, what is he--" Robin cut her question short. The vein pulsed in Alistair's neck. His hands had turned into fists.

"They take our jobs and still can't manage to get by! Now, they're out here begging. Moving around our kingdom begging. No self-respect."

Several other patrons grunted and raised their mugs.

Alistair grabbed his bag from the table. "Are you ready to go?" he asked, not looking at Robin.

Still, she nodded and moved behind Alistair to follow him outside.

As they made their way to the exit, the drunkard who had been yelling turned in his chair and his gaze landed on Robin. She watched him from her peripherals and saw the spark that flashed in his eyes. Lesser men, particularly when drinking ale, always seemed to have that spark in their eyes.

The man leaned forward and lunged his mug, spilling the ale over several other patrons.

"Now, see here, men! This one here is a fine lady, middle-born, of course. Not like those dirty refugees."

Alistair's hands encircled Robin's wrist and pulled her closer to him as they pushed through the crowd to the door.

The man's eyes landed on Alistair but hardly. His gaze roamed over Robin and her skin crawled. She had no idea how he could find her attractive in her current attire. She leaned into Alistair.

The man stood and started forcing his way through the crowd. "Not like those dirty easterners," he slurred. "I'll treat ya right. Like a proper lady." A sloppy grin moved across his face.

Hatred built in Robin's chest and bile in her stomach. She wished she had brought her daggers.

They reached the door. Alistair pushed it open and immediately began running, the moon their primary source of light. He kept a tight hold on Robin's wrist as she ran behind him. Despite him leading her, Robin knew she wouldn't be able to keep up. Her movements still felt awkward and wrong. Not to mention the shoes.

Compared to when she first stepped from the tree, Robin felt much more herself. That didn't mean her body agreed.

As expected, she fell. The drunkard had made it to a corner and was looking down the road. Before he could turn his head right, Alistair scooped Robin up in his arms and ran into the nearest alley.

Robin could smell the blood before he placed her behind the barrel. Flashes from her dream came back to her. Arrows protruding from her back, her own blood pooling around her. She counted to five before swallowing down the vomit, letting the acid burn her throat.

Now is not the moment for weakness. Breathe.

Alistair was resting on the balls of his feet, peering from behind the barrel. Robin looked at him, copied his stance and pressed her shoulder into his.

"Maybe he'll only be a drunken fool?" she whispered. The words didn't even sound comforting to her.

"I don't take threats lightly," Alistair said. "Especially when coming from men like that."

"Giant foul-mouthed ogres?"

"Correct. Now, listen, if he finds us, you run back to the stables. I'll distract him for a while and then, sneak away."

She rolled her eyes. "Do you really think I'm going to leave you?"

"No, but I think you should," he replied, still peering out into the road.

A fluttery anger grew in Robin's chest and she took a long inhale to calm it.

"Woman or not, I'm not running. You're my friend, Alistair."

"You are so stubborn. Has anyone ever told you that?"

Yes. Arthur did many times.

She dug her fingers into the ground and set her jaw. "There's one of him and two of us. If he finds us, we can defeat him."

Alistair reached into his satchel and pulled out the rusty knife. "Since I don't have a choice in the matter, I suppose so. I'll move in first and kick him in the knees, then punch him in the throat. We need to get him down to our level. He's drunk. He probably won't feel much meaning we have to hit hard. When I get him down, step behind him and wait for him to fall."

"And if he doesn't?" she asked.

"Use the back of the knife to knock him out. Here, back against the neck." He pulled his hair aside and rubbed the area.

Robin nodded. Alistair went to say more but there was a loud belch. They both fell into silence and turned their eyes to the road.

He stumbled in front of the alleyway. First forward, then, backward and finally from side to side. He belched again and looked to where they hid. With shaky steps, the drunkard made his way.

"Oink, oink, little piggies. Are ya here?"

Only a few yards now. Robin prepared to pounce.

The drunkard paused. He looked around the alley and as his eyes landed on their barrel, he smiled.

"I got--"

Alistair moved. Robin noted how well he did so. Left foot first, still using the balls of his feet to spin and face the man. Then, quickly stepping forward and kicking the man's knees.

As he had predicted, the man fell. Alistair turned his elbow out and hit it into the man's throat. Saliva sprayed from his mouth and he clasped his throat as he coughed.

Robin stepped out and to the side, moved behind the drunkard and waited. He started to fall forward. Alistair looked at her and nodded, before moving to the side of the alley as well.

She began to make her way to the road when there was a thump and a hiss. Robin spun around. The man had Alistair by the ankle and had slammed him against the wall.

"I'll get ya," he wheezed and began to stand.

"Run!" Alistair screamed.

Robin ignored him, ran back and slammed her knee into their attacker's face. Blood flowed from him and he released Alistair. She pulled her companion to his feet and they begin to make their way.

There was a whistling sound like someone was cutting air and then, Alistair fell to the side.

"What's wrong?" Robin tried to pull him up. His body was becoming slack.

He grabbed at his thigh and grunted as he pulled out a knife. The tip was dripping green.

"Poison," he huffed. His eyes started to cloud over.

"No, Alistair!" She grabbed him by his shoulders and shook until his eyes refocused.

"Leave me," he said.

"I-I can't."

A shadow cast over her. Robin's blood ran cold. She didn't look up, didn't want to see his disgusting face or smell his ale-coated breath.

Alistair's eyes reeled from the side to side in his skull. And then, they were still.

"Alistair," she whispered. "Alistair."

He did not respond.

She watched Alistair, or what was left of him. Still, unmoving, unresponsive, unable to speak or comfort her like the others she had lost. Her uncle, Arthur...

His red hands gripped her shoulders. His fingers pressed into her collar bone.

"I'm going to have fun with you. Just be quiet." The drunkard's words sloshed around in his mouth.

Are you? Are you going to have fun?

He tossed her to the ground and bent over her. A large rough hand cupped one of her breasts and the other felt between her legs.

"Are you?" she asked, staring up into the sky, gazing past the giant above her to the stars. "Are you going to have fun with me?"

"Lot--"

Robin moved her hips forward so his hand slipped away. Then, she wrapped her legs around him and though the feeling of his manhood pressed against her thigh made her sick with revulsion, she continued to press closer. She entwined her arms around his neck.

He smiled. "Good girl."

Robin said nothing. What she did instead was lift her body and pushed her face to his. When he was close enough, she opened her mouth, clutched his nose in her teeth and bit down until she felt his blood in her throat.

The drunkard howled and tried to shake Robin off, but she had him captured like a fly in a spider's web.

The nose was easy. It was soft and right in front of her. In a few moments, she was tossing her head back and spitting out the lumpy piece of flesh in the alley. He continued to cry out, to scream, his hands no longer grabbed for her breasts. Now they pushed at her shoulders. But Robin was not done yet. She was going to have fun with him.

So much fun.

She inclined her head to the side some and dug into his cheek. Fresh blood pooled into her mouth again.

The man grabbed a hold of her hair and tried to pull her away.

But with every tug, he tore away a bit more flesh. A quick move to the left and part of his cheek was gone.

He wailed and wailed and wailed.

No one came to rescue my uncle. No one came to rescue Alistair. Why would they come to save you?

The man beat at her back and though it hurt, Robin let go only when she *decided* to. He clutched at his face. Robin sat up, tightened the hold she had on the rusty knife and shoved it in his throat. The man stilled. She pulled the knife back and red showered her and Alistair. But something moved in the shadows.

There was a *thunk,* and then the man fell sideways. It didn't really take much effort. Robin was sure he was already dead.

But as he fell, a young woman stood behind him with a large branch raised in the air. She was breathing hard as her eyes poured over the scene. An unconscious Alistair, a man missing pieces of his face, and a girl covered in blood.

The young woman closed her eyes, flashed them open and her breathing had calmed. The anxiety and fear disappeared from her face.

Her eyes landed on Robin. "Help me grab Alistair. We need to get him home. The guards will be coming. They're only slow because they're at the other end of town dealing with a matter."

She stepped over Robin and draped Alistair's arms around her shoulders. The way she held Alistair, the familiarity, she obviously knew him. But Robin was not herself. She was not Robin Leingard. She was a woman covered in red with the irony taste of blood in her mouth who had just been assaulted by a drunk pig. So, instead of helping the young woman, she launched at her and pressed the knife to her throat.

"Who are you?" she said between clamped teeth.

They were at the edge of the alley now and the moon's rays were in full reach. The woman's hair was an odd shade of black, no, it wasn't black. Just a dark green.

The confusion had to be apparent on Robin's face, but the girl didn't show she saw it.

She simply said, "My name is Maddy."

"What should we do?" Alistair's head rested in Robin's lap. She stroked his face while he lay motionless.

Maddy was staring at the poisoned knife. She moved it from

side to side and sniffed. She covered her face and heaved a breath.

"One option left," she stated. With a quick flick, she moved the tip of her tongue over the blade's end.

Robin nearly gagged. Thankfully, she had already vomited enough on their way here.

The young woman closed her eyes and moved her tongue around in her mouth. There was a quiet moment and then, she flung the dagger into the wall.

"I can't tell what poison it is. It's covered in too much blood."

"Well, do you at least have some medicine? Something to slow it until we can figure out what *it* is?"

A green shade had appeared in his face. Robin wiped at his cheeks, wishing she could wipe the color away.

Maddy shook her head. "All my herbs are gone. Sold. I could go into the forest to search for more but I--"

Alistair jerked up an inch from the ground. He wrenched to the left. Shivers ran down his body. His head remained still yet his body tore in every direction. Suddenly, his eyes shot open and he gazed straight up at Robin.

She felt as if her heart was going to spill from her.

Robin pressed her face close to his and let a few tears slip out. His body continued to convulse, knocking at everything close by. Robin whispered soothing words in his ear, shushing him as his body fought with itself.

"Omay."

"What?" Robin moved her face from beside his and stared down into his eyes. They hadn't moved. His pupils were still fixated to the spot where her head had been and his teeth were mashed together.

"Ine."

"Is he speaking?" Maddy moved to her side and placed her ear close to his mouth.

"Ine."

"Listen," Maddy said.

Robin placed her ear by his mouth once more.

The words were short and clipped yet clear now that she had heard them several times.

"He's saying he's fine," Robin said. "He's all right."

She went to squeeze him when a hot pain shot through her arm. She fell backward and his head rolled out of her lap.

"Are you hurt?" Maddy asked.

Robin nodded but she couldn't even look at the stranger. All she saw was Alistair's silver patch shimmer, then turn a bright white.

The torches in the room began to fade, darkness slowly creeping in. And then, the fires died, the light was gone but Alistair's silver still shimmered a brilliant white--their only source of light in the darkness.

Chapter Six

Alistair had never been hungrier and he knew hunger. Actually, they acquainted themselves with one another about once every three weeks. It was a standing appointment.

He stretched and rolled over when he saw strings of dark hair on several of the cushions. The same shade as his but much longer...

Where is Robin?

Alistair jumped to his feet and leapt to the door. He was already stepping out and only noticed them sleeping in the corner because he had to turn forward to climb down the ladder.

Robin and Maddy sat cuddled together, their hair loose and falling around them. They both were snoring, as well, something Alistair would make sure to bring up later.

His eyes fell on Maddy.

She never comes to the stables in the evening...and why is she in my room?

Horses neighed below him and one neigh stood out amongst the others. It was loud and breathy and sounded more like a pig's snort to Alistair, though, of course he would never mention that to Fred.

He started to make his way down the ladder when a burning started in his thigh. He turned his leg to the side while he gripped the ladder. There was a wound on the back of his lower thigh, about two inches across and deep from the pain it was causing. It wasn't bleeding and seemed to have been cleaned.

"Alistair!"

"Oh, my God. Where did he go?"

"We have to find him."

"The guards might be looking for us."

"Yes, we need to stick to the edge of town and move around the perimeter."

The door flew open. Both women stood on the edge of his home, gaping at him as if he had suddenly grown horns and a second head.

Alistair shifted from side to side, before pointing his gaze back at them. Finally, whatever spell they were under broke and Robin began to gush like a child.

She snatched him by his hair and planted several kisses on his forehead. "You fool! You nearly scared us to death."

"Um, all right. I didn't know grabbing breakfast was such a treacherous deed."

"That's not what I mean," she said and released her hold on him. Her hands moved past his head and Alistair snatched the one to his right, catching something wrong in the color. Instead of a pale white, there was a light, crusted red that caked in her palm's crevices.

He turned his eyes back to her. "I think someone needs to tell me exactly what is going on."

"You almost died," Robin shouted and pulled her hand away. "*We* almost died. Then Maddy came and saved us." She wrapped the green-haired girl in a tight hug. Maddy's eyes pinched at the corners as she smiled.

They stood there hugging one another while Alistair stood on the ladder replaying Robin's words in his head.

Died? I think I would have remembered that.

"I didn't really do much. Seems like you had already ki--"

"Shush, shush, shush." Robin pressed a finger over Maddy's lips. She glanced at Alistair.

"Okay, we need to talk," he said not missing her gesture. "I'm coming up."

The women nodded and stepped out of his path. He made his way back into the room and kicked the door shut behind him.

"All right," he said, scratching at his silver patch. "What happened?"

"How much do you remember?" Robin asked.

"We were going around town asking about your friend. We went to the Midnight Tavern down the way yet found nothing. Then, we came home."

Maddy narrowed her eyes.

"What?" Alistair replied.

"This must have been a strong poison. Not only did it make you forget. It replaced your memories, as well."

Alistair pushed his hair back and looked at the ceiling. "Hm. Fine. What else happened?"

Both women stared at him.

"You seem calm at the news someone tried to kill you," said Maddy.

Robin nodded, confusion plastered on her face, as well.

Alistair suddenly knew what a rabbit felt like when it saw the arrow racing towards it.

"I'm just, uh...I..." He went to smooth down his clothes,

hoping to avert his gaze.

His hands felt the dried spots before his eyes saw them. Alistair was coated in dark, stale blood. He took in a trembling breath and turned his head to look back at his companions.

"Tell me everything," he said.

Robin nodded and tucked her hair behind her ears. "We were leaving the tavern after asking about Arthur. This man had been raging on about the easterners and refugees. He saw me, followed us out and tried to attack us in an alley we were hiding in. We almost escaped but he grabbed you at the last second. Then, we were running and he threw this poisoned dagger into your thigh."

She reached behind her. When she faced him again she held a blade dulled with blood.

Alistair took several steps back until he hit the wall. His legs didn't feel right. Nothing was right about what she was telling him. What poison could be so strong he'd forget the previous night?

He slid to the floor and ran his hand over his thigh, trying to force the memory back. It refused.

"You passed out. He...um, tried to hurt me..." Her eyes shifted to Maddy who moved her attention to the floor.

"Anyway," she said and cleared her throat, "I fought him and then Maddy helped me...with the rest, I mean. We brought you here. You weren't responding. Then, you started shaking. Your silver streak started to heat up and it turned a bright white. After that you just fell asleep."

He wiped his face and clutched his jaw as it tightened to the point of throbbing.

"When you say, 'the rest,' you mean you killed him?"

The women exchanged glances.

"We didn't have a choice, Alistair," Maddy said. She squeezed Robin's hand.

He nodded. "Robin?"

"Yes."

"He did more than hurt you, didn't he?"

There was a pause.

"We don't need to—"

"Please, just tell me."

He heard the uneven breaths and the sob she caught in her chest.

"He touched me," she whispered. "He wanted to do more, said he was going to have fun with me...I went cold and then, anger flared up and I...I--"

Alistair slammed his fists against the wall. He dug his nails into his palm until he felt the pain in his whole hand. He chewed on his bottom lip, grinding until the flesh became sore.

He wanted to have fun with me.

Alistair brought his knees up and hung his elbows there while he stared at the floor. His eyes burned, and he twisted his fingers, imagining they were around the drunkard's neck. His throat felt tight.

"I failed you," he wheezed.

"No, Alistair—"

"No, Robin. I did." He looked up to meet her eyes. "I did. When you needed me the most I was useless."

"You had no way of knowing," Maddy said.

"It doesn't matter." Alistair shot to his feet. "I'm going to take a walk. We have some things to discuss later."

"Where are you going?" Robin asked. "And what more is there to discuss?"

He closed the door behind him and headed outside. The early morning air turned his breath into mist though he didn't feel the cold himself.

A single feeling consumed him. The feeling when Robin said those words.

He touched me.

Alistair balanced a bucket on his hand and a plate of food on his elbow. He leaned against the ladder and stretched his other hand up to knock. Maddy smiled down at him as she opened the door.

"Hello, there. Welcome back." She took the plate and bucket from him, then, moved aside for him to step up.

"I got some food from the storehouse," he said. "We were so busy yesterday I don't think we ate much. I brought some for you as well, Maddy."

"Are you sure?" she asked, her eyes already glued to the meal.

"Considering you saved my life, I think I can spare some bread and broth."

She grinned, the corners of her eyes pinching again. "Thank you. I've always got room for good food."

"Has your appetite returned yet, Robin?"

She shook her head. "Not really. I'm more interested in what you need to discuss with us."

"Right." He cleared his throat. "Let's eat a bit first."

Maddy took a hunk of bread and shoved it into her mouth. She rocked from side to side and smiled as she chewed away before draining a cup of water. Alistair ate with her though with less eagerness and Robin only nibbled.

They went on like that for a few minutes, a strained silence Alistair wished to stretch out until, finally, Robin sighed, crossed her hands in her lap and stared at him pointedly.

His patch began to itch again. "Fine," he said. He put his food to the side.

Alistair grabbed the silver in his hair and lifted it. "This is why the poison didn't kill me."

Robin raised a brow. "Because you have some early graying?"

Maddy snorted and covered her mouth with a slice of bread.

He sighed. "No, it's not early graying. It's a witch's curse."

Robin eyed the silver but shook her head. "You mean you...a witch tried to kill you?"

Alistair nodded.

"But witches are...I guess I can't say that now. What I mean is most adults don't survive a witch encounter much less a child."

"You're right but when they do, they get a mark on their body wherever the witch last touched them."

He pulled at his silver hairs. "For me, this is the last place she touched me before I was saved. My father came in and tossed blessed water on her. She was in the process of *taking* me."

Robin's eyes fixed on his hair. She stared and then leaned forward and stroked the strands. Immediately, the itching grew worse.

"This must be how I got out. Yes, yes, it is! I grabbed your hair. I felt the magic." She dug both hands in his hair again and was pulling in either direction with an excitement Alistair was sure was going to leave him bald.

"You can sense magic too, can't you?" Maddy sipped on her cup of water.

"Yes," he said and placed Robin's hands back at her sides. He looked back at Robin and frowned. "I think that's also why I can remember. Everything from *before*."

He kept his sights on her.

His words settled and her eyes became fiery slits. Her hands turned into balled fists.

"You lied to me."

He took a long breath. "I did."

"Why?" she barked. "This entire time I thought I was the only one. But you knew. You knew and--"

"It's called a curse for a reason, Robin." Maddy placed a hand on her shoulder. "Most think children who have the curse are possessed by witches. They're killed."

"What?" She gaped at her. "No, those are barbaric rituals from the past. My uncle banished such before Cadfen stole the throne."

"The king can't be everywhere all the time," said Maddy.

"That fact is why my parents sent me away," he said. "They didn't want anyone to catch on. At the time, most people thought the curses were fairy tales yet many still believed. Even today. That's why we're all still terrified to go into The Cursed Forest. If anyone had caught me, I'd probably be dead."

Robin fell back onto her knees then pulled her legs up close to her chest. "I see why you lied to me."

"Truth be told, I've tried to lie to myself about that night. My uncle and aunt told me what I had acquired as soon as I moved north. Their thoughts were only confirmed when I ate a poisonous fish and still lived."

Maddy nodded. "Those with a witch's curse are reversers of fate. That's why poison doesn't affect him. Magic can't affect him either unless cast by the witch who marked him."

Alistair narrowed his eyes. He glanced at Robin who had a similar expression on her face.

"How do you know so much about witches?" he asked.

She leaned her head to the side and stared out the window. "In the middle kingdom, some have lost faith in the old beliefs. That wasn't the case in Issin's or Orof's kingdom. I've been lectured on witches and ghouls since a child."

Robin rested her chin in her hand. "Maddy told me more about the eastern wars. Essen and Issin could never agree to anything. My uncle would complain about their bickering all the time. Whoever thought it would come to war?"

The green-haired girl gave a small smile though she seemed to be only partially listening. Maddy kept smiling and nodding but she wasn't looking at Robin. She was staring at a spot just above Robin's head, a spot where some wood was chipped and scarred.

Alistair recognized the look.

Once, he had rushed to stop some children from harassing Maddy. They ran behind her throwing stones and manure. After Alistair scared them away, she responded with a flat "thank you" and gave him *that* look. It was bland and empty. It didn't match the charming southern girl he was accustomed to.

Her wavy green hair drew more hate than curiosity. She still refused to dye it even if for her own protection. To be honest,

Alistair was a little relieved when she told him she was keeping her hair color. He liked the way her hair was, the way it made her look, like she was a fairy from a children's book, waiting to sprinkle her magical dust.

"You said you had been asking about Arthur?" Maddy inquired.

The name jerked Alistair back to reality. He looked at Robin.

"I didn't say a word," she said to him.

Alistair sighed.

She must have let it slip last night.

"Based on both your reactions, I'll say yes you were." Maddy moved her eyes between them, finally landing on Robin. "What's his last name?"

"Pendragon," Robin replied. She glanced at Alistair.

He shrugged. Maddy and he hadn't been lifelong friends but considering how the townspeople treated her, she didn't have any chance to be a blabber mouth. She wouldn't know anything besides a name. Unless she was a witch--and she wasn't-- what harm could that do?

Maddy had taken more bread from the plate and was dipping it in her third bowl of broth. She stared at the ceiling.

"Hmm. I haven't heard his name for some time."

Alistair could nearly feel the explosion.

Robin grabbed Maddy's arm and pulled her so close, their noses were almost touching. Despite Robin's hold and the beaming hope in her eyes, Maddy remained stoic.

"You...you know Arthur?" Her shoulders were shaking.

For a moment, Maddy said nothing. Then, she moved closer to Robin's face, pressed her nose against Robin's cheek and took a deep breath.

The beaming hope had left Robin's eyes. Instead there was a mixed look of amusement and worry.

Maddy pulled back. "I'm not sure where you came from, Robin. There must have been a lot of magic. Up close, I can smell it all over you."

If Robin's jaw dropped any farther, Alistair was sure she was going to lose it.

Maddy turned away from Robin and gave her attention to Alistair.

"When you said you remembered from before, you mean before Cadfen was king?"

Now it was Alistair's turn to be surprised. "You remember, then?" he asked. "You remember King-"

"Terryn?" She bobbed her head.
"And Arthur?"
All of Robin shook. Maddy looked at her. She smiled.
"I know where he is too."

Chapter Seven

ark blue rested over Satbury as the sun made one last attempt to stretch out its rays. But it was the moon's turn to hang in the night sky. The azure hue grew darker and darker until its remnants were outshined by the night's stars.

Maddy had kept her head turned upward to the sky for most of their walk. Alistair, in turn, had kept his eyes on her, wondering what in the sky had captured her interest.

It had been two weeks since the drunkard. The guards had informed everyone it was an animal attack. Alistair was sure even they didn't believe that. Still, no one had question them. Actually, many were becoming accustomed to seeing Robin at his side. They often were asked if they were siblings or cousins.

Maddy's vision was still on the sky. Her eyes were unmoving, though, to be honest, her behavior wasn't exactly unusual. Alistair had never seen Maddy speak with anyone else besides him. It made sense she was used to being in her own head. Except, she was rarely like that with Alistair. She always had a story to tell and a question to ask. However, in that moment, as the two walked along the edge of town by the forest's line, dwarfed by the giant ash trees, Maddy was silent.

Alistair glanced at the sky. It didn't intrigue him really. The northern skies were enthralling, especially during the new year when Helen's Lights, as they were called, appeared. There were striking shades of every color weaving across the sky. Compared to that, the stars in the middle kingdom seemed more like rusty metals.

Despite him being middle-born, Alistair couldn't deny he felt a little out of place in the kingdom. He had spent sixteen years with his uncle, aunt, and cousins on the icy shores of their home. He left the middle kingdom when he was young, before he could really understand what it was like to be middle-born, to say the phrase with pride, and to understand the culture of his mother's land.

Maddy drew more attention but the land was as foreign to him as it was to her. So, he wondered why she didn't wish to return to a place she had once called home.

"Are you sure you don't want to go with us to search for Arthur?" he asked for the eighth time that night.

Maddy turned from the sky and smiled at him. "You're not going to let up, are you?"

"Eventually, but not now. I still have time to convince you."

"You won't," she said and her smile grew bigger.

Alistair nodded. "If you say so. Are you worried about returning to the east?"

"Why would I be worried?"

"Because I..." He inhaled through his nose and closed his eyes.

"Alistair?"

"Because..." The word tasted bitter in his mouth. "Because of what happened to Robin. Because I, I let her get hurt and—"

Maddy stopped her tread, grabbed Alistair by the shoulders and spun him around to face her.

"That wasn't your fault," she said. "None of it was any of our faults."

Then, why did shame bore into him every night he heard her crying in her sleep? Or puking behind the stables in an attempt to rid herself of any remnants of the drunkard's blood? It had been two weeks. She told him nothing ailed her. That was what people always said when they were the most ill.

And Alistair was to blame.

"I would never let anything happen to you or Robin," he said, his voice louder than necessary. He straightened his back. "Never again. If that's why you're scared, please—"

"There is nowhere safer than with you, Alistair. Why do you think I always stop by to see you?"

Her words brought his shaming to a halt.

He liked that.

He liked the way her eyes had grown wide with her words and the way her mouth had set into a straight line. She meant everything she said.

Alistair's face immediately grew hot. If his northern cousins could have seen him, the taunts would have never ceased. The effect was only intensified when a small patch of pink rose to both of Maddy's cheeks, as well.

She removed her hands from his shoulders, stepped away and tucked her hair behind her ears. She wasn't looking at Alistair any longer. Instead, she stared at her beaten shoes.

"Anyone with eyes can tell Robin is high born," Maddy said. "Even with those clothes you've let her borrow."

Why does that matter now?

"But she's not exactly what comes to mind when you think of high born. I find talking with her very easy, actually." She turned her head up to meet his stare. There was a glint in her eyes now and her lips began to curve up.

"She's really curious too. Do you know what she asked me?" Maddy started their walk again. Alistair followed beside her not sure how they got on the topic. Either Maddy ignored his lack of a response or she didn't really need it. She just kept talking.

"Since she knows magic is more than a fairy tale, she asked if I was related to trolls?"

Alistair nearly tripped over his own feet. What sort of question was that?

"She asked because of my hair. It's not even common in the Southern Kingdom. People make up tales." Maddy laughed. "I didn't know the stories had traveled this far. Do you believe them, Alistair?"

He raised both brows and pulled them together as he stared at her. "Do I believe that you're part-troll? Uh, no, the thought never crossed my mind."

"What about the other stories? The tales of the green-haired people of the south." She wiggled her fingers at him and glanced around in the darkness. "I even heard they especially love to eat young men with black hair and purple eyes."

The tips of her fingers tickled his cheek as she continued to play ghost. Alistair stepped out of her fingers' reach and smiled.

"I thought I was the jester between the two of us."

She rolled her eyes. "I'm not sure how you came to that thought. You're always working. When do you have time for jokes?"

He gawked at her. "I tell jokes all the time. Fred, that horse, never misses a show. My biggest fan."

Maddy laughed now, really laughed. She bent forward first giving her joy to the earth, before tossing her head back and singing her joy into the sky.

And Alistair laughed, too, only slowing when he realized how wonderful their laughter sounded together.

Maddy took in a deep breath, her arm wrapped around her stomach and held her side. "All right," she said and came to a halt. "This is where you'll leave me."

Alistair looked around. Currently, they stood behind the glassblower's home but there wasn't another house in sight.

"Where's your home, Maddy?"

She scoffed. "I'm not taking you there. You know that."

"Then why did you agree to let me walk you this time?"

"Would you have stopped yourself if I said no?"

She has a point there.

"Plus," she continued, "I, well, I like to keep some things private." She looked away.

There was a moment of silence.

"Yes. Of course, I'll respect your wishes. Will you at least stop by tomorrow to see us off?"

She nodded. "There's no other place to be."

"Well, I'll see you tomorrow then."

"One more thing, Alistair."

He stopped his departure and turned to face her once again.

She smirked. "I want to further prove how much I trust you. I'm going to give you my full name. It's a southern tradition. Only family and the closest of friends know and use our full names amongst us."

The butterflies in his stomach were flapping full force now. His hands began to sweat.

"Well, I'm honored. What's your full name?"

"Madelia," she said. "From now on, when it's you and I, you will call me Madelia."

Robin wiped her mouth. She hated the fact she was becoming accustomed to the smell of her own vomit. But she couldn't help herself. She needed to get as much of *him* out as possible. She had done what she needed to survive. Still, in her mind, his blood had contained a thousand parasites and now they roamed freely in her body, little pieces of him that refused to leave.

Fred neighed in the stables.

It was a good thing horses couldn't talk because if Fred had a chance, he'd spill all her trips to the stables' rear to Alistair. Then the guilt she knew he already felt would increase. She didn't want that, especially not on her part because the truth was she should have listened to him. If she had, her stomach wouldn't be heaving right now, and Alistair wouldn't have been poisoned.

Then again, if none of that had ever happened, Robin wouldn't know Arthur was living in the fallen eastern kingdom of King Issin who had gone mad after he lost the war with his brother King Essen. Well, if Robin was being honest and if her uncle's stories were true, he had never been all there. The war just pushed him over the edge.

Her stomach clenched and she released another mouthful of

slimy liquid from inside her. Her head was starting to get light again. She needed to at least get back to the room before she passed out and Alistair went insane himself wondering where she was.

She stumbled her way back to the stables, giving Fred's nose a quick pat as she headed up to their small room. Robin all but thought she was going to die climbing the ladder. Somehow, she managed and as soon as the room door was open, she tossed herself on the mat. She had given up arguing with Alistair about it. He refused to take the mat, even when she said all she needed was a pillow. Whoever his uncle was, he had engrained a gentleman's qualities into Alistair and Alistair would not negate them for a moment.

Robin moved the pillows around, adjusting them to give her body more support. But even with the pillows, the mat wasn't much of a bed. She now understood how Alistair slept on it every night before her arrival. People grew used to things and despite her upbringing, Robin found herself longing for the poor excuse of a bed like it was made from the finest wool and the pillows stuffed with the smoothest feathers. There was only one thing she wanted more and that was to get to the eastern kingdom and find Arthur.

She clutched the bracelet in her hand, toying with the dragon charm in the middle.

Robin wondered what he would be like now. Ten years was a long time after all and people changed, especially if war was involved. War rakes at a man's soul and leaves all the bad things in his soul to grow like weeds in a clean and fertile garden. That was what her uncle used to say, at least.

Uncle Terryn.

Her fingers moved from the dragon charm to the one shaped like an apple. Terryn had given it to her when she was a child. She didn't remember any of this but supposedly, she would call Terryn Applebeard because he enjoyed apples very much and sometimes the pieces would fall in his beard.

She chuckled at the thought and then, she cried. Because she had lost two fathers in one lifetime and that didn't seem fair at all. High born or not, it didn't seem right. She'd trade her royal blood and all the jewels in the world to have everyone with her, well and alive.

Yet she knew that wasn't going to happen. People didn't come back from the dead.

Robin turned onto her back. She wouldn't go to sleep until Alistair returned from walking Maddy home, so, there was no point in pretending.

I wonder what Arthur looks like now?

She had caught a few glimpses of herself in windows. From what she saw, the tree had somehow kept her looking like the same foolish nineteen-year-old who ran into that damn forest. Arthur was nineteen when they separated, as well, meaning now he'd be twenty-nine. While, she still appeared a child.

She balled her fists and let the anger run through her. She had to do that lately since Maddy had told them where to find Arthur. Everything felt an extreme to her. Her entire body was on edge and her limbs full of anticipation. After ten years, she'd be with him again. Finally.

But that was still ten years they missed together.

It was a gap of time in which they could have been married, been together as man and wife, even had children, a thought that filled Robin with so much joy and longing, she thought her skin was going to evaporate.

Children.

She hated the way women were expected to bare offspring like a tree bearing fruit. It was one of the main reasons she had decided before she was considered a young woman, she would never have children. Her husband would have to be satisfied with a few horses.

And then Arthur came along, and they fell in love. She understood the maternal wanting her mother had discussed with her. Of course, not every woman had the desires, but Robin did, at least when it came to Arthur.

She began to finger the charms again. The movement became methodical and then, it slowed. Her eyes grew heavy, her mind, too. All wants fleeted into a corner, waiting to be picked for a dream. The image of Arthur was standing at the front.

Chapter Eight

"Do you think he'll remember me?" Robin placed her chin on Alistair's shoulder as they rode towards the lower-eastern border. She had been silent most of the ride. The question had been on the tip of her tongue for some time and had blocked any other words from leaving her mouth.

He kept his face forward but when he spoke there was a steady lightness to the sound. Robin, now having been around Alistair long enough, recognized this tone as the sound of his smile.

"Of course, he will. After our initial encounter, I'm sure you always leave others with a memorable first impression."

Now she was smiling. She tried to take that smile, that feeling, and push it through her whole body, soothing the odd mixture of excitement and anxiety. It had been ten years, ten long years and now, less than a day's travel separated them.

Though her blue dress was no longer in fashion, Robin had worn it instead of trousers. Arthur had always been a bit old fashioned. And he loved her in blue.

They had ridden as far south as they could before turning east towards the forgotten kingdom. Patches of wood had thinned out to open pastures. Satbury gave way to small villages, and eventually, to nothing aside from the expansive fields.

Robin tilted her head back and admired the clear blue above them. Before *that* night, she had traveled very little and never to the east. What had it been like then? When Issin was still somewhat sane and still king?

Maddy had informed Robin that after King Issin lost the war with his brother, he fled into the wilderness and no one had seen him since. The aftereffects of the war, as well as Issin's unexpected departure, left the kingdom in pieces and his people with nowhere to go. King Essen, the older of the two brothers, only took in a handful of his brother's citizens, mostly physicians and scholars. Others, like Maddy, were granted temporary access into the middle kingdom. The rest, well, they were left to fend for themselves in the ruins of their home.

Needless to say, there wouldn't be any guards at the capital, Rowan, much less the borders, to inquire about Alistair and Robin's travel. The biggest concern they had were bandits.

Robin placed a hand on her waist where one of her two

daggers was concealed. The other she had given to Alistair. She gripped the hilt.

This time, she would be ready.

"Maddy said he was rumored to be hiding in Issin's fallen castle," said Alistair. "Once we reach the border, it should be a short ride."

"If that old map is correct, you mean?" Robin countered.

When Alistair had first brought the map out to show her, she swore it was going to fall to pieces on the room floor.

He tucked his hair behind his ears, revealing his face to Robin. "No one bothers mapping out Issin's Kingdom anymore. The country is no longer functioning and not many people venture there."

"Deserted, you mean?"

He nodded. "Overall, yes. Besides those who couldn't find refuge anywhere else."

Robin turned her head to the side on his shoulder. "Why do you think you and Maddy are the only ones who remember my uncle?"

"We've wondered ourselves. The only thing we have in common is we're both foreigners and I'm not sure how that plays a role in our memory."

She chuckled. "So, you're a foreigner now?"

"Well, I spent most of my life in Herald's kingdom, so I'm as close as I'll come. The customs here are odd even to me. When I think of home I" --his eyes glanced to his left --"I think of the north."

Robin watched him.

It must be a strange feeling--belonging to two places yet only able to identify with one. Is this how Maddy feels too?

"Why didn't Maddy want to come again?"

When they left several mornings ago, the green-haired girl only waved them off and wished them well. Alistair had never explained why she wasn't accompanying them. She knew the land better than they did, especially with an old map as their guide.

"I'm not sure," he said. His voice sounded like a heavy weight was pulling him down.

Robin squeezed his shoulder. "You know," she said, "I like Maddy. She's a sweet girl. Close to your age, too, isn't she?"

"Four years younger than me. I enjoy her company, as well" he replied, his lips had started to curve up at the edges.

A grin played on Robin's mouth. "Oh, I *know* you do."

"What-what do you mean?" His back had become very

straight suddenly.

"I mean you have feelings for Maddy, Alistair."

Alistair jerked his shoulders back as short, breathy denials sprang from his mouth. This movement sent Fred racing in the opposite direction they had come from which Alistair didn't notice until he fumbled over his words so badly, he stopped talking completely. Then, red rushed to his cheeks. He pulled the reins to the side and started Fred racing back to the border.

After a short moment of quiet, he began his repeated denials of having feelings for Maddy. When those words dried up, he puffed out his cheeks, seeming to hope others would land for him to store in his arsenal.

Robin's laughter was beyond control, happy tears streaming down her cheeks and her stomach aching from taking hard, repeated joyous breaths.

This only flustered Alistair even more. He spun around to counter her accusations, and as he spun, Fred jumped. Then, he hit the ground and Robin landed--laughter postponed--on top of him.

"Are you all right?" she asked, touching the back of his head to ensure there was no bleeding.

He sighed. "Yes, I'm fine. I think it's my back that took the worst of it."

"Oh, sorry!" Robin scrambled up and offered him a hand which he took.

Alistair stood, placed two hands on his lower back and pushed it forward. A crack echoed over the plain and Robin felt guilt slipping inside her.

"I guess I shouldn't have teased you so much," she said, taping a finger against her chin. "I didn't know you were so embarrassed about it."

He gave a heavy exhale and shook his head, before looking back at her. "Is it really that obvious?" he asked.

She nodded. "To me, at least."

"Lord, I hope she hasn't noticed."

"Alistair, why would it matter? I believe you two would make a fine pair."

He shrugged.

"Are you really that embarrassed?"

He closed his eyes and took a deep breath. "Yes, I am."

"But you're a wonderful man, Alistair. Why should you be embarrassed?"

"Because," he said looking her straight in the eyes, "I don't have anything to offer her."

Again, Robin wanted to smack herself for pushing him. It was becoming a bad habit and one she'd have to fix. Then, again, Arthur always said she was a bit pushy. Perhaps the habit was already there even before the tree.

She looked over Alistair who had now broken their eye contact. He had never shown any insecurity before. None at all. Alistair was a young man who was very aware of his situation and was doing what he could to live a good life. He wasn't rich, but he had more than enough to be happy from what Robin had seen.

But what she saw in front of her now was someone full of shame.

He turned his head and stared back in the direction they had traveled. He tapped his fingers on his hips.

"Made-Maddy, I mean, she hasn't told me everything. Still, I know she hasn't had an easy life. From the south to the east with only her mother and younger brother. Then, war broke out and she had to live through that, only to find herself with no country to call her own and alone in Satbury where the people treat her like dirt. There's a reason other refugees only pass through. After all that, I think she deserves something more than I can ever give her. I'm not a rich man and it's not likely I ever will be. Best to leave her open to another, seeing what a bellibone she is and swooping her up. I mean, I—"

Robin lunged forward, wrapped her arms around Alistair's neck and buried her face into the little crook there.

Alistair softened. "You are a hugger, aren't you, Robin?"

"Hush up. You quite enjoy my hugs."

He chuckled. "I do."

"And you need them because you're not seeing what I see."

"A horse staring at us with raised brows? Wait, they don't really have brows I guess."

She bit her lip, refusing to laugh. She needed to let him know.

Robin lifted her face from his neck and stared into his eyes. She placed a hand on his chest and kept her gaze steady.

"Great men wear golden armor but not on the outside." She tapped the center of his chest. "They wear it on the inside, their golden armor. And I see yours here, shining, Alistair. I only wish you could see it too."

Any hint of play left his face. He sighed and placed a hand on the back of Robin's head. He planted a kiss on her forehead and smiled.

"I'll keep working on it, then?"

She nodded. "Agreed."

Alistair hissed and stumbled out of her grasp. He dug his nails into his silver strands and pulled at them, gritting his teeth.

"What's wrong?" Robin stumbled after him, her hand outstretched.

"Something's coming," he said. The purple in his eyes was more evident now, like a candle lighting them. "We have to go."

No other words needed to be spoken. Alistair mounted Fred and Robin sat behind him. The horse immediately took off at top speed, racing towards the border. While Alistair directed Fred, Robin kept her eyes open and watched the land around them.

Like Maddy and Alistair had told her, the lower-eastern land wasn't a common destination since the war. They should have been alone and they were, except for an shadow-like figure running behind the tree line, across the land and towards them.

Robin felt her stomach drop. All the air left her. She could only squeeze Alistair's shoulder. He followed her line of sight. She imagined he must have felt the same way she did. His eyes doubled in size and his mouth fell into a downward curve.

As if it knew it had been seen, the creature turned to them and grinned. Its face was like a blurry black mist that wasn't sure how to form. The only features hinting that the creature had a face were three splotches of bright red to create the eyes and mouth. The red had been carelessly thrown onto the black, almost like something a child would have done if handed a paint brush.

The creature cocked its head to the side, not missing a beat as its body continued to race forward. Its smile grew. Robin's heart raced.

"It's going to try and meet us at the border," she said, more to herself than to Alistair.

"I know," he replied. "But it won't."

"Alistair, you don't have to do this," she stated, eyes steady on the creature and its eyes steady on her, as well. "We are no match for whatever that thing is. A witch?"

"We're never going to figure out what happened to your family and friends that night if we don't reach the castle. Turning back will do nothing."

She lowered her forehead to his shoulder and breathed.

"You're right," she said to his back. "It could be here again if we returned later."

He nodded. "Exactly but I have a plan. You're not going to like it."

"I won't leave you," she replied.

Alistair sighed. "Because of my sliver, I'm likely to be resistant to its magic. If we cannot outrun the creature, while I distract it, I want you to take Fred and go."

"I am not going to leave you in the bloody hands of a monster!" She tightened her hold on his shoulders, wanting her words to sink in to him.

"Robin, listen to me," he shouted. "You have to. There is no other option. If you find Arthur in time, he can use Excalibur to save me. I've heard the tales. You must find Arthur."

"But—"

"Robin, please!"

It went against every natural instinct in her. She had never abandoned a friend and she didn't want to start now. But she had to admit, Alistair had a point. She wasn't resistant to magic like him. She'd be more of a burden than an asset because he'd try to protect her. She knew that.

Her gut wrenched and she sucked in a sharp breath that felt like spikes in her windpipe, before barking out, "Fine!"

Alistair nodded. They braced themselves.

The border grew closer and so did the creature.

Only yards now.

Robin gritted her teeth and kept her eyes locked on the figure.

They crossed the threshold, breaking the first line of tall trees and stomping onto the carved-out path. The thing was only a few yards from their right. It smiled, its eyes narrowed and it lunged forward, barely missing the tip of Fred's tail.

Robin swiveled her head back to see if the thing planned to follow. But it didn't. It just stood there, inky black, the splotches of red and adorned in a dress. Blue silk, slim fitting like the one Robin wore the night she was imprisoned by the tree, the same dress she was wearing at that moment.

Air became harder to take in as Robin registered what she was seeing. Her lips trembled for words and breath but found none of either. She tightened her hold on Alistair, attempting to grasp something to help her breathe.

Warm hay in the sun, warm hay in the sun, Alistair is warm hay in the sun.

Her eyes were still frozen on the creature that now waved at Robin...

Suddenly, its hand stopped moving. Alistair groaned. Robin turned to look at him and she swore his silver stands moved of their own accord. There was a gasp and she turned back. Where one stood, there were now two. The second figure was taller than the first and well-formed. Even at a distance, Robin could tell it was in the shape of a woman, but she had no splotches of red like the smaller one.

The second figure moved its head to look in Robin's direction but only briefly. It quickly focused its attention on the first creature who now stared at the ground. The second figure grabbed the first by its head. The small creature let out one sharp shriek that left Robin's ears drumming before vanishing into nothing.

The remaining figure followed suit, seeming to disappear into itself. Robin wasn't sure if it screamed like the first. Everything sounded hollow to her now. The only noise that made it through was the sound of Alistair asking, "Robin, are you all right?"

Fred wouldn't stop moving. Robin had never seen the animal so distraught. He neighed wildly, raising on his hind legs and kicking out his hooves in the small clearing they had found.

Alistair approached with small steps and raised hands. Like the horse, his chest sunk and rose with shuddering breaths. His hands and legs shook. Even as he attempted to calm Fred, he was still trying to calm himself.

Robin looked down in her lap and saw her folded hands were trembling, as well. She pulled them apart and shook them loose, knowing it wouldn't get rid of her fear but enjoying the temporary distraction.

Alistair continued his approach. He reached out a hand towards Fred's nose. The horse neighed a few times and kicked its legs before returning to all fours. Heavy bursts of air rushed from his nostrils.

None of us seem to be able to breathe.

Robin placed a hand on her chest. While she watched Alistair, she counted her heartbeats.

Alistair brushed his hand against Fred's nose and the horse pushed his head against his palm.

He smiled. "Good boy, Fred. It's all right. Whatever it was, it's gone now. It's only us, okay?"

He smoothed his hands over the horse's neck and then, down his back, whispering words of comfort.

Once Fred seemed to relax, Alistair took a seat on the ground by Robin. He placed a hand on her back.

"Are you sure you're fine?"

She swallowed down the truth and nodded.

"You don't seem fine."

Robin let out a breathy chuckle. "Well, I don't think any of us are what most would view as fine, now, are we?"

His hand paused on her back.

Robin shut her eyes. Suddenly, she wanted to bite her tongue out for the way she had just spoken to Alistair. He didn't deserve that, not after saving them.

She moved to turn in his direction to apologize but there was a tight pressure on her neck. She peered up from her peripheral vision. Alistair's face was turned towards her yet his eyes were on the surrounding trees. His hand grasped her neck.

"Robin," he said, still peering into the trees, "I don't want you to react. I only want you to listen."

She nodded.

"Some people are here. They're watching us."

She nodded once more.

"I want us to appear like we're talking. When you look up, toss your head back, almost like you're praying and focus on the tree tops."

Her even breathing disappeared. Images of the black creatures formed in her mind. Alistair's grip tensed on her neck.

"I'm here with you. It's fine. They're people, not witches. My patch isn't itching."

"Good."

"We don't want them to know we've noticed. When you see them, stand with me and we're going to continue to the capital. If they make a move, stand back-to-back with me and Fred. I have the dagger you gave me. Be prepared to use yours."

Robin balled her fists and let the pain run through her. So many times before she had to be strong. When Liz betrayed her, when the tree took her, when she escaped and with the man in the alley...now she'd have to do it again.

Her heart was pumping so quickly but Robin was becoming familiar with the beat.

"I'm ready," she said.

He released her. Robin turned her head up and back like he had directed. If a person didn't stare too hard, it almost looked like the trees just had very large branches or extra limbs. But there were too many on a few of the trees to be normal. She could see it now. Alistair was right.

She closed her eyes as she faced the sun. Then, turned back to stare at the ground. Finally, with Alistair's hand now on her back, she stood and walked towards Fred.

Alistair helped her mount the horse, before climbing on, as well. Together, they continued through the trees at a slow stroll. Robin observed how the path they were on was carved out. It had to be man-made but not used often, considering all the agriculture that now grew over it and narrowed their path.

"I think we should dismount," she said leaning into Alistair's ear. "The road is too narrow and if they come now, we won't be able to climb off fast enough."

The tree branches creaked and snapped from either side of them.

He swallowed. "You're right. I'll pretend to have some back pain."

Alistair pulled at the reins, before moaning in agony as he pushed on his back.

"Oh, what's wrong?" Robin asked, raising her voice.

"Bumpy ride. My back can't take it after the fall."

"Of course, let's walk, then."

Alistair slid to the ground, ensuring the simple movement appeared to take more effort than it did. Robin followed suit and soon the pair were on either side of Fred, walking at a casual pace.

"You see them moving?" she whispered.

"I do. Don't think it's going to be much longer."

"How many have you counted?"

He glanced from side to side again. "I'm counting six but there could be more. They blend in with the trees. Better than the hunters from up north."

Robin wasn't sure what that meant. She nodded nonetheless. "You're not going to ask for me to leave again, right?"

He shook his head. "That plan won't work here. We're outnumbered. Some of them would give chase. We have to fight and make our escape when the opportunity presents itself."

Robin itched to get her hand on her dagger. Neither her father nor uncle had thought fighting skills were necessary for a woman. Of course, Robin could see their logic. Men went to war, not women. Men were primarily charged with guarding the home, women on rare occasion.

But she enjoyed the strategy behind fighting, the challenge, not to mention, as she would always ask her father and uncle, what if the men aren't there?

This question always shut down any objections because they knew the answer. When the enemy killed all the men, the women were only trophies for the taking.

Robin had experienced that fear in the alley with the drunkard. She was alone, Alistair was unconscious, no men were present to help and she still survived. Of course, Alistair was awake and alert now, but Robin would not allow another's strength to be her own. Not completely. They needed to support one another. He'd slash someone's throat for her and she'd press a blade into someone's gut for him. It was only fair.

There was a large cracking sound, followed by several grunts. Both Robin and Alistair moved back behind Fred and turned their backs to one another, daggers already glistening in the sun.

They were surrounded. There were six as Alistair had said, all holing rusty battle axes or dull swords.

"State your name and your purpose." The young man who spoke stood at a distance on the road side. He faced Alistair, but Robin could see him from her side vision. He was stout and stocky. He didn't hold himself with the grace of a knight. However, he seemed built for combat with large, defined muscles and an easy hold on a battle axe that almost matched him in height. What struck Robin as even more odd was how young he was, younger than Alistair even.

"My name is Clark and this is my wife Thea."

"Purpose?" he repeated.

"Visiting. We're newly married and have never been to the kingdom." The lie slid easily from Alistair's lips. Robin made a note to compliment on his skill later.

The young man huffed. "Newlyweds with daggers? Jeweled daggers at that? Do you think I'm daft, *boy*?"

Robin pressed her tongue against the back of her teeth as laughter erupted around them. *He* was calling Alistair a boy?

"Well," Alistair said, an obvious strain in his voice, "Since I don't know you very well, I wouldn't be the best judge. How about you let us go and our conversation can come to an end?"

The young man scoffed. "That's not going to happen. Now, tell me the truth. Why are you here and who is the woman?"

A chill ran up Robin's spine. The boy was watching her.

"I already told you the truth," Alistair replied.

"What kingdom do you call home, then? And don't mislead me."

"The Middle Kingdom."

Robin could hear their grips tighten on their weapons. The sound of leather against metal signaling they didn't like the answer.

"Ah, a couple middle kingdom bastards." The boy made the

small jump from the land to the road. His eyes moved between Alistair and Robin.

"Cadfen's people, huh?"

"Yes," Alistair barked out. "We don't want any trouble. We'll leave. Just let us go."

The man threw back his head and chortled. His men followed his mocking gesture.

Again, Robin pressed her tongue against the back of her teeth. If ever given the opportunity, she would have more than a few choice words for them. Alistair was a better man than all of them combined.

Once he had finished making a fool of himself, the young man thrust out his battle axe and pointed it at Alistair. "How about this, middle-born? Since you're so set on fleeing with your beautiful wife, why don't you fight me for your freedom?"

He pulled the axe back and threw his arms wide open. The most arrogant smirk decorated his face. Robin wanted to slice it off.

"Fight me," the young man said. "If you win, you and your wife go free. If I win, we take you both back to our camp and figure out what you're really doing here."

There was a quiet moment as everyone waited for Alistair to speak. Everything in her told Robin this was a trap and the boy couldn't be trusted. On the other hand, there were two of them and six of the enemy. That meant three men for Robin and another three for Alistair. A few of the men were scrawny. They'd be easy to kill if the need arose. But Robin and Alistair were still out-armed and outnumbered.

There weren't many good options.

Alistair stepped away from where he stood with Robin. He faced the stocky young man. "Fine. Give me your word and it's a deal."

He placed a hand over his heart. "I swear on my men," he said. "Win and you and all your company are free."

Alistair nodded. Robin moved behind Fred, so her back wasn't facing any of their opponents.

Alistair rolled his shoulders and let the dagger hang loose at his side. With them facing one another, Robin could better see the differences in their physiques. The young man was shorter than Alistair but he had more built muscle whereas Alistair's muscles were leaner.

If this came down to brute force, Alistair wouldn't win. But he hadn't relied on brute force in the alley and he wouldn't rely on it now. He was quick and smart. He could win. Robin smiled.

Of course, the arrogant fool moved first.

Impatient.

He swung out the ax horizontally a few times, attempting to catch a slice of flesh from a distance. Alistair, in turn, gracefully stepped out of its reach, moving one foot behind the other and then back.

After completing a quarter of a circle, his opponent drew his weapon back and rushed forward. He screamed as he swung, and his axe sliced into the earth. With ease he pulled the weapon free and moved closer to Alistair.

"You're good on your feet," he said, his breaths heavy as they left him.

Alistair only nodded.

The young man pushed ahead to Alistair and swung again. This time, however, he grabbed for Alistair with his free hand.

A distraction.

He gripped Alistair's arms and pulled him to his body. There was a victorious smile on the man's face. He didn't know Alistair wasn't done yet.

When there was less than a foot of space between them and his opponent's elbow was curved, Alistair stepped forward, pushed his arm up and then, pushed himself back out of his opponent's grasp. It all happened so fast Robin thought she may have imagined it. She didn't though. Because Alistair was free, standing right in front of her.

Then, he moved once more. He had pushed himself back from the man's hold and now he slammed the butt-end of the dagger into the man's nose. His opponent staggered. Alistair took his chance. He grasped his opponent's hand that held the axe and turned it with enough force the axe fell. His palm was open and shaking now.

Alistair lifted his dagger. He grimaced and brought it down directly in the middle of his palm. The man hadn't screamed before but now he was howling in pain.

Robin would have been lying if she said the sound didn't bring her some pleasure.

Alistair tossed the man away from them.

The young man held his shaking hand and stared at his bloody palm. There was a gloss over his eyes. Robin could have sworn he was on the verge of tears. And then he did something very stupid.

He glanced to his left. One of his men jumped down onto the

road behind Alistair.

I knew it.

Robin ran ahead and put all her weight into her shoulder. She thrust herself into the new enemy and he landed on the road's short wall. He "umphed" as he landed before blinking up at her. His reaction was stalled.

Robin raised her dagger, sent up a silent prayer, and brought the weapon down.

"Wait, stop!"

That wasn't Alistair's command. That was the other one. Robin continued her thrust downward until the blade pierced her opponent's throat. There was some gurgling, lots of blood and finally, two unwelcome hands on her shoulder.

She mimicked Alistair's movements and managed to get one shoulder free which was more than enough for her to spin around and slice her dagger out. Blood sprayed in front of her and her other shoulder was set free.

She quickly took her place at Alistair's back. The other men had now leapt into the road and were pressing upon them.

"Fred, clean the hay!" Alistair pulled Robin to the ground.

The horse thrust his back legs into the air and his hooves smashed into two of their enemies, knocking them to the ground. Only one stayed down.

"Everyone, stop," the young man screamed.

But his men didn't listen. There was fury in their eyes and in the way they held their swords. They took another step.

"Stop!" he shouted.

Another step.

"No!"

Robin raised her weapon. Alistair pressed his back against hers.

"By order of Arthur, I order you to stop!"

The name brought the men and Robin to a sudden still. She spun around to face the arrogant young man. He was still sweating and shaking from his fight with Alistair.

She marched over to him and pressed her blade against his neck. His men turned their weapons on her.

"How do you know Arthur? Where is he?" she hissed.

He glanced down at her wrist. "If you hadn't hidden that charm bracelet so well, all of this could have been avoided."

She pressed the dagger into his flesh. "Answer the question or I'll slit your throat."

He shook his head. "Honestly, it's my fault, as well. When

your friend hit me with the dagger I should have recognized the symbol. There was so much blood everywhere though. More now that you've killed two of my men. They had no families so don't feel too bad."

"Do you like to be a fool?" She spat the words out at him.

He grinned. "Actually, no but sometimes I find myself in that role. I think we got off on the wrong foot. My name is Lancelot."

Chapter Nine

Robin's feet ached. They had been walking for hours and despite her insistence they ride Fred, Lancelot and his men preferred to guide, not give directions.

Well, that's what they said at least. Robin thought the arrogant Lancelot was looking for an excuse to stare at her.

When the battle was settled and they started the long march, Alistair placed himself on the left of Fred and Robin on the right. Lancelot immediately directed one of his men to the left of the road side and he took his place on the right.

Now, his eyes were still unwavering. His gaze made her want to crawl out of her own skin and she was sure she would have if possible.

He didn't have that spark the drunkard did. But there was something in his eyes, an iron clad curiosity he was trying to press onto her.

Lancelot moved onto the road. Fred came to a halt and Alistair was suddenly standing in front of them, glaring at the young man.

"What do you want with her?" Alistair asked, not holding back the bite in his words.

The young man grinned. "Only to talk. If I wanted harm done to her or you, it would have happened already."

Alistair's lips curved but he forced the smirk away. Robin found herself smirking, as well and she refused to hide it. She turned to Lancelot, lips curved and eyes sparkling, when she said, "For a man who was just bested, you speak very highly of yourself. You've even given your axe to your comrade because you can't hold it in the hand my friend sliced open. Am I right?"

There was a strained tick in his jaw that made Robin wary. She watched his face harden and tried to do the same with her own.

And then, he smiled.

"Arthur told me a lot about you."

Robin shrugged. "I hope I don't have to learn much more about you."

She turned her back to him and began their march again. She inclined her head towards Alistair and he slunk back to his side of Fred. Lancelot followed quietly behind, before stepping closer to her side.

"Hair as black as night, eyes such an ice blue you'd think they'd pierce your soul. He was very right."

She continued staring ahead and said nothing. Yet, her hands were shaking. She tightened her hold on the reins to stop the involuntary movement.

Arthur had talked about her.

The knowledge sent a flurry of feelings in her chest. They all fluttered about looking for an escape but there was none. She would only express her feelings of longing, desire, and heartache to Arthur, once they were together again and alone.

He deserved all of it after waiting ten long years for her to return. She wanted all he could give, as well. They'd take back Camelot, send Cadfen to the gallows and then...perhaps they could be together properly as man and wife. Maybe eventually children too.

What would our children look like? What shade of blue would their eyes be? More like mine or his?

Excitement tingled in her. She placed a hand on her chest to relax her breathing.

Everything was coming together. Yes. It would be fine now.

"Where have you been these last ten years?" Lancelot was close enough Robin could feel the heat from his body. She took several large steps ahead putting more distance between them.

"Arthur thought you dead," he continued.

"Well, obviously I'm not."

"Then, where have you been? It must be quite a tale."

"It is none of your concern where I've been," she retorted, slamming her words out at him.

Robin hoped she had finally silenced the fool.

He took a deep breath and the trail of words continued.

"We're almost there. Since I am a gentleman, I think I should tell you th—"

"A gentleman?" She stared back at him with raised brows and laughter on her face.

He only shrugged. "Once you get to know me better, you'll see that I am quite the gentleman, Robin."

He squeezed her shoulder. It took everything she had not to turn and press her knife into his belly.

The rest of the journey was made in silence. Alistair, occasionally, would peek under Fred's head to check on Robin and she, in turn, would stick out her tongue at him.

Lancelot had returned to his position along the roadside. Still, his eyes were on her. She fought back the cold feeling he caused her with thoughts of Arthur.

The last time they met, he had smelled like the gardens. She doubted there were any gardens like those in Camelot. Still, there was plenty of nature. What would he smell like now?

Honey, perhaps. This kingdom was known for its honey farms. Maybe he took up the trade.

The thought brought a smile to her lips.

Soon, the narrow road expanded, and then opened into a square. There was a large crumbling wall which, at either end, had a fallen tower. The rubble surrounding the area was covered in moss and ivy.

Robin stretched her neck back and tried to imagine the wall's appearance ten years past. If Issin had structured his capital like her uncle's, what she was staring at was the remnants of Rowan's outer wall.

What it once had been.

The group marched on. Together they traversed over and through the rubble until they reached, once more, the grassy land of the capital. Barely any homes or buildings were left. There were no people, none that Robin could see at least, and everything had been conquered by nature.

As they continued their tread, a castle came into view. The structure was surrounded by a destroyed wall, as well, and as they entered what looked to have once been a courtyard, they stepped over large wooden gates.

The courtyard was several acres in circumference. In the very middle stood the remains of Issin's keep. Only two towers still stood properly and more than half of the main structure was rock. The entire castle was overshadowed by trees that moved upward into the mountains.

However, unlike before, the area was moving with life. It was full of people running this way and that, carrying wood, tools, and cloth. There looked to be several gardens near the edge of the space and a workman's table for daily tasks. Robin realized that though Issin and his kingdom were gone, his people were still prospering.

Lancelot moved in front of the group with one of his men at his side. He leaned towards his comrade and said, "Fetch Arthur. We'll wait here."

The man raced ahead into the collapsed structure.

Perhaps it was her imagination or maybe it was all the traveling finally catching up to her. Suddenly, the air seemed too thin. Robin couldn't get enough. Her dress felt tighter, too tight, like it was attempting to suffocate her. Her palms had started to sweat, and she began to play with her charms.

The man Lancelot had sent ahead returned from the ruins. Behind him, another man stepped out. He was taller with broad shoulders and blonde hair just above his brow. Even from a distance, Robin knew this man had eyes as blue as the seas. She knew this man was Arthur.

She clasped her hands together and placed them on her chest. She wanted to wait, to be patient and savor this moment to ensure it was not a dream. Yet, one small step became two and two three, before several sobbing breaths of air left her and she was racing to him at a full sprint.

With each step, he was getting closer, moving better into her view and becoming fully formed. She wasn't even sure if she was breathing anymore. All that mattered was Arthur and getting to him.

Then, he looked up and his slow stroll with the guard came to a halt. His hands fell by his side and on his beautiful face realization broke like a sunrise. He tore into a run but Robin was already halfway there.

She leapt into his arms and held him so tight, she thought her shoulders would break.

"Tell me I'm not dreaming. Tell me you're really here." His voice had deepened. It had a raw edge to it that made her reflect on the young man that courted her those many years ago.

She pressed her face into his neck and inhaled deeply. As she had thought, he didn't smell like gardens. Instead, he smelled like salt, honey, and fresh water. At that moment, Robin decided it was her new favorite scent.

She could feel his fingers running through her hair, twirling the strands.

"Your hair's gotten longer."

She laughed and pulled her face away, so, she could stare up at him. For some reason, his jaw seemed to be wider, more set in its place than before. There were also a few lines at the corner of his eyes, though they were hardly visible.

He was still Arthur.

Robin stood on her toes and pressed her lips against his. Her chest was in full flutter now and everything inside her turned into a burning, light airiness that she needed to share with him, to push into him.

His lips were a testament to his scent. They were sweet, salty, and delicious, awakening a hunger in her she hadn't felt in years.

She teased his bottom lip with her tongue and his mouth opened to let her in. She could feel his body become rigid around her. She pressed closer to him, and tightened her hold, one she intended to never let go.

He placed his hand on her lower back and twisted the other in her dark tresses. He pulled them apart, just a bit; only to move his lips back to hers with a slow, deliberate pressure. Finally, he hovered his lips over hers, before opening his eyes and gazing down at her.

"Robin," he breathed into her.

And she would have smiled at the way he said her name, except when she looked into his eyes, the initial joy was gone. Instead, there was a strained wariness that tossed a cold bucket of water on the heat he had spread through her body.

"What's wrong?" She placed her hands on either side of his face.

"Arthur?"

Robin turned to her right. She may have been wearing pants and men's boots but there was no mistaking Morganna. She was a little shorter than Robin with the same narrow shoulders, brown eyes the color of acorns and blonde hair that Uncle Terryn once said put the sun to shame.

For a moment, Morganna's face had the same happy light Arthur's did when he first saw Robin. She glanced at Robin's arms, following the path to her hands which rested on Arthur's face. The light faded and a tense smile spread across Morganna's lips.

Morganna took a step back, and as she did, the sunlight caught on something around her neck.

Robin felt her throat swell. She stepped away from Arthur and moved towards her cousin. There, around Morganna's neck, was a golden charm in the shape of a dragon. Almost the same design as the charm on Robin's own wrist.

A clammy sweat broke out over Robin's body. Her mouth became dry and there was a heavy feeling in her stomach. She tried to breathe through her nose, but her body didn't want air. It pushed it out in a hacking cough. She placed her arm around her middle and bent over as her breath fought against her.

Suddenly, there was a gentle weight on her shoulder. She turned her eyes upward.

Alistair was smiling down at her. It wasn't a happy smile. "Let's return to Fred."

She shook her head. "No, please, just, just take me into the woods." She closed her eyes. "I don't want anyone else around."

He nodded and placed her arm around his shoulders.

"Robin?" The sound of his voice made her head spin. Everything was supposed to be okay now. Yet, it was all so wrong.

"Robin?"

Just stop saying my name.

"She's fine," Alistair said. "We need to rest. We'll return in a few hours."

"I think she should—"

"Arthur," Robin said, not even glancing back at him. His name seemed to bring an immediate silence to everyone around them.

"Get away from me," she said. "Please, just get away from me."

"I can't blame him, can I, Alistair? I can't blame her either." Robin sat back-to-back with Alistair staring down at the ruins. They were on a small hill about a mile up. From a break in the trees, Robin could see Arthur still standing in the clearing.

Alistair sighed. "I guess not...no, you can't."

She swallowed down a bitter taste in her mouth. "It's been ten years. Did I really expect him to wait for me?"

Yes.

She scoffed at her answer and shook her head. "How could I be so stupid?"

"It's never stupid to want for love, Robin."

"Then, why does it feel that way?"

"Because you're hurting."

Robin rested her head on her knees and continued to stare down at Arthur.

"I'm so angry with him yet I can't look away."

"I know what will help. Come on." He moved to a seat on a nearby rock and waved Robin over.

She looked at the clearing once more, before moving to stand by Alistair.

He pointed at the space in front of him. "Sit," he said.

"Why?"

"I'm going to help."

She raised her brow and crossed her arms. "Is this a trick?"

"When have I ever tricked you?"

"Well, my count so far is twelve and, yes, that includes when you lied about your name."

"And the other times?"

"Do we really need a list and explanation?"

"I'm always in the mood for a good story." He propped his chin up in his hand and grinned. "Serenade me."

Robin shook her head but laughed. She pinched his cheek. "You're the worst, do you know that?"

"If it makes you smile, then, I'll gladly wear the title. Now sit."

She huffed but tucked her legs under herself and sat where instructed.

Alistair pulled her hair to the side. He ran his fingers through it, starting from the scalp and moving down to the ends.

"I'm not sure what that tree did while it had you, but it took good care of your hair. I think you'd put any show horse to shame."

She squeezed his calf between her thumb and finger.

"What? Should we ask Fred to be certain? I'm sure he'd agree."

She captured his calf flesh again and twisted it until it turned red.

"Okay, okay! No more jokes. Only business."

Alistair brought her hair to her back and spread it out across her shoulders. She could feel his fingers at the front of her hairline. He grasped a few strands and, slowly, his fingers begin to move around one another.

Is he doing what I think he is?

She tried to turn to get a better view only to be yanked forward.

"Was that really necessary?"

"You're going to mess it up," he said.

"Why are you braiding my hair?"

"Because you told me your mother would braid your hair when you were feeling ill as a child."

Robin leaned into him and let the tears burn behind her eyes. "How could you remember that? I've barely mentioned my parents."

"Because I could tell it was important to you. Not to mention, two of my cousins from the north are girls and they love when I play in their hair."

Robin closed her eyes and rested her head against his abdomen. "They are lucky to have kin like you."

Alistair reached the end of her hair and tied it in a loose knot.

"Here, pick one."

In front of her, he held two flowers. One was a yellow dandelion and the other a blue thistle. They were the few remaining from summer.

"The thistle," she said, and his hands returned to her hair. As Alistair tied the flower into her braid, her eyes fell back onto the clearing. Arthur was still standing there and for a moment she felt like he was staring up at her.

She closed her eyes and shook herself. *There's no way he can see me up here. I'm only imagining it.*

"You think you're ready to go back? We've been up here for hours and I think Arthur's going to send out a search party soon."

She laughed. "I agree though I'm not sure if I'll ever be ready."

"You're stronger than you think, Robin."

"I know but..." Tears rushed to her eyes and she bit her lower lip to force them back. She turned away from the clearing and to the sky instead.

"Up here, it's fine," she said. "Up here, it's like it's just us back in Satbury. But once we go down there to Morganna and Arthur, it all becomes real again."

"If you want, we can leave. It'll be night soon and we can sneak out to where they've placed Fred."

The idea was tempting. She could run, put the horrible memories behind her, start anew as someone different who never even heard the name Pendragon. Still, even if she left without speaking to Arthur or Morganna again, Cadfen would be king. Her uncle would still be dead, and Arthur would still be the only one who knew what happened that night.

"No," she said, nearly having to choke the word out. "I can't leave yet. I need to know more."

"All right. What would you like to do, then?"

"It's not so much a want as it is a need," she said. "I need to figure out what happened to my uncle and how Cadfen became king. But with the way I feel right now..."

The churning started in her stomach. She grabbed her middle and pinched her abdomen, hoping she could untwist the knots. She needed to pull herself together. She couldn't be angry at either of them; she knew that.

But a part of her didn't. A part of her was tearing itself apart on the inside, clawing away skin, muscle, and everything she was and would continue to until there was nothing left. Once there was nothing, she wouldn't be able to feel anything. Once she had destroyed herself, all the pain would go away.

Robin wanted to smack herself. How could she let someone

have such a hold on her?

The more important question was how could she become free without breaking herself completely? She only needed to shut everything down for a little bit, until she could afford to be weak.

An image of Maddy in the alley with a stick raised above the fallen drunkard flashed in her mind. She played the brief scene once more.

Her eyes focused on the clearing.

None of this is really happening. Not to you. Keep telling yourself that.

She stood, eyes fixed on the clearing below them. "I'm ready."

Chapter Ten

Alistair wished he knew how to stop Robin's pain. He had seen her face when her cousin stepped into the field wearing the golden necklace. She had crumbled like the fallen castle and even when she stood on the hilltop looking down on Arthur's group, she seemed not herself. It was like she had been thrown off balance. Robin was raw, damaged but she was not broken, not until that moment at least.

He could tell by the way her shoulders fell and her lips quivered only to be replaced by a nearly ear-touching smile. Every time she was close to crying, she would grin instead--a big toothy smile fit for a royal playing pretend.

They breached the line of torches surrounding the clearing. A few people still milled about in the dark, probably guards. Alistair couldn't really focus. His eyes were on Robin and the tension in her face that was revealed as they crossed the line of torches.

Arthur was standing in the middle of the clearing staring straight at her, holding his own torch and with another pushed into the earth beside him.

When they neared, he offered a hand, but Robin didn't take it. She stopped within arm's reach and maintained their eye contact. Her shoulders shook for a moment, and then she smiled widely.

"I am so glad we've found one another again after all these years," said Robin.

The words were spoken slowly and with additional emphasis on their pronunciation.

Without the sun, Arthur's face was darkened. Still, the torch provided enough light that Alistair didn't miss the widening of his eyes.

He made a step towards Robin. Like a spooked cat, she stumbled backward and turned her eyes away from him. Alistair grabbed her and before Arthur could take another step, he had placed himself in front of Robin.

Like any boy his age, as a child, Alistair had heard countless stories about Arthur. Some of the stories were probably more tale than fact but that was irrelevant. What mattered was in a fight against Arthur, Alistair didn't stand a chance, not unless he fought dirty. Maybe not even then.

It wasn't about Arthur's size or bulk really. He and Alistair were *almost* equal in height. What mattered here was experience and Arthur had tons compared to Alistair. As a knight, not only had he been trained to fight since young, he had gone on numerous missions where he returned to Camelot with a stained blade.

When Terryn was king and the two eastern rulers were in one of their usual skirmishes, he had sent Arthur to end the conflict. He fought two of their best men from each side and won. That wasn't sheer luck.

And though Alistair had learned to survive as the runt in a town of massive northerners, he wasn't a fool.

Arthur's gaze slid from Robin to Alistair where his eyes scowled at the human barricade. Like when he first met Robin, Alistair could see the storm brewing but behind Arthur's eyes this time. It made sense when Alistair thought about it. Arthur probably wasn't used to being challenged and, once again like Robin, he was in a raw, emotional state.

Still, Alistair wouldn't move. Robin didn't want Arthur near her. She didn't want him touching her, and if Alistair was the one thing that gave her some peace then, he'd take the punches as they came.

Arthur stepped back. He crossed his arms over his chest.

"And who are you exactly?"

Alistair straightened. "My name is Alistair. Pleased to meet you."

Arthur didn't respond for a moment. He was working his jaw from side to side, grinding his teeth. His eyes fell on Robin but quickly returned to Alistair.

"Yes, all right. I've had dinner brought to my chambers for us. Please follow me." He looked past Alistair again and his jaw stilled.

"I've arranged for some chocolate berries to be brought in, as well. I remembered they were your favorite import."

The hold Robin had on Alistair's back nearly made him push her away. She had quite the grip when she needed it.

"That'll be fine," Alistair said, attempting to relax into the pain. "Please, lead. We'll follow."

There was a flicker of anger as his eyes passed over Alistair. Arthur handed him a torch, turned on his heels, and began walking while Alistair and Robin followed a few yards behind.

When Arthur had turned his back to them, Robin stepped from behind Alistair, and walked by his side.

"I'm a coward," she said.

"You are not. This can't be easy for you."

She took a deep breath. "Easy or not, it must be done. I

thought I had a hold on it but...I'm not as good at this as Maddy."

"What?" Alistair turned to look at her. "Good at what?"

"That day with the drunkard. After Maddy hit him, her eyes filled with terror," she said. "But then, she took a deep breath and the fear disappeared. There was nothing on her face. As if we hadn't just killed a man."

"Maddy never told me—"

"Can you help me for a moment?" Robin wrapped her arm around Alistair's.

Quietly, they walked behind Arthur. Despite being dark, Robin had closed her eyes. She kept one hand on her chest, and with a finger, she had started a steady beat. Repeatedly, she took deep breaths, in her nose and out her mouth. Just before they entered the ruins and passed into a temporary darkness, Robin let her arms fall to her side. She stepped into a torch's light as they crossed the threshold.

Alistair looked at her. Her face had stilled and dulled, her piercing blue eyes faded into haziness, but she was smiling. A great big smile.

Alistair was never one to pass up a good meal and the plates of food in front of him qualified as a good meal. But he was dumbstruck by what he was seeing.

Robin, the Tree Woman as he once called her, who barely ate, was stuffing herself with meat, bread, cheese, and apples. She chewed fervently and swallowed with a grin.

The food had, apparently, made her oblivious. Because as she ate, Alistair and Arthur gawked at the speed she was consuming the meal.

Alistair finally shook himself and turned his attention back to his own plate. He glanced at Robin.

"What's gotten into you?" he whispered.

"Hmm?" She stared at him while she pushed a slice of boar into her mouth.

He raised a brow. "You never eat this much. I can barely get you to eat bread when we're home."

"And where is home exactly?"

Their eyes shot to Arthur. He had asked the question without indicating a responder, yet his sight didn't falter. He watched Robin with a shaking earnestness in his eyes.

Alistair paused. He glanced between the two.

Robin took down the last bit of her food, sipped from her cup, and cleared her throat. Finally, she looked directly at Arthur, her stare flat and bland.

Alistair saw Arthur's hand quickly clasp around his cup only for him to release his hold a moment later. He tapped his finger against the metal.

"We're residing in Satbury, right below the northern border." There was a strong, pointed clarity in her voice. "Arthur, I need you to tell me what happened that night. What happened to my uncle?"

The knight cast his eyes downward. "I don't want you to have to live through that."

"And I don't want to be left in the dark."

"Robin." He pushed his plate to the side and spread his hands across the table. "Listen to me. It is hard enough to have to tell you King Terryn is no longer with us. I won't give you the details of his death."

She leveled her gaze at him. Alistair had a feeling the power play had turned in her favor.

"*My* uncle's death is what got me here," she said, taking in sharp breaths. "*My* uncle's death is what got me locked in a damn tree for ten years, only to wake to...to nothing."

She closed her eyes and placed her forehead in her palm.

Alistair reached for her but she held out a hand to stop him. When she opened her eyes, they were like daggers aimed at Arthur.

"Tell me. Everything," she stated, raising her head.

Arthur sighed, a tremor in his clasped hands. He sat back in his chair, yet he did not look at Robin. His eyes had found something particularly interesting about the stone floor.

"As King Terryn and I thought, Cadfen was a traitor. Both you and Morganna had fled safely, so, I proceeded to meet with the other men."

He ran a hand over his face. A tense red began to appear in his cheeks.

"Your uncle was in the throne room as we planned. We waited in the hallway that led to his bed chamber, the opposite side of the entrances. Cadfen and his traitorous lot appeared to murder King Terryn. We ran in and took our guard around the king. They were outnumbered. We thought we had them bested."

His voice hitched. He suddenly leaned forward, grasping his cup until his knuckles turned white.

"Cadfen knew everything about the king. Terryn trusted him too much. He knew the king was supposed to be alone in the throne room that night. We thought it would be an easy battle. We were wrong."

Arthur's eyes moved from the floor to the cup and became stagnant.

"We couldn't kill them. Cadfen is a castor."

The word sent a shiver down Alistair's spine.

Castors were humans who could manipulate magic. In exchange for their powers, they gave up a piece of their soul to a witch.

Having a witch's curse like Alistair was rare. Castors were almost unheard of. Most people weren't foolish enough to deal with a devil.

Arthur took a hard breath. "These shadows stepped from the walls and they tore into my men, into the king, splitting their bodies in two. The king fell and, then, soon, I was the only one left."

Robin's lip quivered. Her lids fluttered as water filled her eyes.

"And then?" she asked in a voice that was barely a whisper.

Arthur turned to her. The cup now hung loosely in his hands and he peered at her from over the rim.

"And then, Cadfen attacked me. One on one. He said he was a fair man and he wanted a fair fight. I didn't believe him. I stepped in to fight him. He landed a blow to my gut; I got a slice to his chest but when I had my chance, I ran. I gathered any men I could, and I fled though I wasn't sure if I would even be alive to lead them. Excalibur is the only reason his magic had no effect on me. As I was running from the castle, Morganna was turning back. I think the fire started when the men tried to resist Cadfen's traitors in the tower. She had seen the flames and raced to Camelot. There were only two dozen of us. We tried to run north but Cadfen was on us and the journey across the fields would have left us exposed for too long. King Essen refused us, said he didn't want to get involved. And—"

Robin slammed her fists on the table. "That hypocrite! My uncle was the only thing that kept him and his brother from each other's necks for years."

Arthur nodded. "He seemed to have forgotten that. Though Essen's mental state was preferred over his brother's, Issin agreed to take us. Then the war broke out. He fled, and we're here, hiding in the ruins, trying to blend in with those who were left to fend for themselves."

"Have there been attempts to retake the castle?" Robin asked. She was tapping her foot under the table.

"There hasn't been a chance. Between trying to raise our numbers and survive in the turmoil..." He sighed. "No opportunity has presented itself. I've sent out scouts. The place is well guarded, rounds every hour, three stationed on all sides on the ground. I'm not even sure how to train men to fight a castor. The risk is too high."

Robin raised her brow. "But Cadfen hasn't come looking for you. He thinks you dead, then?"

"That's what it seems. The blow he landed was not an easy one to heal from," he said, pressing his finger into the cup's rim. He turned his eyes up. "Robin, I need you to know—"

The door swung open sending an echoing creak throughout the room that made them jump in their seats. Their eyes fell onto the doorway and there stood Morganna with a plate in her hand.

She pulled her cheeks up into a grin and closed the door behind her. "I thought to join you all."

Arthur's mouth fell into a flat line. "Morganna, I asked you to eat with the others. Just for tonight."

Her smile stretched higher. She waved her hand at him and strode across the room to the table.

"Everyone's already finished and you know I often eat late. Plus," she glanced between Robin and Arthur before settling on Robin, "today is...it's a miracle. I don't want to miss a moment with my cousin." She took a seat beside Arthur and beamed.

Alistair was sure if she smiled any harder her face would crack. He was also very sure she couldn't get any closer to Arthur without physically merging.

"Morganna, please—"

"I want to be here, Arthur." She gave him a direct nod.

He took a long breath and turned to face them. However, this time his eyes did not meet Robin's.

"*We* tried looking for you, Robin. You and Liz."

Robin scoffed. "Elizabeth is a traitor. She was working for Cadfen." She took a sip from her mug and looked at the table.

A quiet fell over the room.

Arthur shot back from the table and jumped to his feet.

"I sent you with her. Dammit! Liz was always so doting. She wasn't mentioned in any of the journals. I never thought..." His words trailed off.

"Neither did I," Robin stated. There was a catch in her voice. "But she did. It will probably please you to know you were right,

Arthur. Cadfen did want me for a bride. Liz was instructed to capture me. I escaped her, but his men were soon following me on their horses. They shot arrows in my back to slow me down." She cleared her throat. Her hand was not steady any longer. "I would have never made it to King Herald, so, I ran into the forest for cover."

Morganna's eyes bulged. "Cousin, why would you—"

"I didn't have a choice," Robin barked, glaring at her. "It was either that or be forced to lie with Cadfen every night. I took my chances."

"I didn't mean any offense, Gwynevere."

Alistair and Arthur snapped to attention. Their eyes slid between the two women.

Robin gripped the table's edge. "You know not to call me that name."

Morganna sighed. "Very well. I did not mean any offense, *Robin*."

"It seems you've done quite more than offend, cousin," Robin spat. The words hung in the air like a raised sword.

Robin took a deep breath. She grabbed the dingy knife by her dish. She scratched circles into the wood but kept steady eyes on Morganna. The sound of carved wood grew louder the deeper she cut.

"Somewhat identical," Robin said, still staring at her cousin.

Morganna looked from Robin to the knife and back again. She jutted out her chin. "What do you mean?"

"This sound, right here that I'm making." She gestured towards the circling knife, letting her face open in an exaggerated innocence. "Don't you hear it? It sounded like this when the tree took me and covered me in bark. Suffocating me, blending me into its body. The moment the bark wrapped around my throat, sound seemed to fade. All I could hear was the steady creaking of the tree as it took me prisoner."

With a sudden pull, Robin freed the knife from the wood and flung it across the room. She stood, never breaking the stare she held on her cousin.

"Who knew I would be there for ten years?"

Robin switched her gaze to Arthur. She smiled. "I'm not really in the mood for berries, Arthur. Thank you, though. Goodnight."

She left. Alistair followed.

Chapter Eleven

Robin knew he was going to come. It wasn't in Arthur's nature to run from a challenge or to leave a matter unresolved. Robin knew that and she was fine with him coming to see her because this time she was ready.

She wasn't dizzy with impatience and longing like when she first stepped into the clearing. Not at all.

She placed those emotions at her core and let her anger for everything loss form them into something hard, something distant. Where once there was love, there was now only a quiet stone-like acceptance.

This was the world she now occupied. She would have to adjust.

The bottom of the door slid softly across the stone floor. "Robin?"

He had rarely visited her room when they lived in Camelot. Of course, it was viewed as inappropriate and even dangerous. There was always the looming threat of lust and losing control.

Robin would have been lying if she said she never dreamed of such, that she never wondered what it'd be like for her and Arthur to place customs aside and see where the day led...

But these were not those times and Arthur was now courting her cousin.

"You can come in, Arthur." She sat up from the small bed and moved around the room looking for a torch to light.

Arthur stepped into the room and the space was illuminated.

"You've come prepared, I see." Robin straightened out her dress and perched herself on the edge of the bed.

He closed the door behind him. There was an attempt of a smile on his lips.

"It was a habit of mine you used to hate."

She shrugged. "Not hate. I only loved to tease you about it. You could never let things be. I'm sure that's why you're here now."

He opened his mouth and then closed it. His shoulders slouched and his eyes fell to the floor.

"I'm not a fool, Arthur," she said. "I know what this is."

"Do you?" His eyes remained on the floor.

"Yes. I do. I think it was most apparent when you made sure Alistair and I had separate rooms, despite me informing you we live together in Satbury."

Finally, he looked up at her, his gaze sweeping over her dress. "How well do you know him?"

"He's saved my life more than once. There is no need for you to be concerned."

His gaze turned to the wall. "Doesn't seem he's provided you a proper gown?"

Robin stared down at her dress. She hadn't bothered to pack any night clothes. It was going to be a short journey and the only other clothes she had to wear were a borrowed set from Alistair. The dress was the closest she had to a night attire and so she hadn't changed.

"Sleep comes just as easily," she stated.

Arthur nodded. He grabbed a stool from a corner and took a seat in front of where she sat.

"How do you like your accommodations?" He motioned around the room. "I know it's not like—"

"How long are we going to do this, Arthur?"

He tensed. "Do what?"

"Talk around the subject," she replied with a deep exhale.

He straightened in his chair though the effort seemed halfhearted. He found her eyes and stared into them unblinking. Robin stared right back, making sure to convey the little interest she had in the conversation.

"I thought you were gone," he said in a cracked voice. "I looked for you so many times. I just...I never thought you'd run into the forest. And I couldn't venture far into the Middle Kingdom. Robin, I am so sorry. I abandoned you. I should have kept looking. I should have done more ...something!"

He was pulling at his hair as the repeated apologies flew from him. Robin felt an opening inside herself, a little alcove of sympathy.

She bit her cheek and quickly closed it.

"How long?" she said.

"How long what?" he asked.

"With Morganna? How long have you been courting her?"

His body became rigid. She leaned forward, making sure he would see her face clearly.

"Just tell me. How. Long?"

Arthur jerked as the question was repeated but the tension soon slid from his body.

"Only the last two years," he said. "In the beginning, we both were too distraught to even think about romance. She wept for you, Robin. We both did."

She wept for me? Is that supposed to make me feel better? What else was she supposed to do? Dig my grave and dance on it?

The thought brought a quirk to Robin's lips.

"Why are you laughing?"

She shook her head. "No reason. Was there anything else?"

His brow furrowed above narrowed eyes.

"Yes. I think it goes without saying you are welcome here. You and Alistair both, if you like. Stay here a—"

"I refuse."

"You're not going to make this easy, are you?"

"Excuse me!" Robin shot to her feet.

Arthur followed behind her at a slower pace. He put his free hand on his knee and grunted as he stood his full height.

"Do I really need to say it, Robin?"

"Say what?"

"That I want you to stay!"

Bubbles. Bubbles of light airiness grew within her. She hadn't expected him to say that. Until then, the conversation had been going as she thought it would. But then he said *that*.

Arthur stepped towards her. Before Robin could move there was a gentle hand on her arm. Both their faces were warmed by the torch's light. As she peered into his eyes, she saw the coldness of her own reflected in them. It was a coldness that disturbed her and a coldness being melted by Arthur's proximity.

He moved his eyes to the left. Robin followed his path.

Her left shoulder was bare, only a portion of it. The dress had become loose since she left the tree and she had undone a few of the buttons before lying down.

She directed her focus back to Arthur and a spring of heat spread through her body. She loved when he looked at her like that, as if she were a goddess from the old religions and he was completely under her control. She had the power.

What would happen if I dropped the gown even farther? Only a little? Maybe we'd lie together and he'd be mine again.

She searched his face. Lust was present in his sea blue eyes, present like the stars in the night sky but Robin needed to see something else. She needed to see love. It was a word they had never said to one another. Still, she knew it was between them...or it had been. But now?

She sighed and stepped around him.

"Robin?"

It has to be there. Maybe I just can't see it? I could always before.

"Robin?"

"Yes?"

She could feel his fingers gliding through her hair.

If I slept with him, it would be for nothing. Lust does not become love.

"Morganna... what's happening between her and. . .it doesn't change how I feel about you."

The words were absurd, yet she wanted them to be true. She turned to face him.

He continued to speak. "Since the day you arrived at Camelot, I have never felt for anyone the way I feel for you, Robin."

"And yet she wears your seal around her neck?"

"I never planned to be with her."

Robin closed her eyes. The feelings, the warm ones, they were rearing their ugly heads again. She placed a hand in her middle and swallowed them down.

"Are you all right?"

She opened her eyes and nodded. "I'm fine and I do not fault you, Arthur. I was a fool to think you'd wait for me forever."

"I wanted to," he said, grasping her hand. "Even before you arrived today, there would be nights I couldn't get you from my mind. You were always there."

"And now you're stuck between the two of us, hmm?"

He dipped his head. "I do not want to do wrong by either of you."

Of course, he wouldn't. Arthur was too kind. He'd want to find a way to make everyone happy. Even now, the way he clutched her hand and his eyes moved from side to side, Robin knew he was thinking what the best course of action would be.

The only problem was he wouldn't be able to save everyone, not this time. There was no optimal solution. Someone was going to get hurt. In that moment, Robin decided.

Better to cut your wrists now than to wait for the enemy to slice your gut.

She pulled the dragon charm from her bracelet and held it out to him.

He stepped back, his expression flattening. "I gave that—"

"I know," she said. "But things have changed. We have changed, and it is time we stop playing like we're the same people from ten years ago."

"I refuse."

She bit her lip. She would have to say it.

"So, will you leave my cousin, then? Will you choose me over her?"

"Robin, I can't—"

"Then take it." She grabbed his free hand and slammed the charm into his palm. "And go. There is nothing more for us to discuss."

"We—"

"If your honor as knight means anything, Arthur, I am asking you to please leave."

He hesitated, his fist tightening around the charm. Robin pointed at the door.

He nodded and walked to the exit. As he stepped into the doorway, he turned back to her. His hand was loose once more and the charm dangled from his fingers.

"Will you at least join me for breakfast tomorrow?"

She looked at the charm. It glowed in the fire's light, calling to her like a beacon. However, she preferred darkness at the moment.

"Please, Robin. Breakfast tomorrow. Only you and me. I'll send Morganna to help with a chore."

She shook her head as she stepped towards him.

"Why?" The pain in his voice would have broken her if she had been the same as before. But she wasn't.

"Because," she said, "tomorrow I'm leaving."

She closed the door and the room fell into darkness.

"Anything else you wanted to pack?" Alistair leaned on Fred's back, peering over at Robin.

Robin smoothed her hand over the horse's back and rested her chin on her flattened hands. She looked past Alistair to the forest beyond the clearing.

"Have you ever seen something very ordinary, but it looks so different when you see it again?"

He stared behind him, before turning back to her. He placed his chin on his hands, copying her movements, and smiled.

"Yes. I think I'm looking at something like that right now."

She raised a brow. "What do you mean?"

"Well, you look a bit more at peace," he said and his gaze fell to the side. "An unsteady peace but considering what's happened, peace, nonetheless."

A ball formed in Robin's throat. She tried to swallow it down. Instead it rested uneasily in her chest.

She stepped away from Fred and turned her line of sight downward.

"I think I'll grab some more boar before we depart. The note Arthur left this morning did say we were more than welcome."

"I think we have enough. Don't you?" Alistair asked.

"If we arrive to Satbury quickly, the leftovers can get us through another day or two and save us some coin."

A grin broke across his face. "Well, look at you. Concerned about money? You're a regular peasant now, *my lady*."

"Always the jester," she said, placing her hands on her hips. "You'll pay for that later. I'm going to get more food."

He nodded. "I'll feed Fred while we wait."

Robin walked back into the crumbled castle and stumbled along the halls. Most of the flooring was uneven and there were pebbles everywhere.

She turned a corner and fell backwards to avoid colliding with Morganna. Her back slammed into the stone floor and she cursed louder than intended.

"Are you hurt, cousin? I'm so sorry. I was rushing to see you off."

Morganna's brown eyes were open and wide as she reached out to Robin.

Robin tucked her hair behind her ears.

"I'm fine," she said and pushed herself up. "I was rushing, as well. I guess I got lost."

Morganna smiled. There was a warm red in her cheeks. "We all got lost a few times when we first arrived. Where do you need to go?"

"The kitchen. I was hoping to get more boar."

"Ah, the beast is quite delicious with the first tastes," Morganna said. "After being here for so long, I'd die for a slice of cow, though. Here, I'll show you to the kitchen."

"Thank you." Robin let her cousin take the lead and followed behind her.

Morganna hummed as they walked through the dark, damp halls. She seemed perfectly adjusted. The mossy stones of what was once King Issin's castle were a far cry from the decorated, pampered rooms Morganna had once lived in at Camelot.

But it has been ten years, you fool. Remember.

Robin held one arm with the other and took a deep breath.

Soon the whole ordeal would be over. She'd be back in Satbury with Alistair and Maddy and she'd lock these last two days away from her memory. Maybe she'd even be able to forget Arthur.

You're being silly again, Robin. You still need to re-take Camelot.

"Right here, cousin. Boar, correct?"

"What?"

Robin looked around her. To her right, there was a long dark hallway. To her left, Morganna stood in the doorway to a spacious room filled with tables and stools. The tables were lined against the walls and covered in cutlery.

"Are you having one of your spells?" Morganna asked, her brows pulled together.

Robin gave her a small smile. "No, I'm just distracted. Thinking about the journey ahead."

She nodded, before looking away from Robin. "And do, do, you plan on coming back?"

She wept for you.

Arthur's words rung in Robin's ear in odd opposition to the hopefulness in Morganna's voice.

Robin raised her brow and crossed her arms over her chest.

"Are you really that happy to see me go?"

The question hurt more than Robin had imagined. She and Morganna had never been close. Robin knew that. She once considered Elizabeth more of a sister than Morganna could ever be, but they were still blood, still kin. She would never wish Morganna gone from her life and, yet, her cousin was wishing her away right now.

Morganna turned her head up so she was looking into the kitchen.

"Let me fetch the meat for you."

Robin darted pass her cousin.

"Please, do not trouble yourself, Morganna." She slammed cupboards and drawers.

"Robin, I—"

"No!" Robin snapped. She pierced Morganna's brown eyes with a deadly stare. "No. I'll pack it myself. Don't want to take a bite and find myself poisoned."

Morganna shook her head. "You're being dramatic. I would never do anything to hurt you."

"But you have," Robin said, tossing a cloth on the table. "You have done many things to hurt me, cousin, including the words you spoke to me only a moment ago."

"You don't understand."

Robin rolled her eyes. "Everyone keeps telling me that. I think I have a fine grasp actually."

"I've loved him since we were children."

Robin's hands paused over the cloth.

She could feel her eyes moving upward to look at Morganna, her mouth opening to question her statement, but she stopped. Robin would not listen to another apologetic rant. Arthur was enough last night and now Morganna?

No.

She quickly wrapped the cloth around the meat and slid the package into a cloak pocket. Then, with a control she wasn't sure she had, Robin walked past her cousin without a second glance. Her hands itched to slap her but what good would that do?

"Robin!"

Dear Lord, does the woman not know when a conversation is over?

Morganna's blonde curls bounced as she ran up to walk beside her cousin.

"Do you hate me, cousin?"

Yes.

"No," Robin replied. She searched the hall for some sort of reminder this was the path they had taken previously. Everything looked the same, though. Robin wasn't sure if she was going the right direction And she wasn't going to ask Morganna.

"If you do not hate me, cousin, then why are you not speaking?"

"What's done is done, isn't it?" she retorted. "What else is there for us to say?"

"Say you're happy for me."

The words turned Robin's feet into statues. She came to an abrupt halt. A fire was rising in her chest.

"Say you're happy for Arthur and me," Morganna pleaded, tears building in her beautiful brown eyes. "Say you're happy I'm *finally* with the man I've loved since childhood."

Robin moved to face her cousin. The fire was at its peak, raging inside her when she realized, with a smirk, she wanted to burn something.

"So, that's what this is about, Morganna? Because he chose me over you." The words left her mouth, full of hate and dripping with acid.

By now, the tears had fallen down Morganna's cheeks. Her shoulders were shaking with the threat of more to come. Still, she straightened her back and took a deep breath before looking Robin directly in the eyes.

"Before you even arrived, before he met you, I knew Arthur was meant to be with me."

Robin gawked and then laughed outright. "I don't mean to make offense, cousin, but I wasn't privy to your feelings for Arthur. More importantly, I'm sure he wasn't either and still you know Uncle Terryn would have never allowed you to marry him. He's a knight. You're a princess."

"All the more reason for you to give me your blessing," Morganna barked. "Because now *we* can finally be together." Her hands turned into fists by her side.

Robin almost stumbled backwards.

Gone were her tears. Morganna's brown eyes had lost their light and she was glowering at her cousin with such a dark intensity.

Robin felt goose bumps on her skin.

"You've gone mad," Robin said and spun on her heels to walk down the nearest hallway, not caring if she got lost as long as she was away from her cousin.

Morganna's footsteps echoed behind her.

"You are not the only one that deserves to be happy, Robin."

That's apparent, isn't it?

"You don't know what it's like to be me."

Thank Trithian.

"He only doted on you because your parents died."

Robin had Morganna on her back and her hands around her throat before she even realized she had moved.

"Who the hell do you think you are?" Robin spat as her grip tightened.

She leaned down almost nose-to-nose with her cousin.

"My father was his brother. Lord Allen, brother of the king. *That* is why he took me in because *that* is what family is supposed to do, you cox-comb. I don't suppose you'd know anything about that?"

Suddenly, Robin lurched forward as air was forced from her lungs. She rolled on her side and wrapped her arms around herself, pain spreading out from where Morganna had kneed her.

Her cousin scrambled to her feet, keeping one hand around her neck. She stared down at Robin, eyes big and wild.

It took Robin a moment to understand what was happening. She got a nice jolt of pain when Morganna kicked her ribs.

She crawled to the side, flipped on her back and staggered to her feet. The two women stood facing once another.

"Perhaps you bested me when we were children, Robin. But living as a rebel has taught me a few tricks." A glee-filled smile spread across Morganna's lips. Her fingers ticked by her sides.

Robin realized her cousin had become a different person entirely.

Morganna lunged forward and Robin moved to the side but she was too slow. Her cousin had her arm in a bruising grip. With one hard swing, Robin's back collided with the wall, knocking any remaining air out of her. She tried to stand, yet before she could, Morganna had her by the shoulders.

Robin slapped her cousin across the face. She smiled when she saw the blood dripping from Morganna's lips.

"Looks like I can still do something, can't I?"

Morganna's elbow smashed against Robin's face. For a second, the world went black. She heard heavy breathing and saw Morganna's bouncing curls. Most things were coming in as a blur. She forced herself to her feet. The world slipped from side to side.

Her surroundings were clearing up. They were facing one another again. Then, she felt a tight hold on her throat. Morganna was closer than she had thought. Close enough to encircle Robin's neck and squeeze the breath from her, not that there was much left at that point.

But as suddenly as it appeared, the pressure on Robin's throat was gone. Air filled her lungs and noise filled her ears.

Voices.

"What are you two doing?" Arthur had Morganna by the shoulders and pushed against the opposite wall.

He went to her first.

"Robin? Robin?"

Alistair.

"Your face. Oh, my God. We need to—"

"Leave," she wheezed. "We need to leave."

"But—"

"Alistair," she shouted, clenching his shoulder. "Please."

He darted a glance at Arthur and Morganna, then nodded. "Let's go."

Robin stood, using Alistair's arm for support. He wrapped her arm around his shoulders and they begin to make their way.

"Robin!"

Both he and Morganna are truly intolerable.

She shuffled forward faster, Alistair almost dragging her along, like he sensed her need to be free of the ruins and the memories it held for her.

Sunlight brushed her face and Robin had never been happier until she realized there was an audience. The people in the clearing must have heard the argument.

They all stared at Robin, including Lancelot.

Maybe this is what he was trying to warn me about before. About Morganna and Arthur.

She scoffed. "The arrogant boy."

"What happened, Robin?" His hand on her shoulder. She didn't think she had the strength left but Robin jerked free from Arthur's grasp and turned on her heels to look at him. Worry turned into utter shock.

"Robin, your face…" He reached for her. She moved away.

"Forget that I ever loved you."

"I will never…"

She turned away from him.

I am so tired of this.

The man she once loved continued to protest. Robin ignored him. She mounted Fred with Alistair in front and when Arthur grabbed her arm, she pulled away.

Alistair flicked the reins, Fred started down the main path, and soon the clearing was nothing more than a fading image in the background.

Fred was running hard. Robin wondered if they should stop for a rest. Still, everything in her said they weren't far enough yet.

Alistair had tried to speak with her. She had no interest in conversation. The rush of the fight had gone and now Robin was left with pain. Her face ached where Morganna had elbowed her and her abdomen was tinder to the touch. She was sure it had bruised.

Perhaps, you could best me when were children, cousin ..

Morganna's words caused a flash of embarrassment to run through her. She hadn't only been bested. She had been completely humiliated.

Robin tried to lean in closer to Alistair but the pressure was too much on her face. Instead, she rested her forehead against his shoulder. She listened to the sound of Fred's hooves against the earth. They were constant and steady with a direction and a purpose.

Robin could feel her body shaking. She wanted to pretend it was only from the ride. And then, her lips started to tremble and her eyes begin to burn.

"He has a purpose," she whispered. "He has direction."

"What?" Alistair asked.

Robin tangled her fingers into his top, biting the inside of her cheek hoping pain would cancel out pain. A physical hurt in exchange for the ease of her emotional grieving.

She was not so lucky.

Robin screamed into Alistair's back as the tears poured from her. They were hot and burned like poison running from her body, leaving stinging, salty paths across her cheeks.

"Robin?"

She wanted to lie to Alistair and tell him everything was all right yet the only sound her vocal chords could produce was a guttural scream. She clenched her teeth together, trying to stop the noise, trying to regain control of herself, trying to remember she was fine. She was strong. Wasn't she?

Her body yanked upward of its own accord and her mouth flew open despite her hold on her jaw, releasing all her anguish into the world.

Everything hurt so much.

Robin balled her hand into a fist and banged it against her chest.

"Stop it, Robin!"

Again.

"Stop!"

Again.

Maybe it was because Fred came to a sudden halt or maybe Robin fell of her own choosing. She couldn't really tell. Her body had become a rattle and she found herself on the ground, screaming into the earth.

She didn't want any of this. The tears, the pain, the screams that were rocking her body, yet this is where she found herself. Hands wrist deep into the moist soil as her agony poured from her eyes and throat, leaving the seeds of torment to fester in the ground beneath her.

Because Robin couldn't do it anymore. Her womb could not bear the spawn of her suffering any longer.

The lost years, the dead parents, the murdered uncle, the mad cousin, and the stolen love.

No, she had to give it away.

"Let it out, Robin. It's fine."

Alistair's arms were like a rope in dark, choppy water, only Robin wasn't ready to take it yet. She had so much more torment to give.

And so they sat there, only a few miles across the border, in the open field. His arms around her, her body convulsing and everything being given to the earth.

Chapter Twelve

This man was angry. As soon as he had come around the corner Maddy had seen the narrowing glint in his eyes. He kept his teeth gnashed together and grumbled his responses to her through them. The veins in his neck looked nearly ready to burst they were so tense! Most importantly though, he would not meet her eyes.

"Hurry up, will you!" he barked, standing behind the shop.

"Of course, sir," Maddy said as she dug through her pockets. The cloak she wore was more like a ragged blanket when viewed from the exterior. But the inside was lined with pockets which made it useful for carrying her goods around. Her mother's idea. Kept bandits away.

The only problem was misplacing items.

She searched through all the pockets on her left. The man's requested herb was not in any of them. She started to shuffle through her right pockets. Her fingers slipped into the smallest by the bottom corner of her cloak.

The last place I would look, of course.

She offered her hand to the man palm up to show the herb. With a smile on her face, she said, "Here you, are, sir. The root from a willow flower dipped in sap to sweeten the brew for your wife. It should clear her head pain quickly."

The irritation on his face vanished, replaced by a lighting joy that loosened his jaw and brightened his eyes. He grabbed the herbs from Maddy's small hands and stared down at the plant as if he had struck gold.

"And this will help her?" he asked, looking back at Maddy for confirmation but already nodding for himself.

She could feel a cheer in her chest.

Maddy grinned and gave him a hard nod. "Yes. There's enough there for a week. After a week, wait a few days and she should be completely healed."

He clutched the herbs to his chest, closed his eyes and sighed. He had found a solution to his problem and now he could rest easy.

Maddy knew his anger was not directed at her, well, not for the most part. Though he refused to have her address him by name, Maddy knew the merchant Chapman and she knew his travel store had been doing poorly the last few years.

But what else was to be expected? Hardly anyone from the middle kingdom traveled anymore, besides a few knights by order of Cadfen. Other than those few men who stopped in once a year or so, tourism to the surrounding kingdoms had come to a halt. And with Issin's kingdom an utter mess, the supply of travelers from the east had cut off, as well. He could hardly feed his wife, much less pay a healer.

Maddy was his last option. She was also a southerner, in birth at least, whom the citizens of the middle kingdom often viewed as barbaric because of their religion and customs. But what mattered most to him was she was a refugee, the current scourge of the middle kingdom.

He was supposed to hate her. Instead, he needed her. His pride was hurt more than anything else.

"It's fall. Must be a blessing of the coming Salvation Day," he said, still smiling at the small bundle in his hands.

Salvation Day?

"Pardon me, sir. What is the Salvation Day?"

Almost like he had forgotten she was there, the man looked up and blinked at her a few times, before slipping the mask of anger back on.

He pushed the herbs into one pocket and reached into another. He tossed some coins at her but Maddy let them fall to the ground, waiting for him to reply.

Chapman scoffed. "Something a dirty refugee like you will never understand. I can tell you this. It'll be the only blessing you'll receive. Best hope The Divines find you worthy."

With his hatred properly spewed, he turned his back to her and walked from behind the shop, down to the eastern side of Satbury.

Maddy waited until he was gone before picking up the coins.

"Must be some sort of religious holiday," she mumbled as she placed each coin into a different pocket. "Knowing King Cadfen, I'll be forced to participate. So, will Alistair."

Maddy sighed. Religious freedom and expression were not common in the middle kingdom, unless one was following the capital's "suggested" belief system of Trithian. And though Maddy kept her presence in Satbury limited to make the locals think her a traveling refugee versus a permanent fixture, she was sure several of them had informed the royal guard of her presence. Still, despite this knowledge, the guard had not ridden up and cuffed her in shackles. Either Cadfen was too busy in Camelot to see to one refugee or Maddy was very lucky.

She wasn't sure which of those two she preferred.

The earth is shaking.

Maddy felt the horses coming before she heard them. Their approach sent a ripple like quiver through Satbury that reached her ears like a roaring wave.

Oh, no.

She scrambled to her feet and made her way to the western end of the village, staying behind houses and shops to keep out of view. When she was far enough down, not too far from Alistair's home above the stables, Maddy pressed into the woods. She wouldn't go far.

If the royal guard had finally come to take her, they'd travel deep into the forest, knowing southerners were most at home among the trees.

Maddy planned to stay close. Once she was less than a mile into the woods, she raced back east towards the shop where she had met with Chapman. She attempted to make her steps weightless, so, if anyone tried to track her, the trail would run cold.

The shop was right in her line of sight now. As were the eight guards stampeding their way into town.

Maddy held her breath, waiting to see if they would split into fours to make the capture quicker. But they didn't. As a unit, they turned right, headed away from her.

A part of her sighed with relief but that relief turned into a knot when she saw what they carried in the last wagon. There was a woman, a small boy, and a box with the symbol of the Trithian on it.

Someone had died and she knew who.

Against her better judgement, Maddy followed the guards. Instinctively it made no sense, but instinct wasn't what carried her. Guilt did and she wouldn't have toyed with the emotion if she hadn't seen the drunkard's family in the wagon with his casket.

They must have had to save up to make the journey.

There was no other explanation. No one else had died in Satbury since him and no one had come to claim his body until now.

The guards came to a halt outside the lord's house. The Captain, Maddy assumed because he was leading the charge, climbed off his horse and approached the house. Before he could even knock, the lord of Satbury, also probably one of the laziest men Maddy had ever known to live, swung the door open and stepped out in front of them.

The two men begin conversing. Maddy wished more than ever

she had some magic to make her invisible. What was the good of spying if one couldn't hear anything?

After a few moments, the woman and child climbed from the back of the wagon to approach the lord. As soon as the woman's feet hit the ground, sobs dripped from her throat. Her son grabbed her hand though Maddy guessed he was crying, too.

She felt a warm pain tighten her chest. He was so small, probably the same age as Endlun.

She needed a better view. Maddy stood back from the closest tree and eyed it. She wasn't very tall, a trait she acquired from a father she never knew.

She thought she could reach the lowest branch. With a quiet grunt, she stood on her toes and grasped the branch. Her hands found a steady hold and she planted her feet flat against the tree trunk. Using her arms and her legs, she climbed the tree until she reached the next branch and the next one, finally sitting on a thick trunk of a limb about seven feet in the air.

She moved on the branch to take in the scene below her.

The pair was in front of the lord bowing. There was some more conversation, before he shouted into his home. Two men appeared carrying the drunkard's body wrapped in cloth. The woman, definitely the drunkard's wife, fell to her knees. The boy, his son, kept a hold on his mother's hand, his eyes focused on the unofficial procession.

Maddy shook herself. She couldn't be fazed. The man got what was coming to him. Only if they didn't remind her so much of her own mother and brother...then, she wouldn't be feeling any remorse. She wouldn't have followed the guard. She wouldn't be sending up silent prayers for the family.

Yet she found her lips moving with pleadings for mercy, forgiveness, and good wealth to the drunkard's kin. It had been a long time since she had prayed.

The body was loaded into the box. As custom dictated, his body was now claimed by his loved ones, and so, the box would not be opened again.

The woman and child climbed into the wagon, as well.

The captain reached into his saddle pocket and pulled out a stack of parchment. At the sight of the stack, the lord bowed, clasped his hands together and nodded vigorously as the captain said a few last words to him.

Then, as quickly as they had come, they were gone. The wagon with the woman and boy shadowed in dust as the group raced away from Satbury.

Maddy leaned forward, hoping to catch one last glimpse but they were gone and she found herself longing for her own family.

The lord disappeared onto his porch and three loud *thunks* sounded throughout the small town. People began to gather around the lord's home. They talked among one another, their voices rising in happy chatter.

"A day has been selected! Salvation is coming."

"We must all do our best to prepare. Did you read the notice?"

"The Divines will come here first? To Satbury for the Salvation?"

Maddy raised a brow. Whatever this Salvation was, it was extremely important to the locals. She had lived in the village for nearly a year and never heard any mention of the event until now.

Her mind drifted to Alistair. If everything had gone right--and she hoped it had--Alistair and Robin should return soon. Maybe she would know more about the holiday.

She climbed down from the branch and landed softly on her feet.

"I think that's enough excitement for today. Back to work, now, Madelia."

She dusted her clothes off and then laughed when the adjustment made no difference in her appearance. Her cloak, pants and top remained as dirt stained as ever.

She waited until the crowd around the lord's home thinned, then stepped out from the forest. There were only a few people left now and they barely paid attention to her as she made her way to the parchment that hung on the lord's house.

She expected the usual sneers, perhaps a few threats or hostile comments but the stragglers seemed to be transfixed by the announcement.

Maddy turned her eyes to it, as well. The notice read as follows:

Salvation Day Celebration:

Salvation will come in two days' time. The Divines will leave the temple of the holy three to offer blessings to our blackened souls.
Attendance is mandatory if residence or citizenship is to be maintained or considered.
Attain blessings from those who are the earthly representatives of the holy three.
Blessed thou are not, blessed we shall become.

-King Cadfen Demure of the Middle Kingdom

Alistair had never been happier to see the sign for Satbury. The ride back had not been as easy as the ride to the lower eastern lands. Besides worrying about Robin throwing herself off Fred again, Alistair was completely exhausted from the trip. He had never longed for his old bed mat so badly.

Robin snored behind him. She had her arms locked around his waist and her chin propped up on his shoulder meaning he heard every snort and sniffle as she slept. He pinched his hand to stop from laughing.

She had barely rested since they left Arthur and his people so it was good she was sleeping

Still, he wished he knew how he could have prevented it all.

He had stood by Robin's side during their time in the east but she had also made it very clear this was her fight.

"No, no, no, Alistair. Fred likes his apples in quarters not halves."

Alistair caught the burst of laughter in his mouth and pushed it down to his gut.

"Yes, Maddy, please, tell Alistair how Fred likes his apples, will you?"

Madelia.

He had tried not to worry about her while they were away but worrying was becoming a habit. Excluding himself, not one person in Satbury cared for Maddy's wellbeing. He had seen her spit on, kicked, cursed at, and worse. And each time an anger rose in him only for her to soothe it away with a pat on his shoulder.

The memories made him take a deep breath.

He had never met anyone like Maddy. He wanted to know so much about her, yet she was always side-stepping his questions with a light joke or a question of her own. Maybe it was the mystery around her...or maybe it was the way she waited and listened to rainstorms in the stables. The way smiles crept across her lips without warning or how she still showed kindness to those who were cruel to her.

He wasn't sure. All he knew was that Robin was partially wrong when she said he had feelings for Maddy. No, Alistair, was certain he didn't just like Maddy.

I love her.

His heart suddenly felt too big at the very thought.

Of course, he had courted other young women on *the hunt* as northern men called it.

The event referred to a young man's search for a wife. For many of these same young men, the event was a disguise for another ritual they had in mind...

Every summer Alistair found a young woman, sometimes more but the relationships never stuck. The fact they didn't never bothered him. For some time, he thought maybe he'd spend his life alone. It wasn't unheard of.

He thought he'd start a shop before passing it on to a second cousin when the time came. Then, his parents died, he moved back home, and a young woman with green hair and green eyes knocked on the stable doors asking if he was in need of any herbs. They'd been friends since.

"That's wonderful, men, just a bit higher."

The center of the town was coming into view now. Even from yards away, Alistair could see people moving about. There were several men standing in the middle of town, using ropes to pull two poles upright with a banner of leather locked in the center.

As Fred crossed the threshold into Satbury, Alistair was nearly toppled over with what he saw. The town had never been this active before. Even the town guard was standing alert, a direct contrast to their usual casual manner. It seemed like everyone was out on the streets at the same time, all of them racing from one house to the next, carrying baskets of food, grinning from ear to ear.

"What's going on?"

Alistair jerked a bit. Robin had been so quiet during the ride he almost forgot she was behind him.

He turned to her. "Feeling better?"

She shrugged and her eyes fell away from his. "Sleeping helped. I'm much more interested in what's going on here though."

He tugged on the reins and Fred started in the direction of the stables. Alistair had no formal training in horse riding. However, he had never had any problem riding Fred in Satbury until now. If he didn't know better Alistair would have thought Fred had suddenly become invisible the way people were walking into him. He had to pull the reins this way and that to avoid knocking anyone over but he seemed to be the only concerned about a horse hoof to the head.

"They all seemed a bit mad, don't they?" Robin rested her chin on his shoulder. "Alistair, look, there's your landlord."

He looked to his right. The tall broad man strode from the butcher's shop with a piece of meat wrapped in cloth and a big grin on his face.

"Hello, sir!" Alistair called to him and raised a hand. His landlord turned in his direction, before turning away.

"He looked right at us," Robin said. "This is odd."

"Very. I think we should find Maddy."

"Agreed. I'm afraid by the end of the night everyone will be deemed delirious and put away."

Alistair laughed. "That's quite a conclusion."

"And this is quite a show they're putting on for us. A tantalizing combination of horror and comedy."

He leaned forward as laughter erupted from him and Robin chuckled behind him. He felt a pressure on his back and saw that Robin had pressed herself against him again.

"Would it be strange of me to say it's nice to be home?"

He found her hand around his waist and placed his own over it. He squeezed.

"I don't think it strange at all."

"Can I say something else, Alistair?"

"When did you start asking permission for anything? Ouch!"

"Would you like another pinch?" She leaned forward and grinned broadly.

"No, thank you. Go on with what you were saying."

She took a hard breath and looked ahead.

"It's nice what we have here," she said, eyes facing straight ahead. "You, me, and Maddy. It's like we've made our own little family, our own clan if you will."

Alistair watched her from his side-vision. Her eyes fell downward, and her grip tightened around his middle.

"Yes, Robin?"

"We need to stick together now, all right?" Her voice was high and loud and if everyone wasn't busy with whatever they were doing, he would have feared they'd notice the urgency in her question. She was staring at him again. Her blue eyes seemed to have lost some of their vigor since Arthur, darkened by her bruised face. But in that moment, it returned, flaring and blinding.

With a quick motion, he pressed a kiss on her forehead.

"Don't worry. I'm quite hard to get rid of."

Her eyebrows rose. "Really? Like a fungus? Or, no, maybe you're more like a wart?"

"Hm. They could all be accurate descriptions. Since we're family now I guess I should call you Grandma."

There were several jabs to his ribs.

"Home at last," he wheezed as the stable came into view. As usual, the doors were open to give the horses fresh air. Not as usual, Maddy was hiding behind one of the doors and with the way she peered around something was evidently wrong.

Alistair smashed his teeth together.

What have they done to her?

Robin jumped off Fred before he came to a full stop.

That's becoming a nasty habit of hers, isn't it?

She raced over to Maddy and placed both hands on her shoulders. Alistair climbed off Fred and followed her.

"Maddy. You look terrified," Robin said. "What's happened?"

Now that he was close enough, Alistair could see Maddy was shaking. From her head to her toes, she was nothing but tremors.

The green-haired girl placed her hands on Robin's shoulders and they both stared into one another's eyes.

"Please," Maddy said. Her eyes became liquid. "Get me out of here."

The door slammed shut with a resounding thud. Maddy had backed into a corner and was pulling her hair from her face. She wasn't shaking so much anymore but her feet were tapping quickly on the floor.

"Maddy, you need to tell us what's wrong? What happened?" Robin squeezed beside her in the corner.

She turned to Robin but her mouth stopped mid-motion. "Your face-how did it—"

"It's all right," Robin said. "Well, not really but that threat has gone. I need you to tell me what's happened to you."

"Everyone has gone mad," she whispered, darting a glance out the window. "They've been up for two days preparing for the Salvation."

"The what?" Alistair and Robin asked in unison.

Alistair tossed his satchel to the floor and sat across from the two women. He looked Maddy over. There wasn't a bruise or scratch on her.

Maddy leaned her head back and stared at Robin. "I was hoping you'd be able to tell me. It's all anyone around her has been talking about since the Camelot guards arrived. They won't even let me leave."

"They won't let you leave?" Alistair asked.

She shook her head. "I've tried. But more guards have arrived."

"They seem to be happy to see you go any other time," Robin said. She rested an arm around Maddy's back and squeezed her shoulder.

"And that's why this is so disturbing. It's like they've been possessed." She moved her head in disbelief. "Two days ago, Camelot guards came to pick up the body of that drunkard. They left the lord with a stack of parchment announcing Salvation Day. They're all over town."

Robin looked at the ceiling and pinched her brow. "Salvation Day? No, during my uncle's reign there was no such holiday. Alistair?" She looked at him.

He shook his head. "I've never heard of it, but I haven't been here a full year yet."

"Neither have I," said Maddy.

He nodded. "So, we must have just missed it when we arrived."

"That still doesn't explain what this holiday is," Robin stated. "Or why they won't let Maddy leave."

"Maddy." Alistair scooted closer and grabbed her hand. Her gaze flickered from their clasped hands to his eyes.

He could feel his tongue go dry.

"Did you, uh--did you hear anything else? About the Salvation?"

"Not much. I was selling herbs to Merchant Chapman and he told me Satbury would be receiving a blessing. That's all I know."

The ladder creaked beneath them. All movement paused. Maddy darted her eyes between Alistair and Robin. Robin looked at Alistair and nodded towards the window.

Slowly, he turned, stepped to the right, and looked down to the ladder that led to his room.

His landlord, Grant, was staring back up at him.

"Hello, Alistair," he said, still smiling. "How are you? Welcome back."

"I'm fine. Thank you. Is, is something wrong, sir?"

"No, no. I only wanted to remind you about Salvation. The Divines should be here in a few hours."

"Of course." Alistair nodded. "And, Mr. Grant, could you tell me more about this celebration? You know I was in the north most of my time."

The man's cheeks pinked as his smile grew. "We will be blessed because our souls are blackened. Make sure your company attends, as well."

"Could you tell the lord that Maddy isn't feeling well? She won't be able to attend and she doesn't live in Satbury anyway."

His face fell. His cheeks paled. "The Divines want blessings for all. Even those who may not be worthy. I will see you all there as the sun sets."

With those words said, Grant climbed down the ladder and left the stables, closing the doors behind him. Alistair's room fell into darkness and there was the distinct sound of a lock turning.

Chapter Thirteen

A listair wanted to rip his scalp off. The itching had never been this bad. It felt like his entire scalp was on fire.

He reached up for a little scratch only to have his hand tugged down by his side. He looked back at Robin. She shook her head and tightened her hold on his hand.

He nodded. She was right. He couldn't keep scratching. He was sure he had already broken skin and bleeding wasn't going to help them blend in. Well, they really didn't have a chance of blending in with Maddy in tow.

She marched quietly behind Robin. The townspeople were crowded all around them. They had come to "retrieve" them for the celebration.

Alistair could hear loud chatter from the center of town and he could see it was lit with torches. He had never seen all of Satbury together at once. And he had certainly never seen them as excited. Children and adults alike were nearly jumping out of their skin with joy.

"Mr. Grant, have the Divine arrived yet?" Alistair asked peering through the crowd. Everyone he saw were those he interacted with daily. There were no strangers.

Grant, who was leading their little march, said without looking back, "They will be the last to arrive. Trust me, you'll know when they've come. The air itself will smell cleaner."

"Can you tell me more about what they'll do when they get here?"

"And ruin the fun?" He let out a hardy laugh.

Soon they were amongst the others in the center of town. Torches lined the perimeter but what Alistair hasn't noticed while they were walking was a large burning pyre.

At their arrival, the crowd parted and split into two: a line on either side of the blaze.

Grant led them to the line closest to his left and placed all three--Maddy, Alistair, and Robin--beside him. Immediately, the man next to Grant began talking to him in elated tones about the Salvation.

Alistair took his chance.

"As soon as we can, we run. My patch hasn't stopped itching. It's nearly driving me mad."

"There isn't going to be a chance," Maddy said. She nodded

her head to the right and Alistair followed her gesture.

There, behind the line across from him and tucked partially in the shadows, were Camelot knights. They wore their full attire and their swords were brandished in front of them.

Alistair dared to look behind him. The Camelot knights were poised and ready.

He turned back to Maddy.

She shook her head and briefly closed her eyes. "More than this morning. And knights, not simple guards. Alistair, we—"

"We may not be leaving." Robin whispered the words. Maybe she meant to keep them to herself but both Maddy and Alistair had heard her.

Alistair leaned in to offer some words of comfort, some amazing escape plan he didn't really have. But he couldn't. His mouth grew slack and he was very aware of his body falling though he could do nothing to stop it. All he could feel was a throbbing cold that spread over him and pierced his legs, rendering them immobile.

Robin pushed herself under him and leaned upward so his side was against hers. Maddy flanked his other half and forced him into an odd standing position.

"Their power has that effect." Grant's voice traveled to his ears. He looked down the line of people. His landlord met his eyes directly. "The Divines. They're here."

Both women tensed beside Alistair. They looked to the right and at the end of the line were three figures draped in hooded cloaks. They walked in formation with one in front while the two walked behind on either side. Each of them carried a basket in their hands. A hush fell. The torch flames seemed to grow brighter.

"Blessed thou are not," croaked one of the figures.

"Blessed we will become," everyone replied.

The cold piercing pain was spreading from his legs to his abdomen. He had started shaking and his scalp suddenly felt like it had been scrapped off with a hot iron.

"All thanks to the three," shouted another of the figures.

"All thanks to the three," they replied.

The three figures split up. The two from the back stepped in front of the third and moved to either line. They begin offering the basket to each townsperson.

The third figure took a step closer into the light.

"Do you wish to cleanse your dirty souls?"

"Yes, Divine One, yes. Cleanse us."

"Do you wish to start your purification from the inside out?"

she asked, looking around.

"Yes, yes, yes."

"Then, come forward and take from our baskets the holy food of Trithian."

The two Divines continued their march down the row of townspeople. A chill ran over Alistair and he tossed his head back from the effect. His heart was beating so quickly, yet, he still felt he was freezing from the inside out. His legs were numb and the girls were slumping under the weight of his body.

Then, his heartbeat grew louder until the Divine speaking in the front was silenced. The townspeople still bobbed their heads at the figure's words, but Alistair had no idea what the Divine was saying.

He so badly wanted to fall over, to let whatever it was that had him, run its course, so he could at least stand on his two legs. But Robin and Maddy stayed strong under him.

He had never felt magic like this before. The noise of his heart became deafening. He couldn't hear anything else and, then, the basket was being offered to him. He stared up into the face of the hooded figure. No eyes reflected back at him and suddenly his body felt ablaze.

Alistair wrenched from his friends' grasps and fell to the ground. He clutched his silver patch, scratching at the scalp and screaming into the earth.

Every ounce of him was a burning piece of flesh, offering a painful contrast to the internal cold that pierced his body. And his heart was going to burst. He was sure of that.

Someone had a hold of his mouth. He tried to look up, but his head was jerked back down. His jaw unclenched and something was thrown into his mouth. It was acrid and mushy. He wanted to vomit.

There was a mounting pressure on his back. Alistair turned to look up. Shadows were all around him. Not the hooded ones. Maybe the townspeople.

They surrounded him. The heat of their breath was on his ear while they whispered. Still, he couldn't hear them. Trying to catch their words was like grasping at air. Pointless.

Alistair fell to the ground and covered his head. Whatever was happening to him, he couldn't fight. It was inside him, burning and alive. But for how long?

More shadows appeared. The torches became distant lights, dimming into nothing.

"Time to wake up..."

Alistair jerked forward and sucked in a gulp of air, his eyes moving around him.

"Alistair? You're fine. It's all right." Robin was resting her hands on his shoulders. "Lie back."

His body felt stiff and out of use. Something wet landed on his forehead. He glanced up. Maddy was wiping a cloth across his face. Her eyes were red and swollen.

"Madelia." It was the first word he thought to say.

Smiling and releasing a shaky breath, she pushed the hair back from his face. She was worried. Alistair decided he didn't like that look on her.

"What happened?" he asked, though his voice was not as loud as he hoped it would be.

Maddy shook her head and her shoulders began to tremble.

"What's going on?" He turned to Robin.

She was holding Maddy's hand but her own face was distorted, as well.

Alistair closed his eyes. What could he remember?

Grant leading them from the stables, everyone lining up, the Divines appearing, bread, an acrid mushy taste in his mouth...

"I passed out," he said. "Again."

Robin nodded.

"But everyone-" he shuddered- "everyone was around me. Shadows. I couldn't see anything. Everything hurt."

"When you fell to the ground, the Divine said you were blessed and gave you the bread," Robin stated, glancing out the window. "Then they all started chanting that you were blessed and they swarmed you."

She took a strained swallow and looked back at him. "Once they were done *blessing* you, we were finally allowed to leave."

Alistair searched for the memory. "All of that's blank to me. I most clearly remember the bread. It tasted horrible. Did you two eat it?"

They both shook their heads.

"We spit it out during the chaos," Maddy replied. She placed the cloth in the water and reapplied it to his head.

The coolness felt nice. He closed his eyes and focused on the water trickling over his skin. Yet it was only a temporary relief.

Alistair sighed. "We need a plan."

"Where will we go?" There was a tautness in Robin's voice. "I can't—"

Alistair jolted up, knocking the water bowl over in the process as he tried to stand only to crumble to his knees. It felt like something was digging into his skull.

"We have to leave now!" he screamed. But the room suddenly became cold. The space quickly filled with a presence he couldn't see, yet it was there. Dominating and overbearing. Powerful and familiar.

Alistair opened his eyes to see what thing had invaded his room, only to realize he was staring at the ground. He tried to turn his head but his neck was rigid. His fingers were digging into the wooden floor. The veins in his hands were prominent and pulsing.

Still, in the midst of it all, there was a hint of humidity--a wet, sticky warmth. It encircled him, tickled his ears, calling to him accompanied by the putrid smell of rot.

There was a witch in his room. *The* witch.

"*I never thought I'd see you again.*" Her words floated in his mind. "*You're no longer the little boy I tried to steal.*"

"Alistair." Her voice was a whisper, but it broke the fear that gripped him.

He turned to look behind him. Robin was propped up on one knee with a dagger in her right hand. Maddy sat slightly behind her, eyes moving between him, the door, and the witch.

Now that he was staring at her, Maddy's eyes bore into him.

Alistair gulped and moved to greet the witch.

He couldn't see her face. She still had her cloak on from the ceremony.

"What do you want?" The words didn't sound like they were coming from him.

"*I want what is mine which you hold.*"

"The curse?" He pulled at the silver strands and held them up. "Have it. I never wanted it anyway."

"No!" Maddy screamed.

"*It's not that simple.*" The witch had taken a few steps closer to them. "*The piece of magic I left with you is a part of you now. I cannot have one without the other.*"

Another step.

Realization wrapped around him and Alistair suddenly felt like he was suffocating. The witch held her arm out and a crooked hand twisted in odd angles. Alistair's throat grew tighter. He grabbed at invisible hands.

"I have to catch your soul right before you die. Before my magic, your energy, is released into the world. You need to be on the brink, Alistair."

His breath became a wheeze and the edge of his vision became cloudy.

"Robin, no!" Maddy's voice.

The sound of feet scrapping against wood.

He wanted to see but the witch held him in place. Despite his cloudy vision, her face became clearer. It was smeared with splotches of red.

Alistair opened his mouth for one last breath.

I don't want to die. Please.

A blinding light filled his vision. Alistair was vaguely aware of his body hitting the floor. He was too busy trying to suck in all the air he could get.

Arms wrapped around him.

Robin.

She was saying something. He couldn't focus.

The blinding light faded. A child who seemed to be made of mist stood with his back to Alistair.

The evil that had overtaken the room receded. The witch stumbled away.

The child raised his hand and what can best be described as pure light itself poured from him.

The witch withered into tendrils of smoking blackness, screaming as the light consumed her until she was silent. The smoking stopped. All evidence of her had vanished.

Both Maddy and Robin were pushing at Alistair now. He still couldn't hear what they were saying.

The boy turned to face him.

He looked to be about eleven. Alistair couldn't tell his hair or eye color, but his clothes were neat and pressed. His boots would have been considered fashionable more than a decade ago.

The child crossed his arms and scowled.

"Well?" he said, glaring at Alistair.

When Alistair remained silent, he uncrossed his arms and shook his head. "Aren't you going to thank me? Haven't you any manners?"

"I...uh, yes, thank you..."

"The names Edwin by the way. And you are Alistair, I assume?"

"How do you know my name?"

The child raised his brows. "Why wouldn't I? You're the one

who called me here."

Chapter Fourteen

Robin held Fred's reins in one hand and smoothed out her dress with the other. She couldn't believe she was doing this, yet she knew there were no other options. They had nowhere to go but back to the east, back to Arthur and Morganna.

She shook herself.

None of that matters now. What matters is finding refuge and figuring out a plan.

She nodded to herself, though she cringed when an image of Arthur flashed in her mind. Her stomach suddenly felt light and watery. She swallowed the feeling.

Maddy sat atop Fred, humming as she stroked his mane. Her dark green hair was in a braid that hung down her back.

Robin watched her. The young woman hadn't spoken since they left Satbury. After the witch burned up, a result of a boy Alistair called "Edwin," there really was no other choice except to pack their things and leave. So, they did. Everything they could carry on their backs, as well as Fred's had been stuffed into pouches.

Initially, Robin thought Maddy was upset because she had been dragged into their mess. But that wasn't it. It didn't seem like Maddy to hold grudges, especially with the way she had dove into the crowd in an attempt to retrieve Alistair. The villagers had given her no mind and continued to grab at him.

Robin shuddered. That was a memory she'd never be able to forget. That and the sight of the witch, strangling Alistair.

Her eyes burned.

Don't cry. Not now. Maybe later.

Her gaze darted to Alistair whose once raven black hair had turned a snow white. He was riding behind Maddy on Fred and staring to his left. Robin inclined her head to see what had him entranced.

There was nothing there. There had been nothing in the room back in Satbury either, but Alistair called the nothing Robin saw, Edwin. He told her Edwin was a young boy, about eleven, and he was who saved them. Then, he had fallen into his current trance.

Maddy couldn't see Edwin either. Still, Alistair was certain he was there.

If there are witches and women who escape from trees, why not ghosts?

What was real and what was not should always be questioned. She knew that now.

Her eyes moved to Alistair again, specifically his hair. She looked at her own dark strands. Their hair had once been the same shade of black. A few of the townspeople had even mistaken them for siblings. But now, his hair was in direct contrast to hers. Pitch black to blinding white.

Could the witch have cast a spell on him before she died?

Robin didn't know. Maddy continued to hum beside her.

"What tune is that, Maddy?"

She continued stroking her fingers through Fred's mane, eyes transfixed forward.

"It's a song from the south. My mother would sing it to me when I was a child."

"Does it have a story?"

She nodded.

Robin stared at the trail ahead of them. "We still have some time. What's this story?"

Maddy's humming had come to a stop. She was silent for a moment just staring at the path ahead of them.

Finally, she spoke.

"In the story, monsters attack the village of a young child. His parents are held prisoner with the other villagers as the monsters prepare to eat them." She pulled at her braid. "The child sneaks in to see his parents and they tell him he must find bravery if he is to defeat the monsters. It's an ancient gift locked in a treasure chest across the widest river, in the lowest valley, and atop the highest mountain to the east."

Robin grinned. "That's quite a journey for a young child to make."

Maddy nodded. "True but he had no choice. So, he went east across the widest river. He traveled across the lowest valley and climbed the highest eastern mountain to find the treasure. It was beautiful, and he felt its power as soon as he grasped it."

Robin fiddled with her charms. The nausea returned when her fingers grazed the air where the dragon charm had once been.

She swallowed. "What happened next, Maddy?"

"The child returned to his village, held the treasure out to the monsters, and then a blinding light consumed his home. He blacked out. When he woke, he was still standing with bravery in his hand and all the monsters were slain."

"What a tale," Robin said. "As good as the sly fox and the bear, right, Alistair?"

She turned to him, but he did not awaken from his trance.

Maddy continued. "This child grew up to lead the village and he became a very brave warrior. But on his death bed he revealed a secret to his daughter."

"What did he tell her?"

"He told her the tales about him were wrong, that he didn't find bravery in the chest but a rusty sword in its place."

Robin knitted her brows. "Then how did he really kill the monsters?"

"He found a rusty sword in the chest, but he found bravery on his journey. That is what he used to defeat the monsters."

"A plot twist, hmm?"

Maddy bobbed her head. "And when he died, his soul was placed in the rusty sword and locked in the treasure chest by his daughter."

"What?" Robin surprised herself at how loud her voice was. "Isn't this supposed to be a happy story?"

Maddy finally looked at her. She smiled.

"Not as a punishment. As a gift."

"How is being sealed in a chest a gift?"

"Because," Maddy replied, "he wanted to be present for another's journey."

Robin's gaze fell to the ground for a moment, before returning to Maddy. "I suppose that makes it a happier story. At least his imprisonment was of his choosing."

"The man was glad to do it," she said as her fingers trailed down her braided hair. Maddy curved her finger into the end of the braid and began to untangle it. With her hair wild and free again, she tossed it over her back so it spread out across her shoulders.

Robin's nausea subsided.

The crumbled wall was coming into view. They only had to continue until they crossed the inner wall and stepped into the old capital.

She took a deep breath.

There are no alternatives, Robin. Do you want to be Cadfen's wife?

Bile rose in her. Being with Cadfen was the only thought worse than seeing Arthur and Morganna again. She made a note to keep that in mind during their stay.

Several heads turned as the trio stepped into the clearing of the fallen castle. Robin suddenly became very aware of her bruised face. The swelling had gone down and the coloring wasn't too bad, but it was still a nasty sight to see.

She peered around the clearing in search of a familiar person. Her eyes landed on Lancelot chopping wood far to her right. He had an ax raised in the air and was staring straight at their small group.

She sighed. *Apparently, I'm cursed.*

Smoothing out her dress, she walked over to the young man with Fred at her side.

Lancelot brought the ax down just as she approached.

"I see you're back."

"I am."

"Didn't expect to see you so soon?" He smirked.

She scoffed. "You're not alone in that regard. Where is Arthur?"

Lancelot tossed his shoulders back and moved a hand through his brown sweat-soaked hair. He stared at the trio, glancing between them. His eyes widened when they landed on Alistair.

Robin cleared her throat. "Can you please tell me where Arthur is? It's urgent. Please."

"Seems that way," he said, finally breaking his eyes from Alistair. His brows furrowed.

"Are you all right, Robin?" he asked.

Now it was her turn to raise a brow.

Why would he care?

"I only need to speak to Arthur. If he is here, please, direct me to him."

Lancelot looked between them again. Then, he grabbed another log and placed it on the stump. "He's gone."

"Where?" she sighed, tightening her grip on the reins.

Maddy reached down and squeezed Robin's shoulder. She sent her a thankful smile.

"Hunting with some of the others. I stayed back to manage things while he's gone."

"Right. Fine. Then, I need your assistance." A heavy feeling built in her chest with the words.

He split the log and rested the ax in the stump. "I am at your service, Robin. What can I do to help?"

"For now, my friends and I need to rest. That's all."

He nodded, letting his eyes roam over her.

She cringed.

"All right. Follow me," he replied.

Lancelot used his forearm to wipe sweat from his brow and started towards the castle. Robin followed alongside him.

Travel east and find shelter. One task is complete.

Relief eased the stress that had built in her shoulders.

Lancelot tapped his hip repeatedly while they walked. He glanced over.

"I...I hope your face is healing well."

The heat rose to her cheeks faster than she could fathom. She balled her fists by her sides and spun on him.

He was going to receive a word lashing he'd not soon forget. Yet as Robin prepared to chastise him, the flaming anger was doused.

His eyes were large and searching hers.

Robin's lips parted in surprise and she found herself almost falling backward. She used the reins to keep steady.

When she had found her footing again, Robin lightly coughed and started walking once more.

"It's much better than it was. Thank you for asking."

He nodded. "I know it doesn't count for much but I'm on your side. Morganna's mad for what she did to you."

Robin hated to admit it, yet those words were nice to hear. He was on her side. One of Arthur's closest men could see things from her perspective. The relaxation she had found in her shoulders traveled down her back.

"Thank you, Lancelot."

As they reached the entrance, Lancelot looked around and whistled. Almost like she appeared from nowhere, a little girl came racing over to him.

"Elanor, I need you to take Robin's horse to the stables. Then bring some water and fruit to the chamber in the farthest western hall. The one at the very end."

She gave Lancelot a hard nod, then turned to Robin.

"May I, miss?" She held her hand out.

Robin forced back a giggle. Every time the little girl spoke, she could see a gap where her two front teeth should have been.

Maddy dismounted and helped Alistair down. She handed Fred over to the child.

"Here, you are."

"Thank you, miss. He's in safe hands with me. Come on, now, horsey." She pulled at the reins and Fred complied stepping behind her.

"She's quite the littler helper," Robin noted.

Lancelot bobbed his head. He went to speak but his eyes drifted from Robin. She followed his gaze to Maddy standing at her side.

Unlike Alistair, who was still staring at the nothing Robin assumed was Edwin, the green-haired girl was watching Lancelot without abashment. Her eyes moved from his head to his muddy boots and back again. She narrowed them.

He crossed his arms and his lips turned up at the corners.

"See something you like?"

She shook her head. "Not really."

Lancelot blanched at her statement. Robin pinched her side to stop from laughing.

"You must have bad taste," he retorted.

Maddy's vision briefly moved to Alistair. Then returned to Lancelot.

"No, I don't think that's it. I'm actually a good judge of character."

A muscle ticked in his jaw. He turned, speaking to Robin. "And your friend is?"

"Maddy," Robin replied. "And you know Alistair from our...from our last visit."

"Looks quite different. Can't wait to hear the story behind that transformation. All right, follow me."

His eyes fell on Maddy again. "Is it fine with you if I lead, Miss Maddy?"

She nodded. "Yes. I said I'm good with judging character, not directions."

Perhaps, this wasn't such a good idea.

"You need to stay here, Robin." Arthur had made the statement approximately six times since they sat down to talk.

"The journey will only get more dangerous from here on out."

"I know that," she snapped.

Morganna cast a sharp glance at her cousin. Robin stared straight at her.

She flexed her fingers under the table. She wanted nothing more than to have Alistair at her side. But he was still sleeping. She couldn't blame him for being so exhausted. Nearly dying twice in one night would take the strongest man down for a few hours. Not to mention the journey east.

Still, she wished he was there with her.

I guess I've become quite selfish with him. At least Maddy's here.

The green-haired girl sat in a large wooden chair in the corner that placed her directly across from the door. From her position, she had a full view of the room and everyone in it.

Lancelot had placed himself in the corner opposing Maddy.

Morganna and Arthur sat at the table with Robin.

What horrible company.

"I've come too far to stop, Arthur." She tried to speak calmly, folding her hands in front of her on the table.

"Not so far you can't turn back."

"Arthur," she sighed, "this isn't only about Cadfen or my uncle. The witch, it attacked Alistair. He's been in this trance since and I—"

"We have healers. He'll be treated well here." The veins in his neck were showing. Always a sign he was worried.

Robin pulled her attention back. "Do any of these healers specialize in witch curses?"

His mouth moved but no words came out. With a heavy breath, he ran his hands through his hair.

"No, they don't."

"Then, I need to find someone who does. We can't stay here. We only need to rest until our next step."

"Which is what, cousin?"

Robin swallowed back the chain of insults ready to leave her mouth. Arthur looked between the two women.

Robin cleared her throat and stayed focused on him. "I came here for refuge, Arthur, and because I have a theory I wanted to get your opinion on."

He raised his clasped hands to his mouth and narrowed his eyes. "Are you trying to distract me?"

She laughed. "There's no need to distract you, Arthur. You no longer have say over what I do."

The words just tumbled out. She hadn't even meant to say them. They were a small thought in her mind that had raced to her mouth without her awareness.

Morganna took in a hard breath. Robin swore she saw Lancelot flinch in the corner. But Arthur did nothing. His gaze remained steady on her.

"What theory do you wish to tell me?"

She couldn't believe she was going to say it. She had toyed with the idea during their unexpected journey. Still, she wasn't certain. Yet, it was the only explanation.

She straightened her back. "You said Cadfen was a castor?"

He nodded.

"I think I know how Cadfen is controlling the people of the middle kingdom," she said. "I know how he's making them forget."

Arthur's eyes flared. He and Morganna both leaned forward, Morganna's palms now shaking a bit.

"You have to tell me everything," he said.

She took a deep breath. "I told you about the Salvation and how the villagers eat the bread blessed by the Divines."

"The witches in disguise, yes."

"You and I both were raised to follow Trithian but we never celebrated Salvation Day. I believe Cadfen started this holiday to cast a spell on the people. He does it through the blessed bread."

Robin stared into Arthur's eyes, hoping he'd trust her. She balled her hands into a fist to still them.

Arthur leaned back in his seat. His brows were raised, and his eyes rounded as he watched Robin.

"After all this time," he said.

The knot in her chest unraveled. Robin bobbed her head repeatedly. Arthur trembled in his in disbelief, his mouth turning up into a smile.

"We've figured it out," he said, looking back at her.

"Yes," she replied. Robin reached across the table for Arthur's hand just as Morganna's thin arm reached across his back.

She halted mid-motion and dug her nails into the table top.

You fool. Why'd you let yourself get carried away?

Morganna had now wrapped both her arms around Arthur. Tears ran down her cheeks and a thin pink-lipped smile was on her face.

Robin tucked her fist under the table, blinking rapidly and looking away from the couple. Her sight landed on Lancelot. There, behind those brown lashes, his eyes gouged into her and Robin suddenly felt naked. She tugged at the collar of her dress, glanced back at Maddy because she needed to know she wasn't alone, and then faced her cousin and the man she once loved.

She cleared her throat. "This also means he has witches working for him. More than one if The Divines are any hint."

Morganna had released her hold on Arthur but kept a hand on his shoulder, smiling at him.

"So, if we disrupt the ritual, you think the people will remember?" He curved an eyebrow.

"Exactly," Robin replied. "And then, a rebellion will be much easier to lead."

A warming hope filled her.

"You're all forgetting one thing."

They turned to Maddy sitting in the corner. She moved to take a seat beside Robin.

"We're not sure what sort of spell they've put on the blessed bread. We can't say for sure they'll remember. Who's to say Cadfen won't just start killing villagers as their memories return?" She stared at all of them.

Robin bit her tongue but forced the words out. "He may be a traitor, but Cadfen is no fool. He knows how to lead. Killing villagers would only spark more outrage. He can't kill them all. A king needs someone to lead."

Maddy took a long breath. "I'd like to believe that yet it's hopeful thinking. Selling your soul to witches has an affect on the body and mind. We can't be certain he's the same Cadfen from before."

"Then, what do you propose?" Morganna had released Arthur's shoulders and held her palms out towards Maddy. "I don't see any other plans, yet you are Southern-born. You know more about witches than we do. If you have something, offer it up."

Robin moved in her seat so she was facing Morganna directly for the first time. She met her gaze.

"Be careful how you talk to my companion, Morganna. An offense against her is an offense against me." She folded her hands in front of her.

"I'm only asking to see if there is a better choice," Morganna replied.

Robin didn't miss how her cousin's eyes lingered on the blue and purple spot on her cheek.

"And I don't think we need another duel to know who not to offend, do we, *cousin?*"

Robin shot up from her seat, her teeth clinched together and grinding against one another.

Morganna stared up at her. She smirked.

Maddy tugged at Robin's arm. "She's egging you on. Don't let her win," she whispered.

Robin knew Maddy was right. Still, there was something about the way Morganna looked at her, the way she called her "cousin" that made Robin want to cut the woman's tongue out. To think, she ever cared about her.

As Maddy held Robin, Arthur pulled Morganna down to her seat, though her eyes never left her cousin. Eventually, Robin followed suit and sat, as well.

"Look," Maddy said, forcing a fixed stare on everyone in the room, "the best way to dethrone Cadfen is to kill him directly. Once, he's dead, the witches will take his soul and the throne will be open. Salvation Day will cease because the witches will have no reason to poison the people. You all can start rebuilding the kingdom from there."

No one said anything. Robin and Morganna still glared at one another.

Lancelot sighed from the corner.

"Well, Miss Maddy," he said, "I think your plan is brilliant. But how will we ever get close enough to Cadfen to kill him?"

"We need to lure him with something he wants," she said.

"Which is?"

There was a silence.

Robin rolled her eyes. "Me, obviously."

"Absolutely not," Arthur shouted.

Maddy shook her head. "No, Robin, I did not mean—"

"But it's true," she replied, staring into her friend's eyes. She thought she should be sad, that maybe she should cry, but Robin didn't feel disturbed. She had had ten years to process his unsolicited desire for her.

A warm hand grasped hers.

Arthur.

She turned to him.

"I will not use you as bait." His grip tightened around her hand and, despite knowing better, she squeezed his hand in return.

"I know you won't, Arthur," she said. "But remember, the choice is no longer yours. It's mine."

She pulled her hand free and he stood from his seat.

"I do not care whether I am courting you or not. I will not see you harmed."

Haven't you already?

She shook herself. *Stay focused.*

"There's no sense in worrying about it now. No decisions will be made tonight. Before we defeat Cadfen, I have to help Alistair."

"And how do you plan on doing that?" Lancelot asked, leaning against the wall again, his brown eyes roaming over her.

She turned away from him and squeezed Maddy's hand. "That plan we're still trying to figure out."

Chapter Fifteen

Alistair still hadn't woken. Three days of mumbles and brief requests for water. That was all he had given Maddy and she found the weight on her chest growing heavier. When would he wake?

He rested in the bed while she sat on the floor of their room. Robin had gone out, probably to walk Fred for some exercise. That seemed to be the only thing she would do now. Wake, eat, chat with Maddy, and then leave to spend time in the stables.

There had been no other meetings since the day they arrived. Still, Maddy was sure the conversation was not over. She and Robin had agreed to try to not leave Alistair alone. But when they would venture out together and run into Arthur, his eyes locked on Robin like a child who had just watched their toy fall apart. And by the way Robin cringed at his sight, Maddy was sure she knew he was watching her, as well.

He'd never agree to use Robin to lure Cadfen into a false pretense. Maddy wasn't so crazy about the idea herself. She hadn't meant for the conversation to take that turn.

Alistair stirred. He fumbled under the blanket and tossed his head from side to side.

She moved from the wall where she sat and squatted beside him. She ran her fingers through his hair, staring into his face and smiling as he visibly relaxed.

"You know I'm here, don't you?"

His chest rose and fell.

She grinned. "Not an answer exactly but I trust you do. You need to wake soon. Robin and I...we miss you."

She rested her hand on his forehead.

"I think you miss us, too. You're quite boring by yourself, Alistair." She smiled before leaning back from him and placing herself by the wall adjacent his bed.

"If my mother were here, she'd know how to wake you. Of course, she doesn't have magic, but she was the best healer in our village in the south."

Maddy turned her head to the stone ceiling. She had pulled her knees to her chest and now rocked them from side to side as her eyes drifted over the ceiling above her. She hummed and imagined the stones were flowers and the walls were trees. In her mind, everything became lush and alive.

The gray of the room faded. There was now only nature's beautiful green and splashes of color from flowers. Red, purple, and orange tulips hung from the walls.

Everything was quite beautiful here, in her safe place.

In the center of the flowers, Maddy could see her mother's face. She saw the waves of dark green that rippled over her mother's shoulders. The woman still refused to cut her hair more than once every two years.

It was an old belief that hair was like the roots of a tree. It connected people to nature and the longer the hair the more connected.

Her mother's face was round and her eyes narrow like she was always thinking about something.

Then, in the shrubbery, her brother's face appeared.

What would Endlun look like now? He wouldn't be the same child he had been when they were separated, would he?

Maddy blinked until the image became blurry. Her eyes suddenly felt like they had been stung with smoke. The beautiful green faded, the stone walls of their room spread out in front of her and Alistair's light breathing brought her back to reality.

Deep breath.

"I'll return to you soon, Mama. I'm still saving up for the entrance fee to Essen's kingdom."

Yet as she spoke the words, an uncertainty spilled over her.

She had been selling herbs for two years now and she still didn't have half the entrance fee. And now, Satbury, the only place she had been able to earn some income was no longer safe.

She thought of her last days there. Maddy had never been so scared in her life. During the war between Essen and Issin, she had seen things she wished she could unsee. Yet nothing she had experienced disturbed her as much as the people of Satbury's relentless smiles and praise for the Salvation Day.

To Maddy, there was a peace in death, even if it was a slow one. But to be alive and manipulated by evil was a torture she did not want to experience. At least in death, one was free.

The door creaked open and Maddy jerked upright.

Robin stood in the doorway, dressed in Alistair's clothes. The only thing of hers she wore were her traveling boots, usually only matched with her blue dress. Her hair was twisted up into a bun and there was a small smile on her face.

"Good afternoon, Maddy," she said.

"Noon, Robin. How's Fred?"

She shrugged. "Fine. I think he misses Alistair though." She stared at him for a moment. Then, moved her sights to Maddy. "Do you want to go for a walk with me? There's some work around here that we can help with."

"You think it's wise to leave him alone today?" she asked. "He was talking quite a bit. I think he may wake up."

"Well, if he does, he won't be alone." Robin stepped to the side. Behind her, little Elanor stood with a bucket in her hands. By the way she was struggling to hold it, it had to be completely full.

"Elanor has agreed to watch over Alistair while we work."

The child nodded. "I'll take good care of him. Miss Robin said he's been thirsty, so I grabbed the largest bucket."

Maddy smiled. "Thank you, Elanor."

The girl arched her back and lifted the bucket until it was barely an inch off the floor. She, then, slowly walked to Alistair's side and put the bucket down, careful not to let any water spill out. When she was done, she heaved a sigh and wiped her brow.

Robin covered her mouth while she watched the child and Maddy found small chuckles leaving her, as well.

"I suppose we shall be off, then?" Robin leaned against the door and looked at Maddy.

She stood from where she sat, glancing back at Alistair briefly as she stepped into the hallway.

"We'll be back shortly," Robin called into the room before closing the door.

She and Maddy made their way through the halls. They had managed to learn the entrance and exit routes from their bed chamber. Navigating the rest of the castle was still a puzzle.

As they broke into the clearing, Robin turned to her left where women and children lined up in front of Calvin who managed the daily work tasks.

Maddy walked slightly behind Robin whose legs were much longer than hers. From her side vision, she saw Lancelot. He was standing by the trail that led into the clearing and was staring in their direction.

Robin tugged her shirt up but the poorly weathered material sagged right back down. She had noticed his attention, as well.

Maddy had no magic. She didn't even have an *aerin* as her people called it. In her land, there were tales of those who were blessed with a special gift that allowed them to master one specific ability. She once thought her mother had a Gift but her mother always denied it. She'd say her skills came from practice and study, nothing more.

Still, Maddy's mother had always been impressed with the

child's instincts. Currently, her instincts were telling her Lancelot was not someone she'd want to call friend. There was something about him...he was off somehow.

Then, again so was Morganna. The woman was completely jealous of Robin and utterly obsessed with Arthur. Everywhere he was, she seemed to be nearby. The few times Arthur and Robin were caught in a conversation, she latched onto him like a maggot did a dying man.

They reached the line. Robin looked around her.

"Is he gone?" she whispered.

Maddy turned back to where Lancelot had been. The spot was empty. She peered around the clearing.

"I think so. I don't see him anymore."

Her shoulders slacked. "Thank Trithian. I could feel his eyes on me the whole time I was with Fred."

"Did he approach your or say anything?"

She shook her head. "No. It's quite disturbing."

Maddy turned to the sky and clucked her tongue on her teeth. "Seems he has an unwarranted affection towards you."

Robin glanced behind her before speaking. She turned back to Maddy. "I'm not sure if it's affection."

"Then, what do you think it is?"

She shrugged. "I don't know. I only know I don't like it."

The line moved on and soon they were standing in front of Calvin. He was a round man, looking to be in his forties with permanently red cheeks and a beard to match.

"Afternoon, ladies," he said, his cheeks rising high as he smiled.

"Afternoon, Calvin," they said in unison.

He reached under his makeshift table and pulled out two battered pouches. They both had holes in them and the seams were unraveling in the corners. He handed one to Robin and the other to Maddy.

"Just follow the others. We're collecting apples today and anything else you can find," he said.

"In preparation for the cold weather?" Robin replied.

He nodded. "Getting colder each day. The days are getting shorter too."

"Hopefully, it's not too harsh a winter. We'll be off then." Robin and Maddy turned to leave.

"And make sure you stay with the others. Don't go too far off on your own," he called after them.

Robin stopped walking. She closed her eyes and took in a

sharp breath through her nose. She looked back at Calvin.

"I assume Arthur told you to tell me that."

The man grinned. "I'm not one for spilling secrets."

She shook her head and started marching behind the others. Maddy jogged to catch up to her long strides.

"The man won't let up," Robin snapped.

Maddy nodded.

"Does he not understand he can't have both? He no longer has say over what I do." She clenched her teeth together and released a slow exhale. "I'm trying to ignore it. I really am, Maddy, but if it's not Lancelot, it's Arthur. Always watching, always commenting. And then Morganna..."

Her words trailed off and she sped up her pace, stomping hard on the ground.

Maddy sighed. Her own legs were not meant for this amount of speed.

"He's just a fool," Robin spat.

"Hm. I agree but do you wish he was your fool? At least sometimes."

Robin kept her eyes ahead. "Sometimes."

The two fell into a silence. They followed the women and children onto a path that appeared behind the trees. The path crawled up onto the hill top. The trees grew thicker, and the higher they climbed, the more Maddy found herself relaxing. It felt so nice to be surrounded by nature's green again though the approaching winter had snatched most of it. She ran her fingers through her hair and looked up into the trees.

If it were either of the hot seasons, she'd blend in quite well.

The trees seemed to be having a similar effect on Robin. Her fists were loosened and her hands hung by her side. She had stopped gnashing her teeth together and the tightness in her jaw had disappeared.

After about a twenty-minute walk, the trees thinned out and small red bulbs hung from their branches. Here, the group stopped, and everyone started working on their own tree.

Robin walked past everyone else until she and Maddy stood alone under an apple tree. Maddy picked the lower-hanging apples while Robin snatched the ones just above those.

"Are you a big fan of apples, Maddy?" Robin asked.

"They're not common in the south. I grew accustomed to them once I moved here though. You?"

She bobbed her head. "Yes. I used to call my uncle applebeard he loved them so much. When I was young, my mother would always make me apple tarts, as well."

"I've never tried apple tarts before," Maddy said, reaching up on her tiptoes.

"Really? That won't do. I'll have to make you some when all this is over."

Maddy smiled though she was sure neither of them knew when their current predicament would end. She needed to start selling herbs again--soon. The quicker she earned money, the sooner she'd see her family again. Still...

She looked at Robin, dressed in her peasant clothes, sweat on her brow and dirt on her hands. A lady turned into a field hand. She was quite something and Maddy found herself smiling at the thought of them baking tarts together, at the memory of Robin braiding Maddy's hair while they waited for Alistair to return home in Satbury. Leaving them would be much harder than she had initially anticipated.

"You know, Maddy. Things will be very different once we dethrone, Cadfen." Robin stuffed an apple in her pouch. It was filling quickly.

She continued. "Morganna is the rightful heir and since Arthur is now courting her, I assume they will rule together." She forced a smile on her face. "And they'll be happy. Yes, um, anyway I'm not sure if Morganna will feel comfortable with me staying in Camelot. If we were following old customs, I'd live with them or be given my own home to build a life."

"He may be a fool, but I don't think Arthur would see you homeless, Robin."

She nodded. "I don't think so either, yet I've...I've also reached a decision."

"Hm?"

"Whether they provide a home or not, I no longer want to live in the past. Things are different now and I need to be, too. I think- I think you, Alistair, and I could all live together. Does that sound odd?"

Nothing could have stopped Maddy from grinning at that moment. She felt a heat creep into her cheeks and her heart seemed to swell inside her chest, despite her knowing this could never be a reality.

Robin tried to meet her gaze but Maddy quickly looked away.

The royal stopped picking apples and sat on the ground, staring at the rows of trees in front of her.

"When I left the tree, everything I knew was gone. Family, friends, Arthur...but I still wasn't alone. Alistair found me, and then, I met you and it seems, without me knowing, you all have become my family."

Maddy sat cross-legged across from her. She placed the full pouch in her lap and gave her attention to Robin.

"I'm not sure where we'd go," Robin whispered. "But I'm sure we'd have options. Many more than we have now. How would you feel about that?"

Should I play along?

"It won't be proper living arrangements," Maddy said. "People would spread rumors about us like wildfire."

Robin shrugged. "As I used to tell Arthur, proper isn't always interesting."

Maddy smiled. "That's true."

"So, then?"

The green-haired girl huffed. She picked at a nearby flower and twirled it.

"My mother and younger brother are still in Essen's kingdom. I won't be able to do anything with myself until I see them."

"Why haven't you gone to visit?"

"I told you about the war and becoming a refugee. Essen also put an entrance fee on refugees who were not picked at first selection," she said. "My mother is a healer and my brother was young at the time, so, they had immediate entrance. I, on the other hand, was not skilled enough in healing and was too old to be considered a child. They had no choice but to leave me."

Robin leaned towards her. "Maddy, I'm—"

She held up a hand. "Don't. I don't need apologies. Life could be much worse."

I could have never met Alistair or you.

Robin nodded. "I understand. How much is the entrance fee?"

"Two hundred shillings," Maddy said.

Robin's eyes bulged. "Is he mad? No one who is not high born will ever be able to afford that amount."

She shrugged. "I don't have any other option. I have to find a way."

"No." Robin stood and held the pouch over her shoulder. "We'll find a way. We're in this together now."

Maddy clenched the pouch in her hands. She hated crying. She thought most people did but Maddy especially hated it because she didn't do it often. When she did, the sensation was always odd to her. Yet, she could feel the tears brimming in her eyes and their desire to spill over.

Robin placed a hand on her back. Maddy kept her head

bowed.

"This is the beginning for all three of us, Maddy. New beginnings."

Maddy did not speak. She only nodded as the tears fell from her.

Chapter Sixteen

"It's cold here, Edwin." Alistair's teeth were chattering as he and the young boy walked through the thick fog.

The boy shrugged. "I don't notice the chill anymore. It bothered me when I first died, but I guess, I've gotten used to it."

"Where are we even going?"

"I have to show you something."

Alistair sighed. He felt like they had been walking for days in endless directions. Since Edwin killed the witch, Alistair had felt his mind slipping. He filtered between the foggy realm the boy called Ether and the real world.

He even heard Robin and Madelia calling out to him sometimes, would see faded shapes of their faces. He would reach out to them, only to return to the Ether, unsure of when he would be among the living again.

Alistair knew they had reached the eastern kingdom, so, they were safe. But with their luck, how long would that last? He needed to get back soon.

The boy stepped in front of him.

"What is it, Edwin?"

He looked at Alistair. "If we're going to be working together, I need to show you."

Alistair wasn't sure when they had become partners.

"Show me what?"

"How I died."

"What!" His footsteps came to a halt and he stared wide-mouthed at the boy. "Why would you want to show me that?"

"Because I need you to understand what you'll be facing. What you could have faced too."

"Do you mean-you mean the witches?"

Edwin nodded. "You weren't like me. You got away before they killed you. I only escaped after." He sighed. "My parents were having a gathering. They didn't hear me scream."

Alistair squatted so he was eye-level with Edwin. He placed a hand on his shoulder.

"I am very sorry for what happened to you. I wish I could change it," he said, though he didn't believe his words brought much comfort.

The boy shook his head. "It's too late for me, but you may be able to help others."

"Others?"

"Think, Alistair. When was the last time you heard of a witch attack?"

He rubbed his brow. It had been some time. But he had only returned to the middle kingdom less than a year and the time of tales was long gone. The period of science had begun with King Terryn. Cadfen had carried it on.

"When, Alistair?"

"It has been a long time since an attack in the middle kingdom. What does that have to do with anything?"

"The witches have stopped killing children."

"That makes no sense. I doubt they've found any morals lurking in the shadows."

"They've stopped because Cadfen has been feeding them souls."

If Alistair thought he was cold, that was nothing compared to the chill that ran through him at that moment. Cadfen...feeding souls to witches?

"You have to listen to me." Edwin grabbed his arm. "You know he's a castor?"

"Yes, but—"

"Castors sell their souls."

He nodded.

"Why would the witches grant him so much power? For one soul? An adult's soul at that, not even a child's."

Alistair's mouth felt very dry all of sudden. "I-I don't know."

"Because they're getting their fill!" the boy screamed. "All of them. With Cadfen as king, they no longer have to hunt, always worrying about getting caught or splashed with holy water. They give him power, he gives them souls, everyone forgets witches even exist. I've seen a memory of it. No one cares about orphans, beggars, and criminals."

Alistair shook his head even as the words rang true. He dug his fingers into his thighs.

The Devil has become a man. Cadfen is a murderer.

"Now, you need to see." Edwin begin running, tugging at Alistair's arm as he did so. "We're almost there. I don't come back to watch it often. I forgot where I placed it."

"Your death?"

He nodded. "The memory. Oh, here it is."

"Edwin, I—"

He was in a large room. There was a rug on the floor and toys in every corner. Music and laughter echoed in the distance.

In the middle of the room, there was a bed and in the bed there was Edwin. He was curled up with his fists pressed firmly to his face. His chest rose and fell in steady rhythms.

Alistair peered around him.

"I'm here."

He jumped back and grabbed at his heart which racketed against his ribcage.

"You have to stop doing that, Edwin."

The boy laughed. "I only do it because you scare so easily."

"You have a very wicked sense of a humor for a little boy."

"You sound like my nursemaid."

"Well, then—"

"Shhhh." The boy placed a finger over his mouth. "She's coming."

Alistair's body reacted before his mind had fully grasped the words.

He stumbled into a corner and gazed into the darkness that was only broken by a tiny candle placed near the boy's bed.

The floor seemed to ripple, and from an opposing corner, a shadow rose to stand on two legs. Alistair smashed his lips together. He knew this was a memory, Edwin's memory. Still, the scream pushed at his throat, begging to be released. He had survived two witch attacks, yet that knowledge gave him no solace.

He wondered if he had been like Edwin. Sleeping with his fists balled to his face, chest rising and falling, completely unaware death was approaching.

She crept over to him, leaving black mist trailing behind her. Her arms stood hunched by her sides and her hands--which were more like talons--jerked around in every direction. Perhaps, she was excited, anxious to capture a child's soul. And on her face, there were smears of red, painting her mask into a wide smile.

The creature stood by Edwin's bed.

Edwin's ghost moved over to Alistair. He grabbed his hand.

"Here it comes," he whispered. He squeezed.

The witch raised her right talon and plunged it into the boy's chest. Immediately, his eyes flew open and he began to wriggle beneath her grasp. His eyes found the witch's face, a realization appeared, and then he screamed.

Alistair couldn't help himself. He covered his ears. There was nothing worse than a child's scream. High-pitched but hollowing, digging into Alistair's breast like the witch did to young Edwin.

The boy fought, he struggled, swinging at the monster

anywhere he could. But then, he began to still. His swings slowed, and a light faded from his eyes.

Cackles filled the room. The witch raised her hand and as she did, a golden orb appeared from Edwin's chest.

"My soul," he stated. He grabbed Alistair's hand again. "Don't let go this time."

Alistair nodded, hoping he could keep his promise.

The witch loosened her hold the orb. The ball of light tried to zoom away but the witch was too quick. She reached both hands out and grasped Edwin's soul until it stilled again.

The monster growled, directing her anger towards the orb.

"She's telling me she'll let me go if I'm good," he said. "I still think I'm alive. I think I'm having a nightmare."

Certain the soul would not run again; the witch placed her hands on her chest. With one long nail she dug into her breast bone and sliced downward. A horrible smell filled the room. It was rot mixed with dung and something Alistair wished he didn't recognize so quickly.

Death.

The creature leaned her head back and took in a deep breath. As her chest rose, whispers spilled from the opening. Alistair itched to cover his ears even though he couldn't understand what he was hearing. The voices were light and quick. Here one moment and gone the next.

"The voices of the other children she's taken." Edwin's grip tightened. "They're asking for help, for their parents."

The witch moved forward. She took Edwin's soul in her hands and moved it towards the opening in her chest.

There were stumbling footsteps and giggling. The door swung open. A man and woman came to a halt in the doorway. The witch screeched at the sudden burst of light that spread across her. She lost her grip on Edwin's soul and he moved away from the gap in her chest.

There was a vial hanging around the man's neck. Holy water.

He took it off and began to douse the witch in the blessed water.

She screeched once more, before fading into a corner and disappearing into the darkness. Everything after that happened very fast.

The man and woman screamed into the hallway. The room filled with people. An older couple cried beside Edwin's bed, all the while the golden orb swirled around the room, bumping into *walls, sometimes bumping against his own body but never entering it.*

"I was trying to figure out how to get back in but I didn't know how." He sighed. "My time had run out anyway, I'm sure. The soul can't be apart from the body for too long."

Alistair listened to what Edwin was saying yet the scene around him held his attention. The woman by Edwin's bed tossed her head back and wailed.

The boy shook. "That's enough now." He stepped back, pulling Alistair with him and the mist consumed them again.

Alistair fell to his knees and took in several sharp breaths. He felt like he had suddenly been saved from drowning. Edwin sat beside him.

"Now, you know," the boy said. "You know what you're going to face. It's time to go."

"What?"

"Your friends. They won't stop talking to you. I think they want you back now."

"But what about you?" Alistair asked.

"I'll be coming, too. There's a lot of work to be done." He stood and began walking farther into the mist. Alistair followed behind him, away from the memory of Edwin's death.

"Are you stirring, sir?"

Who is that?

Alistair felt odd. His body felt taut and rigid as he opened his eyes.

There was a young girl with missing teeth staring down at him. When his eyes fully opened, she immediately began to smile.

"Hello, sir. My name's Elanor. Don't worry, I'll go fetch the misses for you." And then, she was gone. He tried to move his head. His neck refused.

He could only hear the girl scramble across the floor and a door closing.

Again, Alistair attempted to move, hoping to lean up and see where he had been sleeping. He made the effort, yet his body only trembled in response.

What is wrong with me?

His chest started to rise and fall quickly as his nostrils flared in panic. Why couldn't he move?

Alistair attempted once more, wanting to turn his body to one side. He remained where he lay. He felt like an animal beating against its cage, except his cage was his body. It was something he should have been in control of and yet...

He grunted and groaned with his efforts. He just wanted to sit up, to turn his body over, to--his finger moved.

With as frustrated as he was feeling, Alistair was surprised he detected the slight movement. He focused on moving the finger again, then, he moved the next one, and the next one. The mobility stretched up from his fingertips to his arms and shoulders.

Air released happily from his lungs when he could finally move his upper body. Soon, he was in command again and--being in no sort of hurry-- he pushed himself upright and leaned against the wall.

Alistair scanned the room. Edwin wasn't in it.

A moment later, the door swung open and slammed against the room's back wall. Alistair jumped as Madelia and Robin rushed in. Without hesitation, they both threw their arms around him, and hugged him so hard, he worried he'd turned purple.

"So, I'm assuming you missed me, then?" He chuckled as Robin slapped his shoulder.

Tears were spilling down her cheeks. "Of course, we missed you! You're such a fool."

He nodded. "It's true. But at least I'm a living fool, so, there's that to count as a plus."

"Did you hear me, Alistair?"

He turned to his right where Madelia had wrapped herself around him. He felt his heart run away from him and he knew his cheeks had turned crimson.

"When you were...sleeping, I mean?" Her eyes were greener than he remembered.

He nodded, still staring at her. "Yes, I heard you, Maddy."

Her hold on his arm grew and she looked away, her long hair acting as a curtain to cover her face. Suddenly, Alistair wanted to lean into her. He wanted to caress his face against Maddy's hair and breathe her in. He didn't realize how much he had missed her, both of them.

"Should I fetch anything, miss?"

Elanor stood in the middle of the room, rocking from her toes to her heels.

"What would you like to eat, Alistair?" Robin asked.

"Do you have any of that boar?"

With those words, little Elanor raced from the room.

Robin ruffled Alistair's hair and beamed at him. "You have no clue how happy I am to have you back. Things haven't been as easy without you."

He grinned. "What can I say? I'm a lucky charm."

That earned him another slap.

Elanor darted into the room with a plate of meat and bread. A small cup rested on its edge.

"Arthur said he'll be around to see you in a bit," she stated, handing him the plate. "He's talking with a few of the scouts."

If Alistair had been drinking from the cup, he was sure he'd have spit it all over the poor child. Arthur was going to visit him? He was concerned about Alistair?

He turned to Robin who shook her head and shrugged. She turned to the child.

"Elanor, do you think you could give us some time alone? Alistair's still tired and we need to talk."

"All right. If you need me, I'll be in the stables or with Lancelot."

The arrogant boy's face flashed in Alistair's mind. He sighed. *I need another nap already.*

Robin nodded at the child. Elanor left the room, closing the door behind her.

"I nearly forgot about that one," Alistair remarked.

"Who?" Maddy asked.

He motioned towards the door. "Lancelot. I was planning on never seeing him again."

"Sadly, fate has a cruel sense of humor." Robin heaved a heavy exhale. She looked up at the ceiling. "I will say he's been less of a fool this time around. Hopefully, he keeps it up. Now, tell me how you're feeling? Do you remember anything from before—"

"Before I almost fell into an eternal slumber?" He let out a dry laugh. "Oh, yes, I remember everything. I need to thank you, both of you." He glanced at Maddy who had now released his arm and was sitting cross-legged adjacent him.

"What for?" the green-haired girl asked.

He curved a brow. "For packing up all our things and getting us out of Satbury. Away from that damn Salvation Day."

She shook her head. "You're such a silly man, Alistair."

"What's so silly about helping me live through another witch?"

"Because," Robin interjected with a touch on his shoulder, "you would have done the same for us."

"Doesn't mean I shouldn't thank you. However," --he grabbed a piece of meat and placed the plate aside--"I do have something to tell you. Something I learned when I was...you know, with Edwin."

"In the afterlife?" Maddy said.

"Edwin calls it the *Ether*. I'm assuming they're the same but that's not what I need to tell you."

He stuffed the piece of meat in his mouth and quickly chewed.

"What is it?" Robin asked.

He took a moment. "Cadfen is...he's—"Alistair clenched his teeth together. His lips curled into a snarl and he could feel his skin prickle with anger. His hand turned into a fist as he gripped the tip of his shirt.

This man is a bloody monster.

Alistair shook himself. He closed his eyes and let the words spill from him. "He's feeding the witches souls. Those of children."

At the very words, the air in the room seemed to darken. When he looked upon his friends again, Robin was gaping, her blue eyes the roundest he had ever seen, and Maddy was sitting straight as a stick.

Robin tapped her knee with her fingers and pressed her lips together. "No, no, that can't...even he wouldn't—"

"Wouldn't he, Robin?" Alistair grabbed her hand and squeezed until she stopped shaking her head. She found his eyes. "Wouldn't he, Robin?"

"It's too horrible to imagine," she said.

Maddy shot up from the bed. "I have to go."

"Where?" Robin asked, her brows raised.

The girl didn't respond. She was already rushing to the door.

"But there's more we need to tell him."

"You tell him," she said, giving them one last look. "Please."

And then, she was gone, the door closing quietly behind her.

"Dear Lord," Robin said, staring at the door, "she ran out of here like the Devil was on her heels."

Alistair stared after her. *It's okay to be scared, Madelia.*

Robin stood, grabbed a chair from across the room and sat opposite Alistair.

"If what you say is true," she said, wringing her hands together, "then we need to kill Cadfen sooner than hoped. I also discovered something about him."

She tucked her hair behind her ears. "The bread from the Salvation Day?"

He bobbed his head.

"It's how he makes everyone forget. The Divines--the witches, I mean—I think they cast a spell on the bread before having everyone eat it. Because the holiday is compulsory in the kingdom, no one has had a chance to remember."

Alistair flexed his fingers.

There weren't many people Alistair really *hated*, really wanted to *hurt*. Though the list was short, Cadfen's name was at the top.

"We're going to have to kill him, Robin." He repeated her sentiment.

She nodded. "Yes, we agree on that but what about you?"

"What about me?" he asked. He roamed over his body feeling for wounds or an injury. "Besides what Edwin told me, I feel fine."

"Uh..." Robin looked between him and the floor. "I suppose I should just show you. Here, I found this mirror around the clearing."

He took the mirror from her hands and stared at his reflection. A white-haired version of himself looked back at Alistair.

He nodded, cocked his head to the side, and hmphed.

"Is this some sort of trick, Robin?"

"I'm afraid not."

Another nod.

Alistair jumped to his feet, clutching at his hair and shouting at the reflection.

"What the hell happened to me?"

"We're not sure. After Edwin saved us the black faded."

"I look like an old man!"

"Alistair, it's not that bad," she said, stepping next to him.

He shook his head and gave her back the mirror. "How did this happen? Do you think the witch cursed me again?"

She shrugged. "I'm the worst person to ask. But before we even think of attacking Cadfen, we need to make sure you're well. We can't run in to fight already weakened."

"I'm assuming no healer here is trained in witch attacks?"

"Not one. Arthur says the training isn't common these days."

Not in the middle kingdom, it's not but elsewhere...

He released a long breath and fell back onto the bed. "I know where I have to go."

"Where *we* have to go," she corrected taking her seat again, as well.

"I don't think you're going to like this idea."

"Try me."

"Like in the south, the people in the north still believe in the old ways, though the legends are a little different," he said. "My aunt was the first one to tell me I had a witch's curse. Our local healer confirmed her thoughts. Together they'll know what to make of this." He pointed to his hair.

Robin smiled.

"So?" he asked.

"When do we leave?" she replied.

"Are you sure about this? It's not an easy journey."

"I don't expect it to be," she said. "But I'm not going to leave you. I expect Arthur will grumble. Though, that's nothing new. You should have seen how red his face got when I told him about Satbury. I thought he was going to pop."

Alistair chuckled. "He does seem to be quite protective."

She shrugged and pulled at the fabric of her pants. "Perhaps. You are, as well, though."

"You think so?" Alistair quirked a brow and smiled at her.

"Of course. You took me in off the street, Alistair. The difference between you and Arthur is I want your opinion on my decisions. I do not desire his."

He examined Robin. She was putting so much focus on a stray strand of cloth. He reached over and grabbed her hand.

"It's okay to feel sad," he said.

She sighed. "Sadness is a luxury I cannot afford. We need a plan for after we return from the north. Cadfen still needs to be dethroned."

Alistair grabbed his plate and began stuffing his mouth. "What have we come up with so far?"

Robin cleared her throat. She turned her attention to the floor. "Well, I was thinking Cadfen wants me so—"

"No."

She scoffed. "You sound like Arthur."

"This is one thing he and I will agree on. There has to be another way, Robin."

She huffed and fell back against her seat. Her eyes landed on Alistair's plate which he offered to her.

"You should eat. You must be starving."

"And you were probably starving yourself worrying. Everyone thinks better on a full stomach, too."

Robin placed a hand on her abdomen She moved her gaze between Alistair and the plate.

"Fine," she said. "Seems it'll be of use since we need a new plan to rid ourselves of Cadfen."

"Exactly. One that doesn't involve you being captured."

She filled her mouth with bread. "Hm."

Chapter Seventeen

The way the moon touched her skin made Lancelot's knees weak. Her hair seemed to have grown longer since their last visit. Her tresses were still dark as ever almost like Trithian had taken to the night sky with a paint brush when he made her. She was a sight for the eyes, sitting perched above the clearing with the grass as her blanket, her head turned up to the moon like it was her own personal candle.

He gripped the stone that lined the entrance to the tower. Lancelot had never wanted a woman as badly as he wanted Robin. She was like a goddess of old come to life, something that shouldn't exist, yet did.

He took in a sharp breath when she craned her neck even further. He wanted to feel the warmth of her skin, to line her neck with kisses, to roam over her with his hands.

A smirk pulled at his lips.

His age did not escape her notice. He was quite aware of the difference in years between them, as well, but it mattered not to him. He had enough experience to know how to make her feel good and how to make her happy.

It was true Lancelot was one for the ladies. He had no shame in admitting it. Yet, if Robin were his, he knew all women would fade into the shadows. They'd be a gray night and she'd be the shining star among them.

He released his grip on the stone and leaned against the wall. He sighed and turned his head so one eye was still on her. Their camp was safe. They hadn't had an attack in years. Still, after his parents had paid off some bandits only to be killed by them the same night, Lancelot had learned it was better to be safe than sorry.

What are you doing out here, my Little Robin?

He wondered how she'd react if he called her that. Probably a tongue lashing and a good smack.

The thought made him smile.

The hallway echoed with heavy footsteps. Without even thinking, Lancelot sidled his way down the wall and just barely ducked into a side passage. He pressed himself against the stone and waited to see who would appear though he already had a good inclination.

Arthur walked by him without a glance in his direction. That was good. If this were a few years ago, Lancelot would have been caught. Thanks to Arthur, he had learned to fight, to be brave, and to blend into his environment.

Still, why was Arthur here?

It was a dumb question to ask himself. He already knew the answer.

Robin.

His mentor stood exactly where he himself had only a few moments ago. He was gazing at Robin, his shoulders hunching up as his gaze lingered. The man let out an exasperated sigh and shook his head. He began to pace the entrance, shooting glances in her direction every now and then. He had one hand on his hip and the other stroked his face.

Lancelot knew that look. Arthur was in deep thought.

Though he had tried to breach the subject of Robin's arrival with Arthur on several occasions, the man would always dismiss the issue. It was odd for him to keep secrets from Lancelot which spoke to his distress. Stuck between two women, cousins at that!

There was no doubt Morganna was beautiful. Her brown eyes and golden hair were a perfect combination. Yet, Lancelot could never force himself to be attracted to her. Perhaps, it was the slight pinch in her nose or the shape of her face. There was also something off about her. He wasn't sure. All Lancelot knew was he would have chosen Robin over her cousin any day.

The fact Arthur hadn't showed how incompetent he was in terms of relationships. Yes, Lancelot loved Arthur. He saved him, became his hero, and taught him how to survive. But on the matter of Robin, Lancelot was not willing to budge.

As far as Lancelot was concerned, Arthur had made his choice during her initial departure. Robin's face was covered in blood and bruises, yet he didn't ban Morganna immediately? The woman was mad with jealousy, what attraction could be left? He had thought of slicing the blonde sheep himself for what she had done to his Little Robin.

The only good that came of that whole ordeal was now Robin could be his. Arthur would come to accept it one day. And in truth, it was all his fault Lancelot fell for her. She was the lost woman, the name Arthur whispered in his sleep when they camped outside, the creature who captured his heart the first time he laid eyes on her. For hours, drunk or sober, Arthur would go on about the woman who should have been his wife, advising Lancelot to never let go of his true love once he found her. Well, he had and he had no plans of letting go. Not one. This dark-haired beauty would be his.

Arthur stopped pacing. He now stood in the middle of the entrance openly staring at Lancelot's woman. He itched to push him away. Arthur didn't deserve Robin.

Arthur ran his hands through his hair. "Robin, you will never know how much I miss you. I never meant for us to end up like this."

He sighed and leaned against the entrance wall, keeping his face turned out to look at her. "I want you back but Morganna will not let me go easily. And I do owe her my loyalty, at least, after all these years. But even when you weren't here, sometimes I'd look at her and I'd hope to see you. Robin..."

He covered his face with his hand and took in a long breath. A whimper escaped his lips while he shook his head.

Lancelot almost reached out to him. He almost wanted to lend a comforting ear. Then, he remembered Arthur was not his mentor at the moment. He was an obstacle to Robin. So, he stayed in the shadows, clenching his teeth and digging his nails into his arm to stop from helping the man. Arthur would have to fight this one alone.

There were a few more shaky breaths and a dry heave that could have been a sob before Arthur took his leave. He walked quickly. Lancelot assumed he was headed to his room. Before leaving his hiding spot, he waited. Arthur didn't come back. Yet just as he was about to resume his position at the entrance, Robin started her way across the clearing. She had worn her dress today. He loved her in that dress.

She stepped into the tower and came to a halt. Robin peered around her. She started walking again but at a much slower pace, constantly staring into the darkness. Soon she stood right beside the hall where Lancelot was hiding. She stopped, turned, and looked at him.

She can't see me. She can't possibly see me.

Robin shivered and turned her head away before hurrying down the passage.

There was no question he was going to follow. Just as soon as she got a large enough lead.

I guess what my mother said about women's intuition is true. Too bad my father didn't listen.

He stepped into the hall and sidled along the walls, careful not to get too close.

He only needed to make sure she got back to her room safely. Many of the men were honorable but he didn't know everyone's history. Most of them could be lying thieves for all he knew.

Better to be safe than sorry.

She turned down the last hall to her room, the one she refused to leave despite her male companion being fully awake now. Lancelot hated that they were so close. Still, they seemed to only be friends, and if the boy was too forward, he'd just kill him.

Yes, her companion had bested him during their first encounter but even he wasn't immune to poison.

She opened the door but not before taking another glance down the hall. Finally, she closed the door behind her.

Lancelot released a breath.

She's safe.

A smirk pulled at his lips as he thought of her last look down the hall.

That woman's intuition is going to be a problem.

Morganna held her hair back and vomited into the chamber pot. Her stomach ached from the constant heaving. She seemed unable to hold anything down since becoming pregnant. It shouldn't have surprised her though. According to her father, her mother had been the same way when she carried her. Everything would end up right back in the pot. She'd need to clean it out before Arthur returned.

Where is he?

Dinner had ended long ago. When she started feeling nauseous, Morganna excused herself but she remembered there had been little on his plate. He hardly ate anything and what was left was mostly crumbs. So, where was he?

Could he be with Robin?

The thought brought another wave of nausea to her and Morganna lunged for the chamber pot once more.

She had been waiting for the right moment to tell Arthur about their child. Then, her cousin returned. In need of shelter and food, no less, looking all the beautiful maiden in search of a knight. She had always been good at that, making men do what she wanted, manipulating them. She had done it with Morganna's father too. He never seemed able to say no to his niece.

Morganna grabbed a cloth and wiped her mouth. On shaky legs she stood, before grabbing the chamber pot and walking out to the back of the clearing. She had become so familiar with the halls now candlelight was unnecessary.

She poured the pot's contents out by the forest's edge, then, rinsed it out with a bucket of water left by the tower.

Clean pot in hand Morganna returned to their room and sat on the edge of their bed. She wouldn't go to sleep until Arthur returned. She had to make sure he returned to their room or else she would just have to go looking for him.

Please, come back soon. Don't be with her.

There were footsteps in the hallway. The tension loosened in her shoulders. Morganna prepared to stand to greet her love. But the footsteps walked past her door, down the hall, leaving her with an empty feeling in her chest.

She gripped the comforter on their bed and dug her teeth into her lips while her eyes ached. She began to rock back and forth. The motion reminded her of how her maids would hold her when she was a child. They were always so gentle, always so kind to her. Everyone was really, except Robin.

The tension built in Morganna's neck as she thought of their childhood days. After Robin moved in permanently, nothing was ever the same. The girl was wild. The guards would be sent out into the town in the middle of the night because Robin had disappeared from her bedroom. Sometimes the cook would make Robin a special meal because she refused everything else.

Morganna's father had told her, her cousin was grieving, and it would take time for her to adjust. But from what Morganna could see, Robin had never quite adjusted to life in Camelot.

She fingered the dragon pendant around her neck and pressed it firmly against her skin.

Arthur had nearly snatched it from her neck after she and Robin's altercation. Once Robin and Alistair had disappeared down the trail, he had pulled Morganna into their room and screamed for what felt like an eternity. All the while, he glanced between her face and the necklace where the charm rested. She was sure the only thing that had stopped him from taking it was she had tucked the necklace into her top to keep the charm out of sight.

Anger was out of character for Arthur. Irritation or annoyance was somewhat common, yes, especially when he was stressed. But never anger. Red faced, eyes bulging, gritted teeth anger. That was not like Arthur at all and though Morganna would never admit it to anyone, she had cried that night. And of course, his anger immediately faded. He began comforting her but Morganna only remembered bits and pieces of what he said.

Because she wasn't upset about him screaming at her. Yes, it hurt to see him so out of sorts and for his frustration to be directed towards her. What hurt the most was knowing Robin had caused it. Only Robin could force Arthur so far from his natural state, only Robin could make him turn on Morganna, only Robin could make Arthur say he loved her without actually saying it...

He loves her.

Morganna had tried the words several times aloud and each time they felt wrong. Arthur wasn't supposed to fall in love with Robin. He was supposed to love her. Since they were children, Morganna knew they were meant to be. Why hadn't he?

Was it because Robin was such a pitiful story to tell? Beautiful dark-haired girl born too soon with a poor constitution who loses her parents a bit more than a decade later.

Morganna scoffed. The tale nearly sold itself.

The truth was Robin had been soaking up sympathy from everyone since the day she was born. It only got worse when she lost her parents and moved to Camelot. Because then, she cast Morganna in shadow and no one saw how badly Morganna was suffering, as well.

Yes, Robin had lost two parents. That also meant Morganna had lost an aunt and uncle, not to mention her own mother had died years earlier, even before Morganna could know her.

She wanted to grieve, she wanted to experience sorrow, but it seemed her dark-haired cousin was the only one allowed to do so. She had always been the only person allowed to feel without restriction due to her health and great loss.

And now she was back, and it was happening all over again. The overwhelming sympathy and eyes of admiration.

Morganna had seen the way some of the men looked at Robin, had heard Lancelot gallivanting around telling Robin's sob story to any ear. She was sure he had heard it from Arthur.

While all this was occurring, everyone in camp looked at her differently. Morganna wasn't known for a harsh tongue. She supposed the identity of the culprit behind Robin's bruised face was getting to anyone who'd listen.

A hard anger settled over Morganna.

Once again, her horrid cousin was invading her home. Everyone was looking at her like she was their new queen. Or more like a precious lamb who had managed to escape the slaughter.

The thought nearly made Morganna laugh. It would have been a very bitter laugh. Because while everyone groaned for poor

Robin, they all forgot Morganna had lost just as much as her cousin.

Like Robin, now both her parents were deceased. Unlike Robin, she had also lost a whole kingdom of loyal followers. The ones who survived the fire that night at Camelot had forgotten her completely.

Arthur was the only person she had left. The fact she had ran back to Camelot at the sight of the flames and Robin had ran away should have been proof enough who really loved him.

Why can't you see it, dear Arthur?

The door creaked open. She sat up from where she was lying, not even realizing she had done so, as Arthur stepped through the door. The candles had burned low and there were shadows cast across the room.

"Good evening," he said and shot her a quick smile. His voice seemed hoarse.

"Good evening, Arthur. How was the rest of your dinner?"

"Fine. Do you feel better?" he asked. "A few of the men had some stomach complaints, as well. Hope the cook didn't use some bad berries."

He didn't.

She moved towards him to help him undress. He held a hand up to stop her.

"I'm fine." Then, he stepped behind a curtain hung in the corner.

Morganna quickly wiped her eyes.

Because of her.

She crawled into bed and waited for him to follow. Once he was changed, Arthur blew out the candles and climbed in beside her. He pulled Morganna's hair away from her face and kissed her forehead.

"Night," he whispered and turned his back to her.

They had never slept like that before. He would always hold her until they both found rest. Now...

Morganna took a small breath. She reached her arms around Arthur and tickled his waist, moving them further south.

"It's been so long since we—"

"You're ill, Morganna, and I'm exhausted." He removed her hand from him, gave it a gentle pat, and placed it beside her. "Maybe tomorrow, dear. Goodnight."

She leaned away from him. "Yes. You're right." Another wave of nausea rolled over her just as a dark rage plunged into her gut.

"You're always right, Arthur."

Robin hated how Arthur was staring at her. They were in a room full of people, Alistair and Maddy at her sides, Morganna by his and he was giving her *that* look.

He was leaning on one elbow with his fingers tenting his mouth and his sea blue eyes narrowed on her. Even though his fingers covered his lips, she could still see the edge of his mouth straining to stay down. She almost wished he'd just laugh already if it'd stop him from staring at her. He knew she was stalling.

Robin poured another dose of honey on her griddlecakes and began to slowly slice the cakes into small squares. She tried to get twenty-four squares each time. That was six rows and four columns for each cake.

She glanced up. He was still looking at her. She clutched the fork in her hand to stop from swearing.

Robin wanted to move forward with her life, wherever it may lead, but Arthur's stolen glances threatened to pull her back to the past.

The fork scrapped her tongue as she put four squares in her mouth. She looked down ready to poke the next four only to realize her plate was empty.

I lost count. Damn it.

"I think it's time we begin, don't you, Robin?"

Arthur smiled at her as he leaned up from the dining table.

She could feel her stomach flutter and with the flutters came the feeling of bile, as well.

Robin looked at her cousin. Morganna was surprisingly quiet. She wasn't even staring daggers at Robin like she usually did. No, she seemed to be in her own trance, her eyes never leaving the window above Robin's head.

Where are your claws, cousin?

"Robin and I have an idea," Alistair said.

Robin turned to him and saw as his eyes slid from her to Arthur.

Yes. I called this meeting. I'm supposed to be leading this conversation. Time to speak up.

She cleared her throat and wiped her mouth, before casting her gaze on everyone in their small group.

"We've decided on our next step, the next course of action."

The smile faded from Arthur's face. "And what is that

exactly?"

Why was her heart beating so quickly?

"We are going north to Alistair's family," she said, keeping her voice steady. "His aunt is the only one we know who holds any healing knowledge on witch curses. We have to move north."

He had begun shaking his head even before she finished.

Robin fixed her gaze on him. "This is not your choice Arth—"

"Since you have reminded me of that fact on several occasions, I am quite aware my vote on the matter is nulled." He wiped his face with his hands. Then, crossed his arms and leaned towards her.

"And as I've told you before, I don't care. I will not see you hurt, Robin." He set his eyes on her.

She had never wanted to hit someone so badly, well, except Morganna that is. The way he was watching at her brought on a fresh wave of rage...and wanting.

The softness in his eyes, the determination...he shouldn't have been allowed to look at her like that. Not anymore.

Morganna's vision moved between the two. Her teeth dug into the corner of her lips. She had noticed, as well.

Robin steeled herself and let the rage gleam in her eyes. "I never knew you as one to try and lock women in cages, Arthur?"

"You know that's not what I'm doing," he said, gaze still locked on her.

She quirked a brow. "Isn't it?"

"Robin—"

"Let me make something clear." She stared around the room, before finding his eyes again. "Dismiss my decisions all you want but they will still be mine and I will still do as I please. With or without your blessing, I am still leaving for the north."

The veins were pulsing in Arthur's neck.

She rested her head on her fist and looked at him directly. "No one will tell me what to do. I make my own choices."

Maddy patted her knee under the table and Alistair grinned from ear to ear beside her. She could feel their pride building with her own. The flutters stopped in her stomach.

"How dare you speak to him that way?" Morganna had finally managed to find her voice. "After everything we've done for you. After—"

"Lady Morganna," Maddy chimed in with a smile on her face, "I don't think your cousin was done speaking. Were you, Robin?"

The green-haired girl nodded to her friend. Robin sat tall and turned to her cousin. Her blonde tresses seemed more frizzled than they had a moment ago.

"No, I wasn't. I wanted to tell you both I think we may have a plan for killing Cadfen."

Arthur eyed her. "I assume you want to offer yourself up as bait, then?"

"Actually, no." She grinned at him. "We've come up with a different strategy."

"Infiltration," Alistair said with a nod.

Morganna narrowed her eyes. "What do you mean?"

Alistair pulled his white hair from his face. He grabbed utensils from the table and lined them up.

"Here," he said pointing at Robin's plate "is Satbury. And here is Camelot." He gestured to his own dish.

"Camelot knights don't often travel between the two cities," he said. "When they do, it's because of one of four reasons. Either an important event is about to occur and the surrounding counties need to be informed, there is word of an attack, someone from Camelot has died, or the guards need to switch posts."

Arthur nodded. "So, you want to use one of these four methods to get into the castle? Now, the question is which one."

"Exactly," Robin said. "We can't wait around for someone to die or Satbury to be attacked. We need to speed up the process. The only sure way is when the guards switch stations from Satbury to Camelot. Maddy knows the route the guards take and she knows how many switch at once. If we distract them as they make their way back to Camelot, we can attack them, disguise ourselves as knights, and sneak into the castle."

Maddy leaned over the table and followed the trail of utensils from Robin's to Alistair's plate.

"Midway will be safest because it's far enough from Satbury no one will notice any commotion. Plus, it's closest from here. Five guards come and five return. I've watched them from the trees. There's a sort of backroad that leads them to the castle and around the Cursed Forest. Cadfen may have erased it from the maps but it's there. I can describe the route to Alistair and we'll have to stake it out before trying, of course."

"And who exactly will be sneaking into the castle disguised as knights?" Morganna used her own fork to flick at the laid-out utensils. "We can't send anyone and we need a plan for what happens once we're inside." She moved down the trail and turned over a fork and knife, before gazing up at the three friends from under her lashes. "Did you three manage to think of that?"

Alistair moved his hand over the utensils and straightened

them out again. Morganna watched him. Her fork hovered over his hand and Robin was ready to slam her cousin's head against the table if she stabbed him. But she didn't. She placed her fork on the table and tucked her blonde hair behind her ears.

When he was done, Alistair sat up and nodded at his work. He turned to Morganna and offered his hand. "May I have your fork, Lady Morganna?"

Why he and Maddy feel the need to call her "Lady" is beyond my comprehension.

She handed him the fork.

"Thank you. All right. If this is halfway down the road—" he placed Morganna's fork midway--"it is at this point we're going to attack. As I said, there's not much travel between the two, so it's not likely we'll run into any other wagons. But we shouldn't chance it. Maddy will act as the distraction. We'll need two or three others for the infiltration."

"I will be one of the three," Robin said.

Arthur opened his mouth to speak.

"And," she continued, "we believe Lancelot and Alistair should accompany me."

"And why am I not included in this plan?" Arthur asked. He pointed at Morganna's fork. "What I mean is why am I not one of the three?"

"You're too valuable." Everyone turned to stare at Maddy. Her eyes were locked on him.

"I am not of royal blood," he replied. "I understand why Morganna should not be included but fighting and protecting is what I do as a knight."

She nodded. "Yes, and who will protect these people if you were to be captured, tortured, and, eventually, killed?"

Robin could feel a chill run over her skin. She would need to keep that in mind. Death and worse were all real possibilities for this mission.

Arthur's bright blue eyes seemed to dull at Maddy's statement. He shook his head and inhaled a heavy breath, before turning his sights on the table top.

Then, as if it were something she did every day, Maddy reached out and patted Arthur's hand. She peered into his eyes as his gaze lifted to hers.

"These people need you, Sir Arthur." She squeezed his hand. "If the mission fails, there needs to be someone left to make a rescue attempt. Or at least incite a rebellion. We all must play our part. I'll be the distraction and you must remain here. These people would not have even lasted this long without you."

"She's right," Alistair said on Robin's other side. "We need to be strategic about who goes in case…" He met both Maddy and Robin's gaze.

Her heart swelled and Robin could feel her eyes begin to burn. *Later, Robin.*

"In case you fail." Morganna reached out where Maddy held Arthur's hand and gently moved his hand under the table with her own. She turned to Robin. "I understand your thinking, but if that is the case, why is Robin going? True, I am the heir, yet my cousin has no battle experience. I am much better at holding my own than she."

What would it feel like right now if I reached out and cut her throat? Robin eyed the knife less than an inch from her hand. Arthur had his eyes on Morganna. He wouldn't even notice. *Then, at least one of my problems could be solved and maybe I could finally be with--*

Alistair slid the knife onto his plate.

"As tradition dictates, what Cadfen did was an offense against your bloodline and so a representative of that line should be present." He nodded towards Robin. "And believe me, she is quite capable of taking care of herself. Ask the men who tried attacking us during our first journey."

With his white hair and purple eyes, Alistair turned on Robin and shone a huge grin. The dark thoughts receded from her mind. Robin wanted to do nothing more than wrap him in a hug. Sometimes it felt like he was her own personal sun, always warming her, comforting her.

She took in a gulp of air and moved to look at her cousin.

"He's right, Morganna. I will see Cadfen dead in the name of your father, my uncle. If he managed to kill you, the direct line would end."

"So, you've changed your mind about being used as bait, then?" A blonde brow rose.

Robin eased the words out. "When we kill the guards and take their place, Cadfen won't even know I'm among them."

Morganna rolled her eyes. "I—"

"They aren't wrong, Morganna," Arthur said.

Her eyes bulged. "But I can help. I can kill Cadfen. If you come, we can kill him together. And Robin hasn't received half the training I have."

His eyes turned on Robin. She refused to look away and she found herself searching his face.

The lines were creasing under his eyes. There was a strain on his lips.

"Though I think she should remain here, as well, I understand I no longer have a say in the matter."

If Robin was made of air, she was sure she would have deflated that very moment. She clasped her hands together in front of her and beamed.

Finally, he's letting me go.

"When will you all be leaving for the north, then?" Morganna had pressed herself by Arthur's side again.

The three looked at one another.

Robin said, "A week for preparation. Then, departure."

Morganna smirked. "God's speed."

"Would you like me to leave?" Robin asked.

Alistair glanced from Robin to where Edwin stood in the corner of their room.

"You still can't see him?"

She shook her head.

"And I look mad, don't I?"

Robin smirked. "All the more reason for me to leave you to it. I'm sure Maddy's with Fred. We can take him on a short ride around the clearing."

Alistair sighed. "Are you sure? I don't want you to feel put out."

She waved a hand. "Not at all. After this morning's conversation, I could do with some fresh air. I'll leave you to it."

Robin headed to the door.

"By the way?"

"Hm?" She turned and stared at him.

"You were great today, Robin," he said with a smile. "Morganna took quite a few of her own hits." He winked.

Robin's lips curved and she pushed her shoulders back. "I think so, as well. Thank you, Alistair." She stepped through the door and slid it shut behind her.

"Do you like her?" Edwin asked, looking at the door and rocking on his feet.

Alistair chuckled. "Not in the way you may be thinking. She's more like a sister I stumbled upon."

"And how did you stumble upon her again?"

"I thought I told you this story already." Alistair plopped down on the bed and stretched out his legs.

"I want to hear it again," Edwin said. "I don't have many chances for stories now. Well, not good ones anyway."

Alistair cringed as he thought of eternity in the Ether. One's only companion, a constant gray mist and other wandering souls. According to the boy, he could sometimes cross back to the world of the living. When he did, the act always drained him and he wasn't able to stay long, except this time.

Alistair was acting as his anchor.

"Are you going to tell me the story or not?" He tapped his foot and crossed his arms.

Alistair released an exhale. "Fine. I will but the short version. I have other things to tell you, too."

Edwin sat cross-legged on the floor and turned his eyes upward to Alistair.

He started. "I was running late on my deliveries after working an odd job for an innkeeper. I decided to cut through the Cursed Forest to save some time. What I didn't know was my life would be changed forever."

Alistair paused and waited for a reaction.

Edwin sighed.

Guess, it's only good the first time.

"Me and Fred slowly made our way through the twisted and tangled trees. The forest allowed little light inside but something caught my eye."

"The bracelet with the dragon charm?"

Alistair nodded. "Exactly. You have a good memory, Edwin."

He sat straight and smiled. "My parents always told me I was quite clever."

"I'd agree."

He moved his misty form a bit closer. "What happened next, Alistair?"

He cleared his throat. "I found the bracelet hanging from a tree branch. I grabbed it but I noticed something was pulling at my hair. I thought it was Fred. Instead," --he stretched his eyes and stared down at the boy-- "it was the tree branch and it refused to release me. Oh, how we struggled!"

Edwin giggled as Alistair threw himself on the bed and began to roll around. "The tree tried to take me. It had quite a grip. Still, I refused to give up. When I finally got free I grabbed my rusty knife—"

"You should start saying it was a dagger," Edwin chimed.

Alistair narrowed his eyes. "But it wasn't. It was a rusty knife."

The boy shook his head. "Dagger sounds more dramatic. No one wants to hear about an old butter knife."

It's not exactly a butter knife...

"All right," Alistair said, sitting back up. "I grabbed my dagger, prepared to fight whatever creature escaped from the possessed tree."

He puffed out his chest before quirking a brow at Edwin. "An arm emerged. I gripped the dagger. Another arm and, then, I pounced!"

Alistair leapt from the bed and landed in a squat position beside Edwin who watched him with amusement in his eyes.

Alistair held up a finger. "But, at the last second, as I was ready to end the creature, I curved my blade to the side. For it wasn't a monster that emerged from that tree. It was a lady."

"And her name was Robin," Edwin finished.

He nodded and fell back on to the floor. "Yes, it was Robin. Now, are you ready for the other news?"

"That sounds like a very simple name," he said.

"It's actually just her middle name. Her birth name is Gwynevere. She prefers Robin, though."

Edwin looked at the door. "She seems like quite an odd woman."

Those manners definitely need some work.

Alistair had no clue where all this curiosity was coming from. Still, he couldn't blame him for seeking out entertainment when he could.

"Edwin, have you ever heard about the sly fox and the sleeping bear?"

The child's eyes widened. He shook his head.

"Would you like to hear it?" Alistair smiled.

For a moment, Edwin looked like he was going to nod. Then he turned his eyes to floor and his shoulders slacked.

"No," the boy said. "There'll be times for stories once we defeat Cadfen. What else did you have to tell me?"

"Are you sure?"

He nodded.

"All right," Alistair sighed. "Well, first, we'll be going north. Me, Robin, and Maddy."

"The green-haired southerner?"

"Yes, though, you can call her by her name. Once, we reach the north and I figure out if this" --he pointed to his hair--"is another curse, we'll return here and start our plan to defeat

Cadfen."

Edwin perked up.

Alistair smiled. "A good story, isn't it?"

The boy grinned. "The best I've heard. Tell me more."

Chapter Eighteen

obin slipped on her cloak and clipped the hood around her neck. She slid the door closed behind her and made her way down the hall. In her right hand, she held her boots as her bare feet palmed the cold floor. She couldn't risk putting the boots on and someone hearing her leave.

The crumbling castle was quiet. Even the cook had not stirred yet--a fact Robin was very proud of actually. The woman had almost caught her last time. She had made a note to wake earlier in order to avoid the cook and so far it was paying off.

Robin tiptoed to the back of the western tower. She pressed her ear to the door and waited.

It was silent, but she had to be certain. Moving slower than she thought possible, Robin pulled the door open and looked outside.

There weren't any guards. They must have been switching positions around the clearing.

Perfect timing, Robin.

She stuffed her feet into the boots and started outside, making sure to shut the door quietly. Another quick look around and she was off. She reached down to pull up her dress, before remembering she was wearing a tunic and pants.

A smile tugged at her lips. Without hesitation, she ran full-speed, pumping her arms and legs with all she had. Her breath came out in fog in front of her and Robin's chest burned like an evening hearth as she moved deeper into the trees.

This was her time.

She stretched her long legs, enjoying how easily she could move in her new attire.

Dresses may be pretty, but pants are quite useful.

When she reached the crest of the hill, Robin's run slowed to a jog then a walk. She slumped to the ground, landing on her back, and gazed up into the early morning sky. It was a murky, cloudless gray. Always a sure sign of a harsh winter.

She tilted her head back.

The gray was endless and empty. The only intrusion to her vision were tree branches. Their leaves were falling; a few were bare already and in the place of leaves, Robin was left to stare at the thin, ragged branches.

The wind blew and, for a moment, it looked like the branches had stretched, further blocking her view of the sky.

A tension wrapped around her heart. Her mind went back to the feeling of bark covering her, merging her into the tree. The slow *creak* that engulfed her.

She had been a prisoner. She had been without the sky for ten years but there, on the hill and alone, that's all there was.

An endless expanse of sky.

And it was hers.

Robin pressed the bracelet to her chest and closed her eyes.

I'm one step closer today, Uncle Terryn. You will be avenged.

She opened her eyes and stood. As she had done for the past few weeks, Robin turned to face the tree to her right. She took in a small inhale, before reaching under her cloak and pulling out her dagger. She gripped it by the hilt, keeping her hold firm but relaxed.

Another breath.

She pulled her arm back and flung the dagger forward. It scratched the bark, then, fell to the ground.

Robin mentally cursed. She pulled out her second dagger, repeating the motions again. This time the dagger stuck. A joy erupted in her but quickly deflated as the dagger grew limp and then dropped to the earth.

She shook her head.

I'll barely be able to nick an enemy at this rate. Perhaps I should try to improve my close combat skills.

Her mind went back to the men she had slain on her first trip to the east. She was lucky because Alistair was there and they likely didn't expect a woman to fight back. She was proud of herself for proving them wrong. Still, what if Alistair hadn't been there?

Robin huffed and marched over to the tree to retrieve her weapons. A cracking sound reached her ears.

Robin spun around and tossed a dagger forward. Arthur stepped to the side. The knife punctured the earth behind him.

Well, at least that's an improvement.

He glanced between Robin and the blade.

"A little early for weapons practice. My men aren't even up."

"Perhaps, you need to have a conversation with your men, then?"

Robin slid the dagger into her belt, then pounded across the earth as she walked past him to retrieve the other. She turned and glared at him.

She had expected a smile at least. He only stared at her.

"What do you want, Arthur?" Robin sighed.

"I was hoping we could speak."

"About?"

His eyes turned to the clearing. Then, they returned to Robin.

"About us—"

"There is no us." She shook her head. "Not anymore."

"Is that how you really feel?"

"I do." She didn't meet his stare.

"Why won't you look at me, Robin?"

She closed her eyes. She could feel the tears coming, the traitors they were.

"Robin?"

"Because," --she clasped her hands together-- "there is nothing to discuss. Please, Arthur. I hoped I'd be alone. The matter of what we were has been handled. What else is there?"

"I choose you."

Robin heard the words. They filled her mind with a disarming fog that made her narrow her brows and shake her head.

It couldn't be real. She had to be hearing things.

"I choose you, Robin."

She had heard them again--the words that whispered her secret desire, something she knew was still present but had long since stopped acknowledging.

All the cold left her, replaced by a spark of hope.

Why are you so stupid?

She attempted to keep her breath steady.

"You shouldn't say things you don't mean, Arthur."

"I mean it. Every word." Not a hesitation or a flinch.

The hope grew brighter, burning from her core through her body.

"Robin," he said and took a step towards her.

She did not retreat.

"What happened between Morganna and me... I think we both needed it. We were both looking for something to help the pain. It seemed right at the moment." He cleared his throat, before meeting her eyes again.

"What I've realized since you've returned is that I-I want to do right by Morganna. But I want to be with you. I want you, Robin."

There was a hitch in his breath and Robin's own chest was rising and falling rapidly.

With familiarity and ease, Arthur closed the space between them. He reached his hand up and took hers in his, never breaking eye contact.

"There has never been another and will always be only you, Robin."

Foolish.

She pressed her lips against his and enclosed his face between her hands. The light stubble on his jaw prickled against her palms and chin. His mouth moved with hers, a growing intensity in their pressure. Soon, his hand had pressed against her back and pressed her to his body. With the other, he tilted her head back.

Robin succumbed. His tongue swept across her bottom lip and she realized there was too much separating them.

She broke their kiss and unclipped her cloak. Her mouth moved down to his throat and a satisfied moan escaped his lips. He moved his hand across her shoulder and turned her vision upward to him.

"I am so sorry for all the pain I caused." Arthur moved a stray hair from her face. "I will never leave you again. And when we take back Camelot, Elizabeth--if she did not die that night--will pay dearly."

Robin snuggled against him. She pressed her face into his neck and inhaled.

Sweet and salty like honey by the sea.

"I am not the same person I was ten years ago, Arthur," she whispered. "Are you sure you still want me?"

"There is no greater desire in me."

She closed her eyes. Robin had waited so long for those words.

"Do you doubt me?" he asked.

She removed her face from the crook of his neck. She shook her head. "No."

His blonde hair was like a halo even under the foggy sky.

"Good," he said. "Because I have something for you."

Still smiling, Arthur reached behind him and pulled free a dagger. Gripping the knife by its blade, he offered it to Robin.

Her eyes traveled from the tip of the blade to the end of the hilt. The hilt itself was bone white and shaped into twisted curves like vines. The vines moved around one another, tucking above and under each other. The blade was beautiful. Robin knew it had to be metal but at just the right angle with the right amount of light the blade appeared translucent. Almost like glass.

"It's yours," he said.

"Why? I don't think I'm exactly in need of another dagger." She gestured towards the two in her belt.

He sighed. "You're not. But this isn't any dagger, Robin. Here, let me show you."

Arthur stepped under a tree's shade. He held up a finger and pressed the knife's tip into the flesh until blood dripped. The drop trickled down the blade and Arthur was wrapped in shadow.

Where he had been standing, there was now nothing.

Robin stood frozen. It was almost like her arms and legs were pinned in place. She blinked but what she saw remained the same. Arthur was gone.

"Robin."

She knew his voice, but she still jumped, stumbling backward and almost falling to the ground. He had appeared a few trees to the left of his original spot. She looked him up and down. Her heart pounded in her chest.

"When did you become a ca—"

"I'm not," he stated and stepped from under the tree. "I have no magic. It's the blade, not me."

Robin crossed her arms and glared at him.

"Do you really think I'd sell my soul?"

"I'm not sure what to think right now to be honest with you."

"The dagger is the same as Excalibur except while Excalibur repels magic, the blade uses it."

She narrowed her eyes. "And what did you do to get it?"

"It was given to me," he said. "Almost the same way Excalibur was."

"No witches?"

Arthur shook his head. "None that I saw."

He walked to Robin and offered the blade again. She watched him.

"Its name is Carnwennan," he stated. "It has the power to shield its user in shadow. Simply prick your finger to disappear. Then, wipe the blood clean to reappear. Here, take it."

Robin eyed the blade briefly, before rolling her eyes and grabbing the hilt.

"Why are you giving this to me, Arthur?"

A smirk played across his lips. "For one, Carnwennan acts as an insurance policy you'll return."

Now it was her turn to smile. "And why wouldn't I?"

He put his hands on his hips and blew out his cheeks as he took a long breath.

"Well," --he rocked on his heels-- "You were always one for a little adventure. I don't want you gallivanting off on some other journey before you return here. Not to mention..."

He clasped her face between his hands. His eyes roamed over her features.

"I want to protect you even when I'm not beside you. If you ever need to escape a situation, the blade can be useful. You can't come in contact with any light while using it though. It breaks the spell."

Robin placed a palm on his cheek. She stared into his eyes. "All those years in that damn tree and I never forgot your eyes. Blue like the eastern seas."

He pressed a soft kiss to her lips. "Return to me and I'll take you there. It's only a two-day trip by horse."

She raised a brow. "You're giving me no choice but to return, aren't you?"

"I've missed too much time with you already. As soon as we can end all this, our real lives can begin."

Robin gave him a small grin. She stared at the blade between them.

"And have you told Morganna of your decision?"

Arthur nodded.

"And what did she say?"

He stepped back and wiped his face. "Nothing. She just turned away from me and left the room. I'm not sure how to mend the wound I have inflicted. I--I will never forgive myself for what I have put both you and your cousin through."

"What's done is done," Robin said and slid the dagger into a belt loop.

I will not live in the past. This is another step forward.

"Yes. I'm afraid it is," he said, rubbing the hairs on his chin.

"You know, Arthur, you never did tell me how you got Excalibur."

He quirked a blonde brow. "Another reason for you to return then."

"Really?" She scoffed. "Why can't you just tell me?"

"You seem to like men of mystery. I have to keep something unspoken between us."

"Yes, and you seem to like being a pain," she retorted.

He grinned. "That's usually what I say to you."

"I guess it's true for both of us, then." She clasped her hands behind her back and walked up to him. "I was shocked when you returned with Excalibur. You nearly scared the life out of me when you used Carnwennan. I wonder what other magical weaponry you have stumbled upon?"

His smiled widened. "I'll only say you should think of that dagger as an engagement gift."

Robin's eyes doubled in size. Arthur grabbed her and pressed his mouth against hers. She fell into him, his familiar touch pulling her in. Yet when their kiss broke, and while he stared down at her with glossy eyes, Robin could only say one thing.

"No."

Morganna thought of drowning herself. She could steal a horse, ride to the sea and tie stones round her ankles. Then she'd walk out until the foamy water consumed her.

It would be so simple and yet she hesitated.

She hadn't been back to the room since Arthur had confessed his love for Robin the night prior. He had spilled everything to her then. Every word was like a slice to her chest and her abdomen. It was as if both her heart and the baby had spilled from her. She felt empty.

Her mouth was salty from tears, the earth underneath her was cold, starting to freeze with the approaching winter.

Maybe I'll just lie out here until I'm dead.

She wrapped her arm around her stomach.

"I am so sorry you never had a chance, little baby. I know you would have been beautiful."

She tucked her knees under her chin and held them there. The wind blew and a chill ran over her skin.

Morganna was sure her nose was red. It had started dripping some time ago and she now sniffled like a child. Except before, when she actually was a child and the cold gave her a dripping nose or a harsh cough, someone was there to take care of her. Usually, one of the servants.

They'd cover her in blankets and braid her hair as she fell to sleep. They'd rub a warm cloth over her face that had been soaked in water and rosemary. Her father would worry like a mother hen.

Yes, everyone cared about her. Everyone worried over her.

But then Robin...

The cold acceptance turned into icy spikes. Morganna balled her hands into fists.

The day she arrived nothing was the same. She took everything. Everything!

The forest was quiet around her. Yet, her mind roared with memories.

The first day Robin arrived, her father had no time for her. He was so busy getting his niece settled, though she didn't seem very grateful for any of it. At first, she hardly spoke. She wouldn't eat, and then she began to throw tantrums like a toddler.

"The ungrateful brat," Morganna whispered to herself through clenched teeth.

There was her first birth celebration at Camelot, as well. So much work for one person, particularly one who wasn't even in line for the throne. Still, everyone put forth their best, only for Robin to run to her room halfway through and refuse to return to the party.

"Wasteful."

Morganna had begun rocking herself. The arm around her stomach tightened and she grabbed the charm around her necklace.

Memory after memory assaulted her, pushing into her mind whether she wanted them to or not. She didn't remember them all, some seemed more fiction than fact, but she knew they were real. She knew they had happened and only she knew how horrible her cousin truly was.

She pulled her blonde hair over her face and took in several breaths.

You're safe now. She's not here.

An image of Arthur appeared in her mind--a younger Arthur, before he was a knight. His face had been a bit rounder. His jaw was not arched and defined like it was as an adult. No, he was quite simple actually. Even his hair had grown blonder the older he became. But Morganna had loved him as soon as she laid eyes on him.

A tear slipped down her face as she remembered the heat that had blossomed in her cheeks upon meeting him for the first time. She had seen Arthur's father before. His mother had died in childbirth, so, Morganna never had the chance.

She would have loved me, I'm certain.

His father had quickly became notable for his skill with a sword. The two had started at some small village in the kingdom before finding their way to Camelot and, eventually, into the castle alongside her father.

Morganna had been twelve. It was Arthur's first time at such a royal event and he was obviously uncomfortable. They found comradery in their distaste for adult discussions and the boring happenings of the party. After that night, she pined over him for a year until...

"Robin."

Morganna turned on her knees. Her hands dug into the

ground beneath her and she screamed into the earth. The dirt was cold and moist between her fingers. She imagined them being warmed by Robin's blood. Nothing would be right until she had it. The throbbing cold inside her wouldn't wane until Robin was dead.

It was the only way.

She pressed a hand to her abdomen, her head pushed at an angle into the earth.

"She will not win. She will not take you away from me."

Morganna moved her hand from her stomach up to her neck. Her thumb and forefinger rubbed the dragon charm. She wrapped her fingers around the necklace. Her jaw ached at how tightly she had it clenched.

A flash of young Arthur confident but uncomfortable at his first royal affair.

Robin, dark-haired, blue eyed and evil.

She yanked the necklace free and tossed it away.

Her breath was fog in front of her as she sat straight and looked forward.

Morganna's whole body shook but no longer with cold from the weather, no. With a chilling determination.

Tremors continued to run through her as she struggled to her feet. Her legs had fallen asleep at her immobility. She was ready now.

Morganna stood and swayed from side to side.

"I will win," she whispered and took her first step forward.

The trees rustled around her as if in agreement.

She smiled and nodded to them as she moved deeper into the trees.

"Yes. I will."

Maddy stood in the nearly empty clearing and yawned into the daylight. She stretched her arms and smiled up at the sun, though the gray sky tried to dull its shine.

"Excited for tomorrow's journey?" Alistair stepped beside her with Fred and another horse in hand. He had been taking them out for exercise.

His purple eyes were full of light and he hadn't stopped smiling since they had started their morning. She knew he had not seen his northern family in nearly a year.

"I don't think I could ever be as excited as you," she replied. "You've got more than enough for all three of us."

He laughed and ran his fingers through his hair.

"We're only taking two horses?" she asked.

He nodded. "Arthur offered three but Robin and I refused. They need the horses for work and winter is fast approaching."

"Hm. I assume he and Robin argued about this."

"Your assumption would be right. Common sense won out in the end though."

"Well that's one victory."

Alistair stroked Fred's mane. His eyes turned north. "I know the trip won't be easy. Still, I'm happy at the thought of seeing my home." He paused and tapped his finger on the reins. "And for my family to meet you...and Robin."

A warmth blossomed in Maddy and she knew her cheeks had turned a light pink.

Alistair cleared his throat. "I should...maybe, someone—"

"Has there been any news about Lady Morganna?" Maddy asked, turning to him, a small smile on her lips.

This question seemed to sober him. He lost all his fluster and shook his head.

"Not since yesterday."

"And how is Robin handling it?" She already knew the answer.

"Considering her cousin tried to kill her, I can't blame her for the lack of love. I don't suppose you would either?"

"No." Maddy sighed and turned her eyes back to the sky.

Alistair watched her, and she could feel more heat rising in her cheeks.

She cocked her head and stared at him. "I know it's been several weeks, but it's still odd seeing you with white hair."

He scoffed. "You think you feel odd about it? I feel like I've aged several decades."

Maddy giggled. "You don't look old, Alistair. It's only the color that's different."

"No, no. I assure you there are some wrinkles creeping up too."

"Where?"

He gestured to his face. "All over. I look like a rotten vegetable."

"I thought we women were supposed to be concerned about our looks," she said, a teasing tone in her voice.

Alistair sighed and leaned against the new horse. "Perhaps I am just a sensitive soul."

"Hmm. Perhaps. I always thought of you as sweet."

The rising pink in his cheeks contrasted the white of his hair. Maddy chuckled, her own hear beating a little fast.

Alistair cleared his throat. "Madelia, could I ask you a question?"

"Of course."

He took her hand. She glanced from their clasped hands to his eyes. The humorless look he had punctured her core and something enticing spread through her.

"Robin told me a bit more about your mother and brother," he said. "I...I'm not sure when this will all be over. But when it is, I want to go to King Essen's lands with you and reunite you with them."

He took hold of her other hand and Maddy found her stomach had turned into knots.

Alistair's eyes briefly drifted to the ground, before returning to hers. He moved his thumbs along her wrists.

"Maddy, I'm not sure what my aunt will tell me when we arrive home. We don't know right now what the creature inflicted me with before Edwin killed her."

He took a hard swallow. His hands trembled.

Her eyes searched his face. "You're scared, aren't you?"

"Yes," he whispered. "I feel fine, but I have a bad feeling the witch still has her claws in me somehow."

He shook his head.

"If I am to leave this world or lose my mind," --the words were slow and heavy-- "I want to spend my time making sure you, Robin, and my family are taken care of."

Maddy's throat began to constrict.

"Because," he continued, "you, of all people, Maddy deserve to be happy. After everything—"

She closed the space between them. Her arms wrapped around his shoulders and the smooth skin of his neck became her comfort. His breath breezed into her hair, tickling the strands and his chest rose and fell beneath her own.

Alistair's muscles tensed, then, eased under her. His arms encircled her, and his fingers found their way into her dark green tresses.

Maddy's mind had a single thought.

You can never leave me.

Chapter Nineteen

A listair was certain he was going to lose a thumb. He had accepted his fate. He was going to be a thumb-less white-haired old man and live out the rest of his days as such. There really was no other option and since neither the cold nor snow showed signs of letting up, he figured better to be thumb-less than dead.

I've been gone from the north too long. The cold never bothered me before.

He looked to his left. Maddy's teeth hadn't stopped chattering since they left the last village. It had been small, mostly farmers and travelers. The sky had been clear, so they had stopped at the local inn to rest and warm themselves with a bowl of soup.

Little did they know, less than twenty minutes into their departure a storm would hit, releasing every snowflake there was from the sky.

And now both they and the earth were covered, the broth's warmth a distant memory.

"Are you all right?"

Robin's voice broke Alistair's thoughts. He turned to respond but her sights weren't on him. She was staring at Maddy, brows knit together and eyes narrowed.

The hood of Maddy's cloak bobbed up and down but the movement was staggered.

Alistair tugged Fred to stand closer to the horse Arthur had given them, Mary. He placed a hand on Maddy's shoulder. Short bursts of vibrations ran through his palm and Maddy's teeth chattering echoed in the storm.

"Maddy, may I pull down your hood?" he asked.

Another nod.

Alistair released his hands from the reins and shook them a bit, before tugging Maddy's hood down. Suddenly, the cold was not what chilled him.

We should have taken the third horse.

"What's wrong?" she asked. "Is it bad?"

"Here." He reached into one of the pouches and pulled out a small blanket.

"I want you to wrap this around your face like a scarf and tie it tight. Do you hear me, Maddy?"

"Yes," she stuttered out.

"Alistair, what's going on?" Robin darted her gaze between the two of them.

"You and Maddy have to go ahead without me."

"What!" they both shouted.

"Listen," he said with a slow exhale. "Frost has started to coat Maddy's face. Her cheeks are becoming a dark red."

"I don't understand," Maddy said voice still quivering.

He took her face in his hands, hoping to transfer some heat to his companion.

"It means you've been exposed to the cold for too long and your body is suffering."

"What are we to do?" Robin's voice was shrill. "Your family's home is still nearly a day's trip away. We won't reach until nightfall."

Alistair shook his head. He pulled at Fred's reins and the horse came to a stop.

He hopped off Fred. "We're going to reach there before nightfall. You and Maddy take the horses and go ahead."

Robin's eyes squinted into a glare. She opened her mouth, but Alistair waved a hand.

"Robin, you can give me a lashing later. If you two don't go now, Maddy will—"

At that moment, the green-haired girl turned to him, her light green eyes glassy and distant.

He bit his tongue and moved back to Robin.

"Continue heading east now. A carved-out path will appear. Follow it. When it comes to the fork, take the road to the right and ride until you hear the ocean. Make sure Maddy keeps moving, even if it's a little kicking."

"What about you?" Maddy asked.

She reached for him and he grasped her hand.

"I will be fine," he replied. "Once you get to my home, ask for Garron and Una. Have them send my cousins back for me. Two horses are better than one, so Robin will ride Fred and guide you on Mary. No discussions."

He released Maddy's hands and grabbed another pair of gloves and a canister of water while she adjusted in her seat.

"I will keep her safe and we will come back for you," Robin said, daring a look at him.

He nodded. "I know you will. Now go."

Robin pulled their horses along, lightly kicking Fred's sides until he picked up speed and Mary matched it.

They stayed in Alistair's sight until the large white snowflakes blocked them from his vision.

Alistair could still manage to walk easily in the snow, though he wasn't sure how long that was going to last. Already it was reaching his ankles and he didn't expect his cousins would come looking for him for several hours. Not until the evening at least.

Walk as fast as possible, drink plenty of water, and then find shelter somewhere I'll be easily spotted.

His uncle Garron had taught Alistair and all his children how to survive in the snow. Thankfully Alistair had paid attention, though he never thought he'd find himself caught in a storm. His aunt Una always ensured everyone was accounted for before a heavy snowfall came in.

What I would do for a pot of her bone stew...

His mouth watered. Alistair tried to focus on that memory as he trudged forward.

The memory of warm soup eaten around a raging fire and being surrounded by his large cousins with their cozy nature.

Yes, that's what he felt. Comfort, warmth, ease. Not the freezing cold.

His aunt would wrap him in blankets. Since he was the smallest of the bunch, she always took extra pains to ensure he was suited and ready. A fact his cousins never let him live down.

Alistair's cloak rushed left and hung flailing in the wind. The wind whipped by him, simultaneously pushing him forward and trying to knock him to the ground.

He stomped his feet hard into the ground and grabbed his cloak. Not focusing on the razor-like cold that had snuck across his body, he wrapped the cloak around him once more and marched.

Do not stop. Your journey is not over yet.

As the snow continued to fall around him, Alistair wondered how well he blended in. He doubted there were any robbers out in the weather but if there were, he'd be a hard target to find.

His hair had blown in his face and he tucked the white strands back behind his ear.

Perhaps, you're more useful than I think. I doubt Robin and Maddy are fond of you though.

His pulse quickened. He shouldn't have thought about Maddy.

The idea he could reach his family's home and she be taken by the frost made him walk faster. But panicking would do him no good.

The snow had passed his ankles. Moving a foot forward was becoming more difficult.

Alistair had to reach her. He had to return to all of them.

There were many things unsaid, especially with Maddy, especially when she had embraced him without hesitation, something she had never done before.

Maddy had always been friendly and kind, yet her space was her own and touching was limited.

And she had never said, much less done, anything to make Alistair think she could have feelings for him. But that day, the day before they departed, the way she sighed into his neck and pulled him to her, he thought maybe there was something there. He only needed to get a hold of it.

A light sizzle of heat swept over his scalp. He closed his eyes while the pain subsided and then turned to look at Edwin.

"You decided to stop by then?"

The boy was almost impossible to see being translucent and surrounded by white.

"Not exactly. I wanted to see how your plans were going." He peered around him. "It doesn't seem you've reached your aunt's yet."

"Uh, yes, you could say that," he replied. "So, you haven't come to keep me company?"

Edwin nodded but he did not look at Alistair.

"I came to tell you something too."

Please tell me Cadfen is dead, Morganna has been found and has ascended the throne and that my aunt has bone stew waiting for me.

"It's about your parents."

Alistair nearly tripped over his own feet. He spun around—as well as he could—to face Edwin. The cold became irrelevant. His blood pumping fast enough to keep him warm for a fortnight.

The wind blew past him and his mouth dried.

"What did you say?" he asked after several deep breaths.

Edwin floated through the air and took hold of Alistair's hands.

"I found your parents," he said. "Well, they found me actually."

Alistair clenched his teeth together. His mind was racing with questions and they all wanted to come out at once.

"I didn't know...could I have seen them in the Ether? When we were there?"

The boy shook his head. "No, they're in a different part. Somewhere I've never been."

"What do you mean?"

"I mean that I can't go where they came from. They had to find me."

Alistair was sure his palms were covered in sweat, despite the temperature.

"And what did they say? Did they—"

"They told me they were proud of you," he stated. "That they love you and they're glad you found a home with your aunt and uncle."

Foggy wisps of steam were leaving Alistair's body as he released trembling exhales.

"And," Edwin continued, "they said they like Maddy. She'll be good for you. Does that mean you're going to marry her?" He gazed at Alistair.

That was not a question he was prepared to venture into with his young friend.

"How were they, Edwin? Did they look well?"

He nodded. "They looked...happy."

A flood of relief pooled from his gut, easing all the tension away. He could feel his eyes burning but refused to cry. He needed to conserve the water, after all.

"One more thing," the boy said. "They wanted you to know they think you're doing what's right. You've done justice to their name."

It made no sense to do so, but Alistair squatted down and hugged Edwin to him.

The young boy hugged him back.

"You have no idea how happy you've just made me," Alistair said.

"Really?"

He nodded. "I have to ask one more thing of you, though, Edwin. If you happen to see my parents again, tell them...I was angry for a while, at them. But I understand now. I know they had to send me away."

Alistair blinked to clear away the tears. "And...tell them I love them. Will you?"

The ghost smiled. "If they visit again. I'll relay the message."

Alistair sighed. "You're a good boy, Edwin. A proper young man." He stood up. "Will you be staying with me until my cousins arrive?"

"If you'd like," the boy replied.

"I would but you should prepare yourself."

"For what?" Edwin asked, his lips pouted and brows drawn.

Alistair smiled. "To run. We have a journey to complete."

He tugged his cloak tightly around him and lifted his legs as high as he could, then began pounding through the snow. He pumped his arms in sync with his legs and kept his eyes forward, looking towards home.

"They're coming," Edwin shouted as he flew through the storm.

"Y-you s-saw them?" Alistair asked.

"Yes, they'll be here soon."

He tried to respond but his mouth was too jittery. Instead, he nodded and kept moving through the snow that was now nearly to his knees.

Night had fallen and with darkened sky came freezing temperatures. He had only stopped once to drink water. The snow had somehow caught up with him.

His muscles ached in protest to his movements. His mind was becoming stagnant. He could only think of the cold.

"I see them!" Edwin screamed. "They're there. Look, Alistair, look!"

Alistair tilted his head up and stared into the distance. There were two figures approaching on horseback. Still, they were too far away for him to know they were his cousins. The wind that had been whipping around him died down for a moment and deep voices reached his ears.

"'Ello, 'ello! Where's our middle-born cousin?"

"Alistair! If you've turned into an ice sickle, I'm taking your share of the bone stew."

They were still several yards away yet at the speed they approached, Alistair knew they'd be hauling him on one of their horses soon.

The sound of thudding hooves grew closer. Alistair breathed a sigh of relief.

He was home.

"Aw, Alistair, you look a bit like those caterpillars the children read about in their picture books." His cousin Brima tucked another blanket around him. He had forgotten how blonde her hair was. All his cousins actually. Blonde hair with piercing silver eyes. Except Brima had streaks of gray in her hair now.

She smiled down at her frozen cousin. Her squared jawline matched well with her smooth cheekbones and round eyes. Brima was nearly an identical match to her mother.

"More like a newborn waiting to be fed," his cousin Farren said as he wiped soup off his mouth.

Aunt Una swatted a spoon against the back of his head.

Farren, in all his timber and muscle, flinched and scooted away from his mother.

"What was that for?"

"Eating like a heathen. We have guests and you can't manage your dinner properly."

Uncle Garron tipped his head back and slurped, drips of soup getting into the long beard that coated his face. Aunt Una raised the spoon in his direction and the bowl found its place back on the table.

He cleared his throat. "Forgot myself for a minute."

Una narrowed her eyes once more before walking around to the other side of the fire where Maddy and Robin were seated.

"More soup girls?" she said. "Bone Stew's a hearty meal for these harsh storms."

Maddy, who had square bandages on her cheeks and was almost as wrapped up as Alistair, glanced from her empty bowl to Una.

"If you're sure it's okay—"

"More than okay!" Una snatched her bowl and filled it to the brim. "We don't get guests often. Have to make sure we leave a good impression."

She handed the bowl back to Maddy and turned her grin on Robin.

"And you?"

"I'm quite full actually." Robin had finished her soup and now sat cross-legged around the fire.

Una gave her a pat on the shoulder. "Well, if you change your mind, we've got plenty. Brima?"

The young woman stood to help her mother. Alistair's eyes drifted over the room.

Not much had changed. The stone walls were mostly bare aside from knitted blankets and decorative flags. The back rooms were separated from the main room by thin blankets and in the center of the ceiling was an opened window where the smoke from the kitchen and living room could blow out.

The door swung open and in stepped Olen, Alistair's second oldest cousin, and Deanna, the youngest.

"Horses are put away and the stables are locked up," he said, kicking the door closed behind him. Deanna skipped over to Alistair.

She perched her chin in her hands, grinning.

"Hi!"

"Hello, Deanna."

"Are your hands warmed yet?"

"Um," --Alistair tried to move his hands. He wasn't sure if their immobility was from the cold or how tightly his aunt had wrapped him.

Deanna pulled her white covered hood down and fluffed out her hair. Like Brima, it had the streaks of gray running through it.

"If they are, I'd like my hair braided now."

"Is that all I'm good for?" Alistair asked, his lips turning up at the corners.

She turned her head to the side. "Hmm, no. But it's something you're really good at." She grabbed her neck-length hair and pulled it over her shoulder. Then, her eyes landed on a strand of Alistair's hair. It had fallen out from under all the covering.

"Where's your silver?" she asked.

"It wasn't the snow?" Olen took a seat beside Alistair, a large bowl in hand. "I thought you had just been covered."

"Oy, Alistair. Don't tell me ya dyed ya hair white?" Farren chuckled.

"Maybe it's popular for men in the middle kingdom," said Brima. She took a seat next to Alistair and showed her hair. "Gray streaks are very popular here. Deanna and I like to stay up on the latest fashion, isn't that right?"

The little girl nodded.

"So, why did you dye your hair?" Olen asked again.

Amidst his cousins, he found Maddy and Robin. They both gave a short nod.

He cleared his throat.

"There's a lot I have to tell you."

Chapter Twenty

Morganna pinched her shoes together and leaned slightly forward on the branch. She stretched her neck as far as it could go before peering at the earth below her. She kept her breaths short and shallow.

The forest was quiet, not even the wind blew. Animals did not scurry, chirp, or howl. The only noise touching her ears was the nearly inaudible sound of her breathing. Aside from that, there was deadly silence and the trees stood like statues in a graveyard.

Snap!

Morganna's eyes eased right. The tree branches were blocking her full view, but she could still see them. Between the crooked and tangled twigs, six men approached the tree she hid in. They walked slowly and with deliberate steps. Their eyes peered around them and the closer they came into view, Morganna saw they were walking in formation. Their weapons were sheathed, though.

She leaned back with her toes still pinched together. Her back rested against the tree trunk.

Don't breathe. Stay quiet.

The last two men of the formation were under her tree now. If they looked up and leaned their head at a good angle they'd see her. But they didn't. They barely glanced at any of the trees as they moved beyond her. After using an agonizing amount of patience, Morganna released a breath.

She knew hiding in the trees would not be an option next time. The faster winter approached, the fewer leaves there were to shield her. She had been lucky.

Morganna tested her limbs, waking them from staying poised for so long. She climbed down the tree and jumped the last few feet. Once she had dusted her clothes off, she moved perpendicular to the direction the men had been walking.

She didn't run. A rapidly moving image would sooner be spotted with so many eyes in the forest. Morganna was surprised they had continued their pursuit. Since her first day among the wild, she had moved deeper into the woods, past two crests at this point. Yet Arthur's men still came searching for her every day. Only now they didn't shout out her name, their voices echoing in the forest to announce their presence.

Now, they were quiet and they were tense. She was their target but they no longer wanted her to know they were searching.

At times, she wanted to return to the castle. She wanted to reveal herself to the men and be escorted into Arthur's arms who surely was concerned about her. Why else would he continuously send out search parties?

But he never came himself and Morganna was forced to accept the truth.

He wanted her back not as his lover but as his queen. She was the heir to the middle-kingdom throne. They needed a trophy to conquer Cadfen and she was it.

Her stomach knotted. She fell against a tree and covered her face as tears burned behind her eyelids.

How did my life come to this?

Tears streamed from her eyes, but she shook them away. Her hand moved from her face to her abdomen. What once was flat was now slightly rounded. She had finally started to show, though it was only a small bump.

She smoothed her palms across her stomach.

We have no time for tears. There's too much to do.

Morganna continued her way through the forest. Soon she came to a little dip in the land. On the opposite side of the dip were several broken branches. Behind those branches was her new home.

She looked around before moving the branches aside and climbing in to her hovel. Based on the size, Morganna had thought the structure had once belonged to some of Issin's people who fled once Essen's army invaded. They could have hid in it for days until they were either captured and sorted or made their way to one of the other kingdoms.

Once she had made her way inside, she crawled as far back as the tunnel could go. There it opened into a large room. She couldn't stand at her full height. Her neck would have to bend slightly or she'd have to fold her knees some. Still, there was plenty of space for her legs to stretch out.

Morganna reached around for the torch and stones. Once her hand wrapped around the torch, she quickly lit it with the stones and placed it against the wall. It was time to get to work.

She grabbed extra blankets and wrapped them around herself while she gazed at the dirt outline. Last time she snuck back into the castle, Arthur hadn't been there and snatching materials had been easy. She knew the guards' rounds and avoided them, walking through the halls with relative ease. That wouldn't be the case on her next attempt after being gone for so long. She'd also be carrying Robin, much heavier than food and covers.

Morganna reached to her side and grabbed some strips of meat from a pouch. Her eyes roamed over the map.

She should be back from the north in two or three weeks. Then, they will attempt to take back Camelot. I will only have a small window to take her.

She sighed and ran her hands through her hair. The blonde tresses her father had once compared to the sun were now dingy and tangled. Even her fingernails had darkened with mud caked under them.

Morganna flicked dirt from under her thumbnail, then returned her attention.

Robin was hardly ever alone. If it wasn't Arthur, it was Lancelot peeking at her like the mongrel he was. She had never understood Arthur's fondness for the boy. She knew he was of bad character after two weeks of him staying at the castle. His eyes always followed the young women around as they went about their daily tasks. Arthur said he never noticed it. Men seemed to be oblivious about things like that.

And then there's that filthy southerner and the peasant. If he was really attacked by a witch, they've apparently lost some of their skill.

A smirk pulled at her lips. She traced the map with her fingers until they landed on the stables--the only place Robin was likely to be alone.

She walks that work horse every morning. I could get close, wait until she came for him and—

The torch flame went out. A cold settled in the hovel.

Morganna again grabbed for the torch and stones but they fumbled in her hands. The cold had pierced her, and her teeth chattered as her hands trembled.

"Damn winter winds," she cursed.

Her hand clasped the torch's base, the fire immediately came to life, and the room lit up with another visitor present.

Morganna screamed and stumbled backward from the shadow. The light fell from her hands and she raced to hold it up again. Once she could, Morganna gazed around the room, turning the flame in every direction. The figure was gone but her heart would not quiet.

She took in long, hard breaths. Then, a rotting stench filled the space and a feeling that could best be described as a sharp rock nailed into her skull, spread across Morganna's face. She groaned and leaned forward, running away from the pain and odor.

The torch fell beside her, casting its glow opposite where she rested. And there she saw the shadow again. Wisps of black fog that held together in a disgusting form and smears of red for a face. The thing was small enough that from a distance one would have thought it a child wearing dark clothing. But Morganna was very close to the creature and its spew of red.

It leaned its head from side to side, each time at a perfect cornered angle. What appeared to be the mouth turned up into a smile.

Morganna's mind blanked but for one single thought.

My baby.

She lunged for the tunnel. The monster was quicker. It blocked her path, still smiling, still leaning its head side to side.

Morganna backed herself across from the creature. She held up the torch's flames towards it and gritted her teeth.

"Whatever hell hole you've climbed from you will return to," she spat. Her hands weren't steady and her dirty hair hung wild around her.

Still, she pushed the torch towards the inky black creature.

The monster paid no attention. Its sight was leveled on Morganna.

When she lunged again, the creature moved to the side and squatted where she had drawn the castle's outline. It picked up the stick Morganna had used and scratched out her drawing.

"What are you doing," Morganna screamed. "Leave it alone!" She moved forward, yet the tremors that ran through her body held her back.

It looked at Morganna and began writing in the dirt. After a few minutes, the monster stepped back. It pointed to the patch of earth between them.

Morganna gnashed her teeth together and gripped the torch in her hand. She sidled along the wall, then leaned forward, glancing between the monster in front of her and the dirt beneath her.

I WANT TO HELP.

The message was little more than chicken scratch, but it came through clear enough. Morganna looked at the shadow.

"What are you?"

The shadow jerked. It turned its head to one side but its eyes looked at the ground. Then, again, it put the stick into the earth.

A WITCH. I DON'T WANT TO LIE.

A new fear erupted inside Morganna. It felt like her heart had dropped into her stomach but still beat within her, sending shots of childhood nightmares pulsing through her. Her hearing became hollow and her gaze slid to the tunnel.

A scratching sound.

DON'T. The message read.

Morganna waited.

I WANT TO HELP.

"Help?" The word broke her like a hoarse cough. She shook her head. "Help with what?"

MURDER.

She narrowed her eyes. The thing had been spying on her.

YOU CALL HER ROBIN. YOU WANT TO KILL HER. BUT YOU CAN'T.

"And how the hell would you know what I can and cannot do?"

It pointed at Morganna's stomach. She instinctively placed her hand over the area.

"You will not have my child's soul."

IF I HELP—

"I said no!"

The torch went out only to relight a moment later. The monster's mouth had shaped into a long oval that slowly shrunk, releasing a shrill creaking noise. Morganna covered her ears but did not move her eyes away. She stared the monster straight into its spew of red.

The noise came to a halt. Morganna stepped towards the beast.

"Never," she hissed.

It tapped the stick on the ground.

I CAN HELP YOU BECOME STRONG. WE KILL EVERYONE YOU WANT.

She raised a brow. "And what would you be getting in return?"

FREEDOM. NOT SUPPOSED TO BE HERE. BUT I WANT FREEDOM.

"From who?"

FATHER.

Morganna blinked. "Your father? Do witches even have fathers?"

It nodded.

HE FED ME UNTIL I WAS BORN AGAIN. HE WILL FEED ME NOW. HE IS MY FATHER.

Cadfen.

Morganna tapped her fingers against her waist. If the creature wanted her dead, she would have been, and the baby inside her empty of life. But it hadn't attacked. It had only watched and offered.

WINTER WILL BE HERE SOON. YOU WON'T SURVIVE. BABY WILL DIE. I WILL HELP YOU LIVE.

Morganna's fingers steadied on her hip. "And how could I help you escape? How can I help you find your freedom?"

WE SHARE BODY. BUT SOUL IS YOURS. I ONLY WANT ONE THING.

"Which is?"

TO TAKE BODY FOR MY OWN ONCE A MONTH. AND TO EAT ALL I WANT WHEN I COME OF AGE. NO PUNISHMENT LIKE FATHER DOES.

So Cadfen keeps the witches in line. The peasant boy was right.

Morganna reached for her dragon charm, then, cursed herself for doing so. Her neck had been bare of it for over a week now and she still had the need to clasp it. Before, she and Arthur had worked together to rebuild Issin's castle and start their new life. They were each other's consultants and until Robin's return, she had trusted his judgement.

What would Arthur advise in this situation?

She smiled.

He'd hate it.

"I will keep my soul?" she asked.

It bobbed its head.

SOUL YOURS. BODY OURS. WE TORTURE, THEN KILL ANYONE YOU WANT.

Morganna had stopped trembling. Her teeth had stopped chattering and the nausea in her stomach had subsided.

She eyed the witch.

"How will you help me survive the winter? I need proof."

The inky figure nodded.

Another creaking noise escape from it, before the monster's chest split open. The smell of rot and decay returned. Morganna's head began to swim and she covered her nose, though it had little effect.

The figure leaned forward, so its chest was directly above the earth.

A sound that reminded Morganna of a man who had had too much ale filled the room just as a rabbit's carcass fell from the shadow's chest.

Morganna heaved and turned away from the sight in front of her.

Dear God.

The sound filled the room again but before another rabbit's body could fall at her feet she turned and faced the creature.

"That's, uh...that's quite enough."

It nodded.

I CAN CATCH LOTS OF RABBITS. EASY TO KILL.

"I see that."

WILL YOU LET ME HELP YOU? I NEED YOU TO AGREE OR HE WILL KNOW.

Morganna's eyes darted from the dead rabbit to the cavity from which it had fallen. They landed on the eyes of the monster.

I could kill her easily with the aid of a witch. Perhaps in ways I didn't think possible. I could make her suffer.

Her heart raced at the thought.

And my soul would still be mine. I won't be like Cadfen. He is damned but I could keep my soul and rid myself of Robin once and for all. Maybe then Arthur...

Morganna started to reach for the charm but forced her arm by her side. She pushed back her shoulders and exhaled slowly.

"You will not enter my body until after my child is born. Is that clear?"

It nodded.

NOT UNTIL BABY IS BORN. YES.

"And you will not harm my child, understand?"

I WILL NOT HARM THE BOY. NO.

Morganna gaped. "How do you know it's a boy?"

WITCH'S EYES SEE WHAT HUMANS CANNOT.

"I have one more question. Since we'll be *working* together I need to know what to call you. What is your name?"

WE HAVE NO NAMES.

"Your father never named you?"

It shook its head.

"Hmm, then I think I have a name for you. How about Lilith? It's an old name."

The figure cocked its head to the side. It picked up the stick and dug into the earth.

LILITH IS A GOOD NAME.

Chapter Twenty One

"Come on, dear. We've got a few more stops I want to make before we get to the Amian."

Una grabbed Alistair's arm and pulled him beside her. Her eyes moved around the neighborhood roads that were full of its northern inhabitants. Most of the buildings made from piled stones were family homes, often only one or two rooms. The larger stone buildings with nicely patched roofs were town centers like the lord's home or the messenger's office. And all around, there was snow.

The storm had snowed them in for three days and his aunt, like any other homemaker, had to restock her cupboards. The way Farren, Olen, and Brima ate, he couldn't blame her. The only one who seemed not to always have her eye on the kitchen was Deanna.

Maddy had become quite a fan of Una's cooking the last few days. She was right along with Brima and the others asking for seconds and thirds.

Alistair smiled at the memory. He had wanted her to like his family and she seemed to be getting along with them.

They hadn't had much time alone since they arrived. Still, sometimes he'd catch her looking at him and a blush would creep on her cheeks. Of course, it could all have been his imagination. The small smiles, the stolen glances...yes, his imagination.

"Did you hear me, Merlin?"

"Pardon?" Alistair blinked at his aunt.

She puffed out her cheeks and shook her head. "I said do you think we should buy some whale blubber for the fried biscuits."

"When has whale blubber ever been a problem." He grinned.

"You sound like your cousins, now, don't ya?"

"I guess they're rubbing off on me."

"If that's the case, maybe you'll start using your given name like they do, hmm?" She eyed him, tapping her boot in the snow. "Your parents gave you a fine first name, but you insist on using your middle one. Baffles me what you children do nowadays."

Alistair sighed. "Aunt Una, Merlin makes me sound like an old librarian who spends his days surrounded by dusty books. My middle name sounds better."

She scoffed. "You don't even respond to Merlin anymore. It's a shame, a good name like yours going to waste. Now, come on.

Inlen's home is right up here."

"He moved?"

She nodded. "Sold his home to a family that had moved down from the capital. Used that and savings to build himself a new place."

A few houses down, Una approached another stone building in the shape of a large dome. From the roof, smoke billowed into the sky. Blue tapestries with whale designs hung on the outside.

Una slammed a gloved hand on the door. Rustling could be heard from the house, and a few moments later, the door creaked open. Inlen, a short stout man, appeared at the door with a grin on his face.

"Someone seems happy this morning," Una noted.

The man nodded. "I am. Business has been well today, and considering Alistair's up for a visit, I expect you'll be doing a lot of frying."

Alistair bit back a laugh.

"Oh, really?" she said, crossing her arms over her chest. "Perhaps, I should go see your brother across the way. It's a further walk, aye, but maybe I'll get less lip there."

Inlen narrowed his eyes. "You know as well as I his blubber and butters are nowhere near as good as what I've got to offer."

He straightened in the doorway and began to stroke his beard as his eyes darted around them. Alistair looked around but there was no one standing close by. He turned back to Inlen who was still glancing here and there.

Finally, the man leaned forward. He pointed at Una, then tapped his ear and mouth before slashing a hand through the air. The northern language for *you didn't hear this from me.*

"What'd you gotta say?" Alistair's aunt moved forward, completely transfixed by the chance at some gossip.

Inlen cleared his throat. "Dorren said she found rot in blubber she bought from him."

Una raised a brow. "Rot? In your brother's blubber? Have ye both lost ye minds."

"I only pass on what I am told," he said, hands raised in the air. "I never start the telling myself."

Una gave him a look from head to toe. "That I doubt. Are ye going to let us in or not?"

He opened the door wide and bowed. "Your Grace."

Una slapped him on the head as she walked. As Alistair stepped through the door, Inlen pulled him to his side.

"Don't think I forgot about you, little middle-born! Nice to finally see ya again."

"Thanks, Inlen," Alistair said. "It's nice to see you, too. How are Nano and Nina?"

They were Inlen's twin boy and girl who had been born around the time Alistair left for his parents. He had only seen them a few times before he had to leave.

The man wiped his forehead. "They're full of energy is what they are. Trying to walk now. This week was the first time I've had the house to myself. Wife took them up for a visit to the parents."

"Did she make it through the storm okay?"

"Oh, ye—"

Inlen's jaw dropped and Alistair cursed himself for taking his hood off.

"My, my, my, your hair's whiter than a rabbit's—"

"Inlen, I need three pounds of your latest catch," Una said and stepped between the two men. "And I want the rest of your herbs, too. Don't know when we're going to see those again."

He looked between her and Alistair. "Uh, right. I'll wrap it up."

As soon as he placed the package in her hand, Una spun on her heel and pushed Alistair out the door.

"We'll be seeing ya, Inlen," she called back.

A cold wind whipped through the street. Alistair pulled his cloak around him. A gentle weight rested on his shoulder. He turned and Una was smiling at him.

"Perhaps, it's best we keep the hood up for now. If we don't, we'll never make it to where we need to be."

Una moved through the roads quickly. She stopped at different houses to purchase items and, of course, anyone they ran into she'd pull Alistair along to act as the center of the conversation.

"Aye, he's making his parents proud. Even worked as a messenger, delivering packages all around."

Though his aunt's frequent chats delayed their destination, Alistair found himself smiling.

By the time Amian's house came into sight, Alistair's legs ached with all the walking. On one arm, he carried a week's worth of groceries and the other his aunt had snaked her own arm around.

The healer, Amian, lived a bit outside of the town. Alistair could only remember going to see the man a handful of times during his stay in the north. From what he remembered, he was good at what he did but hated being bothered.

The small hut of a home was quiet as they approached. Una raised her fist but knocked with more hesitation than she did at Inlen's.

As soon as she knocked, the door flew open. In its wake stood a tall and thin framed man with long white hair and dark green eyes. He was covered from head to toe in blankets and didn't look at all pleased to have his comfort interrupted.

"Is someone dead?" he asked.

Una hesitated. "Uh, n-no—"

"Is someone dying?"

She and Alistair looked at one another.

"We don't believe so."

He sighed. "Has a plague swept through the village?"

They shook their heads.

"And are there any major ills or ailments that need immediate attention?"

"We don't think so," Alistair stuttered out.

"Then, why," --the old man yawned--"are you knocking at my door?"

Amian hasn't changed. Storms did always make him grumpy.

Una cleared her throat. "There is a very personal matter I need your expertise on, Amian."

"And what would that be after three days of being locked inside our homes?"

A redness rose in Una's cheeks and Alistair had to fight the urge to back away from the pair.

Una crossed her arms and the two began to stare each other down, their gazes unflinching.

Between his aunt and Amian, he wasn't sure who'd win, only that he didn't want to be caught in the crossfire.

Una worked her jaw, eyes locked in place. "Are you going to keep sassing me, old man, or are ye going to listen?"

He shrugged. "Depends. You going to say anything worth listening to?"

A taut fear wrapped around Alistair's middle. The groceries suddenly felt like weights attached to his arm holding him in place.

Una huffed. She slammed her hand on the door and it went flying back against the hut wall. Amian fell to the side with the door and she stepped inside.

The old man glared at her. She glared right back.

Alistair stood on the threshold.

Amian sniffed. "Well, since you're here..." He gestured to a row of small stools on the left side of the hut.

She nodded, before looking at Alistair.

"Come on in, Mer-Alistair."

The old man shook his head. "Still refusing to use his given name?"

"Aye. He seems to be fond of the middle."

"Children in these times."

"Now that is one thing we can agree on," she said. "But that's not what I wanted to discuss with you, Amian. Our family needs your help."

"With what exactly?"

Una looked at Alistair. "Show him."

Alistair placed the groceries to the side and pulled down his hood. Like everyone else, the old man gaped at what he saw.

He turned to Una. "Is it some new fashion in the middle-kingdom?"

Why does everyone think that?

"I wish it were, but no. Alistair's hair turned white after he encountered *the* witch."

Amian raised a brow. He tossed the covers off him and leaned forward on his stool.

"The same one that cursed him, then?"

Una's voiced cracked a bit as she spoke the words. "Yes, and he says he's been to the afterlife. He met a boy there who speaks with him."

The old man's eyes turned on Alistair. "And I assume your silver is gone, aye? Your witch's curse?"

"Yes," he said.

A sharp intake of breath. "This is not something I thought I'd ever see."

He rose from his stool and kneeled before Alistair. Suddenly, Amian's long fingers were entangled in Alistair's hair and his head was being turned in every angle.

Amian jerked Alistair's head straight. He squinted his eyes. "And you killed the wretch?"

He nodded. "Aye."

"How?"

"I'm not sure."

"Think, boy!"

"I-I," Alistair took a hard breath. He briefly closed his eyes and tried to remember that day, but it was mostly empty spots.

He shook his head. "All I remember is the witch attacking, being terrified and, then Edwin appeared and killed the witch. He said I had called him."

The old man's eyes widened. "Helen's Lights, I've never seen one."

"A what?" Una asked, wringing her hands together. "What's wrong with my boy?"

Amian released Alistair and took his seat again. A large smile spread across his face and he slapped his knee.

"You're a warlock, son!"

"A what?" Alistair said.

The old man straightened. "A warlock. When one with a witch's curse kills the witch who cursed him, he becomes a warlock, the men, at least. Sorceress is the term for women. Think of what you have as buying what you borrowed for some time and using the material in a new way."

Alistair stilled. Una's gaze shifted between them. She placed a hand on Alistair's shoulder before turning to the healer.

"So, he's not ill?"

Amian shook his head. "Not at all. He's actually very lucky. There's only a small window of time between the transition of power that a cursed can use it. Until then you only had a few of the advantages such as being immune to magic and poison. I think you lose the magic bit now. Remember the fish though?"

"Nearly had me keel over that day," Una said.

"Aye, you and me both," Amian said. "But now things are different. The moment the witch used her power to pull it from Alistair, he used it. He called Edwin, killed the witch, and now he has her power. Rarely ever happens."

Una squeezed Alistair's arm. "That's good, though! It means he's well. Alistair..."

What am I?

The hut was suddenly too small, too dark. Alistair needed light. He couldn't breathe as a dense feeling of foreboding snaked its way around him. His body became tremors, yet he couldn't be the one shaking. He wasn't gripped by a chilling fear, his mouth hadn't suddenly lost all its moisture, and his hands weren't shaking like a rattle, no, not him. That was some other young man, one who had just been told he was a monster.

He shook his head. It couldn't be him. Because if it was that would mean she won.

She's still inside me.

Alistair lunged forward, wrapping an arm around his middle and clamping his teeth shut as the bile reached his mouth.

"Alistair!" His aunt's arm was warm around his shoulders.

"What's wrong, boy?" Amian slipped a pot into the space where Alistair was hunched over. "Did you eat some bad cooking?"

"Oh, shut up, Amian," Una barked. "Alistair, you can hear me, can't you? Dear?"

His hair was like a white curtain. It hung loose in front of him with small waves at the ends.

When he was a boy, he had wanted his hair to be lighter like his cousins. He wanted people to stop questioning their relation, even though Una told him his dark hair was a gift from his mother.

The image of the woman who had birthed him flashed in his mind. He pushed it away.

He had finally gotten his wish. His hair was the lightest of all his cousins and now it would always be a constant reminder of what he had become.

Una rubbed his back.

Alistair gripped his sides and screamed. He dug his nails into his arms and let the anguish roll out of him.

Because this wasn't right. This wasn't how it was supposed to be. She, the witch, was supposed to be dead and Alistair was supposed to be free. His parents had sent him away for nothing. He grew up without them for nothing.

He shot to his feet, a hand tangled and pulling at his hair as his eyes flared in search of the answer to his questions.

"I have to go," he said and turned towards the door.

"Wait, Mer-Alistair." Una scrambled behind him, but he would be quicker than her, he had to be. Because his aunt would try to make everything okay. It's what she did, except this time there was no solution.

Amian had said Alistair was no longer cursed yet it didn't feel that way.

"Merlin, stop running!"

He looked behind him. His aunt was jogging after him, struggling to keep the baskets of groceries steady in her arms. She was panting and her cheeks puffed out with touches of red on them.

"Wait," she shouted.

Alistair slowed his run until it became a stroll. His chest burned and his body felt heavy.

Una was still several yards behind him. She staggered and the baskets fell to the ground.

I'm such a fool.

He sighed, spun around and made his way to his aunt. He kneeled beside her and began placing groceries in their basket. She stared at him.

"What happened, Alistair?"

He remained silent.

Una moved her hand across his face, pushing back his hair. Her eyes were watery and her lips were pulled into a thin line.

"This changes nothing," she stated.

He sighed. "It changes everything, Aunt Una."

"No," she replied, her blonde hair moving with the force of the word.

She grabbed his chin and turned his purple eyes, so they were looking directly into her silver.

"No," she repeated. "It doesn't. You are still *my* boy. I know you and I know you are not a monster."

"But the witch...she's inside me." His hands had started to tremble again. "I took her power. I took her."

Una moved her hand from his face to his shoulders. She gripped them into him and found his eyes once more.

"It is not what you have that makes you. It is how you use it. Now, you have magic, Alistair, but it doesn't turn you into the witch."

He clutched his hands to stop the shaking.

"What am I then?"

She smiled. "A young man with a gift."

The cold night air nipped at her fingers. Robin cursed herself for forgetting her gloves but there wasn't much time for packing or preparation.

Alistair had been gone since his aunt returned and only now had Robin found a moment to sneak away. Una refused to tell anyone what happened or where Alistair was, despite their concerns.

Well, anyone, except her husband. The moment the two stepped into the bedroom, Brima and Farren had helped Robin through the guest room window. Maddy, Olen, and Deanna kept watch.

The moment she landed, Brima gave Robin directions to where Alistair liked to go to be alone. Then, she closed the window which barely made a noise and was much quieter than the door as Robin had first proposed. Apparently it creaked though Robin hadn't noticed upon their rushed arrival.

Maddy had grinned and waved at her from the window but she was as worried about Alistair as the others. Only she was more skilled at hiding her feelings, a trait Robin admired about her and if Maddy hadn't caught the frost on their journey, she would have encouraged her to come along.

But Robin was going to make the short trek alone.

She wrapped herself in her cloak and rubbed her hands together. Though she considered herself stronger than she ever believed, Robin doubted she'd ever become accustomed to the northern cold. Of course, it snowed in the middle-kingdom, as well, but without such ferociousness. The temperature was below zero, she was sure.

A wind blew and Robin blinked twice to clear her vision.

Past the first house, you'll see Helen's Tree. Make a left and walk as if you were going to the shore. If you keep walking, you'll find a pile of rocks rising from the ground near a piece of land that looks like a cliff. That's where he'll be.

Brima's words repeated in her mind.

She had passed the first house some time ago but still no tree.

"Nothing worth having is easy in getting," she mumbled to herself. A smile tugged at her lips.

"Only further evidence Arthur was a know it all, even as a youth. Oh, if he could see me now."

The very thought made her laugh. Her walking alone in a foreign country at night after barely making it through a blizzard...he'd probably lay an egg.

Warmth blossomed in Robin's chest.

That was Arthur. Worrying like a mother hen was what he did. He was kind and generous and willing to put the needs of others before his own, always happy to hold the heaviest of burdens.

Then, why did you reject his proposal?

She shook the question away and clenched her hands by her sides.

I will not think about it. I've made up my mind.

She nodded to herself and marched harder across the snowy ground. Soon Helen's Tree came into view. The branches were completely bare of either snow or leaf. What stood in front of Robin was simply a gray-barked tree with numerous limbs. Still, she couldn't deny what Brima and Deanna had told her.

The branches looked like opened hands turned towards the sky either offering or waiting for a blessing. Though Robin was a believer in Trithian herself and had learned little of the old religions, she couldn't deny her growing interest or the logic behind the old ways.

She doubted she'd ever be able to worship Helen like the northerners yet choosing a woman as a god made sense. Women birthed children. Why not believe a female spirit could have birthed all the world? Yes, men played their role, but women were like the soil, the carrier, and the caregiver. She could understand why they believed the way they did.

Robin passed the tree and headed towards the shore. Her hands were catching chill again, so she cupped them together and blew into them. As she began to warm her fingers, the sound of waves greeted her ears.

A gust of wind burst from the shore and blew her hood down. Her hair tossed in the air and she moved her face away to block the sudden gust. And that's when she saw it.

There were five large rocks protruding from the ground, set in a sort of arc with smaller ones in similar standing. From where she stood, they looked to be rather smooth, the opposite of the jagged rocks she had been expecting.

Her eyes made their way east of the rocks. Just as Brima had told her, there was a small outstretched piece of land that looked like a cliff.

She walked closer to the set of rocks. Slowly, in the farthest corner of the arc, hunched over and silent, a figure took shape.

Robin braced a hand against the cold stone and smiled. "Alistair."

"Brima sent you, didn't she?" He sat up and pulled his hood back to look at her.

"Actually, they all did. Well, except your aunt and uncle. They don't know I'm here."

His eyes were in sharp contrast to the white surrounding them. His hair countered the dark stones behind him. Alistair didn't look at all the same young man she had met in the Cursed Woods over a month ago.

He patted the ground beside him and Robin took a seat, wrapping her cloak around herself.

"Robin, where are your gloves?"

She grinned. "Forgot them during my grand escape."

"And you didn't ask my cousins to throw you a pair?"

"I was in a rush," she replied. "I wanted to make sure you were well."

Alistair ran a gloved hand through his hair. "Come here," he said and opened his hands.

She placed her hands in his and he began rubbing them

between his own.

Robin leaned her head against the stones. She watched him as he worked.

"What happened, Alistair? Why didn't you return with your aunt?"

"She won."

"Who is she?" Robin asked. "And what did she win?"

His eyes didn't move from her hands. He was quiet for a moment.

"The witch. The healer told me today." He released her hands and rested his elbows on his knees.

The comfort and warmth he had offered moments ago evaporated. An empty feeling settled in Robin, making her feel hollow.

She gripped at the clasp of her cloak. Her vision was blurring.

"S-she cursed you again? Before she died?" Her voice was uneven and teetering. She could feel her throat growing tight as she fought back the tears.

If Alistair's not here...no, I can't. I will find a way to save him.

She inhaled through her nose and stiffened her shoulders. Alistair was staring at her with raised brows.

Robin balled her hands into fists. "I will not allow you to die. I don't care how far we must travel, how much money we must spend, I will not lose you, Alistair. You will not die."

He smirked. His lips began to quiver, and then Alistair had one hand over his middle while he howled with laughter.

Robin scrunched her face in concern. She placed her fists on her hips and glared at him.

"What the bloody hell is so funny?"

A few tears streamed down Alistair's cheeks. His laughter slowed and he took in several deep breaths before turning back to Robin. His eyes were wide and happy as he looked over her face.

"You still haven't answered my question," she huffed.

"I'm not dying, Robin."

"What?" The empty feeling was replaced with a blazing anger. "What do you mean you're not dying?"

"I thought you wanted me alive," he stated.

"I did but I'm very much questioning my decision now."

He held his hands up, palm forward, still smiling. "Can I explain?"

"I suppose."

Alistair clasped his hands together. The smile now left his

face.

"The witch, she...I-I killed her when I called Edwin from the afterlife, remember?"

She nodded.

"Apparently, when one with a witch's curse kills the witch that cursed him, he gains the creature's power."

He watched her.

Robin stared back at him. "What else?"

"That's it. I'm now a warlock or whatever Amian said."

"Amian?"

"The healer," he corrected. "He told me I absorbed her power by killing her. Now, it's like..." At that moment, he turned away. He lowered his head to his clasped hands and took in a long breath. "Now, it's like she's still inside me. It's like I'm still cursed, Robin. She won."

Robin wanted to smile. She wanted to laugh, grin, and then slap Alistair for worrying her the way he did. There was lightness in her heart now because his life was no longer in danger. She wouldn't have to complete her journey without him.

Yet, what to her was good news was a blight to him. Her mind raced for soothing words and she found none.

Uncertainty circling her, Robin reached out and took hold of his clasped hands. His eyes turned upward.

What do I say?

There were no right words. In one way, Alistair was wrong. The witch was gone from this world, likely burning in hell for her sins. On the other hand, a part of her, her power was still with Alistair and therefore a part of her was still alive. Otherwise, couldn't be argued.

What do I say?

She opened her mouth. Her uncle had held her hands like this after her parents' death. There weren't any words for that situation either. Still, he had found some that were good enough.

"Nothing I say will take away your pain. It is likely nothing I do will cure you from this ill either. But what I can assure you is that time will shrink the pain. And when it becomes too much to bear, I will carry it with you."

Tears filled her eyes again. She squeezed Alistair's hand.

Thank you, Uncle Terryn.

"I think I must be the luckiest person ever to have walked through the Cursed Woods." He tucked her hand under his. "You are the greatest companion, Robin."

She smiled. "As are you, Alistair. And please remember, you

are not the only one who has been cursed. You helped me regain my strength and learn to walk again when I left the tree. In a way, I will being do the same for you."

He nodded. "Together, then?"

"Together."

Robin stood and pulled Alistair along with her.

"You know my aunt is going to likely slap you and my cousins with her spoon for sneaking out."

She gulped. *I hadn't thought of that.*

A smooth material covered her hands. She looked down and saw that Alistair had slipped his gloves off to place on her.

She snatched her hand away and began to pull the glove off.

"I can't ask you to lose your fingers on my account, Alistair."

He sighed. "And if you return home without your fingers, Uncle Garron is likely to toss his ax at me. Which would you prefer?'"

She rolled her eyes. "You're intolerable."

He slipped the second glove onto her other hand.

"I think that's what you like about me the most."

"I've told you this before and I'll say it again, Alistair. Arrogance does not suit you."

She spun on her heels and started to walk in the direction of Helen's Tree. Alistair had caught up with her in a few moments.

"You don't seem to mind it on Arthur," he laughed.

Arthur. The proposal...

"What's that look?" Alistair asked.

"Huh?"

The laughter left his face. "You looked sad for a moment, Robin."

"It's nothing."

"I think you know that I know it's much more than nothing." He gestured to her face. "It was clear as day."

This just isn't the right moment.

She met his gaze. "I want to tell you, Alistair. It was on my mind during our entire journey up here. But I haven't figured it out myself yet, so once I do, I'll tell you everything. How does that sound?"

He searched her face. "Fine. I'll hold you to it, though."

"Agreed."

"How was my aunt when she returned, by the way? It took much convincing to get her to leave me for some time."

"She wouldn't answer a single question about you. She kept glancing out the window, too, which was quite worrisome. Oh, and she referred to you as Merlin."

Alistair pinched the bridge of his nose.

"Is that your middle name?"

"No. Actually, it's my first name. Alistair is my middle but I prefer it over Merlin."

"Hm."

"What?"

"I agree that Alistair is a better choice. Merlin doesn't suit you."

"I wish someone would tell Aunt Una that."

Robin peered at the sky. She shook her head.

"What?"

She shrugged. "It's nothing. Only that the name Merlin makes me think of an old librarian who spends his days surrounded by dusty books."

Alistair laughed. "Exactly."

Chapter Twenty Two

Morganna breathed through her mouth despite the cold weather. She knew it was not lady like. Her father would have scolded her for not acting proper. However, her nose could not afford another whiff or sniffle. With each intake through her nose, the stench of Lilith's muddy flesh on her own made Morganna's head swim.

She knew she had no choice but to smear the black sludge over herself. It was part of the witch's spell, so that when Lancelot arrived he wouldn't see Morganna. He'd see Robin in her place.

She flung her braid to her other shoulder and stared at the monster across from her. Lilith sat like a child on the ground, hunched over with smudged red eyes and a stick in her hand as she drew into the layer of snow.

"Are you sure he will come?" Morganna asked.

She nodded and continued with her design.

The little witch had been following Lancelot for several days. She now knew his habits, behaviors, and patterns—including the paths he traveled.

Morganna peered back out at the road. Lilith had proven herself trustworthy. Not only had she consistently supplied Morganna and her child with food, she had stolen supplies from the capital. As hard as it was to admit, she knew without Lilith's aid she would not have survived the first snow. Blankets and dry firewood were essential when living within the elements.

Morganna stared down at her stomach. Each day it rounded a bit more, her child became a bit stronger, even with the meek meals she had supplied him. Mordred was going to be a strong king.

She placed one hand on her stomach. The other she turned palm-upward to stare at the seed it held.

Lilith would not tell her where it came from. She would not even tell Morganna the seed's name. All the creature had said was that it belonged to her, so it belonged to Morganna, as well and she needed to get Lancelot to swallow it.

HIS MIND WILL BE OURS AND ONLY OURS, Lilith had said.

Witchcraft had been Morganna's first thought.

She took a deep breath and let the thought settle in her mind. Perhaps, her actions were cruel, but her intention was good. She needed to rule Camelot properly with Arthur by her side as it should be. Mordred should know his father as any child should and all this could only be done if Robin was revealed to be the villain she was.

Arthur could not see beyond her light blue eyes and pouty lips. He was dumbstruck by her moon pale skin and dark hair but Morganna would set him free.

Because she knew he loved her. He had simply forgotten..

She nodded to herself. *Yes. I will make him remember.*

She clasped her middle. *He has to remember.*

Snow crunched in the distance.

Will he notice?

Morganna shook herself. "He won't know it's me."

The small sound of punctured earth made Morganna turn to her right.

Lilith sat squatted on the ground. She was using the same stick from their first encounter.

I COULD KILL INSTEAD. YOUR CHOICE.

She shook her head. "We need him. It's the only way for Arthur to see Robin for what she truly is."

YOU HATE THIS MAN.

She scoffed. "He thinks himself a man, yet he is only a boy in truth. Arthur gave him too much freedom."

It nodded. Dark wisps of Lilith moved about as the wind blew. HE'S CLOSE.

Morganna gulped. She looked down at her stomach. "This is really for you, you understand? It is only one sin."

She turned to the little witch. "Is there anything else I need to know? Once I give him the seed and...the deed will be done?"

She bobbed her head.

HE EATS SEED. HIS MIND OURS. YOU SIN. WE CAN BECOME ONE.

Morganna looked back at the path. She could hear footsteps. "And he won't recognize me?" she asked.

Lilith turned her head to the side. The red splotches on her face shrunk for a moment, nearly disappearing. The creature dug into the earth again with the stick, its eyes never leaving Morganna.

YOU WEAR MY FLESH. I MAKE YOU LOOK LIKE HER.

The stick froze for a moment.

I CAN GIVE YOU MORE.

Before Morganna could assure Lilith she had enough rot, the creature offered its arm. What once were wispy tendrils of black solidified into an arm that looked liked possessed wood. It was so rigid and the veins within too large for such a tiny arm.

Lilith reached forward with her other arm which was as deformed as the first. She took a finger and dug into her wrist until an inky liquid appeared. And then, it thickened like spoiled porridge.

She moved her finger down the forearm until the rotten porridge pooled from her. She pushed her arm forward, the liquid becoming a sludge.

Morganna had covered her nose at the sight. Her eyes stung with the very smell. Yet her feet moved her.

Be strong, be strong. This is for Mordred and Arthur. Lancelot's sacrifice is necessary.

She scooped a bit from Lilith's arm and began to rub it on her face. She did not breathe while she did so.

The distant footsteps had become louder.

He's here.

Morganna looked up from her stomach and locked eyes with Lilith. The witch nodded and Morganna stood before taking a deep breath and clasping the seed in her hand.

She stepped out into the road and looked to her right. The sound of crunching snow came to a halt. Lancelot's eyes were fixed on her and Morganna found herself giving him an appreciative once-over, as well.

Dressed in his sparring gear with an old cloak of Arthur's wrapped around him, the boy was quite the sight. His brown hair lightened under the moonlight. He even seemed a bit taller.

She smiled. *I am sorry you must suffer, as well. I can at least promise Arthur will not truly be harmed.*

"Robin? What are you doing here? Did you just return?"

Morganna fought the urge to smile. Their plan was working perfectly. Now all she had to do was play the part.

Her eyes roamed over him. She shook her head.

Lancelot slipped his sword into its sheath and turned to face her.

"Where are your friends?"

"I came to see you," she said. Her dress slipped lower.

He quirked a brow. "Is that so?"

She nodded but turned her gaze away from him. Her thin, delicate fingers trailed over her nearly bare chest. Morganna looked back at him with small, pink trembling lips.

Lancelot stormed towards her and gripped her smooth shoulders under his hardened hands.

"What's happened?" he asked, trying to force her eyes to meet his. "Were you all attacked on your way back to the castle? Were there bandits?"

She closed her eyes and a whimpers slipped from her lips. "Robin..."

He pushed her hair back and ran his thumb along her jaw. "I-I..."

"Yes, Robin. What is it?"

"I don't know what to do," she stuttered.

"About what?"

Morganna met his eyes again, her lips slightly pursed as she gazed at him.

"About you, Lancelot."

His hands froze. "What do you mean?"

Her eyes found Lilith's in the shadows. The witch nodded. Morganna turned back to face Lancelot.

"I don't want Arthur to become suspicious. We need to be patient."

A vein pulsed in his neck. He cupped her cheek and flicked away a stray hair. "I'm done with being patient."

The smirk had faded from his lips, replaced with a smile. His thumbs stopped their circular movements on her cheeks. His gaze bored into her.

Morganna took in a sharp breath, pushed aside the warmth rising in her stomach.

"N-no," she stumbled over her words.

Lancelot's smile only grew. He leaned closer to her lips.

"You come to me like a ghost. Every night, I see nothing but you, Robin."

Lancelot moved his hands away from her face to the small of her back. He closed his eyes and Morganna knew this was the moment. She leaned forward, moving her hands up his chest until she had a good range. Without another thought, she tossed the seed into her mouth and lunged forward until her lips crashed onto Lancelot's.

Forgive me, Arthur.

His arms secured her against him. The weight he put behind their kiss forced Morganna to lean further back.

His tongue smoothed over her lips, before moving between them. Suddenly, her mouth tasted of Cook's stew and roasted squash.

Arthur's favorites.

Morganna pressed her feet into the ground and straightened

in Lancelot's arms. She wrapped herself around him, her own tongue now parting his lips.

She ran her fingers up from his neck through his hair. Her hips pressed against his and Morganna found a tight pressure growing between her legs.

The taste of deer meat, rosemary, and cinnamon coated her tongue. But she wanted more. It had been awhile since she had anything that reminded her so much of home...so much of Arthur.

And so the moan left her. Lancelot unclipped her cloak and they stepped back into the woods.

His mouth moved down to her neck and suddenly she was pressed against a tree. The rough bark was pushed into her back, yet she found the sensation enticing as Lancelot's hands moved up her thighs.

His tongue darted out and coated her lips. With the cloak and if she imagined hard enough, she could even pretend he was Arthur.

She moved her head back as the boy's mouth moved from her neck to her chest. Winter's chill was caressing her skin, only to quickly be replaced with Lancelot's warm lips, his heated palms.

I should stop him.

She had already pushed the seed in his mouth, after all.

I'll feign innocence and he'll let me leave.

But she pressed his face farther into her bosom and when they moved to the cloak he had tossed to the earth, she offered no objection. Morganna only stared at his light brown hair, imagining it was a beautiful yellow like her own instead. And below that yellow were two ocean blue eyes.

His lips moved to hers once more. The spices filled Morganna's tongue again and she was sure it was Arthur who towered above her. She wanted to be so certain.

He's had a long sparring session. I can smell the sweat on him.

Lancelot's hands gripped her hips. Her dress had long been pulled up to her middle, her breasts long been exposed.

If I imagine hard enough, it's Arthur.

Lancelot undid his pants. He leaned over her.

I must convince him I'm Robin. And this is what she would do. Yes...all for Arthur.

The young man nuzzled her nose and, then, kissed her cheek. She closed her eyes because his were not the right color.

His body arched above her as she was filled and her pressure eased.

A shadow passed over the moon. Lancelot looked up. His arms suddenly felt like they were missing something and when the moonlight graced the earth again she was gone.

His arms were stagnant. They had become nothing but tremors.

"Robin," he breathed.

No answer.

"Robin."

His call caused no response.

"Damn it!" He clutched his arms behind his head and began pacing. His teeth gnashed together as the chill of her absence settled into him.

She had been here. I felt her...Robin...

Lancelot kicked at the earth. He slipped his clothes on before starting to the clearing.

Could I have been acting out a dream? No, it isn't possible. But how could she have been here?

He gripped the hilt of his sword as he walked.

"I couldn't have imagined her," he whispered. "Unless it's like what Arthur had described."

The land slanted below him. Lancelot turned his feet to the side and steadily made his way down until the torches came into sight. Several guards circled the clearing, nodding towards him as he came into view.

He lifted a hand to them and they began their march once more.

"Lancelot."

Arthur walked towards him. He was tapping a finger against his chin.

This isn't going to be good.

"Could I have a word?" Arthur asked. "I'm in need of some advice."

"Of course. How can I help?"

"Uh..." Arthur peered around them, before raising a hand and scratching his head. His gaze was again on Lancelot. "I was hoping we could speak in my quarters."

Lancelot dipped his head and proceeded to follow Arthur into the crumbling castle. The halls were nearly empty. Everyone most likely waiting for Cook to open the dining doors.

When they reached Arthur's room, Lancelot closed the door behind him and turned to his friend.

"Has something happened to Robin?" He crossed his arms and tucked his hands under them to hide their shaking.

Arthur slumped in a chair placed at the corner of the room table.

"I haven't received word from them still," he said.

"Perhaps we should go after her? If she hasn't—"

He raised a hand. "Calm yourself, my friend. I trust her with Alistair. She's also proven capable of defending herself."

Lancelot took in a sharp breath. He released it slowly through clenched teeth.

Arthur smiled at him. "Are you still mad because Alistair bested you?"

He scoffed. "Luck was in his favor that day. But no man has an endless supply. You said so yourself."

Arthur nodded. "I did and it's true. However, part of being a knight is admitting when you have been bested and doing so with grace."

He rose from his chair and walked over to Lancelot. He placed his hands on his shoulders.

"One loss does not take away from all you have accomplished. All right?"

He nodded. "I still plan on challenging him once this is all over."

"As you should." Arthur smiled and ruffled Lancelot's hair.

I hate when you do that.

"But I don't want to talk to you about Alistair," he said, releasing his hold. "It's...well, it's Robin. More specifically, something she did. Or didn't do. I haven't been able to push it from my mind."

Arthur returned to his seat and Lancelot took one across from him.

"She rejected my proposal."

"You proposed?" Lancelot asked. He could feel the sweat building on his brow. The emptiness in his stomach had become more apparent.

Arthur sighed and leaned back in his chair.

"I did," he replied. "And she said no."

The corners of Lancelot's mouth urged to be turned into a smile. Instead, he bit the inside of his cheek and cleared his throat.

"Did she say why?"

Because she loves me.

"No, which makes it all the more frustrating. She simply said she couldn't."

"When did you propose?"

"The day before they left for the north." His eyes turned to the floor. "The same day Morganna disappeared. Not exactly the best timing, I know. Actually, while you were—"

Lancelot shook his head. "Still no sign of her. We all know to report to you immediately if we see anything."

Arthur lowered his head to his hands. "I never wanted to hurt either of them. Before Robin disappeared in the forest, I had never considered Morganna as anything more than the princess. Under certain circumstances, perhaps a friend."

Lancelot raised a brow. "Is that why Morganna left? You told her you chose Robin?"

No, no, no, no!

He nodded. "I didn't think she would run. I couldn't lie to her anymore, Lance. Robin has always been…"

She's mine. Mine! You had yours.

"Are you feeling well?"

Lancelot blinked. He straightened in his chair. "I'm fine. Just a bit tired."

"You're sweating, as well."

He slid a hand across his brow. Pellets of sweat decorated Lancelot's palm.

"I…um…I think the cold is getting to me."

"Instruct Cook to make you something."

"I will. You were talking about Robin?"

"Right." He shook himself. "Robin may have rejected my proposal. That doesn't mean I can't convince her otherwise. Things are different now. I can court her properly and I'd like your help in doing it."

A tension was building in Lancelot's neck. He reached back and massaged it.

"H-how can I help?" A forced smile.

Arthur chuckled and froze his sights on him. "I may be getting older, Lance but my vision is still quite well. You have more than a few admirers around here."

But I only want Robin.

"When you're charming a young woman, what do you do?" Arthur asked.

He cannot have Robin.

"Lancelot?"

"Uh, I'm not sure what I do. Honestly, I always thought you'd have more experience."

Arthur laughed. "Perhaps I am not completely absent of female attention, but women have never...shown their eagerness the way they do with you."

A tense nod. "Give me some time to think about it. She's not due to return for another week. I can show you a few tricks by then." He winked.

Arthur shook his head. "Why do I have the feeling getting you to settle down is going to be trouble?"

Lancelot released a dry laugh. "I don't think I'm one for settling down."

Arthur smirked. "I can't wait to meet the young lady that catches you. Is there any—"

"I wanted to ask you something, too."

"I'm all ears," Arthur replied.

"Once before you told me you had seen visions of Robin, correct?"

"Yes, when I thought she was dead. Are you seeing your parents again?" Arthur's brows knitted together. He looked Lancelot over.

"I...I'm not sure. I thought I saw something in the woods during my walk. Then, it was gone. I could have sworn it was real."

"Maybe it's the illness?"

Lancelot shook his head.

"Then, perhaps it's someone you miss," Arthur continued. "A memory of someone you've forgotten that's trying to fight its way back. That's what my father would tell me when I'd imagine I'd seen my mother."

"That sounds...a bit more reasonable."

Arthur smiled. "Good. Now, no more walks in this cold. It's not summer any longer."

"Right. I think dinner's started. We should head down to eat."

Arthur waved his hand. "Go ahead without me. I'll be down shortly."

Lancelot stood to leave. As before, he closed the door behind. His footsteps echoed in the empty halls, though his mind was only full of one thought:

She is mine.

Chapter Twenty Three

The path they treaded narrowed until they reached the crumbling wall. They continued until they entered the city and eventually the inner wall of Rowan.

Alistair could feel some of the tension leaving his body. After a treacherous journey to the north and a long journey back, he was ready for a few days of peace. Yet, as he looked around the clearing, that didn't seem likely.

The boy has no morals.

Lancelot was like a bee to honey. As soon as the trio had entered the clearing, his line of sight fell on Robin and he started to her.

Apparently, she had noticed his intentions, as well. Without skipping a note, Robin had brought the horse to a stop and dismounted. She then helped Maddy do the same, before walking towards the horse stables.

Lancelot's gallop slowed into a stroll.

Alistair had gotten off Fred and walked beside Robin.

"It seems I will never escape him," she whispered.

"He is quite persistent," Alistair noted, glancing back at the boy who slowly walked yards behind them.

"Have you thought of telling Arthur?" he asked.

She shook her head. "He has not made his intentions clear, though I have some suspicions. He's just a boy though. Do you think it's anything to worry about? He's also like a son to Arthur..." She looked at Alistair, her fingers tapped the reins in her hands.

He met her eyes. "I think if he makes you uncomfortable, you shouldn't just have to deal with it."

"And boys do become men," Maddy remarked, standing beside Robin.

Alistair nodded.

The dark-haired woman heaved a breath. "All right. Seems the work is never done. Once this is over, I will speak to him. If he doesn't understand, then I will speak with Arthur about his behavior. How does that sound?" She glanced between both her friends.

The two bobbed their heads.

The stables were alive with neighing and humming. Elanor's head poked just above one of the stall walls.

"Hello, Little Elanor," Robin called out.

The bobbing stopped and the child moved her head outside of the stall. She eyed the trio before giving a large grin.

"Hello, Lady Robin, Miss Maddy, and Mister Alistair," she said, stepping out into full view. "We were all waiting for you to return."

"Just Robin is fine, Elanor," she corrected and pulled her horse into an empty stall. The horse exhaled as she closed the stall door, apparently ready for a rest herself.

"And who is 'we'?" Alistair raised a brow.

Her smile grew and her gaze looked past him. He turned around.

Lancelot had stepped into the stall with a smile across his face that seemed fit for an imp. He nodded to Alistair yet his eyes wandered over Robin.

She glared at him, a light tick in her jaw.

"Good noon, Robin. I thought that was you I saw." His eyes finally found Alistair and Maddy. "Good noon. I hope you all had a safe journey."

"We did," Alistair replied. "And how have things been here? Any reports?"

The boy shook his head. "Just some snow. Aside from the seasons changing, everything has remained the same. I was distressed to not receive a letter about your journey."

He had spoken the question out loud but, again, he had lost sight of the others.

Robin crossed her arms and jutted out her chin. "We agreed to send a letter to *Arthur*. The northern weather prevented it. We'll report our journey to him when we see him next."

Maddy, who stood beside Robin, gave a hard nod in the boy's direction, as well.

Lancelot released what was between a laugh and a scoff.

"Of course," he said. "I'm sure he'll want me there, so we're all on the same page."

Alistair placed Fred in a stall and stroked the horse's nose.

"We shouldn't wait too long," Alistair said. "I'm sure Arthur is anxious to see you, Robin."

He glanced at Lancelot. The boy's face was flushed, his brows slanted and his hands holding just a bit too hard on his hips.

Robin took the opportunity.

"I agree, Alistair. We shouldn't delay. I have something for Elanor, though." She turned to the child and kneeled to her eye level.

The girl's face was smudged in dirt. A light pink colored her cheeks.

Robin smiled. "This is something I saw in one of the northern markets. It made me think of you. Hold your hands out."

The girl's eyes grew round. She did as she was told.

Like watching a shooting star, Elanor was totally transfixed on the small locket that dangled from Robin's hands. The chain was made from polished white silver. On its end was a pendant in the shape of a horse with a flowing mane and runes etched along its body.

Elanor held the necklace in her palms as if it was a king's gem. She fingered the runes on the horse's skin.

"I...I...what do these mean?"

Robin's face lit up at the question.

Alistair grinned while looking at the exchange. He crossed his arms and leaned against the stall, letting Lancelot fall from thought for a moment.

"Well," Robin said, "it is quite a story. I learned it while in the north when speaking to an elder. It's a story of seven horses on a seven thousand-mile journey."

"Seven thousand?" The child gaped.

"Yes," Robin replied. "It's quite a lot, isn't it?"

The child nodded.

"One day I will tell it to you." Robin pinched the child's cheek. "Don't let me forget, okay?"

Elanor shook her head. "I won't. Thank you, L-Robin. I've never been given something so wonderful."

"Well, now you have," Maddy replied.

Robin placed her hands on her knees and stood. She took a deep breath, before looking at her two friends.

"Ready?"

"Always." Alistair moved from the stall.

The group of three left the stables and headed for the castle with Alistair bringing up the rear. The snow crunched beneath their feet. A nice rhythm formed as they made their way. Their feet falling after one another's, creating a friendly song of wintery solitude Alistair associated with the north.

He found himself smiling.

How can I miss it when I've just left?

And then there was the sound of a fourth pair of footsteps, an unwelcome note in their rhythm.

The smile faded from Alistair's face. He turned his neck to look behind and there Lancelot was, following along.

He smirked at Alistair. "We all might as well meet now. No

point in wasting Arthur's time twice."

"Weren't you helping some of the others out here?" Maddy shouted.

Alistair glanced at her. Her big beautiful, green eyes had turned into slits filled with two orbs of poisonous shade. She walked easily beside Robin yet her eyes were locked on the lecher who walked behind them.

Anger was an odd emotion to see on Madelia's face. Revulsion, completely bewildering.

"I was." Lancelot's jaw worked from side-to-side and Alistair was sure his hands had turned into fists under his cloak.

"But I'd say this meeting is more important, wouldn't you, *Miss Maddy*?" Her name came out like a curse.

Alistair's hand moved to his dagger of its own accord. He had clenched his teeth and his breath left him like the smoky tendrils of a dragon's mouth. His cloak was suddenly too heavy. He could feel a steamy heat start on his skin.

Lancelot laughed.

"But then again, what do southern savages know of business?"

He had hoped for a spark of an apology in the boy's eyes. Fear, at the least. But instead, as Alistair stood facing Lancelot, both their eyes hardened and staring one another down, he saw something else. Something that made him nearly step back. Nearly.

His eyes were like those of the people in Satbury on Salvation Day.

"You need to apologize." Alistair took a step forward.

Snow had started to fall again but cold had long since left him.

Lancelot sucked his teeth, eyes still unmoving.

A shoulder pressed against Alistair. As Robin's scent filled his nostrils, there was a light pressure on his shoulder and then a pointed shadow on the snow.

He peered to his right.

Robin had unsheathed her dagger and twirled it in her free hand.

"Alistair is right, Lancelot." Pressed between her two fingers, she moved the blade from side to side. "You need to apologize. And you know something? I've become quite good with these lately. Though sometimes my knives do go askew."

Alistair fully looked at Robin now. Her icy blue eyes could have been daggers themselves the way she was glaring at Lancelot. Yet, he did not falter. Instead, he gave Robin a small smile. The tension around his eyes loosened.

"Apologies," he said, his moving from Robin to Maddy and back again. "I'm truly sorry and beg your forgiveness."

Robin eyed him. She stared back at Maddy.

"Lancelot, I—"

"You all are back!"

Arthur appeared from their right with Calvin in tow. The gruff man beamed at them.

"So, you didn't die?" Calvin laughed and smacked Maddy on the back, not noticing the few feet she stumbled.

She grinned at the man. "No, not this time."

He chuckled. "I'm glad to hear it, though there were some who nearly dug a moat, they paced in front of my work station so much."

The man's eyes fell on Arthur who was standing stiff as a board. Robin's eyes had found his and there was a blush in her cheeks. She turned her gaze to the snow, before pulling her hair to the side and meeting Arthur's eyes again.

Arthur cleared his throat. "Good noon, Robin. I am glad to see you have returned well."

"Thank you," she said with a nod. "I am glad to see you, too. We were actually about to come in search of you."

"News from the north?" He turned to Alistair. "Did your aunt have a chance to look at you? Are you well?"

"Well, I won't be falling over anytime soon," Alistair replied. "Thank you for asking."

"It'd be rude not to," the knight replied.

Alistair smiled. *So, he no longer wishes me dead? Progress.*

"If you'd all like, we can dine in my chambers for the midday meal."

"Caught some stray deer. The stew is sure to be tasty," stated Calvin. He rested his hands on his middle.

"How does that sound?" Arthur asked.

"I have one question." Maddy placed her hands behind her back. She gave Arthur a good once over. He straightened up under her gaze.

Robin and Alistair both stared at her.

She released a slow breath.

"Do you have any more of those southern chocolates left? I'm quite starved."

Alistair forced his body still in its seat. He wasn't sure how much longer he'd be able to sit though, not with Arthur's eyes digging into him. There was only so much a man could take, even Alistair.

"And have you tested your powers?" Arthur asked. He was perched on the edge of his seat with his hands clasped in front of his mouth.

The knight hadn't moved an inch since they had finished their tale of the north and he had begun conversing directly with Alistair. Oddly enough, the conversation had started to feel more like an interrogation.

"I have not used or attempted to use my powers since discovering I have them. This is just as new to me as it is to you," Alistair said.

"And Alistair isn't Cadfen," Robin chimed in. "He's the closest I've ever had to a brother which is why he trusts you enough to confide in."

She glared at Arthur. When he met her eyes, the cold of his seemed to fade. He sighed and sat up in his chair, letting his hands fall to the table.

"I apologize." He took in both Robin and Alistair's gazes. "To both of you. I'm more accustomed to fighting magic, not using it."

"It's fine."

Can we leave now? Alistair's eyes were becoming heavy as he fought several yawns.

"If anything, your power can be an asset against Cadfen."

I guess that's a no.

"Exactly, now all we need to do is to travel to the backroads and—"

"We still need a backup plan."

Lancelot's voice made Alistair want to bang his head against the table. Would the exhaustion never stop?

"Lancelot is right," Arthur said with a nod. "We need to be prepared in case our first course of action doesn't go as hoped."

"Did anyone have anything in mind?" Robin asked.

"There aren't many options, I don't think." Maddy was tapping her fingers against the table top and staring into the fire. "Arthur, you said yourself the place is impossible to get into. Our only option is to go in without being seen."

Lancelot took a gulp from his mug. "Or disguising ourselves?" He slammed the mug on the table and the other utensils clattered to the floor.

Alistair clenched his teeth before gathering his spilled utensils.

"Lance, why don't you get some rest?" Arthur looked over his mentee. "I think your cold is getting worse."

The boy shrugged. "I feel fine."

Arthur narrowed his eyes. Before Lancelot could say otherwise, the knight had placed a palm on the boy's forehead and was inspecting his eyes.

"You're a bit warm."

Lancelot leaned out of his reach. "I'm fine."

"Your eyes seem dull too."

He is quite the mother hen. Alistair felt a good laugh coming on. He cleared his throat and banged on his chest though the smile still tugged at his lips.

Both Arthur and Lancelot glared at him.

"Sorry. Just clearing a few snowflakes."

Robin covered her mouth as she giggled. Lancelot glanced towards her, then turned to face Arthur once more. He scowled at him.

"I said I'm well, Arthur," the boy hissed through clenched teeth.

"Off to bed with you." Arthur rose from his seat. "I can't have my best man getting ill before a mission."

"I—"

"Off with you, Lance. I'll have Cook bring you your supper."

Alistair was certain he had never seen a face as red. Truth be told, at that moment, Lancelot's face would have put the freshest apple to shame.

Yet as quickly as it had come, as quickly as it went. Lancelot released a breath, nodded to the table with eyes lingering on Robin and then left. The approaching storm had disappeared.

Arthur shook his head as the door closed. "I apologize about Lancelot. He won't admit it, but the winter doesn't always agree with him. I'm just cautious."

"No need to apologize." Robin smiled. "A mother must do what a mother must do."

"Yes...wait, Rob—"

"He does have a point though, Arthur," Maddy said, finger still taping the table. "Perhaps, if we cannot access Camelot through the guards' passage, sneaking in disguised is our best option."

"But who would we disguise ourselves as?" Alistair asked.

"Perhaps, we don't need a disguise. Robin entered Camelot with Alistair unnoticed the first time. Why not again?"

"But that was before Salvation Day in Satbury," he stated. "We cannot be sure what the other witches know, so we cannot be sure what Cadfen knows. They may recognize us now."

Robin shook her head. "If they knew who I was, wouldn't Cadfen have sent them looking? There were no incidents while we were gone."

She turned to Arthur for confirmation. He nodded.

"Maybe they don't know who you are," Maddy said. "It's not like Cadfen himself saw you, so walking into the front gates of Camelot under pretense is possible."

"What pretense though?" Arthur turned to her. "And how many of us can go in together without drawing attention?"

"And if we make it inside, what do we do from there? My messenger seal will be no good this time." Alistair raked his fingers through his hair. "I'm sure my employer has spread word of my disappearance. They're likely to be suspicious if I attempt to use it."

Everyone took a hard breath. Endless questions had filled the room and there seemed to be no answers to offer.

"Refugees."

Maddy's head was bowed as they all turned to look at her.

"It's not uncommon for us to wander. Even to places we know we aren't likely wanted."

She sighed and folded her hands in front of her. "If we can confirm from the back roads how the guards enter Camelot, I may be able to ask for temporary sanctuary and let everyone else inside."

"But you're putting yourself in danger," Alistair said.

He closed his eyes and shook his head. "Maddy, we designed the initial plan because—"

"Because I'm not a fighter." She grinned. "I know. I was there, remember? But do we really have any choice? Plus, it's only a backup. How likely is our first plan to go wrong?"

Robin rubbed her fingers along her wrist before meeting Maddy's eyes.

"I trust you, Maddy. You know I do but...but I can't ask you to put yourself in such a position. This isn't your battle after all."

"Robin is right," Arthur said.

"It is if I say it is," Maddy replied. "So, unless there are any other suggestions, I think this is our decision for now?" She looked around the table.

Alistair sighed. "Maddy, I—"

"Do you have another suggestion, Alistair?" She quirked a brow.

He drew his mouth into a thin line.

"You know what I'm going to say, don't you?"

"Yes, and you know how I will reply."

He bobbed his head and held Maddy's eyes. She didn't hesitate to stare right back into his.

Damn it!

"Fine, but only as a last resort. Correct?" He pinched the bridge of his nose.

They all agreed.

Now, can we rest?

"It's getting late," Robin said while she yawned. "I think it's time we head to our chambers."

"It has already been prepared. However, I did wonder if I could have a word with you, Alistair."

What have I done to deserve such a cruel fate?

"I promise, Robin, he will be returned safely to you."

She moved her arms across her chest. "I don't see why you cannot speak in front of us all."

Arthur released a breath. "Do you trust me?"

Her shoulders tensed but she dipped her head.

"Then, know I mean no ill will towards your brother. Are we all right to meet, then?"

She turned to Maddy who only yawned in response.

"I suppose so," she said, before turning to Alistair. "We will see you shortly. I expect to hear all the details of this conversation."

"And I will give no less." Alistair grinned.

The two women rose from their seats and exited the room. The door closed softly behind them and Alistair found himself alone with Arthur.

The noble filled both their mugs. He leaned back in his chair and took a deep breath. He tilted his cup from side to side while his eyes fixated on the table top. He seemed comfortable, relaxed while Alistair was toeing the line of complete exhaustion and dread about the private conversation. Even Edwin's company would have offered some comfort, though the spirit had not appeared again since the storm.

Arthur sighed and leaned forward, so his elbows rested on the table. The burning fire flickered shadows across the room and the royal was partially covered by darkness.

He rubbed his thumbs along the rim of his cup, then met Alistair's eyes.

"I know...I know I have not always been courteous to you,

Alistair. I'm sure, often, I came off as more of an ingrate than a knight."

Arthur took a long gulp of ale. Alistair followed suit and had a small sip of the earthy brew. He had never been one for drink.

"Under normal circumstances, I am sure we would have been fast friends."

Alistair nodded, though he wasn't sure about that himself. After all, he had always been a peasant and Arthur had always been a high-born. Their lives were worlds apart.

Arthur took down another gulp from his mug. He lowered it and rubbed the back of his neck.

"But we did not meet under normal circumstances. You were with Robin, the woman I love and thought dead." The last words came out hard and strained.

Arthur shook his head and took in a sharp inhale.

He continued. "That day, when you all returned, I believed I was dreaming for a moment. But then, I felt her, her arms wrapped around me, her dark hair like silk against my skin. It was as if...as if, when we held one another once more, no time had passed between us. Everything I had felt for her all those years ago had come back including my desire to protect her, to keep her safe."

His hand froze on his neck and he stared up from the table to look at Alistair. "Do you understand? I had always been the one to protect Robin. Yet when she needed me most, I had left her to rot in a tree. And she would have stayed there if you hadn't come along and rescued her. I have failed her. You took care of her when I couldn't. Because of that, I was jealous when I should have been grateful."

He adjusted in his seat.

"So, thank you, Alistair." He offered his hand to him. "Thank you for taking care of Robin when I was unable to."

Alistair stared at his hand.

"Do you not accept my apology?"

Alistair scooted forward in his seat and folded his hands in front of him. "It's not that I refuse to accept your apology, Arthur. I'm just not sure if it's necessary."

"It is," he stated. "Trust me. I was horrible at times and I watched with a suspicious eye when it was unnecessary."

"But only because you care for Robin."

"It's not an excuse," he replied.

"No, yet I hold no ill will towards you." Alistair gazed at the door. His mind drifted to Robin—the first time they had met, the night after the drunkard, their first journey home from the east...

A warmth rose in Alistair's chest. "I understand why you reacted the way you did. Not only is Robin a precious companion, but it's not exactly respectable for a young woman to journey along with a stranger. Most people had questions when they first encountered us together. Still, I ask that you understand, I was not the only one doing the saving. Robin's gotten me on my feet on more than one occasion."

"The tree, though, it—"

"Is long forgotten...mostly." Alistair waved his hand. "What I'm trying to say is thank you for your apology, but it isn't needed. I may have unknowingly helped Robin escape from the tree, yes. Still, I do not consider myself her savior. She would have never made it this far without her own will and determination."

Arthur laughed. "Willful is very much the proper word for her."

They both nodded. Silence filled the room aside from the crackling of the fire wood. Alistair took another gulp of ale and Arthur smiled at him.

"Friends, then?"

Alistair finished his mug and offered his hand to the noble. "Friends."

Both men shook. Arthur refilled their cups.

"One more this eve?" he asked.

"All right."

With both cups filled to the brim, Arthur raised his own in the air. The smile had not left his face and all its joy was directed at Alistair.

"To Robin." The knight grinned.

"And to the retaking of Camelot. Cheers!"

Chapter Twenty Four

"*Lancelot.*"
Something smooth moved along his chest.
"*Lancelot.*"

He wiped a hand over his face before opening his eyes. The room was pitch black save for a few torches hung on the walls. But someone was there. He could feel a presence looming over him and his body was rigid.

Why can't I move?

"*Have you forgotten what I feel like so quickly?*"
"*Robin?*"

Lancelot attempted to turn his head to the left where the closest torch hung. He needed to see her, he needed proof that he was not dreaming. Yet, he couldn't move. The muscles in his neck were rigid.

Again, he felt something pass over him but this time against the flesh of his throat.

It was as if a collar had been taken off. His neck muscles regained their feeling. He flexed them, swallowed a few times before turning to the light.

And there she was, pressed against him, her blue eyes wavering from his face to the darkness.

"*I have missed you,*" *she whispered.*

Even in the shallow light, he could see the pink of her bottom lip as she spoke. The same lip he had suckled on weeks past. He let his gaze linger there for a moment before meeting Robin's eyes once more.

There was a heat in her desire. Her blue eyes seemed darker somehow.

He smirked. "*Have I done this to you?*" *Lancelot turned on his side to face her. He took one hand and moved it from her shoulder to the small curve of her hip. She closed her eyes and leaned her mouth up to his.*

Without thought, he moved his hips against her own. A moan broke from her lips and soon he hovered above her.

His arms were on either side of her head, as he fingered her long tresses. He gazed down at her.

"*Why have you taken so long to come to me again?*"
She caressed his face. "*Patience, my love.*"

He pressed a kiss to her palm. "I am running low on that."
"Our time will come," she said.
"When?" He pushed his hips harder against hers. "When?"
Robin closed her eyes and bit the corner of her lip.
"Soon," she breathed.
Not good enough.
Lancelot reached up with his right hand and gripped Robin's chin. Her eyes flared open. He turned her head, so she was staring directly at him.

For a moment, the darkness in her eyes faded, replaced by the blue he adored so much. For a moment, the woman's face was pure shock...and something else.
"Lancel—"
"Shhh," he whispered. "It is time for me to take care of it."
He released her chin. His fingers trailed down the middle of her body until they reached the bottom of her dress. He moved his hand under the garment and along her thighs. She jerked in response.
Yes, that's it.
He lowered his face to hers, so their eyes had no choice but to meet. The feeling of her shivers around him, made him grin.
"Once we have retaken Camelot, you will have to rule as queen until Morganna is found. Well...if she is found," he corrected. "But when the capital is yours again, I will tell Arthur of your true feelings."
She shook her head. "We will need to wait. At least until late spring or—"
"No," he retorted through gnashed teeth. "No more waiting."
Lancelot cupped his fingers and engulfed himself in her warmth. He lingered there and watched her reaction. The way her eyes closed, the way she shivered, even the tilt of her neck, exposing her jugular to him. It said it all.
She is mine...
There was a rustling from his right. Lancelot jerked, his eyes flew open.
Wait. How the hell did I get out here?
The winter wind blew. Lancelot felt the chill to his very core. He looked over himself. The only clothing he wore was a pair of thin trousers--his night attire.
Another sound from his right. Lancelot reached for his sword, then silently cursed when he touched air. He had no memory of when, how, or why he left the capital, only that he was in the wilderness with no protection and someone was watching him.

Lancelot waited for something to emerge from the darkness but the woods remained still.

Quickly, he looked around himself. He picked up a stray stick, keeping his eyes on the woods as he did so. It wasn't a sword but it was better than nothing.

Something stepped into the moonlight to his left. He swung around, stick already raised when the shadow turned and ran. Lancelot took chase.

He pushed higher into the mountains and deeper into the woods. Careless branches scratched his arms as he ran, the figure only a few yards away from him. He pushed harder.

The figure was tall and slim. More importantly, it was light on its feet.

A woman.

It stepped into a patch of moonlight and for a brief second it looked back at him with beautiful blue eyes.

Robin?

Lancelot fell face forward to the earth. His stick flew from his hands.

"Damn it," he hissed and pushed himself up from the ground. He peered around him. There was only the night. She was gone and he was left with an aching chin.

Those eyes were Robin's. But why is she out here?

His gaze moved around him as he pushed up from the ground and wiped his chin.

"Lancelot..."

His spine straightened at the sensual hiss of his name. Lancelot stared behind him and there she stood. His eyes grew large, his nostrils flared, and his blood rushed through his veins while he took in all that Robin was.

She stood in front of him, her beautiful blue dress slipping down her pale shoulders. Her dark hair was wild and tangled. Still, it was partially pulled to the side so that it cascaded over her shoulder and covered her right breast.

He inhaled. "What are you doing here, Robin?"

Her eyes roamed over him. Then, she shook her head.

Lancelot turned to face her.

"I came to see you," she said. Her dress slipped lower.

He smirked. "If you wanted to lie with me tonight, you should have told me before we departed to our chambers. Of course, I am more than happy to oblige your impatience."

She nodded but turned her eyes away from him. Her thin, delicate fingers trailed over her nearly bare chest. Robin looked back at him with small, pink trembling lips.

Lancelot's chest grew tight. He stormed towards her and gripped her smooth shoulders under his hardened hands.

"What's happened?" he asked, trying to force her eyes to meet his.

She closed her eyes and a whimper slipped from her lips. "Robin..."

He pushed her hair back and ran his thumb along her jaw. Heat raced to his lower region.

"I-I..."

"Yes, Robin. What is it?"

"I don't know what to do," she stuttered.

"About what?"

She met his eyes again, her lips slightly pursed as she gazed at him.

"About you, Lancelot."

His hands froze. "What do you mean?"

She placed both hands on his chest and pushed her lips so close to his, a gust of wind would have concluded the act.

He pressed his hips against hers and the little gasp she released only charged him more. "What are you asking of me, Robin? Whatever it is, I can provide it to you."

She shook her head. "You can't."

"Why not?"

"Because," she sighed, "I'm not yours."

"You are!" he barked. "You have been mine since I decided you were. Camelot will be yours, we will tell Arthur--"

"He will never let me go," she sobbed. "Now that I've returned. I only...I never expected you, Lancelot."

He moved his lips to hers and clasped the back of her neck while he kissed. His other hand had tangled in her hair and held her steady against him.

Lancelot pulled away, certain he had made his point. Her lips had swollen. They looked as if they might bruise.

"Do not fret over Arthur," he said. "When the times comes I will tell him. We have hid this for too long."

She sighed. "You do not understand."

"I do!"

"He will never let you or I live."

"He will!"

"You must kill him Lancelot." The words were a whisper. Her eyes blazed into his, the pouting lip and trembling voice gone.

"If you or I am to survive the retaking of Camelot, you must kill him. Just when the throne is mine, slice his throat," she said.

Lancelot shook himself. "We cannot--"

"Do you love me?"

"I wouldn't be up here freezing my ass off if I didn't."

"Then, kill him. It is our only option."

A different type of chill settled on his skin.

Robin smiled. Her blue eyes had darkened again.

Chapter Twenty Five

Though Robin knew she had to stay still, her body rocked back-and-forth ever so slightly. She broke her eyes from the road and turned them upward towards Maddy.

Her green-haired friend seemed perfectly content perched on a tree branch gazing at the guards as they made their way along the backroads. Her green hair was covered in a pile of snow, her own personal requirement to ensure she wasn't seen in the white-covered trees.

Robin turned back to the road. The wagon moved in and out of her line of vision. Each time it disappeared, she longed to move just a little closer to the tree line, but she stayed steady. Arthur and Alistair's presence behind her helped. Their own tension was like a rope keeping her in place.

Behind them were several other men including Lancelot, all hidden among the trees.

She took a deep breath.

So close, so close.

The wagon moved within her vision again but was gone just as quickly. She silently cursed the tree for not giving her some sort of magic or improved sight.

Several pebbles made hollow *thump* sounds as they landed in the snow. Again Robin looked up at Maddy.

Her friend nodded and pointed to the road.

She mouthed "Almost" before looking back out at the wagon.

It had completely left Robin's sights now. Her stomach churned with anticipation. She placed a hand by her right side and felt the length of Arthur's dagger: Carnwennan.

Her other hand, she placed against a tree, leaning her weight into it.

You are going to pay, Cadfen.

The air moved beside her. Robin drew her dagger, her nerves on edge but all killer instinct died when she saw the arrow in Maddy's shoulder.

The green-haired girl stared up at her, looking at Robin but not seeming to actually see her as she grabbed at the arrow and repeatedly parted her lips as if searching for air.

"What do you mean?"

Alistair.

Robin looked behind her. Her friend's hands gripped at the

muddy white earth beneath him as his purple eyes rounded.

She followed his line of sight and saw nothing.

Is he speaking to Edwin?

The air whizzed around Robin. Arthur's command to "get down" was a secondary thought. She was frozen and Maddy was bleeding out beside her.

Someone or something pushed her to the ground. The shocking cold pierced the skin of her face, the weight of whatever held her pressed harder into her back.

She couldn't move.

Robin screamed and when she had finished she was surprised to hear other screams follow, as well. But they were deeper, shorter--the hollow shouts of men whose lives ended with extreme abruptness.

Maddy still gaped beside her.

No.

"Maddy," Robin shouted.

She attempted to turn her neck to see who was holding her down but they had her nearly meshed with the earth. Robin didn't care though. She was going to escape.

With gritted teeth and a grunt, she flattened her palms against the ground and pushed upward. More pressure was added to her back yet she refused. She had to save Maddy.

"Robin, you have to stay down. They haven't stopped shooting!" She paused at the sound of Arthur's voice.

"Do you hear me?" he asked. "The arrows are still coming. Stay down!"

"Where is Alistair?" she hissed. "Where is he?"

"I don't know. I'm sure he found cover. He was—"

Suddenly, Arthur's weight left her and Robin was pulled to her feet. She looked at the men who held her. They were dressed in armor with Camelot's seal marked on their helmets.

The clink of metal against metal drew her attention. A guard dressed like the ones who held her battled with Arthur.

They begin to drag her away.

Arthur's back still turned. He could not see the man who came from behind him.

She struggled against the men that held her. She thrashed her body away from them, yet they were unfazed.

Her feet made trails in the snow as they forced her away.

"No, Arthur! Arthur, behind you!"

The coward raised his sword.

"Robin!"

Maddy staggered to her knees. She held her hand over the wound but the blood flowed easily. Her legs trembled as she stood.

Robin shook her head. "No, Maddy. Run, run!"

A man yelled.

"No!" Robin moved her eyes back to Arthur, tears already streaking her face.

But it was not Arthur who was bleeding. Lancelot stood behind his mentor with a sword in hand that pierced the abdomen of their enemy.

Even from the distance she then stood, Robin could see the man's blood dribble down Lancelot's sword and onto the snow. She smiled, her lips seeming to stretch of their own accord and the knot in her stomach temporarily easing as the sight of the enemy's blood joyously unhinged her.

Robin laughed. And she laughed even harder when she saw more armor-clad bodies lying on the ground. Her heart was a burning pit of black happiness that rocked joy through her.

"Down with Cadfen," she screamed. "Down with the traitor! Kill them. Kill them all!"

She smacked her fist against the helmet of one of the men who held her.

"I will see you hang and watch your feet dangle," she spat at him..

"You are the one that matters to us," said the man to her right. "King Cadfen said nothing of your friend, so I suggest watching your tongue." He stared behind them and Robin followed his gaze.

The joy she felt quickly dulled.

Another soldier had tossed Maddy over his shoulder and was jogging towards them. Behind him, more guards filled the space where Alistair and the others hid.

The wet cold that touched her feet disappeared as Robin was grabbed by her legs and lifted into the air. She fought the four men that had grasped her limbs. She screamed up into the gray sky that rested above her, hot tears streaming down her face, her throat growing raw.

Why? Why is this happening again?

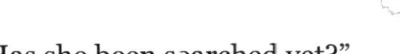

"Has she been searched yet?"

Robin didn't recognize the voice she heard. Her head felt heavy and her lips dry.

"Not yet, my Lord. As you instructed, she was not—"

"Touched by anyone but me. You are dismissed."

There was the sound of several footsteps, a door closing, and finally the slight creak of a chair.

She could feel someone near the bed she rested on.

Though not familiar, the bed was notably more comfortable than anything she had slept on in months. Even the blanket that covered her was heavy and warm, perfect for winter and for keeping her out of the sight of her captors.

She had only been up for a short time. Her entire body still ached from the battle. Her mind still reeled from what she had seen.

Where is Maddy?

Her daggers must have still been attached to her sides if the previous conversation was any indication.

There also seemed to be only one man now—a much easier target. How big he was and how skilled were questions Robin did not have the answers to.

Rough hands ran through the very top of her hair. Small beams of light infiltrated her darkness as the cover was pulled back.

She pinched her eyes shut.

"Robin."

He knows me.

The rough hands that trailed her hair moved down to her face to her bottom lip.

"I am so sorry it came to this, Robin," said the man. "I am even sorrier I did not find you in time. If my men had been quicker that night, all of this would have been avoided. You would have been my q—"

Robin turned her mouth and grabbed Cadfen's finger between her teeth. As his calloused flesh ripped in her mouth, she flashed her eyes open and glared at him.

There was no doubt it was Cadfen. Yes, he had cut his brown hair, so it no longer hung by his shoulders and, yes, he had grown a short beard. But those eyes reminiscent of ash were still there.

All pain dissolved from Robin's body. Her heart pounded loudly in her chest and soon she heard nothing else. She could see nothing else but Cadfen and her uncle's ring that rested on his finger.

The traitor had lunged away from her, but she had broken skin. The taste of his blood excited her. She planned to leave all of his on the floor.

Robin tossed the covers away. She went after Cadfen while he still stared down at his bleeding finger. She barely heard her dagger being unsheathed, hardly felt it in her grasp but she knew it was there. And she wanted to kill him with it.

She raised her parents' blade wide and brought it down. He stepped to the side, out of her target range.

Stupid, Robin. Get him!

Taking only a second to breathe, she used the momentum of her run and moved around to face him once more.

"So, you were awake?" He raised a brow, a slow smile starting on his face. "I assumed such. I am very happy to see you. I apologize—"

"I do not want your words!" she screamed and charged forward.

He easily dodged each move with her dagger. The only one she had not used was Arthur's. She couldn't afford for Cadfen's blood to touch the blade.

He moved several steps back. There was greater distance between them.

"You've picked up some skills on the roads, I see." He gave her a once-over. "I admit I am impressed. However, you're aware of how long I've trained, Robin. You know you cannot win."

Her grip tightened on the dagger she held.

Bastard.

"What will we do here, then, hmm?"

Cadfen removed his cloak and tossed it on the floor. He crossed his arms. "I may have aged ten years, but my stamina is still quite good. I can do this for hours if you'd like. But do not expect me to raise a hand to you in defense."

He placed his arms by his side. His chest was broad and exposed.

"So, what will it be?" he asked.

Robin bit her lip. The anger was still burning in her, but the flames had died. Her body was feeling weighted again. The pain was surely returning.

She glanced around as her focus expanded beyond Cadfen.

The room was nearly barren. There was nothing she could use to her advantage.

The only thing I have is myself. I must.

She raised a dagger and threw it at him. It spun perfectly in the air. If it had been anyone else, she was sure it would have landed in their shoulder. But Cadfen was experienced. Like before, he stepped to the side.

However, she was already running towards him.

Robin watched him. He seemed complacent, not shocked.

Good.

As she moved up to stuff her other blade in his chest, Cadfen dodged, grabbed her wrists and soon she was pressed against the wall, the weapon stuck in her hold.

He moved close to her.

"Have you forgotten yourself?" he asked. "Have the roads changed you so much? You were always stubborn but you're acting like a savage."

She hardened her eyes.

"Have you forgotten who you are? You are Lady Gwyneverre or, because you always preferred it, Lady Robin," he said. His eyes roamed around her face.

Soft, Robin. Soft like Brima said.

"You are a lady of the kingdom, the court."

Still holding her in place, Cadfen placed his palm against her cheek. His ashen eyes were so honest, Robin nearly laughed.

Instead, she allowed some water to flow to her eyes. Her body grew limp. Her bottom lip trembled some.

He sighed yet he had a small smile. "Yes, yes, Robin. Come back to me. You are my lady of—"

Robin angled her feet into the floor and her back into the wall. She jumped into the air and kicked the traitor away from her.

He landed before she did. The dagger had already left her hand. The hiss that escaped his lips brought a smirk to Robin's.

Cadfen was on his knees, holding the right of his abdomen. When he pulled his hand back, blood decorated his palm. He stared at her.

Robin stood, one of the few times she had ever towered over him.

"I am not your lady."

There was silence. She wanted her words to fill the room and suffocate him until he understood.

She had never been and would never be his.

"I didn't want to have to do this, Robin." Cadfen came to his feet. He kept his eyes steady on her.

"You are making me a cruel man," he said.

"I am making you into nothing," she retorted. "Cruelty is in your blood. You are the monster. Not me!"

Cadfen released a sigh. "My men tell me you care for that refugee we have in the dungeon?"

She cringed.

He nodded. "That is answer enough. I ask that you prepare yourself for dinner tomorrow evening. I will give you the day to gather your senses. I expect you dress as any lady of the kingdom would. Properly."

"Where is Maddy?" Robin hoped she hid the quiver in her voice well.

He broke eye contact with her before grabbing his cloak from the floor.

"I will see you for tomorrow's dinner."

And with that said, Cadfen disappeared from the room.

Chapter Twenty Six

*A*listair paced the small room he once shared with Robin and Madelia. Chills ran over his body and his stomach was in knots. He could feel him there. He was just hiding. Edwin.

Somehow the room seemed smaller than before, despite it having fewer people to accommodate. Alistair found his strides were too long for the space. He was sweating despite the tremors and cold that ran through him. Everything was wrong. This wasn't how it was supposed to be.

The temperature in the room dropped. Alistair's sight and hearing dulled for a moment. His skin felt loose, and then the room seemed to fall from under him.

It was if everything was turning upside down, the room was *slowly vanishing until...*

Suddenly, he was covered in the foggy gray he had only seen once before. It surrounded him in every direction, endless, the perfect place for a man to go if he wished to lose his mind. Part of Alistair did.

"Alistair?"

He turned to peer behind him. There stood Edwin, dressed in the clothes of a young boy, face still round like that of an innocent child, yet he was anything but.

"You killed them!" *he screamed, moving so he was fully facing the child.* "You handed them both to Cadfen!"

Swirls of steam rose from Alistair's nostrils. His entire body felt hot. His scalp burned like it had never before, and in the pit of his stomach, there was only a boiling rage. His chest felt heavy.

Why can't I breathe?

Now, his eyes tricked him too. The gray had become blurry.

"Alistair, I-I'm sorry. Please, stop."

His cheeks were warmed by his tears.

"I had to, Alistair! I had to."

He lowered his head and wiped his eyes.

"Please! Alistair, don't send me to the dark place."

The dark place?

Alistair blinked rapidly and forced his vision to clear. He turned his attention back to Edwin. The boy shivered where he stood, his eyes gazed over the darkness that surrounded him. The gray was nearly gone. The place they now stood was the night sky absent of stars. There was only the dark aside from a small area where the boy stood.

Alistair raised his brows. He shook his head. "I'm not doing this."

Still, even as the words left him, the darkness moved forward, shrinking Edwin's space of security. And Alistair found himself smiling, just a bit, as the boy held himself from the approaching shadows. Maybe he could...

"Why did you betray us, Edwin? Why did you tell Cadfen of our plans?" *Alistair screamed.* "I trusted you."

"I had to, Alistair!"

"You made a choice. Now, Robin...Maddy...he could be doing anything to them."

Bile rose in his throat. He swallowed it and used it to fuel his anger. After all, he was hurting because of Edwin. Wasn't it fair Edwin now hurt, too?

Move.

The shadows did as they were commanded. A sob broke from the boy's lips.

"I trusted you and—"

"He was going to kill my sister."

The shadows came to a halt, the fire in Alistair temporarily doused by Edwin's words.

Through whimpering lips, the boy spoke.

"Cadfen called me to him. I tried to ignore him but he's very strong and, I had to go. I didn't have a choice," *he cried.* "The witches must have found the one I killed. They told him what happened when I saved you. He knew all about me. The witch that tried to take my soul was there, too a-and he said if I didn't help him, he'd kill my sister. She's the last of my family, Alistair. My mother was carrying her when I...died."

Edwin looked away from Alistair. He stared down at his feet, his fists balled by his side.

"I wanted to tell you so many times," *he whispered.* "But I'm her elder brother. I have to keep her safe."

The boy's shoulders shook. Alistair chewed the inside of his mouth while his face remained stoic. He thought of Madelia, Robin, and the men who had died during the battle. He focused on the nausea that rolled over him as their faces flashed through his mind, the angry fire that had burned in his stomach.

But in place of the fire, Alistair found a heaviness that weighed both him and Edwin down.

He sighed, his shoulders slouched, and the shadows receded until the gray fog appeared again.

"Why didn't you tell me, Edwin?"

The boy glanced up at him. "I didn't know what you'd say. I didn't want to risk Elizabeth."

Alistair closed his eyes and ran his fingers through his hair. "You should have trusted me, Edwin." *He stared at the boy.* "I thought you did."

"I do. I just—I just—"

The boy covered his face with his hands, his right slanted across his eyes and his left across his mouth. The sobs were muffled.

Alistair sighed. He tried to grab at the hate he had felt for Edwin only a bit ago but the remaining tendrils were quickly evaporating.

He strode towards the boy and crouched in front of him. Edwin continued to cry, covering his face.

Alistair scooted a bit closer before wrapping the child in his arms. Tears stained his shirt, though ghost tears were colder than he had expected.

He pulled him closer. "There, there, Edwin. It's all right. I forgive you."

The boy took in a long gulp of air. He wrapped his arms around Alistair's neck and buried his face there.

"Do you promise?"

"I do."

"I'm so sorry, Alistair."

He patted his head. "What's done is done. We cannot change what happened but you can right your wrong."

Edwin sniffled. "What can I do?"

"The night the witch attacked me, you destroyed her once I summoned you. I need you to do that again." *Alistair squeezed the boy's shoulder.*

His eyes rounded. "B-but Cadfen will—"

"No." *Alistair's grip tightened.* "Not if we kill him."

He shook his head, fresh tears coming on. "I can't. I'm supposed to protect my little sister."

Alistair sighed. "And how can she truly ever be safe if Cadfen is willing to offer her up at any moment? He'll use her against you again. Perhaps she'll just be the next soul he gives to the witches."

Edwin's gaze fell to the ground. "I know but..."

"But you can correct your wrong and save your family, as well," *Alistair said.* "Trust me, Edwin."

The boy's hands were trembling. He looked at Alistair. "Cadfen has many witches. I would need to gather others...more children like me. And maybe their parents too if they're here. I think they'd be willing to fight."

"You can convince them, can't you?"

He nodded. "But you would have to summon us all. It will take a large amount of magic."

"I don't care, Edwin! I'll manage. I need to get Maddy and Robin back whatever the cost."

Edwin sniffled and wiped his eyes. "I'll gather them. As many as I can."

Alistair's shoulders slacked and he breathed in relief. "Thank you, Edwin. However, I must ask another favor of you."

"I'll do what I can," *he said.*

"Could you show me how to leave this place again?"

The child's face pinched together. "I don't think you need me to anymore."

"Why not?"

He stared at him. "You almost sent me to the dark place. You can surely make your way from the Ether."

Alistair nodded. "Uh...yes, yes, I can."

"You have no idea, do you?"

"Not one, no."

Edwin shook his head. "All right. Follow me." *He grabbed Alistair's hand.* "One day you'll have to learn to do this alone, you know?"

Alistair laughed. "I suppose it's good that I have you as a teacher then."

Alistair opened his eyes. Once again, he was in the room he had shared with Robin and Madelia. But someone else was there, too. Not, Edwin.

He could feel them behind him but like before, his body was slow to return to his control.

"Alistair, are you well?"

Arthur.

"Alistair?"

He attempted to move his lips. They refused.

The knight's heavy hand landed on his shoulder and he began to shake him. Alistair nearly fell over from the force, but the paralysis was not as bad as before. He could already feel his body becoming his again and as he tipped towards the wall, he moved his back and kept himself upright.

He held up a shaky hand.

"One moment," he mumbled.

Arthur nodded.

"Isn't he done yet? We need to—"

"Quiet, Lancelot. Give him some time."

Alistair took in long breaths. He tried to flex a different muscle with every inhale until his body felt his own again. He turned to face Arthur and Lancelot. They both looked as bad as he imagined he himself looked. Hair disheveled, bags under their eyes, and balled fists that refused to relax.

He was sure the three of them were quite a sight.

"Cadfen used Edwin's sister. If he hadn't acted as his spy, she would have been killed," he said.

Lancelot huffed. "So the dead boy decides to offer us up instead?"

"It's not as simple as that," Alistair replied. He stood up from the wall now. "I'm not saying what he did was right. I'm only saying I understand he was in a difficult situation."

"And how is that supposed to help us exactly, Alistair?" Lancelot perched in the corner. He gave Alistair a hard look. "How can we be sure you weren't working with the dead boy?"

"What?" Alistair moved towards him but Arthur stepped in his path.

"How do we not know this was your plan all along? Kill us, take the women, move back to Camelot and live with the other—"

Alistair lunged at him only to find himself pressed against the wall by Arthur. He continued to struggle under his grasp.

"Lance, leave!" Arthur glared back at him.

He only stared in return.

"I'm going to kill you," Alistair seethed.

"I said leave, Lancelot. That's an order!"

He remained where he stood, looking from Arthur to Alistair. He lifted his chin and squared his shoulders, setting his hateful gaze on Alistair.

A vein ticked in the boy's neck, he worked his jaw, and his eyes rounded with the hate he felt. Yes, he was angry and so was Alistair.

Tendrils of smoke rose from the floor. Alistair could feel something leave him as they took shape, a piece of him was reaching out. And that piece wrapped around Lancelot's neck.

Fear filled the boy's eyes now. The dark tendrils lifted him higher into the air. The rhythm of his pulse filled Alistair.

Lancelot was still alive but it was slipping away ever so slowly.

Arthur grabbed Alistair by the shoulders and turned him forward, so they were face-to-face.

"Release him, Alistair," he said, digging fingers into his flesh. "You may not like Lancelot but you are not a murderer. Release him, Alistair." His tone was wavering.

Alistair paused. He turned his sights to Lancelot as his feet kicked wildly in the air, his eyes beginning to bulge from his head. He focused on the boy's struggle, attempting to embed it in his memory, to gain some joy from Lancelot's loss.

Yet, he felt none and, so he released him.

Arthur looked back at Lancelot before turning to Alistair.

"Thank you," he said.

Lancelot rose to the floor with one hand around his neck. He peered around him. The black tendrils were gone. His eyes rose to meet Alistair's.

"Leave us, Lance," Arthur ordered stepping into their line of sight. "I will speak with you later."

"How can you—"

"I said, I will speak with you later. Perhaps, after you have found your senses."

"I refuse to—"

"Do you dare challenge me?" Arthur asked.

The boy was silent.

"You may have aged, Lance but I am still your superior, in and outside of the training grounds. Now go."

Once more, Lancelot looked between the two men. His breath came out in heavy pants as he massaged his neck. His face had paled some from the brief encounter.

"You are both fools," he spat, before staggering to his feet and leaving the room.

When the sound of his uneven steps couldn't be heard, Arthur turned to face Alistair.

"Your eyes darkened when you attacked Lance."

"He deserves no less for what he said to me." Alistair grabbed the back of his neck and took in a breath. "I-I didn't mean to attack him. I'm still getting use to these powers."

Arthur nodded. "Thankfully so. Without that fog you created, more men would have lost their lives."

He scoffed. "Yes, a lucky mistake. Cadfen still got what he wanted." He looked directly at Arthur. "He still got Robin. And

Maddy. We must retrieve them."

"That, I'm sure even Lancelot can agree on." Arthur took a seat in the room's small chair. "I think his pride is more hurt than anything else."

Can he really not know about Lancelot's desire of Robin?

"Were you able to gather any other information from Edwin?"

Alistair shook his head. "The witches told Cadfen about Edwin. Cadfen used his powers as a castor to find Edwin. Then he blackmailed him. There's nothing more to it really but I may have found a solution."

"I'm listening," Arthur replied.

"You know that Edwin saved me the night the witch attacked. I want him to do that again," said Alistair. "Except this time, he'll be killing the witches that possess Cadfen's body and he won't be alone. He can gather other spirits. I'll summon them all with my magic."

Arthur nodded and looked away from Alistair. He placed his elbows on his knees, clasped his hands together, and rested his chin. His eyes were focused on the wall.

"That kills Cadfen. Good. It doesn't get us into Camelot though."

Alistair took a seat on the bed, pressing his back against the wall and stretching out his limbs. He watched Arthur and allowed his own mind to wander. They needed a plan that would rid them of Cadfen and get them into Camelot but what?

Camelot was impenetrable; there were security checks at every entrance, and guards roamed the streets. Robin had mentioned how she escaped ten years ago through the water tunnel but her chamber maid also knew of this plan and betrayed her. Wouldn't Cadfen know now, as well?

Perhaps, it's still worth looking into. We'd have to go under the cover of night to—

"I didn't want to do this." Arthur placed his head in both his hands. He shook himself and sat up to meet Alistair's eyes. "But I don't think we have a choice."

He raised a brow. "What are you talking about, Arthur? Whatever it is, I agree. We need to help them escape."

Arthur nodded, though his shoulders were still slacked.

With a hard sigh, he said, "Did Robin tell you of the weapon I gifted her? Carnwennan?"

"No, I've never heard of it."

"It's a dagger I acquired on a journey years ago when Terryn was king. It gives its user the ability to blend into shadow."

Alistair shot up. He was sure his eyes had doubled in size. "Where did you—"

"It doesn't matter," Arthur stated with a wave of his hand. "The point is—"

"It does matter! All of this could have been avoided. If we could have used that weapon to sneak into the castle and kill Cadfen, why didn't we?" He had turned his hands into fists in his lap. "Why didn't you say something sooner?"

Arthur briefly closed his eyes, before looking at Alistair again. They were watery.

"The thought had crossed my mind in the past. I thought it too risky. Once exposed to any light, the wielder becomes visible. It would only take a torch swung in the right direction and..." He clasped his hands on his knees and stared at the floor. "I gave it to Robin before you all left north as an extra safety measure. I'd never used it to kill Cadfen because I wouldn't want it getting into his hands if the plan went folly nor am I sure it would be of any use since he's a castor."

"And where is the dagger now?" Alistair snapped.

There was a moment of silence.

"With Robin."

He couldn't take it anymore. Alistair jumped to his feet and began pacing the room. He gripped his hips as he made quick, long strides, his mind racing through all the possibilities of their current situation.

"If Cadfen has discovered Carnwennan and if he knows where we are, we're pigs waiting for the slaughter." He glanced at Arthur for confirmation.

The knight nodded. "If he gets either Robin or Madelia to confess, we will all be murdered at his hand and those of the devils he commands. That's why I want you to aid me in a decision."

"If it will save my friends, then I vote yes."

"Are you sure about that, Alistair?" Arthur raised a brow.

Alistair stopped pacing. "What are you thinking?"

"The man who gifted it to me called it Rhonogomyniad. It's a spear, supposedly molded by an ancient dwarven tribe if you believe in that sort of thing."

"And what does it do?" Alistair asked. "How is a spear going to help us?"

Arthur stood. "Because this one spear can take down Camelot in a single toss. Two, for good measure."

"How is that possible?"

"How is Carwennean possible? Or Robin living in the tree?"

Arthur countered.

"Point taken."

"I have claimed the spear and so it's completely under my control. However, once I toss it, anything in its way will be destroyed. Buildings will crumble and—"

"The citizens under Cadfen's control could get hurt?"

Arthur nodded. "Yes, but we'd be able to finally take back the capital and rescue Robin and Maddy. Only at the expense of others' lives."

Alistair had no words. His mind was too full.

"There is also a book I'd like to give you but I'll discuss that later." Arthur cleared his throat. "I need to know, Alistair...if you are willing to make this choice with me," Arthur said. "For in truth, I do not think it one I can make alone."

Chapter Twenty Seven

Robin wanted to do nothing more than bash in the helmets of the guards escorting her to the evening meal. Their armor was decorated in the symbol of Camelot and the middle kingdom, yet it was all a façade. They weren't real knights, Cadfen wasn't a real king, and she was not going to be their prisoner.

The false king had insisted she wear a blue wool dress. In the note he left for her, he insisted it was a lovely contrast to her light blue eyes.

The bastard.

But she had little choice. Her own dress was smudged and tearing. It had begun to smell, and he had offered her nothing else to wear aside from the gown. At one point, she sent a reply through the guards asking for pants. As Robin expected, this was met with a swift condemnation of "a lady such as herself" wearing men's clothing.

Robin smiled at the memory. In truth, she had only replied so to get a rise out of Cadfen.

Yes, she was technically in his territory now; she was playing his twisted version of cat-and-mouse but she would play by her own rules. And she had no plans to play fair.

"My lady."

The guards stopped at the entrance to a private dining hall. They both bowed, a favor Robin did not return as she crossed the threshold and stepped into the room.

Not much of the castle had changed. There had been some renovations and certain rooms had different uses. Still, much was familiar to her including the chamber where she stood.

After her parent's death and once she had moved in with her uncle, he had invited Robin for a private dinner. It would become one of many, yet her memories were tainted now. Because where her uncle should have been standing to greet her was Cadfen.

He was dressed in fine attire, a color combination of black and purple suited for any royal, not a coward.

"Lady Robin." He stood from his seat and bowed.

She turned away from him. Without having to look, she could feel his eyes on her.

"I see your mood has improved some."

She spun on him.

"My mood is reflective of the present company, *forced*

company to be exact."

He smiled. "Of course. Your quick tongue was one thing I always loved about you, Robin. Quite intelligent."

"Hm. I feel I cannot say the same."

There wasn't even the slightest flinch in his demeanor. Cadfen remained smiling.

"Please, take a—"

Robin pulled the chair out, dragging the legs along the stone floor, before finally sitting.

He smoothed his hands over his jaw and chuckled.

"Dinner will be served shortly," he said.

"Very shortly, I hope," she replied.

"Hm."

Silence filled the large room. Robin could still feel his eyes on her. She had taken to staring at anything but him. Plus, she needed to plan. Since it was only the two of them dining, stealing a knife to use on his throat later would prove difficult. If they were in the main hall, she could easily slip it into her dress sleeve.

He had confiscated all her weapons including Carnnewenan.

I should have returned it to Arthur as soon as our journey from the north ended. How could I have forgotten?

A creaking sounded through the room.

Robin broke from her thoughts as several servants entered the spacing carrying trays of food. She met eyes with each one of them, no recognition flashed in their vision. They may have aged but many of them were the same people who had waited on her uncle, Morganna, and herself for years. Now, they looked at her as if she were a stranger.

Her throat tightened for a moment. She quickly cleared it, turned forward in her seat, and waited to be served.

The plate in front of Robin was filled with chicken, bread, cheese, and tarts. She noticed the servant left a small plate of extra tarts by her side. No doubt Cadfen remembered they were one of her favorites.

When both Cadfen and Robin's plate were filled, the servers stepped to the sides of the room. He eyed them.

"You may leave use."

They all bowed and departed from the same back door they had entered.

"You know," Cadfen began, picking at his bread, "in the last decade, Camelot has been nearly extinguished of all crime. Yes, yes, of course, there are a few that slip through the cracks. Some greedy pickpockets that have luck on their side. Still, for the most part, everyone lives peacefully."

He looked up from his bread at Robin who only responded by crossing her arms and glaring.

His sights returned to his food. "Disease is rare here. We haven't had an outbreak in several years. For the past seven years, the middle kingdom farmers have been very successful in—"

"Is that why you murdered my uncle?"

A vein pulsed in his forehead.

Robin smiled even as her eyes burned.

"No," he said quietly. "Terryn's death—"

"Murder," she spat, "murder that you committed! And for what? The throne? Me? Two things you shall never truly have."

Robin's jaw felt tight. Her nails dug into her arms through the dress fabric and she took deep breaths through her nose. "Do not speak as if the throne, as if the kingdom, were placed in your blood-covered hands."

Cadfen sighed. He sat up from his plate and leaned back in his seat, stroking his beard and eyeing Robin.

"Tell me about the dagger I took from you, the one with the white hilt."

She fought to control the rapid speed of her heart.

"It's nothing but a dagger I hope to use one day on you. Any other questions?"

Another chuckle, followed by a smirk.

"Well, whatever it is, it seems to have some magic about it. I don't suppose you will tell me where you found it, will you?"

He looked at her, his eyes directly met her own and Robin suddenly felt heavy. A pressure settled over her as she slumped in her seat. Tingling sensations creeped over her skin that now felt too tight and something else dragged her down, another feeling...

Fear. I...it's just like before, the witches...

"I command you to leave me."

Robin attempted to force her head up. What felt like a hand pushed it back down.

"My summons was an accident. Return from hence you came and release my guest," Cadfen said. "She is under my personal protection and not to be touched. Release her. Now."

The weight instantly vanished. Robin fell forward in her seat and landed lopsided on the table. Her chest felt vast as she took in air, attempting to gather as much of it as she could.

"Robin, I'm so sorry. I lost my temper. Are you all right?"

She turned her head and watched concern wash over Cadfen's face. His brows were knitted together and his eyes widened as if to look for any physical ailment.

He had risen from his seat and his hands were planted on the table but even from where she stood, Robin could see it. His arms were shaking. His shoulders too.

A wisp of hair fell in her face as she watched him.

"You can't maintain them," she said between breaths. "You're losing control."

Every inch of the man stilled. Robin grinned.

"Seems all is not well in Camelot, after all."

Light footsteps echoed in the hallway.

"Oswin, no." The sound of a child's whisper came from behind the front door. "Stop, you'll—"

"Young prince, you cannot be here," said one of the guards.

Prince?

Robin moved her eyes from the door to Cadfen. The color had drained from his face and he clutched at the table's edge.

"But I want to see father!"

A loud creak echoed throughout the room as the door flew open. The two guards stood staring at the floor where three young boys were piled on top of one another.

"Father!" the smallest one called out. He placed his hands on the floor and tried to push himself up. However, the weight of the other two prevented him from standing.

The child began to squirm, hoping to break free, when his eyes finally met Robin's. She had a full view of his face now. He had a small nose, large green eyes, and dark hair.

The tallest of the three climbed off his brothers and stood. His eyes, a lovely green like his brother's, found Robin while he bowed to Cadfen. As he did so, golden ringlets of hair streamed from his head.

"I am sorry, Father. I tried to stop him," said the eldest boy. His brothers rose from the ground, as well and stood by his side.

I know this child. Robin stood from her seat. *He looks so familiar.*

"Where is your caretaker, Patton?" Cadfen sighed.

Oswin placed a hand on his abdomen. "She went to fetch dinner. Why couldn't we eat with you, Father?"

Robin was sure Cadfen was watching her as she watched his sons. They called him father, so what else could he be? But their green eyes did not come from him nor the curly golden hair. There was only one lady in the castle with those specific traits when Terryn was king. And Robin knew her. She was her chambermaid.

"Lady Elizabeth?" said a guard.

"Yes, have you seen my boys? I returned to their chambers but could not find them. Have they come looking for their father?'

At first, Robin only heard her voice. Then she was there, standing in the doorway, wearing a fine gown with her beautiful hair plaited down her back. Her gaze fell on the three boys and a smile pulled across her face.

She placed her hands on her hips. "Causing trouble again, are we?"

"I only wanted to eat with Father, Liz," Oswin whined, turning to her. "But he has company."

Robin attempted to blink the image of her away, yet Elizabeth remained and now she was staring at Robin. Her face was in full view including the scar that decorated her cheek.

Suddenly, Robin's thigh hurt from the wound Elizabeth had inflicted ten years ago. Her back rippled in pain as arrows pierced her flesh. Fear and anger engulfed her. Her stomach churned from nausea and the room began to swim around her.

Not now. Please, not now.

She looked down at her thigh. Though it didn't seem to be bleeding she could feel the thick, warm fluid roll down her leg and into her slipper. It was on her back, too, dribbling down from the holes like porridge from a child's mouth.

After so long, why now?

Robin knew she was falling backwards. She also knew people were screaming though the sound was a hollow one to her ears. Yet in the midst of all the chaos, there was still a blur of gold in a mass of darkness.

There was still Elizabeth alive. And Terryn still dead.

Kill her.

The knife slipped easily into her hands. The world still shook, but Robin moved with it, tilting herself in the right direction to keep forward and on her feet as she ran towards her chambermaid.

There was more screaming and something slammed. The golden blur had disappeared, and the knife Robin held was plunged into the door instead of Elizabeth's soft, milky flesh.

"I'm going to kill you!"

Robin pulled at the handle but it refused to open. She slammed her fists against the door, her senses slowly coming back to her.

She pulled the knife free and dug it into the door again and again...

"You traitorous whore!"

"Robin, stop."

"I will see you bleed!"

"Robin!"

Arms wrapped around her and she knew they belonged to Cadfen. Without a second thought, she raised her elbow and slammed it into his face. His arms immediately left her. Blood poured over his mouth from his nostrils.

He raised his hands to his face, coating his palms in red.

Robin wanted to smile at the irony but found she was breathing too hard to do anything but stare.

Cadfen raised his head from his hands. He flexed his face some before looking up at Robin. He sighed.

"I am so sorry."

The presence returned. She felt heavy and tired, very tired. There was some mumbling.

Robin fell forward, unable to move, landing on Cadfen's chest, his blood smearing across her cheek.

He shook his head as he stroked her hair.

"I am sorry, Robin."

Her eyes closed, sleep took her, and everything became silent.

I am not here. I am with my mother in the south. It's hot and she's offering me a cold bucket of water to wash in. Endlun comes and jumps in it before I have a chance. He's squirting water at me. I grab him from under his arms, ready to throw him out of my bath but mother stops me.

"Play nice with your brother, Madelia."

"But he took my bath!"

"I can draw you another," she says, gentle lines showing at the corner of her eyes. "Plus, you are his big sister. You must take care of him."

I look at Endlun. He's grinning up at me.

I sigh. "If I have to."

"Wake up, southerner."

Maddy opened her eyes only to wish she had kept them closed. It was the night guard, Charles, who was shaking her awake. He also had a strong love for onion soup.

She breathed despite herself.

Oh, Spirits, he's added garlic.

Maddy's eyes watered.

"Wake up now, girl, you have been called," he said. "I have to say, I've never seen a young lady sleep as much as you."

Most young ladies aren't prisoners either.

She sat up in the bed, rubbed her eyes, and tucked her hair behind her ears. "Why am I being summoned?"

"Not sure," he replied. "I was only instructed to fetch you."

"Well, where am I going?" she asked, her eyes still heavy with sleep.

Charles sighed and flipped down the face cover of his helmet. "You have a lot of questions, but I don't have time to answer them. Please, let's go." He offered his hand.

She glanced from his palm to her own fingers that were curled around the edge of the blanket. He had interrupted her sleep, forced her from her blissful trance to an abysmal reality.

The decorated walls, feather stuffed pillows, and cushioned bed were shallow comforts.

Her grip tightened on the blanket, a shaky urge ignited in her fingers. She wanted to pull the comforter over her head and hide away from whatever she had to face or whomever.

But I can't.

"Please, miss," Charles said.

She looked up at him.

"I do not want to force you." Again, he offered his hand.

Maddy took it and rose from the bed. Just as he began to lead her, the sound of rattling chains reached her ears and she stumbled forward, landing palms first onto the cold stone.

"Oh, are you all right? I'm so sorry. I forgot about the chains. Here, let me help you."

Maddy gave Charles a small smile as he lifted her from the ground. He and the two other guards who were charged with watching her had been quiet when first given the task. However, their curiosity got the best of them. They had never met a southern-born before especially one of the green-haired.

Maddy hadn't known her ankles hurt so badly until he removed the chains. Suddenly, a dull ache began in them. They felt odd, as well, like they were too light and in need of the chain's weight.

Slowly, she and Charles left the bottom floor of the castle and made their way several floors upward. Traveling the winding stairs was particularly difficult. Having to slightly pivot with every other step altered the dull ache into encroaching numbness. She had to lean against the wall more times than she'd like to admit.

Once they had conquered the stairs, Charles led Maddy down

a series of halls.

He walked in front and she a few feet behind. They had only interacted outside her decorated dungeon once before. A servant had forgotten to put a fresh chamber pot in her room. Maddy felt like she was about to burst, so Charles—who had no clue where the chamber pots were—walked her outside.

The day had been cloudy. The earth beneath her was a soothing cold.

That day he had walked beside her, constantly glancing at her seemingly to ensure she was not on the verge of escape.

When she had finished, Maddy took a few moments to stand in the gray light until he called her in.

"What were you doing?" he had asked, narrowing his eyes. "This was not a trip. Remember that."

Maddy had smiled at him. "Southerners do not do well indoors."

Now she felt there was some sort of bond between them, a mutual respect and trust.That was something at least.

There were voices at the end of the hall. As they rounded the corner, Maddy was met with two large men wearing armor like Charles. The three bowed to one another.

Then Charles placed a gentle hand on her back and pushed her towards them.

His helmet was still down, so she couldn't meet his eyes when she looked back at him.

He only gave her a nod before turning his back to her and exiting the hall.

The two men took post on either side of her.

"Follow us," ordered one.

She bobbed her head but did not smile.

Her palms were sweating. A gust of winter air whistled through the hall and sent a chill through her. She took a deep breath.

I survived the eastern war. I can survive this.

Maddy had wrapped her arms around herself. She now let them fall by her sides.

There is a *peace* in death. I've seen it on their faces.

Her face became slack and she stared ahead, her eyes focused on nothing. The drumming of her heart became a hollow sound because she was not present.

Things were happening, yet she was only watching. It was not her bruised ankles that screamed for relief or her stomach that was twisted in knots. No, it was another young lady. Maddy felt nothing.

She looks tired. I think her feet hurt. She needs to keep walking though.

They turned down a hall and to the right was a door. One of the guards knocked but no one answered. Without a second knock, he pushed the door open and stepped inside, his companion following behind him.

The girl stood in the hallway. The two men stared back at her.

"Come inside, southerner. You are allowed a visit."

Who is she visiting?

The girl did as instructed.

There was a woman standing in the corner of the room. She was glaring at the guards as if they were rodents. Then her eyes found the girl's and there was something there.

Robin!

"Maddy!"

The two companions raced to one another, arms outstretched. For a moment, Maddy forgot about her ankles and her exhaustion. All that mattered was that she wasn't alone any longer.

They slammed into one another, their arms immediately linking around the other. Maddy clutched at Robin's shoulders. She buried her face into the crook of her neck as her eyes prickled. Yet she smiled because Robin was solid in her arms, well and alive.

She placed her chin atop Maddy's head.

"Leave us, now." Her tone indicated the statement was meant only as a command.

"Yes, my lady."

There was the sound of shuffling footsteps, followed by the creaking of wood. They were alone.

As if she had been putting on a show, Robin suddenly collapsed to the floor with arms still locked tightly around Maddy.

"You have no idea how happy I am to see you," Robin said, finally pulling away and meeting Maddy's eyes. "I asked after you. Often. The bastards—"

"Don't like to answer questions?" the green-haired girl offered, a smirk pulling at her lips.

Robin laughed. "Yes, exactly. I knew...I mean, I assumed you were alive but I wasn't sure of the condition."

Her eyes fell to Maddy's shoulder and Maddy followed her gaze.

She had nearly forgotten about the arrow wound. It still hurt but it seemed the worst had passed. Her bandages were changed frequently so she didn't fear infection.

Robin placed a hand there. Maddy looked at her.

Her friend's icy blues were covered in water.

"I am so sorry," Robin said. "I know it does nothing to change the past. I know. But when the arrow hit you..." She closed her eyes and shook her head, turning away from Maddy.

Maddy placed her hand over Robin's. They were silent for a moment.

Finally, Robin took in a long breath, meeting her eyes again.

"I felt the same when I saw them carrying you away," Maddy said.

Robin sighed. "You should have stayed down."

"Would you have stayed down if it were me?"

She smiled. "We both know the answer to that."

Maddy's mouth twitched, followed by Robin falling away as laughter overtook her. Their hands remained clasped while tears of joy rolled down their cheeks. They laughed for several moments, filling the chamber with their happiness until the laughter turned into light chuckles and finally silence.

Robin smiled at the green-haired girl. "I have missed you, Maddy."

"I've missed you, as well," she replied. "But how did Cadfen know our plan? How long have we even been here? Time seems endless when you don't have a sky to look to."

"I wish I had the answers." Robin shook her head. "In truth, I was hoping you'd know something."

"So, we're at a loss for now?"

Robin nodded. "Seems that way. M-Maddy, what happened to your ankles?"

She looked down at her swollen and bruised flesh. The very sight brought back a dull ache.

"What have they been doing to you?" She reached for her but Maddy flinched away.

"They hurt," she said, giving a small smile. "Sore to the touch."

"They've kept you chained?"

She nodded.

"I'll order them to bring some salve immediately. Here, rest on the bed."

Robin stood before helping Maddy to the bed.

Maddy, finally finding comfort in the stuffed pillows, watched as her friend gave specific instructions to the guards.

Her back was straight, shoulders pushed back, and she spoke quickly, no hesitation despite being a prisoner herself.

Once Robin had finished, one guard departed down the hall and she closed the door. She took a seat beside Maddy, resting her head on her shoulder.

"You will be staying with me tonight."

"But Cadfen—"

"I do not care what that false king wishes. You're hurt and I'm not going to have you suffer alone." Robin patted her hand and smiled up at her.

Maddy pushed her hair over her shoulder to cover her face.

Robin wrapped herself around her arm. "It's nice not to be alone."

She nodded, her green hair bobbing along with her.

"I do have something to tell you, Maddy."

She wiped her eyes, before looking back at her friend. "We have nothing but time."

"Right." Robin sat up and turned to her. Her lips were pulled into a tight line. "First, I've been trying to ignore the thought because it's too difficult to imagine. But if Cadfen's questioning is any sign, I believe Arthur and Alistair escaped."

She nodded. "I remember they were still fighting before we were taken."

"Have you heard anything from the guards?"

"No. Besides asking questions about the south, they only talk about their own lives."

"Of course. We can be certain they're fine, then?" She was staring at Maddy but her eyes were wavering.

"I don't think we really have a choice."

"You—"

There was a knock at the door.

Robin placed a finger over her mouth. She hopped off the bed and walked to the door.

"Your items, my lady."

Robin took them and slammed the door in the guard's face.

"I know it's not of their own doing," she said, returning to the bed, "yet it still bothers me to no end. Let me see your ankle."

Clenching her teeth, Maddy placed both ankles in Robin's lap. Her friend applied the salve to a bandage, then wrapped it around each ankle. A tingly warmth conquered the ache.

Maddy found herself sighing as the pain eased.

"Better?" Robin asked.

"Much better."

"Good. Let me know if the pain returns. Now, do you remember what I told you of the night my uncle was murdered?"

Maddy nodded.

"I had hoped she had died or that he had killed her. Fate must hate me because she, I mean...my chambermaid is still alive, the one who stabbed me."

Maddy's eyes bulged. "You've seen her?"

She laughed. "Oh, yes, I've more than seen her. I almost stabbed the wench. Cadfen stopped me. Apparently, since the night they took the kingdom their relationship has blossomed. I met their three sons several nights ago."

Now, it wasn't Maddy's ankles that ached but her head. Nothing was making sense.

"I thought Cadfen wanted to wed you?" Maddy said.

"He does. I don't think he meant for me to discover so soon they had a family. He described her as a convenient and willing temptation."

"Three times?" Maddy raised a brow.

"Exactly. He's a murder and a brute."

"Did she say anything to you?"

"No. We only saw one another for a moment." Robin sighed. "I hate to admit it, but we have to wait for Alistair and Arthur. Then, I'll see dear Liz punished."

"Watch and listen until then?" Maddy offered.

"And eat," her friend replied. "I'll have the guards fetch us some food."

A moment later, "Yes, Lady Robin" followed by shuffling metal could be heard in the hall.

Robin turned, placed her hands on her hips, and exhaled. "I managed to send them both off, so—"

The door swung open.

Maddy stared wide-eyed at the woman in front of her. She was short with pretty golden hair and large green eyes—eyes that barely acknowledged Maddy but had locked onto Robin instantly.

Robin wheezed a breath through her nose. Her hands fell to her side and balled into fists.

Without having to be told, Maddy knew Elizabeth was the woman standing in front of her.

"Why couldn't you have died that night?" the woman spoke through gritted teeth. "Why couldn't you have just stayed away?"

"You gave killing me a good try, didn't you?" Robin's voice was full of tremors. "Even after Cadfen ordered you to save me, you couldn't resist a few arrows in my back, could you?"

Elizabeth narrowed her eyes. "Arrows?"

"Three in my back! After all—"

"We never shot any arrows, you fool. It was night, you were in dark clothing, and we didn't have the range. You quickly left our vision."

Robin shook her head. "I remember. I was bleeding out all over the Cursed Woods. One...one was closer to my shoulder."

Elizabeth smiled. "All these years, you...well, they do say the woods play tricks on the weak-minded."

"What?" Robin's hand grew limp by her side. The prominent rage left her face.

Elizabeth cackled. "The woods imagined it all for you! I suppose you thought we were right on your heels, as well." Her laughter grew as she tossed her head back in glee.

Maddy attempted to stand but a slicing pain ran through her ankles and she fell back towards the mattress.

Elizabeth composed herself. She wiped her eyes and looked at her old friend. "I don't know where you were held up these last ten years. But apparently it was ten years wasted."

Robin marched towards her.

She smiled. Robin was halfway across the room when she stumbled to the ground. The floor shook beneath them and the sound of falling rocks echoed around them.

Maddy clutched at the bed sheets and Liz grabbed onto the door to hold her steady. They all looked to the window across the room.

A tower had fallen.

Chapter Twenty Eight

Alistair dove through the hole straight into the smoke and chaos. He heard screams and wails around him, but the fog of dust prevented him from seeing anything. Guards barked orders at one another. There was also the distant sound of metal against metal where Arthur and his men were facing the Camelot knights.

He turned his head upwards and stared into the sky. His eyes stung. The dust seemed to be as endless as the sky itself. Then, there it was, the western tower as Arthur had estimated.

A quick noise filled his ears. It was like the hollow sound of a bird's wings before—

"Help!"

"We're being attacked!"

BOOM!

Arthur's lance had done its job again.

The tower leaned left, slowly sinking into the mist of dust until only the very tip peaked over. Alistair would not lose sight of it.

Hold on you two.

The people of Camelot came rushing out of their homes in hordes. Some heading towards the walls, hoping to escape through the holes. Others raced to the castle looking for sanctuary. Alistair raced to the tower.

On a normal day throughout Camelot, the streets would have been busy. He would have expected to be pushed and shoved. But today terror drove everyone.

While he wanted to head west through the city, the crowd charged east. It was like swimming against the ocean.

Rubble and grime coated the sky in an ugly brown. The tip was beginning to disappear.

Just keep heading west.

Bodies pressed against him. People pulled and grabbed at his shirt as they tried to push him aside. The bellowing sound of screams had dulled his ears.

What felt like eternity suddenly came to an end. Alistair stumbled forward. Immediately, he covered his head, expecting to be trampled on by the townspeople. Yet nothing happened.

He removed his arms and peered around him.

The crowd had thinned. They were all moving away from him

and the crumbled mess that was now Camelot's western tower.

Time to hurry.

Alistair glanced around once more. There were no guards. No one was watching. He'd doubt they'd be able to see anything if they were.

He quickly got to his feet and ran the length of the tower searching for a guard. According to Arthur, there were always at least two in each tower. So, where were the western guards?

Alistair reached the end where a small opening had been carved out. He ducked his head inside and a few feet from him lay a Camelot knight.

Perfect.

He jumped in and approached the unconscious man. The armor had a few dents in it but otherwise it was fine. But would it fit?

Alistair stared at the knight looking from head to toe. He leaned against the man and took the same position. His feet stopped several inches before the knight's.

He slammed his fists into the wall.

He was too short.

More stone crumbled outside of the tower.

Alistair opened his pouch and pulled out a small leather container. He shook his head.

It's for Maddy and Robin.

Without another thought, he poured the rabbit blood over his face taking caution to avoid his eyes. When the pouch was empty he left the tower and turned in the direction of the castle.

A man covered in blood is harder to turn away, isn't he?

A mass of the townspeople pushed at the castle gates while guards tried to force them into a line. Children clung to their parents, tears rolling down their cheeks, eyes wide in fear and confusion. Their parents' eyes held the same emotion, yet they barked orders at the guards begging, demanding safe keeping.

Alistair watched the mob for a moment. His stomach churned at the thought of being caught in all the dirt and heat that was the crowd, yet he had no choice.

When an opening appeared, he moved, ducked in between a burly man and his petite wife. The crowd pushed forward against the gates so Alistair moved along with the force. He would lower himself to the ground and snuck his way around people, only nudging his way through occasionally.

After some time, he was only a few feet away from the guard.

Alistair placed his head in one hand and reached out with the other.

"P-please, help...my head," he moaned so loudly the few remaining barriers between him and the guard stepped to the side to let him pass.

As the path opened, Alistair fell knees first in front of the guard. He then swayed from side to side before falling to the earth.

There were a few gasps. The guard who stood in front shouted to his fellow guardsmen and Alistair was lifted to his feet.

"Hold on, son. We'll take you in to be looked at," said one.

Alistair gave an awkward nod and kept his eyes unfocused.

"Why is the boy going through?"

"What about my daughter?"

He could feel the crowd's tension rise and smooth over his skin. A small knot built in his chest. He was certain some of them were actually hurt.

Alistair and the guards moved around the crowd and onto the castle's grounds. On either side were makeshift beddings, patients, and healers. As Alistair stumbled along with the guards, a young woman turned his way.

The look on her face said it all.

I must look convincing.

"Place him here," she said. "Do you know what happened to him?"

The men rested Alistair on a mat. He lowered his eyelids and listened.

"We're not sure but we have to return to the gate. We'll be in to start moving the patients inside in a moment."

And then they were gone.

The woman turned to Alistair. She placed a hand on his cheek.

"You poor dear. Let's take a look at you."

She began wiping away the blood. Alistair watched her. Her touch was delicate and her eyes roamed over his head.

She was looking for a wound she would not find.

"Miss, miss!"

An older man beside him grabbed at his shoulder bandage. The white cloth was turning red.

"I told you to stay still. You've reopened your wound. Tsk."

She glanced at Alistair briefly before moving to her new patient.

Alistair wobbled to his feet, still clutching his head.

Water," he groaned.

She stared at him. "Please, wait a moment and—"

He shook his head. "I'm so thirsty. I just want some water."

Blood oozed from the man's shoulder and down his side. The woman closed her eyes and took a deep breath.

Her eyes found Alistair again. "Listen to me. There's a well a few yards that way. If you can walk, bring enough back for us all," she said.

She peered around at the mass of wounded people, her fellow healers running this way and that.

"We're going to need it."

Alistair nodded and wobbled in the direction she had stated. The old man's groans could still be heard in the distance. He looked behind him.

The woman wasn't looking. Alistair ran.

He and Arthur had gone over the Camelot map more than a dozen times. Even if Cadfen had changed the structure or arrangements somewhat, one thing remained true of every castle: there was always a servants' entrance.

True to her word, there was a well several yards away from where the wounded rested. It was tucked closer to the castle walls and just far enough on a curve that no one standing at the front could see it.

Alistair stood straight as he passed the well. He broke out into a run, racing along the castle until he spotted a small door that was partially opened.

He approached the door from the left so if someone were inside they wouldn't see him. Taking slow steps, Alistair peeked into the room through the small crack. Shattered dishes, rags, a table with half-eaten food, and an overturned bucket were the only inhabitants.

He pulled the door open slowly, internally sighing when it didn't squeak.

As he stepped in, Alistair saw that the little room led up to a dark set of narrow stairs. If someone were to come down while he ascended, he'd have no place to hide.

"Now or never," he whispered.

Alistair ascended the spiraling staircase. When he reached the top, he saw a stream of light coming from under the door. The light did not shift so it appeared no one was walking nearby to create shadows.

Still, he listened for any sound. When none came, he pushed the door open.

Like the servant's chamber below, the room was covered in shattered glass but the streaming banners, chairs outlined in iron, and long-stemmed candles spoke to royal quality.

Alistair was in one of the private dining chambers.

He took a breath.

Arthur was right. Thank, God. Now, I need to decide where to go first. The dungeon or the west wing?

The dungeons were closer. He'd have to traverse a few hallways before descending a set of stairs, then to a door, and into the dungeons. The east wing chambers where he resided were on the other side of the castle, almost parallel to the castle's entrance.

Alistair raked his hands through his hair but immediately stopped once he felt thick globs of rabbit's blood.

He and Arthur both agreed the dungeons was the logical place to look first. Yet, they had also agreed Cadfen was not going to be outsmarted by simple logic. He would not place the woman he loved in a cell.

He glanced at the door he knew led to a hallway. He re-adjusted his satchel, listened once and closed the door behind him.

One, two, three, now!

The guards marched by him. Alistair grabbed the door with the edge of his fingers, barely catching it before it closed. The guards made their way and Alistair slipped onto the bridge. From there, he'd only have to go up two floors and check the rooms.

The shrill sound of metal slashed against metal grated at his ears. There were still screams and wails but they had been drowned out by the sound of combat.

Alistair ducked as he made his way across. When he was at the other end, he stole a glance over the wall.

Thank, Trithian.

Arthur's men were moving forward. They were nearly pressing against Camelot's walls. There would be no time to waste especially if more guards decided to appear.

Alistair thought of the approaching army.

Cadfen's men will have their hands full.

Alistair stepped into the next passage, found the stairwell, and moved up two sets where stood another door.

As before, he waited and listened. When no sound came, Alistair slowly pulled the door open and began to make his way along the hall.

"This is you! What have you done, you wench?"

"Nothing yet, you traitorous twat."

Robin.

"Let me get my dagger and I'll show you what I—"

A door flung open and slammed against the hall wall. Alistair slipped between the wall and a large window.

Please, don't see me.

"Where is she going?"

Maddy.

Alistair pressed his feet into the floor. He had to wait.

"I must get to him," said the unfamiliar voice.

He could hear the soft sound of slippered feet moving against the floor. Without one glance, a short, blonde woman sped by him, tears streaming down her face.

Soon a door closed, the woman disappeared, and the hall was silent again.

Alistair stepped from his hiding place and sprinted to his companions. The door still hung open. There were whispered voices.

"Maddy, Robin—"

A candlestick went flying by his head and Robin had another raised in her hand.

Her brows were narrowed and her eyes intense as she stared at the doorway. But then, her eyes found his and her arm fell limp by her side.

"Alistair!" As if she had powers, Robin appeared by his side and immediately wrapped her arms around him.

"I knew you'd come. I knew it." Hot, wet tears moved down his right shoulder.

He pressed her head with the back of his hand. "Of course. I'd never leave you." His eyes found Maddy's. "Neither of you."

Robin lifted her head and wiped her eyes. "We have to go, but Maddy can hardly walk. One of us will have to carry her."

Alistair looked over Maddy. Her ankles were wrapped up in bandages but he could still see discoloring from around the edges.

Spikes of heat ignited in his chest. The magic bubbled inside of him, pushing at his skin.

"Your eyes..."

He closed them. "I know. Give me a moment."

Deep breath, now, Alistair. Deep breath.

"I'll carry her," he said, meeting their eyes again. "We need to start moving."

Without another word, Alistair made his way across the room and squatted in front of Maddy.

"Hop on, Madelia."

"There's one more thing," Robin said as Maddy slipped onto Alistair's back. "Cadfen has my daggers. They're in his chambers."

"Including Carnweenan?"

She sighed but nodded. "Arthur told you, I assume."

"Yes, and I think the chance of us being spotted is too high," he said.

"Did Arthur not tell you what the dagger can do?"

"He did but you and Maddy are more important."

"I have to go alone then." Robin balled her fists by her sides and stared at the ground. "I can't be responsible for all the people he could kill with it."

"No," Alistair stated, glaring at her though she would not meet his eyes.

"I am not being stubborn for the sake of it."

"I'm aware and I'm not going to let you be recaptured."

"Alistair, he could kill all of us—"

"No!" The tone of Alistair's voice even surprised him. And for a moment, after seeing the shock on Robin's face, he almost apologized.

But his scalp began to itch. The room became cold and Maddy's teeth began to chatter.

"When I heard it was Arthur knocking down the walls of my kingdom, I knew there was only one reason he would come. After all this time."

Alistair slowly stepped back and lowered Maddy onto the mattress.

The man in front of him was close to six feet tall with dark hair and eyes. His hands were clasped behind his back. He wore a long cloak that dragged across the floor and a belt around his waist with three loops. In each loop, was one of Robin's daggers.

However, all of this was secondary to the fact that Cadfen was alone and his eyes were locked on Robin.

"I never wanted things to be this way, Robin," said Cadfen. He sighed and shook his head. "I always felt you and I were the same."

Robin scoffed. "I am not a murderer. How dare you compare us!"

"I never wished to be one," he replied, briefly glancing out the window.

His eyes returned to Robin. "I saw a kinship in you and I thought—"

"Well, your thoughts were mistaken," Robin barked through trembling lips. "He...he loved you like a son."

Cadfen smiled. It was rueful.

Alistair glanced between the two, waiting for a sudden attack or guards to storm in yet nothing. His hands grazed over the grimoire in his satchel.

Cadfen's eyes shifted towards him before returning to Robin. He shook himself.

"Not now," he said.

Robin narrowed her sights on him. "Speaking with your demons, then?"

His eyes snapped back to her. "Yes."

Alistair felt fear stirring inside him. He fought to keep his eyes away from the door and pushed down the urge to flee. He had to stay and wait.

The smell of decaying flesh filled the room.

"Over time, you will come to see, Robin," Cadfen said as his back jerked outward and his spine creaked. His posture was hunched as he cocked his head to the side. "I've done this all for us and for a greater good."

"You're insane."

The grimoire was seething to Alistair's touch.

Cadfen shook his head. "No. If I were insane, I'd have done this in front of my men. Why do you think I stand here alone?"

The door slammed shut with an echoing sound of finality.

As Cadfen's body convulsed, trembling streaks of shadow stretched from behind him like arms. The stench grew more intense. All the light in the room began to slowly fade.

Witches.

The thought sent him back to Satbury...when the creature had him by the throat. He closed his eyes, allowing the memory to resurface, to pull him back to his nightmares. All the air inside Alistair seemed to center in his chest and wrap around his heart. He opened his eyes, tried to exhale and light mist escaped his lips. Yet despite the cold, sweat coated his skin. The sound of his heart drummed in his ear.

Yes. Just as before. You were scared. She was taking your soul.

There were ten creatures in the room with them now. And they had formed a semi-circle around Alistair and his companions with Cadfen at the center.

"I will only need a few of my servants to complete this task," he said.

A few witches near the end turned to Alistair. Cadfen twisted his wrist and their attention moved forward once more.

Maddy and Robin are screaming. You can't help them.

There's nothing but darkness and the wails of children.

The witches opened their mouths. The shrill sound of a rusted door released from them. Just like the day he was cursed.

An apprehension exploded inside of him and Alistair gasped as his magic shot out like a beacon. The witches shrieked, backing from him, breaking their formation. Finally, Cadfen turned to him. His eyes had become a dull gray.

Cadfen smiled.

Alistair's magic shrunk back within him. He was left gasping on the floor.

"Apparently, you still don't know how to use it properly," Cadfen said.

Alistair shook his head. He was still reaching out.

There was a moment of silence. All that was heard in the room was the creaking noises of the witches twisted bodies.

They must need more magic.

Alistair pulled his satchel to his chest, gripping the book it held inside and staring at the stone floor.

"Did you sell your soul, as well?" Cadfen asked. "Or..."

Edwin!

He closed his eyes.

"...could you be something else?"

A presence hovered above him.

"Leave him alone!" Robin screamed and something slammed against the wall.

The grimoire became a biting heat. Then the room filled with light.

A piercing noise filled Alistair's ears. He felt light and empty with each soul that passed through him. The chill of the room had faded, the sweat on his skin was nonexistent and all color left his vision. Soon, there were only the children.

They were nothing more than shaped mists that filled the room. But they were there. Boys, girls, men, women, the young and the old came, too. And their eyes were on Cadfen and his demons.

"In the name of Trithian, demons are pierced with his holy sword, pushed back by his sacred shield, and exorcised by his words of prayer." The words echoed throughout the room as if God had spoken them. "In Trithian's name, I deem it so and so it shall be."

The spirits raised their hands as one. The white light filled the room as the witches tried to cower within the bit of shadow they could find. It wasn't enough.

Cadfen no longer looked at Alistair. The murderer stared at the ceiling with his mouth agape and his eyes a striped white. His demons rushed back into his abdomen and were expelled upward through his open orifice. Their howls filled the space, seeming to shake the entire castle.

The spirits' light pooled over them and their master. Their shrieks tore at Alistair's ears. He closed his eyes from the blinding light.

Alistair didn't dare move from his position, not until he was sure he wouldn't be blinded or deafened.

There was a brush on his shoulder. Alistair opened his eyes to Edwin. The little ghost was fading.

"It's done," the boy sighed. And then, he vanished.

"Wait, Edwin. Edwin!" Alistair rushed to his feet but fell to the floor. There was a striking pain in his right shoulder. His knees shook and he suddenly felt listless, barely able to move.

His gaze turned upward.

Tendrils of steam were leaving Cadfen's parted lips, yet he still stood. He clawed at his neck before feeling around his body. Finally, he jerked his head upright.

"No," he huffed, still feeling around himself. "No! Where have they gone? What have you done?"

His gaze found Alistair.

"You've ruined it all!" Cadfen stormed at him.

The young man could not move.

Cadfen drew his sword. His eyes were wild.

"I only wanted to—"

The sword froze in Cadfen's hands. He stared to his right and Alistair followed his line of vision.

Maddy hung onto the edge of a small silver kitchen knife plunged into Cadfen's side. His blood ran down its hilt.

She glared up at him. "I told you to leave him alone."

A pale hand slipped around Cadfen's front. The dagger's blade briefly caught light from the window. He had no time to react.

Robin held it to his neck.

"Say hello to my uncle," she spat. "And beg for his forgiveness."

A guttural sound escaped her as she slashed his neck open. Blood oozed from him in thick droplets.

Cadfen fell to his knees, eyes turned upward once more before finding Alistair's a last time. They widened for a moment. He reached a hand out and then he fell forward as blood pooled around him.

The false king was dead.

Chapter Twenty Nine

Maddy sat in the corner and waited until Robin decided what to do. The situation was interesting, though she had a feeling she knew how most royals would have reacted. It only took one day for the boys' entire world to be changed.

Cadfen's eldest son Patton stood in front of his brothers, arms outstretched to his sides.

Robin offered her hand. "You all haven't eaten in a full day. And you must be scared because of all the...noise. Please, come down and join us for the feast. Things are a bit messy but—"

"You need to kill us to get to the throne," he hissed, narrowing his eyes at her. "The food you offer is poisoned."

The smallest of the boys, Oswin, peeked out from behind his brother. He looked up at Maddy.

She smiled and gave him a small wave which he did not return.

"Where is our maid?" Patton shouted. "Where is Elizabeth?"

Robin stilled at the question. She sighed and swallowed down the words. They had all agreed not to tell the boys what happened, at least not any time soon.

What good would it do them to know she had thrown herself onto a pike after discovering Cadfen had perished?

None. Maddy shook her head.

"Miss, where is our father?" Godwin asked.

Robin didn't hesitate. "He's gone for now. I will be taking care of you."

"You want to kill us!" Patton barked.

"I would never hurt you," she replied. "You all will not lose the throne. You will remain princes, heirs to the middle kingdom."

The three boys glanced at one another.

"Father did say she was to be our mother."

Robin nodded though Maddy could see the vein pulsing in her neck. Apparently Cadfen had had many plans for her. More than they realized.

"We can't trust her," Patton stated.

Robin huffed and fell back into her seat. She crossed her arms. "Fine. What must I do to at least convince you to eat?"

Oswin leapt in front of his brother. "Do you promise to be our mother?"

"I promise to take care of you," Robin said.

Maddy nearly laughed. Her friend had dodged the question well.

"And you'll always be nice?"

"As nice as anyone can be," she replied.

Patton pushed his brother behind him once more. The youngest son still watched Robin warily.

"How about I prove to you my loyalty?"

Robin pulled her dagger from behind her and pressed the tip into her finger. She let three drops fall to the floor as she began mumbling a prayer. When done she looked at the boys.

"Do you recognize my words?"

"Trithian's promise to his people," they answered.

"And so you know I must be true in intention or else I would have been smote down, hmm?"

They hesitated but nodded.

"Good." She stood. "Now, follow myself and Lady Maddy for your food."

Without another word, Robin left the room. Maddy offered the boys a smile, picked up her walking stick and followed behind her friend.

A few moments later, reluctant footsteps echoed behind them.

Robin led to the dining hall, making sure to take the path that avoided the carnage of yesterday's war.

Arthur's men had busied themselves around the tables. Their plates were stacked high with Calvin's cooking and no one—aside from Arthur and Alistair--paid attention to the group of five that entered the hall. They waved but were pulled back by the others who filled their cups and patted their backs.

Together they found five empty spaces at a table in front.

Maddy's ankles and feet screamed for relief. She was the first to sit, taking a long breath while the pain eased.

A small, warm hand wrapped around hers.

Oswin didn't look at her. He only held her hand.

Maddy smiled.

Robin began filling their plates. Before she could even complete the task, the princes had dug into the bread, grapes, and dried meat.

My mama was right about growing boys it looks like.

She smiled at the thought. Tomorrow she'd be able to finally write to her mother. More importantly, she'd be able to tell her she had found them a home—a home where the citizens had forgotten the last ten years but a home, nonetheless.

Robin had began chatting with one of the young servants. Maddy turned her attention to her food, but as she moved forward, she saw Lancelot. He stood across the hall within the side door. His gaze was on Robin.

All boys turn into men.

Lancelot stood in the doorway for a few moments, just watching Robin, before disappearing down the hall. Maddy got to her feet and grabbed her walking stick. Oswin had released her hand in preference of chicken.

She smiled and waved at a few people while she made her way.

When the noise of the dining hall was behind her, Maddy closed the door. Lancelot was nowhere to be seen. She continued down the hall.

What is he doing?

Maddy continued to make her way. Chill entered the hallway and whispers reached her ears as she drew closer to the courtyard.

Like before, Lancelot had left the door slightly ajar. He stood inside the courtyard, pacing in front of the door, raking his fingers through his hair.

"Mine, she is supposed to be mine."

He slammed his fist against the stone wall, then stormed farther along the castle away from the entrance.

Maddy followed him until a smell greeted her that nearly made her run back. Robin had told her they had stacked the bodies there. She had forgotten in her haste.

Her empty stomach churned. She had never been so happy to be hungry.

Lancelot was standing in front of one of the body pits.

"I'm supposed to be with her. If I can't have her...he can't."

She gripped her walking stick. He didn't need to say their names for her to know who Lancelot referred to.

The young man looked away from Maddy and across the courtyard. He cupped his ear as if listening for something.

"Yes," he said, now staring into the pit. "I will have to kill them."

Maddy felt her stomach drop. She peered around her, hoping to see a passing guard or a happy drunk, someone else to witness the moment with her. Instead, she found a sword.

"But Arthur is like...no, no." He shook his head and pulled at his hair.

She placed her stick on the ground and approached the sword.

"She's toyed with me. Yes!" He hit his open palm with a fist. "This is all her fault."

Maddy held the sword out towards him. She approached.

"Why does it have to be this way?"

You won't hurt Robin.

"Why does he get it all?"

I won't let you.

Lancelot looked up at the sky. "I have to kill them, to kill them both.What should I say? You want me to say--"

Maddy gasped at how easily the blade punctured his middle. It had felt light in her hands, but the weight suddenly came to her.

Lancelot turned his neck to watch her. She still held the sword's hilt.

He smiled. "Thank you." He tumbled forward into the pit.

The sword shook in Maddy's hands, but she steadied it and forced herself straight.

I am a good judge of character.

She thought of the drunkard back in Satbury who had attacked Robin. He hadn't crossed her mind in some time.

Lancelot's lifeless body stared back up at her.

The wind blew. Maddy tossed the sword into the pit. She grabbed her walking stick and stepped back inside.

She had killed two monsters.

Lilith moved her twig across the earth.

GONE! OUR PUPPET IS DEAD. Morganna read the words.

WHAT DO WE DO NOW? Lilith looked at Morganna. The pools of red began to fill her face.

The woman sighed.

"We will wait." She rubbed her bulging belly. "Arthur is a patient man and Mordred is his father's son."

About the Author

Natasha D. Lane is a friend of most things caffeinated, a lover of books, and a writing warrior to her core. As a big believer in the idea that "the pen is mightier than the sword," she graduated from Juniata College in 2015 with hopes of becoming a journalist. Instead, her path took her on a different route and Natasha found herself digging up a manuscript from her childhood. This dusty stack of papers would become "The Pariah Child & the Ever-Giving Stone" which would lead her to write "The Woman In the Tree: The True Story of Camelot." If there were a single piece of advice Natasha could give to young writers, it'd be this: Write your way through life.

To learn more about Natasha and her writing, visit her at her website: www.natashalanewrites.com